Copyright © 2022 A.J. Montana

All rights reserved.

The characters and events portrayed in this book are fictitious. Any similarity to real persons, living or dead, is coincidental and not intended by the author.

No part of this book may be reproduced, or stored in a retrieval system, or transmitted in any form or by any means, electronic, mechanical, photocopying, recording, or otherwise, without express written permission of the publisher.

ISBN: 9798355100926

Cover design by: Rachel Coulson & Art Painter
Library of Congress Control Number: 2018675309
Printed in the United States of America

*To everyone who took the time to read the draft - you know who you are but everyone else doesn't, so Matthew, Christine, Kelly Ann, Meg, and Sarah, I'd like to say a big THANK YOU!*

# Chapter One
## Rise and shine

**DING, DING, DING!** My alarm clock suddenly went off, waking me up. A yawn escaped my lips as I stretched in bed before swinging my feet round to sit on the edge. I gazed at the clock to my right on the nightstand while rubbing a hand across my stubbled jaw, the metal hammer ruthlessly knocking between the two bells on top. I then swiftly turned it off before noticing the time, which was 6:45AM.

Mindlessly reaching for the transistor radio that was beside the clock, a lamp and birthday card from my 24th birthday last week, I turned the large dial and tuned into the radio station. "Good morning, citizens of Merribridge! It's Monday 6th July in sunny England, and you're listening to 1959's Elation Station!" A honeyed male voice announced before gentle, almost hypnotic bluesy music began to play.

'III've got yooou under my skiiin. III've got yooou deep in the heaaart of meee, so deep in my heart that you're really a paaart of meee. III've got yooou under my skiiin.'.

I then robotically stood up, my bare feet gracing the rough, pale brown tiled carpet, and stretched once more before making my single bed; it was pushed against the middle of the back cream wall. I then leant across my wooden headrest to the window above it, tugging back the white, flower printed curtains that were so thin the sun was already seeping through.

'Don't you knoooow, you foooool, you never can wiiiin? Uuuse your mentalittty, wake up to realittty.'. The music continued as I turned for my wardrobe that was near my nightstand in the far, left-hand corner; it faced into the room at an angle, a matching dresser was to the left of it with a mirror on top. As I pulled my shoes and work clothes out, the song abruptly came to life. '**III would sacrifice anything come what might, for the sake of having you neeear, in spite of a waaarning voic-**' But then I switched it off.

With my clothes and shoes in hand, I headed to the bedroom door that was in the bottom, right-hand corner; it opened with a little squeak, the carpet from my bedroom continuing onto the landing. Directly opposite me was the bathroom door, and to my right was a nook that had a wooden unit with a vase of flowers on top.

I then ambled into the bathroom; it was small and oblong-shaped with a mishmash of different colours. The walls were baby pink, and the cold, tiled flooring was dark red. On the wall across from me was a light green medicine cabinet with mirrors attached to the doors, a matching shelf was underneath. Beneath that was the porcelain sink with white towels hanging from a metal rail to the left of it.

Ignoring the blue bathtub to my right, I strolled over to the toilet on my left that faced into the room with a wicker laundry basket beside it. Once I put the seat down, I rested my clothes on top and set my shoes on the floor in front of it, turning for the medicine cabinet where I grabbed my toiletries and deposited them on the shelf.

My green eyes absentmindedly took in my fair, sculpted face that was wreathed in smiles, dark stubble was starting to come through and my brown hair was a dishevelled mess. Once I brushed my teeth and shaved, I grabbed one of the white hand towels to dry my face before taking off my blue and white stripy pyjamas, revealing my lean body.

I then changed into my work clothes after using the toilet, a white button-down shirt, a gold and black tie, and a pale grey suit with matching waistcoat. Quickly styling my hair so it was smooth on the sides with a quiff at the front, I grabbed my brown wingtip shoes and sat on the edge of the bathtub to put them on. The wall surrounding the bath was tiled and dark pink, fitted with a showerhead and lime green shower curtains.

Once I had put my stuff back in the medicine cabinet, I opened the bathroom door to the smell of bacon and eggs. My mouth instantly salivated as I headed downstairs, my hand gliding along the wooden banister on my left. Ignoring the white front door at the bottom, which had two little, oval-shaped windows at the top, I bypassed an archway on my right and turned left under another that led into the dining room, my shoes clipping against the light wood floorboards. Sunlight beamed through the large, bay window to my right; vibrant yellow curtains were tied either side, complimenting the pale green walls that were decorated with pictures of flowers. Skirting round the long, dark wood table in the middle that had a matching cabinet against the back wall, I advanced on the archway along the left-hand wall where hustling and bustling was coming from.

I then came to stand in the spacious, colourful kitchen where I instantly saw mother stood at the hob across from me, she was looking out at the garden through the window in front of her. The ding of cutlery then gained my attention, and I gazed over to my left where my younger sister, Carmen, was setting the breakfast table; our Golden Retriever, Max, was underneath watching the bacon sizzle in the frying pan.

Taking a further step inside, my shoes squeaked against the dark blue lino flooring that didn't suit the pale pink walls, and I automatically said in my usual, upbeat tone, "Good morning, mother. Good morning, Carmen."
In unison, they spun round to face me, smiling broadly, "Good morning, Nathaniel." Before turning back and continuing what they were doing.

I then made my way over to the breakfast table, pulling up a chair beside the glass double doors that opened out into the garden. Carmen had just finished setting the table, her long, blonde hair that was up in a curly ponytail trailed over her shoulder; the bow holding it in place matched her blue and white checkered dress, which clung to her pale, petite frame. Her green eyes momentarily met mine, a smile growing on her face that had very little make-up.

Carmen then turned on her heels to help mother, her black shoes clipping against the floor.
While she piled the plates up with bacon, eggs and a side of toast, mother queried with a radiant smile gracing her made-up face, "Where's your father?" Before hollering, "Jeremiah?!" She then brushed aside a loose strand of dark brown hair, which had fallen from the pinned up beehive, before advancing on the bright yellow counter along the right-hand wall where Carmen was.
Grabbing a plate, she set that down at father's spot opposite me.

"Coming, sweetheart!" Father called from the living-room, his shoes suddenly rapping against the dining room floor before he appeared with a newspaper tucked under his arm.
"Smells delicious, sweetheart." He gleamed before sitting down where his breakfast was waiting, his dark blue eyes staring eagerly at his food.
He then shifted his attention to mother who was removing the floral apron from around her tiny waist, revealing a light pink dress underneath.

Once mother and Carmen had served breakfast and sat down either side, father brought a forkful of food to his lips; his eyes rolled into the back of his head in delight, a pleasing groan escaping him once he took a bite.
"And it tastes just as good as it looks!" He happily proclaimed as he brought a napkin up to his clean-shaven face, dabbing it either side of his thin, beaming lips.
He then tucked it into his light brown shirt, hiding his dark brown tie from view; his coltish body was emphasised by his pale grey suit, a black and gold badge was pinned to the lapel.

The rest of us then tucked in and the flavours tantalised my taste buds; I couldn't help but moan as did mother and Carmen.

Once I had swallowed my mouthful, I grinned, "Thank you, mother. Thank you, Carmen." And in unison, they looked at me and beamed, "I'm glad you're enjoying it." Before continuing to eat.

"What's your plans for the day, sweetheart?" Father asked mother between mouthfuls, skimming a hand over his brown hair that was combed to one side.

"Oh…" Mother lazily sighed, her dark brown eyes shifting to him as she smiled, "Well, I plan on making raspberry jam and pottering amid the rosebushes; however, I'm sure Mary will ring and ask me out to play badminton at the club, and then we'll have a spot of shopping with the girls followed by lunch."

"The jam isn't going to make itself." Father grinned, and mother briskly added, "But the shopping tempts, so I acquiesce. Lordy, last time I recklessly spent two-thirds of the housekeeping money on an orange girdle, a cashmere overcoat and half a dozen bobby socks."

Father lowered his fork at mother's confession, his smile never lessening as he asked, "I thought we were saving up to get a washing machine?"

Mother hummed and hawed, "That is more important, I don't fancy washing the clothes by hand. I could get a part-time jo-"

"Are you suggesting I can't provide for the family?" He bit back, both smirking at one another.

Mother then opened her mouth to protest, but father piped up first, "A job would be the ruination of you and that's the end of the matter!"

***

After breakfast, I grabbed my briefcase from my bedroom and headed downstairs, mother was waiting for me by the front door with a metal lunchbox in hand. Passing it to me, she turned her head so I could plant a quick kiss on her cheek.

"Have a nice day at work, honey." She beamed as I put the lunchbox in my briefcase.

Returning her smile with my own, I said, "Goodbye, mother."
I then gazed past her, hollering, "Goodbye, father! Goodbye, Carmen!"

"Goodbye, Nathaniel!" They replied in unison.

Turning on my heels, I ambled down the garden path, ignoring father's blue Austin Cambridge that was parked on the driveway to my left beside the lawn. I then opened the white picket gate before waving goodbye to mother, who was still standing by the door with a radiant smile. Closing the gate behind me, I automatically headed right towards the town centre.

Husbands and sons in neighbouring houses were also leaving for work bright and early, waving goodbye to their mothers or wives. They were dressed in fine suits or blue-collar clothes, depending on their profession. Only top management or executives drove to work in their blue Austin Cambridge's, and they would beep their horns and wave at each other.

"Good morning, Nathaniel." One man greeted with a dazzling smile when I walked past, he was strolling down his garden path with a briefcase in hand.

"Good morning, Robert." I beamed in return.

"Good morning, Nathaniel!" The man at the next house hollered with a grin; he then turned and waved goodbye to his wife and daughter.

"Good morning, Thomas!" I called back.

"Good morning, Nathaniel." Another man smiled as he closed the white gate behind him, now walking side by side with me.

"Good morning, Donald." I acknowledged with a grin.

"Rise and shine, it's a beautiful day in Merribridge! The sun is out and there isn't a cloud in the sky!" A plummy male voice rang loud and clear from speakers erected in the grass verge along the footway.

Suddenly, a young man stepped off his garden path, bumping into my shoulder and dropping his briefcase.

"I'm so sorry!" He apologised with a smile, but I shook my head and grinned, "No, **I'm** sorry." I insisted, helping him pick up his bag before heading on my way again.

"Remember, everyone, keep smiling!" The same plummy voice announced, repeating the broadcast over and over, "Rise and shine, it's a beautiful day in Merribridge! The sun is out and there isn't a cloud in the sky!"

Once I reached the small town of Merribridge, management and executives were starting to arrive, parking either in allocated car parks or alongside the cobbled road.

One man then clambered out of his car, his eyes landing on me as he greeted, "Good morning, Nathaniel."

Shooting him a gleaming smile, I replied, "Good morning, James."

Stores owners were now opening their shops with a ding, waving at whoever was walking by at the time.

"Good morning, Nathaniel." The butcher smiled, waving his hand that was holding a cleaver.

"Good morning, Jeffrey." I beamed back, taking in his blood-stained overalls.

When I finally reached my place of employment, the factory smokestacks were billowing with thick, black fumes. C.S – the company I work for - created and distributed supplements, preferring to make all products in-house. The front of the building was completely made up of glass, providing much-needed light.

Pushing open the door, I came to stand in the cream-walled reception area that had hardwood flooring. Black and white photographs covered the entire left and right walls, and the back wall had a wooden door in each corner; the right led to the nurse's office and the other led to the kitchen.

"Good morning, Mr West." I was greeted by the young, beaming receptionist who was sat behind her desk situated in the middle of the room; she then smoothed out her green dress that emphasised her petite, pale-skinned figure.

"Good morning, Miss Jones." I gleamed, walking past the black, cushioned chairs either side of the door along the glass wall.

Adjusting the black and gold badge pinned to her dress,

Miss Jones commented with a grin, "Mr Sheridan was looking for you." And she lowered her thick-rimmed glasses, showing off her ice blue eyes.
She then gestured with a nod towards another door on my right that led upstairs to the offices, causing her startling blonde curls to bounce.

"Why thank you, Miss Jones." I gratefully dipped my head before going upstairs.

Once I reached the top, I opened the only door that was on my left and entered the large, square-shaped office which had cream walls and wooden flooring; the glass along the left wall overlooked the town below. Desks lined the room in rows side by side, uncomfortable-looking chairs were tucked underneath.

Bypassing the executive offices on my right, I made a beeline for the door at the far end that had a clock hanging above it; this door led to Mr Sheridan's office who was top management.
I knocked twice; there was a moment of silence before a plummy male voice called, "Come in!" And I opened the door with a squeak, stepping inside where my shoes rapped against the hardwood flooring.

Closing the door behind me, I gazed at Mr Sheridan sat behind his mahogany desk that was in the middle of the room; the dark wood complimenting the deep green walls.
Squinting against the light pouring in from the window to my left, I said with a radiant smile, "Good morning, Mr Sheridan. Miss Jones said you were looking for me."

Mr Sheridan then leant back in his dark red, leather chair, momentarily glancing out the window directly behind him that overlooked the alley leading to the factory.

"Indeed, I was." He said with a twisted grin, peering at me with his gunmetal grey eyes – they looked so cold against his pale skin - before slapping the palms of his hands down onto the desk, pushing himself up where he advanced on me.

"I want to talk to you about a promotion." He carried on, burying his hands inside the trousers of his sharp grey suit that had a matching waistcoat; a dark blue tie was fastened to the collar of his pristine white shirt with a black and gold badge pinned to the lapel of his blazer.

"A promotion?" I repeated, shocked.

"Yes," Mr Sheridan murmured in agreement, scrubbing a hand through his swept back, dark hair, "A position has opened up for Quality Assurance Manager. I have you and one other in mind; however, I will need to organise an interview." He explained, now sitting on the edge of his desk, "You will be required to put together a presentation regarding how we could increase our desired level of quality for our products."

"Of course, Mr Sheridan!" I beamed, "Thank you so much for allowing me this opportunity!" And I grabbed his hand, vigorously shaking it, "I won't let you down!"

"I'm sure you won't." He grinned, "You may put the presentation together during work hours; however, I must stress that it **cannot** interfere with your paperwork."

"Of course not, Sir!"

"Good. That is all." He concluded before sitting back down behind his desk, waiting for me to leave.

Dipping my head in gratitude, I couldn't stop a full-blown grin from manifesting as I left.

By now the office was packed with people busying away at their desks. Mine was one of five that faced Mr Sheridan's office; it was on the end nearest the window. Putting my briefcase down, I pulled up my chair and took out my paperwork.

\*\*\*

When five o'clock arrived, I packed away my paperwork and ideas I had written down for the presentation before heading to the stairs where everyone was filing out one by one.

"Have a good evening, Mr Smith." Miss Jones bid farewell to everyone in turn, and they too wished her a goodnight.

Her ice blue eyes then landed on me, and she said with a show-stopping smile, "Have a good evening, Mr West."

"You too, Miss Jones." I grinned, grabbing the door Mr Smith had held for me, and I too held it open for the person behind me.

Once they had grabbed it, I turned left and made my way past store owners who were closing their shops.

"Good evening, Jeffrey." I beamed at the butcher as he locked up, and he replied with a grin, "Good evening, Nathaniel."

"Good evening, James." I smiled at the man hopping into his car, and he waved in reply, "Good evening, Nathaniel."

"It's been a busy day in Merribridge! Have a peaceful night's rest ready for a brand-new day tomorrow!" A plummy male voice rang from speakers fastened to buildings, "Remember, everyone, keep smiling!"

Once I had left the town of Merribridge, I was on the last stretch home when a young man unexpectedly swung his garden gate open into me. My briefcase fell to the pavement with a clatter, bursting open and making my paperwork fly out.

"I'm so sorry!" He apologised with a smile, instantly bending down to gather my papers.

Kneeling to help him, I insisted, "No, **I'm** sorry!" And I shoved everything inside my case, clipping it shut.

I then went on my way once more, nodding my head at whoever passed me.

"Good evening, Donald." I automatically greeted a man who now walked side by side with me.

"Good evening, Nathaniel." He beamed before disappearing down a garden path.

"Good evening, Thomas." I gleamed at another as he turned to close his garden gate.

Grinning, Thomas waved, "Good evening, Nathaniel."

"Good evening, Robert." I acknowledged another who was strolling down his garden path.

Looking over his shoulder, he shot me a dazzling smile, "Good evening, Nathaniel."

"It's been a busy day in Merribridge!" The announcement sounded from the grass verge, "Have a peaceful night's rest ready for a brand-new day tomorrow! Remember, everyone, keep smiling!"

**BEEP, BEEP!** Executives and top management started to arrive home, tooting their horns and waving. I could see father's car was already parked on the driveway, looking as if it hadn't moved all day. Swinging open the white gate, I closed it behind me before ambling up the garden path.

Unlocking the front door, I hollered, "I'm home!" And everyone replied in unison, "Welcome home, Nathaniel!" Before I wandered upstairs into my bedroom.

Discarding my briefcase, I slipped off my blazer and deposited it on the bed, unbuttoning my waistcoat and loosening my tie before going back downstairs.

"Where's your father?" Mother asked as soon as I stepped into the dining room; she had just brought out two plates piled with meatloaf and vegetables, the meaty aroma making my mouth salivate.

"Jeremiah?!" She hollered when I sat facing the bay window, putting my plate down and then his plate at the head of the table closest to the hallway; Carmen sat opposite me once she set the table.

Rustling was heard from the living-room before father responded, "Coming, sweetheart!" He then appeared moments later, pulling up a chair; mother sat across from him once she had brought out hers and Carmen's plates.

"Let's say grace." Father said, cupping his hands together and bowing his head, continuing once we all copied, "Bless us, O Lord, and these, Thy gifts, which we are about to receive from Thy bounty. Through Christ, our Lord. Amen."

"Amen." We said in unison followed by the sign of the cross; I then grabbed my knife and fork, the first bite overwhelmed my mouth with a diverse range of flavours.

"How was your day at the office, honey?" Mother asked father between mouthfuls, and he dabbed a napkin either side of his beaming lips before answering, "Busy as always, sweetheart. We're currently looking into new ingredients for the supplements, but there's too few men on board."

"Sounds like you need an extra hand." Mother grinned before looking to me, asking, "How was your day at the office, honey?"

"Mr Sheridan approached me about the Quality Assurance Manager position that has opened up." I replied, making father grin from ear to ear.

"Has he now?" He beamed, "Well, that would be interesting. Father and son working together."

"So you've got the job?" Mother gleamed at me, her dark brown eyes shining with pride.

"No, he would like me to put together a presentation ready for the interview." I responded through a mouthful, making mother coo, "I'm so proud of you!" But then she suddenly glimpsed under the table, unexpectedly snapping with a toothy grin, "Max! Get out this instant!"

There was a brief moment of scuffling before I felt something whack against my legs.

Our Golden Retriever, Max, then poked his head out in-between my legs, resting his muzzle on my lap before abruptly shoving his way out, almost knocking my plate off the table.

"That dog needs to stay in the kitchen during dinner!" Mother hawked, beaming at father who nodded compliantly, "Yes, sweetheart." He sighed with a smirk.

He then grabbed the dog by the collar, dragging him towards the kitchen while saying, "Come on, to the kitchen with you."

***

"Has Mr Sheridan explained to you what is expected in the presentation?" Father enquired with a radiant smile, leaning on the armrest of his brown club chair.

He was sat in the far, right corner of the orange-walled living-room; I was sat to his left on an orange Hillcrest chair, a wooden table was in-between us with a white china lamp and black rotary dial telephone on top.

Nodding, I replied, "How we can increase our desired

level of quality."

"That's my boy!" Father exclaimed in delight before mother wandered in, her shoes clipping against the hardwood floor.
Bypassing the coffee table in the middle of the room, she advanced on the window that took up the entire back wall near father, pulling the cream curtains shut; they were so thin I could still make out the neighbour's fence.

Mother then turned for the large, bay window that overlooked the front garden, kneeling on the pink tufted sofa underneath that was facing us so she could draw the matching cream curtains. Once she was done, she plonked herself down just as Carmen ambled in; she made a beeline for the television, which was on top of a matching table facing the back window.

"Would you like me to turn the television on, father?" Carmen queried, gleaming.

"Oh, yes, of course!" Father exclaimed, as if suddenly remembering, "We don't want to miss the broadcast!"
Carmen hurriedly twisted the knobs until she tuned into a live broadcast; she then dashed over to the sofa, slumping down beside mother.

The Prime Minister – who had such an unusual-looking face it would put Picasso's paintings to shame - was stood at his podium, the black and white television occasionally crackling. He had light coloured hair, which was slicked back and smooth at the sides; it was so pale it nearly matched his fair skin. His dark fitted suit did very little to conceal his paunchy body.

"Citizens of Merribridge!" The Prime Minister began with a radiant smile and eloquent voice, "As you are all aware, Richard Terrance Brown was a wanted man. He not only broke the law on several accounts, but he severely injured officers of the law trying to escape. Today, Mr Brown was caught on the outskirts of Merribridge, there he was shot dead. I want you all to know that what I did, I did for Merribridge, I did for **you**!" He then fell silent for a moment, as if coming to terms with the death of a civilian.

Clearing his throat, the Prime Minister then carried on, "Merribridge needs people like **you**, people who run the country for me. Without you, Merribridge will cease to exist. **I need you, Merribridge** needs you. So, if you ever think of crossing over like Richard Brown, then I want you to look deep inside yourself and ask '**Is there a darkness inside me? Or is that the Devil?**'." Again, he was silent for but a moment before continuing, "Sometimes, the worst place the Devil can be is inside your head. He will whisper in your ear, plant voices inside your head that make you question yourself. The Devil had Richard Brown's soul, remember what happened to Richard Brown."

Another moment of silence filled the atmosphere, drawn out for so long it felt like a lifetime before the Prime Minister finally concluded, "I'd like to wish you a goodnight. Remember, keep smiling!" And as soon as he finished, Carmen got up and turned off the television.

"Right!" Father proclaimed, slapping his hands down onto his thighs, "It's time to turn in for the night." He then stood up and switched off the lamp, all the while we each said goodnight to one another.

I then followed Carmen upstairs, watching as she turned right at the top of the landing before disappearing into her room next to mine; I quickly went into the bathroom to get ready for bed.

Once I had finished, I headed to my room, switching on the bedside lamp and drawing the curtains. Making sure my work clothes were folded neatly, I put them away in the wardrobe, hanging up my suit jacket so not to crease it. Finally, I clambered into bed, fluffed up my pillows, and switched off the lamp.

## Chapter Two
### Rise and shine

**DING, DING, DING!** My alarm clock suddenly went off, waking me up. A yawn escaped my lips as I stretched in bed before swinging my feet round to sit on the edge. I gazed at the clock on my nightstand while rubbing a hand across my stubbled jaw, the metal hammer ruthlessly knocking between the two bells. I then swiftly turned it off before noticing the time, which was 6:45AM.

Mindlessly reaching for the transistor radio, I turned the large dial and tuned into the radio station.
"Good morning, citizens of Merribridge! It's Tuesday 7th July in sunny England, and you're listening to 1959's Elation Station!"
'III've got yooou under my skiiin. III've got yooou deep in the heaaart of meee, so deep in my heart that you're really a paaart of meee. III've got yooou under my skiiin.'.

I then robotically stood up, stretching once more before making my bed. Leaning across the headrest for the window, I tugged back the curtains. '**Don't you knoooow, you foooool, you never can wiiin? Uuuse your mentalittty, wake up to realittty.**'. With one last stretch, I turned for the wardrobe, grabbing my work clothes and shoes from yesterday just as the song abruptly came to life. '**III would sacrifice anything come what might, for the sake of having you neeear, in spite of a waaarning voic-**' But then I switched it off and headed into the bathroom.

Once I had deposited my clothes, I quickly brushed my

teeth and shaved, reaching for one of the white hand towels to dry my face on afterwards. I then changed into my work clothes after using the toilet before styling my hair, making sure it was smooth at the sides with a quiff at the front. Lastly, I pulled on my shoes, put my toiletries away, and wandered downstairs where the sweet aroma of bacon and eggs invaded my senses.

I made my way through the dining room and into the kitchen, spotting mother by the hob with her back to me; she wore the same light pink dress from yesterday, but her dark brown hair was down in a bouffant. The ding of cutlery then gained my attention, and I gazed over to see Carmen setting the breakfast table with Max peering out from underneath.

Taking a further step inside, I greeted in my usual, upbeat tone, "Good morning, mother. Good morning, Carmen." In unison, they spun round to face me, smiling broadly, "Good morning, Nathaniel." Before turning back and continuing what they were doing.

I then made my way over to the breakfast table, pulling up a chair just as Carmen finished setting it; I noticed she wore a pale green dress today, her long, blonde hair down in loose curls. Her green eyes then momentarily met mine, a smile growing on her face that had very little make-up before she began helping mother pile the plates up with bacon, eggs, and a side of toast.

"Where's your father?" Mother queried with a radiant smile gracing her made-up face, hollering, "Jeremiah?!" She then grabbed a plate, setting it down at father's spot opposite me.

"Coming, sweetheart!" Father called from the living-room, his shoes suddenly rapping against the dining room floor before he appeared with a newspaper tucked under his arm; his pale grey suit was the same one from yesterday, the badge still fastened to the lapel.

"Smells delicious, sweetheart." He gleamed before sitting down, his dark blue eyes staring eagerly at his food.
He then shifted his attention to mother who was removing the floral apron from around her waist.

Once mother and Carmen had served breakfast and sat

down, father brought a forkful of food to his lips; his eyes rolled into the back of his head in delight, a pleasing groan escaping him once he took a bite.

"And it tastes just as good as it looks!" He happily proclaimed, dabbing a napkin either side of his thin, beaming lips before tucking it into his light brown shirt.

The rest of us then dug in and the flavours tantalised my taste buds; I couldn't help but moan as did mother and Carmen. Once I had swallowed my mouthful, I grinned, "Thank you, mother. Thank you, Carmen." And in unison, they looked at me and beamed, "I'm glad you're enjoying it." Before continuing to eat.

"What's your plans for the day, sweetheart?" Father asked mother between mouthfuls.

"Oh..." Mother lazily sighed, her dark brown eyes shifting to him as she smiled, "Well, I plan on making vegetable soup and pottering amid the tulips; however, I'm sure Susan will ring and ask me out to play tennis at the club, and then we'll have a spot of shopping with the girls followed by lunch."

"The soup isn't going to make itself." Father grinned, and mother briskly added, "But the shopping tempts, so I acquiesce. Lordy, last time I recklessly spent two-thirds of the housekeeping money on a blue skirt, a cocktail dress and three pairs of espadrilles."

Father lowered his fork at mother's confession, his smile never lessening as he asked, "I thought we were saving up to get a washing machine?"

Mother hummed and hawed, "That is more important, I don't fancy washing the clothes by hand. I could get a part-time jo-"

"Are you suggesting I can't provide for the family?" He bit back, both smirking at one another.

Mother then opened her mouth to protest, but father piped up first, "A job would be the ruination of you and that's the end of the matter!"

***

After breakfast, I grabbed my briefcase and headed downstairs, mother was waiting for me by the front door with a metal lunchbox in hand. Passing it to me, she turned her head so I could plant a quick kiss on her cheek.

"Have a nice day at work, honey." She beamed as I put the lunchbox in my briefcase.

Returning her smile with my own, I said, "Goodbye, mother."

I then gazed past her, hollering, "Goodbye, father! Goodbye, Carmen!"

"Goodbye, Nathaniel!" They replied in unison.

Turning on my heels, I ambled down the garden path, opening the gate before waving goodbye to mother; she still stood by the door with a radiant smile. Closing the gate behind me, I automatically headed right.

"Good morning, Nathaniel." Robert greeted with a dazzling smile when I walked past, he was strolling down his garden path with a briefcase in hand.

"Good morning, Robert." I beamed in return.

"Good morning, Nathaniel!" Thomas hollered with a grin; he then turned back and waved goodbye to his wife and daughter.

"Good morning, Thomas!" I called back.

"Good morning, Nathaniel." Donald smiled as he closed the gate behind him, now walking side by side with me.

"Good morning, Donald." I acknowledged with a grin.

"Rise and shine, it's a beautiful day in Merribridge! The sun is out and there isn't a cloud in the sky!" A plummy male voice rang loud and clear from the speakers erected in the grass verge.

Suddenly, a young man stepped off his garden path, bumping into my shoulder and dropping his briefcase.

"I'm so sorry!" He apologised with a smile, but I shook my head and grinned, "No, **I'm** sorry." I insisted, helping him pick up his bag before heading on my way again.

"Remember, everyone, keep smiling!" The same plummy voice announced, repeating the broadcast over and over, "Rise and shine, it's a beautiful day in Merribridge! The sun is out and there isn't a cloud in the sky!"

Once I reached the small town of Merribridge, management and executives were starting to arrive.

James then clambered out of his car, his eyes landing on me as he greeted, "Good morning, Nathaniel."

Shooting him a gleaming smile, I replied, "Good morning, James."

Stores owners were now opening their shops with a ding, waving at whoever was walking by at the time.

"Good morning, Nathaniel." The butcher smiled, waving his hand that was holding onto a cleaver.

"Good morning, Jeffrey." I beamed back, taking in his blood-stained overalls.

I then pushed open the door to C.S, coming to stand in the reception area where Miss Jones smirked at me from behind her desk.

"Good morning, Mr West." She greeted, smoothing out her pale pink dress and adjusting the badge pinned to it.

"Good morning, Miss Jones." I gleamed, advancing towards the door that led upstairs.

"Mr Sheridan was looking for you." She commented with a grin, lowering her thick-rimmed glasses once she had fastened her startling blonde hair into a high ponytail.

"Why thank you, Miss Jones." I gratefully dipped my head before going upstairs.

Once I reached the top, I immediately strolled over to Mr Sheridan's office, knocking twice; there was a moment of silence before a plummy male voice called, "Come in!" And I opened the door with a squeak, stepping inside.

Closing the door behind me, I gazed at Mr Sheridan sat behind his mahogany desk; he wore the same sharp grey suit from yesterday with a badge pinned the lapel.

"Good morning, Mr Sheridan." I said with a radiant smile, "Miss Jones said you were looking for me."

"Indeed, I was." He replied with a twisted grin before slapping the palms of his hands down onto the desk, pushing himself up and advancing on me, "I wanted to talk to you about the promotion I mentioned yesterday."

"What about it?" I queried.

"I have arranged the interview for next Monday, all the executives will be present as well. We will be asking you questions before and after the presentation." He explained, now sitting on the edge of his desk, "Timothy Miller, the other person I have in mind for the vacancy, will be having his interview first."

"Thank you for letting me know, Sir!" I beamed, grabbing his hand and vigorously shaking it, "And thank you again for this opportunity!"

"How is the presentation coming along?" Mr Sheridan queried, pulling his hand free from mine, "You may ask for help if you're uncertain, but you should be able to put the majority of it together if not all of it."

"Thank you for the offer, Sir, but I can manage."

"Good. That is all." He concluded before sitting back down behind his desk, waiting for me to leave.

Dipping my head in gratitude, I left.

*** 

When five o'clock arrived, I packed away my paperwork and presentation notes before heading to the stairs where everyone was filing out one by one.

"Have a good evening, Mr Smith." Miss Jones bid farewell to everyone in turn, and they too wished her a goodnight.

Her ice blue eyes then landed on me, and she said with a show-stopping smile, "Have a good evening, Mr West."

"You too, Miss Jones." I grinned, grabbing the door Mr Smith had held for me, and I too held it open for the person behind me.

Once they had grabbed it, I turned left and made my way past store owners who were closing their shops.

"Good evening, Jeffrey." I beamed at the butcher as he locked up, and he replied with a grin, "Good evening, Nathaniel."

"Good evening, James." I smiled at the man hopping into his car, and he waved in reply, "Good evening, Nathaniel."

"It's been a busy day in Merribridge! Have a peaceful night's rest ready for a brand-new day tomorrow!" A plummy male voice rang from speakers fastened to buildings, "Remember, everyone, keep smiling!"

Once I had left the town of Merribridge, I was on the last stretch home when a young man unexpectedly swung open his garden gate into me. My briefcase fell to the pavement with a clatter, bursting open and making my paperwork fly out.

"I'm so sorry!" He apologised with a smile, instantly bending down to gather my papers.

Kneeling to help him, I insisted, "No, **I'm** sorry!" And I shoved everything inside my case, clipping it shut.

I then went on my way once more, nodding my head at whoever passed me.

"Good evening, Donald." I automatically greeted when he walked side by side with me.

"Good evening, Nathaniel." He beamed before disappearing down a garden path.

"Good evening, Thomas." I gleamed as he turned to close his garden gate.

Grinning, Thomas waved, "Good evening, Nathaniel."

"Good evening, Robert." I acknowledged while he was strolling down his garden path.

Looking over his shoulder, Robert shot me a dazzling smile, "Good evening, Nathaniel."

"It's been a busy day in Merribridge!" The announcement sounded from the grass verge, "Have a peaceful night's rest ready for a brand-new day tomorrow! Remember, everyone, keep smiling!"

**BEEP, BEEP!** Executives and top management started to arrive home, tooting their horns and waving. I could see father's car was already parked on the driveway, looking as if it hadn't moved all day. Swinging open the white gate, I closed it behind me before ambling up the garden path.

Unlocking the front door, I hollered, "I'm home!" And everyone replied in unison, "Welcome home, Nathaniel!" Before I wandered upstairs into my bedroom.

Discarding my briefcase, I slipped off my blazer and deposited it on the bed, unbuttoning my waistcoat and loosening my tie before going back downstairs.

"Where's your father?" Mother asked as soon as I stepped into the dining room; she had just brought out two plates piled with fried chicken and vegetables, the meaty aroma making my mouth salivate.

"Jeremiah?!" She hollered when I pulled up a chair, putting my plate down and then his at the head of the table; Carmen sat opposite me once she set the table.

Rustling was heard from the living-room before father responded, "Coming, sweetheart!" He then appeared moments later, pulling up a chair; mother sat across from him once she had brought out hers and Carmen's plates.

"Let's say grace." Father said, cupping his hands together and bowing his head, continuing once we all copied, "Bless us, O Lord, and these, Thy gifts, which we are about to receive from Thy bounty. Through Christ, our Lord. Amen."

"Amen." We said in unison followed by the sign of the cross; I then grabbed my knife and fork, about to tuck in when a scuffling was heard from under the table, distracting everyone.

Glimpsing underneath, mother unexpectedly snapped with a toothy grin, "Max! Get out this instant!" And there was more commotion before I felt something whack against my legs. Max then poked his head out in-between my legs, resting his muzzle on my lap before abruptly shoving his way out with such force I was knocked backwards, causing my dinner plate to slide off the table. An audible gasp was heard from father when the food fell into my lap with an audible squelch, the plate hitting the floor with an almighty smash.

"**MAX!**" Father bellowed with a radiant smile, jumping up and dragging the dog away when he tried to eat it; I had never seen him react so angrily before.

Mother then dashed into the kitchen, returning with fistfuls of kitchen towel to clean up the mess, passing me several sheets so I could wipe my trousers, but the damage had already been done.

Gazing at me sympathetically, mother cooed, "Go and get yourself cleaned up, honey."

Nodding, I rose to my feet and immediately went upstairs to change my clothes, grabbing a pair of beige, straight-legged trousers and a blue and white stripy t-shirt; I then discarded my dirty clothes in the laundry basket in the bathroom afterwards.

When I returned to the dining room, everything had been cleaned up and everyone was sat back down; however, there was no fresh plate of food at my spot.

"Sorry, honey." Mother apologised, gazing sheepishly up at me with a smile, "But there were no leftovers."

"I hope you're happy, Vivian!" Father abruptly growled, grinning from ear to ear, "Now the boys going to go hungry!" And he peered over at me, clearly concerned.

"It's okay." I beamed, "I can wait until breakfast."

*** 

"Has Mr Sheridan told you when the interviews will be held?" Father enquired with a radiant smile, leaning on the armrest of his club chair.

Gazing at him from my Hillcrest chair, I nodded, "Next Monday." Before mother wandered in, drawing the curtains and plonking herself down on the sofa.

Carmen then made a beeline for the television, asking father as she done so, "Would you like me to turn the television on, father?"

"Oh, yes, of course!" He exclaimed, as if suddenly remembering, "We don't want to miss the broadcast!"

Carmen hurriedly twisted the knobs until she tuned into the live broadcast; she then dashed over to the sofa, slumping down beside mother.

"Citizens of Merribridge!" The Prime Minister began, grinning from ear to ear, "It is with great pleasure I am proud to be **your** Prime Minister! It's because of **you**, Merribridge is an efficient town. Merribridge is resourceful, prosperous, and self-reliant, all because of **you**." He then fell silent for a moment, as if allowing his words to sink in.

Clearing his throat, the Prime Minister then carried on, "As your Prime Minister, I've worked hard to maintain this perfect, little town for **you**. All I ask for is your loyalty and labour. Like any other town, **you** are the cog that helps this town flourish." Another moment of silence filled the atmosphere before he finally concluded, "I'd like to wish you a goodnight. Remember, keep smiling!" And as soon as he had finished, Carmen got up and turned off the television.

"Right!" Father proclaimed, slapping his hands down onto his thighs, "It's time to turn in for the night." He then stood up and switched off the lamp, all the while we each said goodnight to one another.

I then followed Carmen upstairs, watching as she disappeared into her room; I quickly went into the bathroom to get ready for bed.

Once I had finished, I headed to my room, switching on the bedside lamp and drawing the curtains. Grabbing my suit jacket, I hung it up so not to crease it. Finally, I clambered into bed, fluffed up my pillows, and switched off the lamp.

# Chapter Three
## Wake up to reality!

**DING, DING, DING!** *Urgh... No... Don't want to get up...* Groaning, I twisted and turned in bed. *Just... Just five more minutes...* And I impulsively slapped the alarm clock, shutting it up.

*\*\*\**

**BANG! BANG! BANG!**
"Nathaniel?!" Father hollered followed by more knocking.
*What the-* Suddenly, my bedroom door swung open, startling me. I sat bolt upright in bed, staring at father who stood by the door with a massive smile plastered across his face; his arms folded over his pale grey blazer, clearly unimpressed.
Confused, I wondered, "What's wrong?"
"Why are you still in bed, son?" He asked, his radiant smile not reaching his dark blue eyes.
*Or face...* Then I realised what he said. *What's the time?!* And my gaze snapped over to my alarm clock, reading 7:27AM. *I'M LATE?!*
"I'll be down in a minute!" I barked, taking father by surprise; he drew his head back quickly, as if trying to process something.
After a brief moment of silence, he said, "You better be." Then he turned to leave, adding over his shoulder, "Breakfasts ready, so don't be too long." Before closing the door behind him, leaving me to get frantically ready for work.
Wracking my brains, I jumped to my feet while trying to

figure out why I hadn't woken up. *How did this happen?!* Ripping open the wardrobe, I grabbed whatever I could get my hands on first before darting into the bathroom, carelessly tossing them on top of the wicker basket.

*Why didn't I hear my alarm go off?!* I worriedly deliberated, tugging off my pyjamas before shrugging on my white shirt. *It can't be broken!* I then yanked on my navy trousers while shoving my feet into my wingtips shoes. *The clock was still working!* Before slipping on my dark brown waistcoat, not even bothering to button it up. *This has **never** happened before!* And I fastened my black and gold tie before pulling on my pale grey blazer.

*Right, what next?!* I panicked, my attention landing on the mirror. *Ah, my hair!* Staring into the mirror, I took in my bedhead hair and stubble. *Do I have time to shave?* I debated, rubbing a hand across my prickly jawline. *Maybe if I do it quic- What the?!* But that thought was short-lived when I spotted my clothes. *Seriously?!* I gawked, my jaw dropping as I gazed from the pale grey suit jacket, to the dark brown waistcoat, to the navy trousers. *How the hell didn't I notice?!* Shaking my head, I couldn't believe this was happening.

*I don't have time for this!* I declared, a heavy feeling growing in the pit of my stomach. *I can't go to work like this! I look like an idio-*

"**NATHANIEL!**" Father abruptly hollered from somewhere downstairs, and I knew I couldn't keep my family waiting a moment longer.

*Great... This is all I need...* I griped, giving myself one last pathetic glance before heading downstairs, going straight through into the kitchen.

Everyone was waiting for me at the breakfast table, their food untouched. Then I realised they were all gaping at me but, somehow, their faces were still wreathed in smiles. *That's creepy...* I shuddered, averting my gaze elsewhere as I wandered over, pulling up the chair by the patio doors.

"What on earth are you wearing, Nathaniel?" Father

questioned as soon as I sat down, gaining my attention.
Not wanting to express my inner turmoil, I blurted without thinking, "Clothes, why?" Which clearly didn't go down well by the slight twitch under his right eye.

"Don't be a smart mouth, Nathaniel!" Father growled through his never wavering smile just as mother piped up, distracting me, "Are you okay, honey?" And she flicked her loose, dark brown hair from her shoulder, the concern shimmering in her eyes not matching her gleaming, made-up face.

"Yeah, why?" I swiftly replied, not even considering whether I actually was or not.

"You just look awful." She bluntly responded while smoothing out her white dress, shocking me.

*Do I really look awful?* I mulled, glancing down at myself only to realise she was right. *I mean, look at me!* I hawked, vaguely aware of Carmen blatantly staring me up and down; her made-up face was wreathed in smiles, but there was an underlying confusion blazing behind her green eyes. *I look like a clow-* But then something dawned on me, and I shifted my attention away from my sister just as she mindlessly twirled an index finger around a strand of her loose, curly hair; a bright yellow headband held it in place, matching her dress.

*Hang on... Why is there a voice – **my** voice - inside my head?!* The heavy feeling in my gut vanished, my stomach now rock-hard. *How is my voice inside my head?!* I panicked, feeling the hairs on the nape of my neck rise before noticing my family were staring at me; it only just occurred to me that they may be hearing this voice too. *Nod your head once if you can hear me.* They didn't, so I focused on just one person - Carmen. *Nod your head once if you can hear me.* Nothing. She continued to stare at me like I was a stranger in my own home, her beaming face not showing any signs that she had heard me.

*WHAT THE HELL HAS HAPPENED TO ME?!* I wanted to scream. I wanted to breakdown. I wanted to curl up into a little ball until the voice inside my head had disappeared. *But I can't do any of that, otherwise they'll think I'm crazy!* I fretted, trying to still my shaking hands. *Even though I am because I'm hearing this voice!* Giving my family one last glance, I knew I needed to get away before I lost my mind.

"Well, I better go before I'm late for work!" I quickly decided, heading straight to the front door and dashing down the garden path, not once glancing back.

*What's wrong with me?!* I cried, yanking open the garden gate with a clammy hand. *Why has this happened?!* **How** *has this happened?!* And I slammed it shut before speed walking towards the town centre. *Did I do something wrong?!*

"Good morning, Nathaniel." Robert greeted; I glimpsed over at him strolling down his garden path with a briefcase in hand.

"Muh-Morning, Robert." I tremulously replied just before Thomas hollered, "Good morning, Nathaniel!" And I peered over to see him waving at his wife and daughter, so I just ignored him and continued on my way; a scream escaped me when Donald suddenly appeared, now walking side by side with me.

"Good morning, Nathaniel." He gleamed, and I gasped in reply while clutching at my shirt, "You scared me!"

"Rise and shine, it's a beautiful day in Merribridge! The sun is out and there isn't a cloud in the sky!" A plummy voice echoed from speakers along the grass verge, gaining my attention where I noticed-

*Wait a minute, is that a camera?* It looked like one had been fitted at the top of every speaker, confusing me. *But why-* **BANG!** I accidentally collided into a young man who had stepped off his garden path, his briefcase hitting the ground with a clatter; paperwork flew out like a flock of doves, drifting down and littering the pavement.

"I'm so sorry!" He apologised with a smile, bending down and gathering his papers.

Kneeling to help, I shook my head, apologising, "No, no, it's my fault." And I handed him what I had scooped up before going to grab my briefcase; however, I couldn't find it.

*Where is it?* I couldn't even remember picking it up. *Oh no!*

And it dawned on me. *I left it at home!* My throat abruptly felt constricted, my mouth now as dry as a bone. *I'm going be late if I go back for it!* Bringing a hand up to pinch the skin at my throat, I tried to decide what to do. *But it's got all my presentation notes inside!* And that thought alone made me realise. *I've got to go back!*

Turning on my heels, I ran back home, getting irritated by the loud broadcast repeating itself.

"Remember, everyone, keep smiling! Rise and shine, it's a beautiful day in Merribridge! The sun is out and there isn't a cloud in the sky! Remember, everyone, keep smiling!"

*Shut! Up! Shut up, shut up!* I growled.

I was a stone's throw away from the house when I saw father get in his car; my worry abruptly vanished, relief now washing over me. *Yes! Thank God he hasn't left!*

Just as he started to reverse off the driveway, I briskly waved him down, hollering, "Wait!" And he abruptly stopped.

Poking his head out the window, he asked with a dazzling smile, "I thought you left for work?"

Cupping my hands together, I begged, "Can you give me a lift? I forgot my briefcase and I'm going to be late."

A look between trepidation and dismay shimmered in his dark blue eyes, but his smile never faltered as he bluntly replied, "No." Shocking me, "What! Why?!"

"I'm an executive, Nathaniel." He explained matter-of-factly, "You are middle management. During work, we **do not** socialise. Remember, routine is key." And he drove off without another word, leaving me staring after him.

\*\*\*

By the time I had grabbed my briefcase and bolted to work, my breath was hitching in my throat and my lungs were on fire. *Never... Run... Again...* I panted, virtually collapsing through the entrance door of C.S, but I managed to hold myself up on the doorframe.

"Mr West?" Miss Jones called, gaining my attention. She was stood behind her desk showcasing her light brown dress, complimenting her startling blonde hair that was down in waves. Her ice blue eyes blazed in bewilderment behind her thick-rimmed glasses, her hand lingering on her parted, beaming lips.

"Are you... Are you alright?" Miss Jones queried further, blatantly staring me up and down.

"Yuh-Yeah..." I gasped, struggling to catch my breath back, "Juh-Just a bit of... Bit of light exercise buh-before... Work..."

"Hmm..." She murmured, unconvinced, "So I see..." And she continued to just stare at me, making me feel conspicuous.

*What's she looking at?* I wondered, following her quizzical gaze; I couldn't help but do a double-take when I noticed the state of me. *Oh dear!* My tie was hanging halfway down my neck, the white shirt untucked from my navy trousers; sweat had seeped through my light grey blazer, the stench hitting me out of nowhere. *God, I stink!* I inwardly gagged, quick to lower my arms in the hopes the smell wouldn't waft.

Suddenly, movement out of the corner of my right eye gained my attention; I had to stop my jaw from dropping in horror when I noticed clients were sat waiting near the window. They were looking at me in apparent disgust yet, somehow, they were grinning from ear to ear. *Oh no!* I panicked, anxiously rubbing my sweaty face when I diverted my gaze elsewhere. *I'm going to be in enough trouble as it is because I'm late, but now I'm also giving C.S a bad image!*

"Anyway," Miss Jones piped up, distracting me, "Mr Sheridan was looking for you, but that was a while ago now..."

"Great..." I muttered under my breath, "Just what I need..." And I brushed aside a few slithers of hair that were stuck to my brow. I then headed for the door to the offices upstairs, but Miss Jones stopped me in my tracks when she spoke up, "Mr West?"
When I peered over my shoulder, she continued, "If I may be so bold, I think you should see the nurse. You look terrible!"

"Why thank you, Miss Jones." I retorted scornfully, narrowing

my eyes, "Terrible was what I was aiming for..." But she didn't seem to grasp my sarcasm.
*Never mind then...*

Shaking my head in frustration, I deliberated. *Should I see the nurse?* But then I realised I couldn't. *I can't tell her I'm hearing voices in my head! She'll think I'm crazy!*
But I didn't get the chance to object as Miss Jones decided, "I'll give her a call and tell her you're waiting." And she gestured for me to take a seat away from the clients before sitting down behind her desk.
Sighing in frustration, I did as she said and sat down, setting my briefcase on the floor beside me.

"Good morning, Nurse Lane." Miss Jones greeted, and I glanced over to see she was on the phone, "I have a Mr West waiting to see you." There was a moment of silence before she said, "Thank you, goodbye." And she hung up.

*What's happening to me?* I couldn't help but wonder as I sat in silence, trying to ignore the clients prying eyes. *Maybe I should've stayed at home and rested?* I debated, biting my bottom lip and rubbing my clammy hands down my trouser legs. *I don't understand why I can hear a voice - **my** voice - inside my head.* Clearing my throat, I ran a jerky hand through my damp hair.

*Has this ever happened to anyone before?* Then the Prime Minister's warning came to mind. **'Sometimes, the worst place the Devil can be is inside your head. He will whisper in your ear, plant voices inside your head that make you question yourself.'.** *Is it the Devil's voice I'm hearing? But... Why does he sound like me?* My stomach suddenly hardened when that thought sunk in, causing the hairs on the nape of my neck to stand on end. *No!* I adamantly declared, feeling my chin tremble in fear. *It's not the Devil! **I'm not** the Devil! This is just a dream!* And I jammed my hands into my armpits, as if hugging myself. *I'm dreaming! I'm going to wake up soon!* **Please!** I sobbed, now shaking uncontrollably. *Wake up to reality!*

"Mr West?" A silvery voice called, distracting me from my inner turmoil, and I couldn't stop my jaw from dropping when my eyes landed on the nurse outside her office door in the far, right corner.

*I **must** be dreaming!* I gasped, feeling a shifting sensation near my heart.

The first thing my eyes locked on were her mesmerising green ones, they were filled with such kindness that was mirrored by the genuine smile on her plump, rosy lips. *She's beautiful!* I exclaimed, longing to get a better look at her dark brown locks that were pinned underneath her white nurse's cap; the little tendrils I saw complimented her milky skin. I then gazed from her heart-shaped face down to her curvy figure, which was clad in a white nurse's uniform. Her slender legs were concealed by white tights with matching shoes, but even the slight heel didn't sway from how petite she was.

"Mr West?" She called again, looking around, and I knew I couldn't keep gawking at her forever.

Without thinking, I staggered to my feet with my hand in the air as if I were in school, blurting, "Yeerrrah… Here! I'm Mr West!" And I instantly regretted it.

*Could I have sounded any more like an idiot?!* I growled, but my embarrassment dissipated when I saw her smile blossom, consuming me with a pleasurable shiver.

"If you'd like to follow me." She stated before disappearing through the door behind her.

For a moment I was left staring after her, unable to move or say anything. *How haven't I seen her before?! Then again, I've never been to see the nurse…* Straightening myself up, I advanced towards the door, trying my hardest not to make more of a fool out of myself.

My feet scuffed against the mottled, dark brown tiles when I stepped into the nurse's office, now gazing around the small, yellow-walled room. My eyes instantly locked onto her bum as she sashayed over to her mahogany desk that had a brown leather swivel chair tucked underneath; it was in front of a window that took up the entire back wall, directly opposite the door where I stood. *I need to get a grip!* I announced with a shake of my head, trying to distract myself.

I then spotted a white medicine cabinet with a glass front fastened to the right wall above the desk; it faced into the room and was low enough to be within reach. *But I can't!* I realised, and my attention swiftly circled back to the nurse as she sat down. *I just want to hold her!* I proclaimed while my fingers tingled with the need to touch her, so much so I had to stroke my left arm as a surrogate.

But then I wondered. *How's she doing this to me?* It was as if a spell had been cast over me. *I've **never** felt this way before about anyone.* I deliberated, but that thought was long forgotten when her mesmerising green eyes locked with mine, and I was suddenly spellbound once more. I couldn't help but take in her porcelain skin that glowed against the sunlight seeping through the window, making her loose, dark strands seem almost auburn. *Wow!* I couldn't help but gawk, my heartbeat now quickening.

"Are you going to come in?" The nurse suddenly piped up, and I immediately took a further step into the room, closing the door behind me.
*I need to focus!* I growled, noticing with every stride I took towards her a fluttering feeling grew in my chest. *I'm here to talk to her about my problems. Kind of...* And I tried to concentrate on that. *Woke up late. Look a mess. Woke up mess. Look a late. Late up woke. Mess look-* Then I realised I was still too distracted by her. I hastily averted my gaze elsewhere, glancing over to my left where I saw a single bed pushed lengthways against the wall; it had white sheets and a privacy curtain hanging from a pole beside it.

"Look," The nurse spoke with a small smile, gaining my attention; there was no denying the underlying hint of annoyance lacing her voice when she continued, "I don't have all day. So, **please**, take a seat." And she gestured to the empty, hard-looking chair in front of her desk with a sweep of her hand.
*Oh, right!* I anxiously exclaimed before hurriedly advancing on the chair, blinking back the sunlight that bathed my face when I

sat down.

*She's going to think I'm weird!* I worried, absentmindedly bouncing my foot up and down. *I need to say something!*
Clearing my throat, I apologised, "Sorry, Miss-"

"**Nurse**." She sternly corrected, her smile never faltering as she continued, "Nurse Lane."
*Of course, I had to go and put my foot in it again...* I uttered in dismay, shaking my head as I done so.
Nurse Lane must have sensed my inner turmoil as she swiftly added, "You're not the first, so don't worry about it." And the smile on her rosy lips looked more genuine.

"Now," She carried on, pulling out a pen and notepad from her desk drawer, "What can I do for you today?"
*That's the thing, I don't even know.* I had no idea what was wrong with me. *Is waking up late and dressing like a clown an illness?* I rhetorically asked, my brow becoming knitted. *I can't not say something, but I can't tell her everything.* I pondered, a sinking feeling in my stomach now apparent. *What do I tell her?* I debated, rubbing my forehead as a headache began to form.

A sigh from Nurse Lane gained my attention, and she uttered in coherent frustration, "Take your time..." But the grin on her plump lips baffled me.
*How can she look so fed-up yet smile like that?* I queried, narrowing my eyes. But then I realised that was the least of my worries. *I need to say something before she tells me to leave.*

Wringing my hands, I tried to muster up the courage to admit at least one thing that was out of sorts for me, but Nurse Lane spoke up first, "If I had to hazard a guess," She began, almost bored, "I'd say you were suffering from anxiety."
Anxiety? I repeated, frowning. *As in worried? But that's not a real thing. It's something people make up in their heads, like that Richard Brown.*

Shaking my head, I bluntly replied, "No, I **can't** have anxiety."

"Oh really?" She countered, shocked, "Then there's nothing you're worried about? No fear? Albeit mild or severe?"

As soon as she said the word '**fear**', something seemed to click into place. *Maybe she's right... I mean, I'm terrified in case someone realises my voice is inside my head.* And then I realised how crazy that sounded. *Nope! I'm fine! This voice will go away soon, and everything will go back to normal!*

"Fine, don't say anything." Nurse Lane commented, adding, "But you're not the first to walk in here with '**anxiety**'." And she quoted with her middle and index fingers before continuing, "They were all adamant too that they didn't have it, but it was nothing a good cup of tea couldn't fix, it put a smile right back on their faces."

"Tea?" I repeated, unconvinced, "How is tea going to fix my problems?"

Smirking, Nurse Lane pointed out, "So, you agree that you **do** have anxiety?" Taking me aback.

"I didn't say that!" I announced while she reached for the medicine cabinet, opening the glass doors and pulling out a box of teabags.

"But you implied it." She added, her smirk growing into an almost triumphant one.

I opened my mouth to retort, but then I realised. *I'm not going to win...* And I softly shook my head while she deposited the box in front of her.

Picking up her pen, Nurse Lane then said, "I'm going to write you out a prescription for these." And she gestured to the box of teabags with a nod of her head, "They have calming properties, so they'll take the edge off your worries."

*Really?* I pondered, sceptical.

"I'd advise having one in the morning and one in the evening." She explained, "You'll be right as rain in no time!" And she gave me a beaming smile but it didn't quite reach her eyes.

Nurse Lane then grabbed the box, ready to write on the label while asking, "What was the name again?"

Circling my attention away from the teabags, I replied, "West."

"No, I meant first name." She stated, peering up at me with a radiant smile.

35

*Then why didn't she say that?*

"It's Nathaniel." I said, "Nathaniel West." And her pen fell from her hand like deadweight; her mouth fell open, a gasp escaping her.

*Why's she so shocked?* I pondered, taking in her beaming, incredulous face staring back at me.

After a moment of silence, Nurse Lane queried, "Did... Did you say '**Nathaniel**' West? As in the same Nathaniel West whose father is Jeremiah West?" And I couldn't understand her surprise.

*I thought everyone knew I was his son.* But I must have been wrong.

"Err..." I muttered, still somewhat bemused myself, "Yeah, I am. Why?"

"He's an executive, correct?" She wondered, and I had no idea where she was going with this.

*How doesn't she know my father? He's been working here for over thirty years.*

"He is." I eventually replied, narrowing my eyes as I asked, "Why are you suddenly so interested in my father?"

Nurse Lane looked taken aback by my question, but she swiftly said, "I think I've figured out the root cause of your anxiety."

"I told you!" I huffed, "I **don't** have anxiety!"

Wagging her index finger, she grinned, "I wouldn't be so hasty, Nathaniel." Then she slapped a hand over her mouth, apologising, "I'm so sorry, Mr West, I overstepped the mark!" And she lowered her hand, "I shouldn't have called you by your first name."

Waving my hands sympathetically, I said, "It's fine, you can call me Nathaniel." And the shock plastered upon her beautiful face abruptly dissipated, instantly replaced with relief.

"Thank you!" She beamed before carrying on, "As I was saying. I believe you **may** have anxiety that's been brought on by the pressure of following in your father's footsteps." And I understood where she was coming from.

*I guess people do expect me to fill father's position when he eventually retires.* I mulled, nodding in agreement. *Then there's the new Quality Assurance position, I'd hate to not get the job and disappoint him.*

"I... I guess..." I murmured, "I mean, I'd hate to let him down and not get the Quality Assurance Manager position."

A victorious spark shone in Nurse Lane's mesmerising green eyes that was paired with a delighted smirk.

"No wonder you're on edge!" She proclaimed, "You need something with a little extra **oomph**!" And she snatched up the box of teabags, shoving them back into the medicine cabinet.

I watched as she rummaged around before producing a pill pot, depositing it on her desk in front of her. *And what's that?* I wondered, staring between the pot and Nurse Lane.

Grabbing her pen, Nurse Lane instructed, "I'd like you to try this-"

"And what is **this** exactly?" I swiftly intervened, not giving her the chance to explain.

"Revivamide." She replied matter-of-factly, "It'll help you bounce back to normality." And just those words alone gave me a spark of hope.

*So, everything will go back to normal?* I mulled. *And this voice will go away?*

Nurse Lane quickly filled out the prescription label while saying, "Twice a day." And she pointed at the instructions with a tap of her pen, "Morning and evening. It's a low dosage, but I will increase it if necessary."

Gazing down at the pot, I read the instructions in her cursive handwriting. 'Take one tablet twice a day. <u>TWICE daily.</u>'. *Sounds simple enough.*

"I'd like you to come back Monday morning." Nurse Lane commented, gaining my attention, "Then we can assess your '**anxiety**'." And she quoted with her fingers again.

Smiling, I nodded, "Will do." Before I stood up to leave, grabbing the pot and pocketing it as I done so.

I then headed for the door, shooting Nurse Lane one last glance over my shoulder as I said, "Thank you."

"My pleasure!" She beamed.

Dipping my head in gratitude, I stepped out into the reception area, closing the door behind me.

"Mr West!" The recognisable voice of Miss Jones rattled my eardrums, and I gazed over to see her stood by her desk with a briefcase in hand, "You left this in the waiting area." She said with a radiant smile, gesturing down to the briefcase with a sweep of her hand.

*I did?* I gawked, taken aback. Then I noticed the clients in the waiting area were staring at me like I were an imbecile, and I instantly wanted to disappear. *Stop looking at me!* I begged, feeling my ears burn with embarrassment.

Swiftly averting my gaze back to Miss Jones, I forced a smile and murmured, "Thuh-Thanks..." Before taking my briefcase.

"My pleasure, Mr West." She beamed before sitting back down, adding, "Mr Sheridan called while you were with the nurse. He asked for you to see him once you were out."

"Sure." I nodded, "Thank you, Miss Jones." And I turned on my heels, going straight to the door that led up to the offices.

*I really just want to get this day over with...* I uttered, coming to stand at the top of the stairs. *I really don't want to go in there...* I murmured, scrubbing a hand through my dishevelled hair. *What are people going to say or do when they see me dressed like this?!* And I peered down at my multi-coloured suit, grimacing when the stench of fresh sweat struck me like a wrecking ball. *God, I stink!* I groaned, making sure to keep my arms firmly pressed to my sides. *I should've just stayed at home...* I realised. *But it's too late... I'm here... Mr Sheridan knows I'm here... So I better go and see him before he wonders where I am...*

Inhaling a steady breath, I opened the door and took a step inside. Everyone was too busy at their workstations to notice me, so I made a beeline straight for Mr Sheridan's office. Knocking twice, there was a moment of silence before he called, "Come in!" And I opened the door with a little squeak.

"Ah, Mr West!" Mr Sheridan beamed; I closed the door behind me before noticing he was clad in his iconic sharp grey suit.

"I was hoping-" He began but abruptly cut himself off, his jaw dropping when his gunmetal grey eyes took me in, "What on earth are you wearing?!"

Feeling a little put on the spot, I nervously ran a hand round the back of my neck, saying, "A suit, Sir." But it only seemed to irk him.

"I can see that!" He snapped a little too readily, his smile never faltering.

Mr Sheridan then shook his head in exasperation before gesturing to the empty seat directly across from him, saying bluntly, "Take a seat." And I instantly obeyed, plonking my briefcase down before fiddling with my hands.

"I had called you in here to discuss the interview; however, I feel that wouldn't be the wisest decision right now." He stated, pinching the bridge of his nose as if he had a headache.

*Why?!* I abruptly panicked, fearing the worst. *Is he going to withdraw my application?!* And I couldn't help but bite my bottom lip while all kinds of outcomes manifested in my mind. *Is he going to give me a written warning? A verbal warning? Will he think I'll never be fit to become a manag-*

"Why do you look like that?" Mr Sheridan interrupted my mental ramblings, his hands now entwined and his gunmetal grey eyes boring into mine.

Confused, I asked, "Like what?"

"You're not smiling, Mr West." He pointed out, "You're not **happy**." And I felt even more baffled.

*He's got to be kidding, right? Can't he tell I've had a bad morning?*

Before I had the chance to reply, Mr Sheridan reached for his phone. *Is he calling father to tell him I'm not fit to be a manager?!* I fretted, watching as he dialled a number before pressing the phone to his ear, beaming as he done so. *And what's father going to think?! That I'm a useless son?!*

Not even a second passed before Mr Sheridan said, "Good morning, Miss Jones. Could you bring up two cups of tea?" And I couldn't help but emit a sigh of relief.

*Thank God it's not father!* I exclaimed, a slow smile pulling at my lips.

Nodding, Mr Sheridan grinned, "Thank you, Miss Jones." He then hung up before his cold, grey eyes circled back to me, stating, "Miss Jones is bringing us up some tea." But I didn't understand why.

*Does he feel sorry for me or something?*

"Anyway," He carried on, leaning back in his chair while resting his hands behind his head, "While we wait, do you care to explain why you're dressed like **that**?" And he gestured with a nod towards my suit.

Sighing, I replied, "I woke up late and just grabbed whatever I could get my hands on."

"But it's Wednesday." He pointed out, "You can't expect your mother to wash your suits throughout the week. Surely you'd only wear the one you wore Monday and Tuesday."

"Yeah, **normally** I would." I agreed, "But Max knocked the dinner table last night, and my food fell all over me."

Mr Sheridan's eyes suddenly lit up, the smile plaguing his face paired with the foreboding gleam in his gunmetal grey eyes put me on edge.

"And I presume there were no leftovers?" He wondered, and I nodded in agreement before he continued, "So let me see if I understand. You woke up late because you're tired, and you're tired because you didn't eat anything last night. In your haste to make up for lost time, your appearance was hindered. Do you agree so far?"

"Erm..." I murmured, bringing a hand up to touch my throat, "Yeah, I guess..."

"Excellent!" He beamed, "Then it seems we're both in agreement who was at fault." And he paused as if for dramatic effect, "The dog."

*Erm... What?* I couldn't help but shoot Mr Sheridan an incredulous gaze. *He's joking, right?* But the seriousness on his face led me to believe otherwise.

Shaking off my shock, I repeated, "The dog?" And he

nodded, "Yes, the dog, Mr West!" He beamed, "The suit and waking up late is because you're tired, and you're tired because you didn't eat. Why didn't you eat? Because the dog knocked it off the table. Don't you see what I'm saying?"
*I'm not arguing over this...*
Nodding once, I chose to appease him, "Sure..."
"Excellent." He purred just as there was a knock at the door, so he hollered, "Come in!"
Miss Jones wandered in with two steaming cups of tea, which she placed carefully on the desk before turning to leave.
"Thank you, Miss Jones." Mr Sheridan gleamed before she left, his attention swiftly snapping back to me, "Have some tea, Mr West." But I instantly shook my head.
"I'm fine, thank you." I replied with a smile.
Mr Sheridan then sat up straight before resting his hands on his desk, entwining his fingers as he done so.
Slowly, he leaned forward while saying, "It wasn't an offer. It was a request." Shocking me.
*It doesn't seem like I have much choice...* I uttered, diverting my gaze down to the cups of tea. With a sigh, I grabbed the closest one and brought it to my lips, taking a tentative sip. The warm liquid instantly soothed my inner turmoil, making a smile pull at the corners of my mouth.
"You can take that back to your desk." Mr Sheridan piped up, gaining my attention.
He was staring intently at my cup before his grey eyes locked onto mine, and he added with a smirk, "Try and get as much of your paperwork done today as possible, then you can get on with your presentation." And I couldn't help but emit a sigh of relief.
*Thank God he isn't pulling my application!*
Unable to stop a full-blown grin, I commented, "Thank you, Sir!"
"Anytime, Mr West." Mr Sheridan offered, "You can always talk to me."

*\*\*\**

When five o'clock arrived, I packed away my paperwork and presentation draft before heading to the stairs where everyone was filing out one by one.

"Have a good evening, Mr Smith." Miss Jones bid farewell to everyone in turn, and they too wished her a goodnight.

Her ice blue eyes then landed on me, and she said with a show-stopping smile, "Have a good evening, Mr West."

"You too, Miss Jones." I grinned, grabbing the door Mr Smith had held for me, and I too held it open for the person behind me.

Once they had grabbed it, I turned left and made my way passed store owners who were closing their shops.

"Good evening, Jeffrey." I beamed at the butcher as he locked up, and he replied with a grin, "Good evening, Nathaniel."

I then smiled at the man hopping into his car, "Good evening, Jam-" But a silvery voice cut across me, "MR WEST!" And I glanced over my shoulder to see Nurse Lane.

"Good evening, Nurse Lane." I greeted, about to go on my way once more but she came to stand before me.

"I just wanted to remind you to take your tablets." She explained; I automatically buried my hand inside my blazer, retrieving the pill pot.

"Of course, Nurse Lane." I acknowledged, unfastening the cap, "I shall do that right now."

Blinking in gratitude, Nurse Lane placed a consoling hand on my arm before saying, "Good evening, Nathaniel." And she left without another word.

I then glanced down at the label where I saw her cursive handwriting; '**TWICE daily**' was the first thing I saw, so I tapped out two pink-hued tablets and swallowed them like candy.

"It's been a busy day in Merribridge!" The broadcast echoed as I made my way back home, pocketing the pot as I done so, "Have a peaceful night's rest ready for a brand-new day tomorrow! Remember, everyone, keep smiling!"

Once I had left the town of Merribridge, copious amounts of sweat formed on my brow; my stomach churned with all the tea Miss Jones had provided throughout the day, threatening to erupt out of my mouth at any moment. Gripping my tender stomach, I hurriedly continued the last stretch home when a young man unexpectedly swung open his gate into me. My briefcase fell to the pavement with a clatter, bursting open and making my paperwork fly out.

"I'm so sorry!" He apologised with a smile, instantly bending down to gather my papers.

I tried to kneel but couldn't, bending over caused hot vomit to shoot up my throat. Slapping a hand over my mouth, I hastily swallowed the sick before snatching everything out of his hand, desperately shoving the papers into my briefcase. I then made a dash for home, hearing the blood pound in my ears while my head reeled like a spinning top toy.

My vision started to blur just before Donald greeted me, "Good evening, Nathaniel." He then disappeared down his garden path.

"Good evening, Nathaniel." Another man waved, my vision now so fuzzy I couldn't tell who he was.

"Good evening, Nathaniel." Someone else acknowledged; I didn't dare look as any slight movement made my head heavy.

Everything around me was now violently whirling, as if I were on the Round-Up ride at a funfair. Voices began to contort, dropping into deep octaves.

"It's been a busy day in Merribridge!" The announcement sounded, feeling like a fracture to the mind, "Have a peaceful night's rest ready for a brand-new day tomorrow! Remember, everyone, keep smiling!"

**BEEP, BEEP!** Car horns then struck my brain as ruthless as the sea, making me stagger the last few feet to my garden gate where I collapsed against it. After a brief moment, I was finally able to push myself up and stumble to the front door, struggling to fit the key into the lock. Once the door was open, I wobbled inside, dropping my briefcase with a clatter.

"Welcome home, Nathaniel!" Everyone called in unison while everything around me spiralled at a sickening pace.

I then tried to grab hold of the banister when I felt myself falling forwards but- **SMACK!**

# Chapter Four
## Everything's a blur...

**DING, DING, DING!** An alarm woke me with a start, the noise perforating my head like a jackhammer. Squeezing my eyes tightly shut, I hoped the pain would subside but it didn't. *Uuurgh...* I groaned, pressing a hand to my forehead. *God... My head, it hurts...* Then my face started to throb, making me feel queasy. *Urgh... I don't feel good...* I tried to shake off the nausea to no avail, so I gingerly sat up but instantly regretted it; my entire body started to sway, as if I were on a boat and moving with the motion. *Nope, nope! Need to lie back down!* And I hastily did while inhaling several steady breaths. *In through the nose... Out through the mouth...*

Once I felt a little better, I tried to gather my thoughts. *What happened last night?* I couldn't remember a thing. *All I know is I managed to get home, then everything's a blank.* But then I wondered. *Hang on, where am I?* And I slowly opened one eye and then the other, gazing around and realising I was in my bedroom. *How did I get up here?* I deliberated, carefully propping myself up onto my elbows before glancing down, noticing I was still wearing my sweat-stained, mishmash suit from yesterday as well as my shoes.

*Why can't I remember what happened?* I mulled while delicately leaning over to my alarm clock, turning it off before it could drill anymore into my head. Pinching the bridge of my nose, I mustered up some strength to swing my legs round to sit on the edge of the bed. *I need to get up... I need to try and get to work...* I didn't want to go, but I knew I couldn't risk my application being withdrawn because of my absence. *I want that job.* And that notion alone gave me another burst of strength to stand.

I then shakily advanced on the wardrobe, opening it and gazing inside. *I need to remember to wear the same colour today.* I pondered, peering down at my navy trousers that still looked clean. *Unlike the waistcoat and jacket...* Which were tainted with my sweat. I then decidedly grabbed the navy blazer and matching waistcoat, a clean white shirt, and a blue and gold tie before making my way to the bathroom.

*God... I need some tablets or something...* I uttered while closing the bathroom door behind me, struggling to work through the pain pounding in my head. Once I had deposited my clothes, I turned for the medicine cabinet only to spot my reflection, making an involuntary scream escape me. *What the?!* I gawked, horrified. *What happened to my face?!* An angry-looking ring of purple/red bruising engulfed my swollen left eye, the white completely blood red.

*What the hell happened?!* I declared, now aware my entire body was shaking. *I look a mess! Mr Sheridan won't want someone who looks like* **this** *as Quality Assurance Manager! What the hell am I going to do?!* I panicked, now pacing the bathroom while biting my bottom lip. *I have nothing to cover it up with! I can't exactly pretend it's not there!* My mouth started to become dry, my throat now feeling constricted. *What am I going to d-*

"Nathaniel?" The recognisable voice of father called before there was a slight knock at the door, "Are you okay? I thought I heard screaming."

"I-I'm fine!" I replied, but even I could hear slight the tremor in my voice.

"Are you sure?" He queried, unconvinced.

"Positive!" I insisted, and there was a moment of silence before father said, "Okay, then. Breakfast is nearly ready, so hurry up." And I could hear his retreating footsteps disappear downstairs, making a sigh of relief escape me.

*Thank God he's gone!* I breathed, now fixing my sights back upon my reflection where a dejected sigh escaped me. *I guess I don't have much choice but to just get ready and hope no one asks any questions...* With another sigh, I quickly brushed my teeth before changing into my clean clothes, about to discard my dirty grey blazer in the laundry basket but remembered. *Oh! My keys!* And I plucked them out but found something else; it felt like a pot of some kind. *Huh?* Grabbing it, I recognised it as the pot of Revivamide Nurse Lane had prescribed.

Once I had stuffed the keys and pot inside my navy jacket, I opened the bathroom door to the smell of bacon and eggs. *Ugggh!* I gagged, the smell making me feel sick, so I breathed through my mouth while making my way downstairs into the kitchen. Mother was stood by the hob with her back to me, the sunlight seeping through the kitchen window matched her yellow dress. The ding of cutlery then made me wince, the sharp, sudden sound stabbing into my brain and making me groan aloud. *Urgh...* I uttered, pressing a hand to my forehead. *I forgot to take something...* Lowering my hand, I gazed over to see Carmen setting the breakfast table, but something was missing from that unvarying scene. *What's different today?* But I couldn't quite put my finger on it.

Shaking my head, I wobbled over to the breakfast table, pulling up a chair just as Carmen finished setting it. *I don't think I've ever seen her wear that before...* I mulled, taking in her chocolate brown dress, the ends of her blonde, curly ponytail trailing over her shoulder. Her green eyes then momentarily met mine, a smile growing on her made-up face; I then expected her to help mother plate up breakfast, but she merely stared at me for what felt like a lifetime. *What's she doing?* I deliberated, averting my gaze downcast; it was then I realised what was missing. *Where is he?* And I peered under the table, searching for Max but he was nowhere in sight.

"Where's the dog?" I piped up, peering over at mother who turned from the hob, frying pan in one hand and spatula in the other; a few dark brown strands had fall from her beehive, trailing down her made-up face.

"What was that, honey?" She queried, smiling from ear to ear, so I questioned once more, "Where's Max?"

"Oh!" She gasped, as if suddenly remembering, "Your father had to take him to the vets." Shocking me, "What? Why?"

"He said he was awfully poorly." Carmen inputted, gaining my attention; she then turned to help mother plate up breakfast.

*Poorly?* I worried, biting my bottom lip. *What's wrong with him?*

"Where's your father?" Mother queried with a radiant smile, hollering, "Jeremiah?!" She then grabbed a plate, setting it down at father's spot.

*He is coming home, right?*

"Coming, sweetheart!" Father called from the living-room, his shoes suddenly rapping against the dining room floor before he appeared with a newspaper tucked under his arm; he wore the same pale grey suit with a badge fastened to the lapel.

"Smells delicious, sweetheart." He gleamed before sitting down, his dark blue eyes staring eagerly at his food.

Just as mother and Carmen had sat down after serving breakfast, I spoke to father before he could bring a forkful of food to his lips, "Where's Max?"

Lowering his fork, father was hesitant for a moment before replying, "He's... He's gone to live on a farm, son." And I instantly knew what he meant.

"I'm not twelve!" I bit back a little too readily, "Just say he's dead rather than lie!" And my retort clearly upset father by the anger shimmering in his eyes, not matching the smile on his lips.

"Don't talk to me in that tone, young man!" He fumed with a shake of his head, so I swiftly countered, "Then talk to me like an adult and tell me what happened!"

"Nathaniel, pack it in!" He warned with a raise of his brow, giving me a glassy stare.

Undeterred, I growled, "Why-"

"**ENOUGH!**" He cut across, his strident tone taking me aback; his face was red with acrimony, but his dazzling smile never once faltered.

*I've **never** heard him shout like that before!* I gawked, gulping.

Father then brought his fork to his lips once more, his dark blue eyes rolling back in delight while a pleasing groan escaped him.

"And it tastes just as good as it looks!" He happily proclaimed, dabbing a napkin either side of his thin, beaming lips before tucking it into his light brown shirt.

*Why won't he tell me what happened?!* I thought, frustrated; then I noticed him eyeballing me, abruptly dragging me out of my ponderings.

"Why aren't you eating?" Father probed, gesturing to my food with his knife.

Sighing, I admitted, "I'm not feeling too good." Which had me wonder.

*What happened last night? And how did I get a black eye?*

"What happened to me last night?" I voiced, and father stated matter-of-factly with a smirk, "You passed out."

*Does he find this funny or something?* I grumbled, biting my tongue.

"Is that how I got this?" I wondered, pointing to my black eye with an index finger, and father nodded, "Yes, you hit your face on the banister." His dark blue eyes then locked onto my bruise, evidently taking it in before adding, "I suggest you go to the nurse and get it seen to. And make sure she gives you a cup of tea while you're there."

*I guess it wouldn't hurt to make sure everything's okay.*

Before I could ask any more questions, father asked mother between mouthfuls, "What's your plans for the day, sweetheart?"

"Oh..." Mother lazily sighed, her dark brown eyes shifting to him as she smiled, "Well, I plan on making a Victoria sponge and sewing up some dresses; however, I'm sure Linda will ring and ask me out to play netball at the club, and then we'll have a spot of shopping with the girls followed by lunch."

"The cake isn't going to make itself." Father grinned, and mother briskly added, "But the shopping tempts, so I acquiesce. Lordy, last time I recklessly spent two-thirds of the housekeeping money on a black cocktail dress, a grey poodle skirt and three pillbox hats."

It was right then something dawned on me. *They have the same conversation every day...*

Father lowered his fork at mother's confession, his smile never lessening as he asked, "I thought we were saving up to get a washing machine?"

Mother hummed and hawed, "That is more important, I don't fancy washing the clothes by hand. I could get a part-time jo-"

"Are you suggesting I can't provide for the family?" He bit back, both smirking at one another.

Mother then opened her mouth to protest, but father piped up first, "A job would be the ruination of you and that's the end of the matter!" And, by now, I had enough of listening to them squabble.

"Let her get a part-time job." I chimed in, "Then maybe she won't waste money on clothes."

Aghast, father declared, "Nathaniel, women are **not** capable of working! They're genetically too emotional and therefore unsuitable in the workplace." And I had to stop myself from laughing.

*Then why did he hire Miss Jones?*

Raising my hands apologetically, I tried to make amends, "Sorry, father."

"That's better." He praised, but I was getting mixed signals by his angry, protruding eyes and the grin on his lips.

*I can't tell if he's happy or not...* I murmured. *He's always smiling...* Then my attention shifted to mother and Carmen. *All of them are always just smiling...* And I couldn't bear to sit there a moment longer with them all gleaming at me, as if they were inpatients from a mental asylum.

"I'm going to leave for work," I explained, rising to my feet, "Try and get some more of my presentation done for Monday."

"Your briefcase is in the living-room, honey." Mother

commented as I headed under the archway into the dining room. Glancing over my shoulder, I said with a smile, "Thanks."

I then ambled into the living-room, finding my case on the orange Hillcrest chair.

By the time I had turned back round, mother was at the front door with a lunchbox in hand. *O... Kay...* I murmured with a furrowed brow, taking the metal tin from her grasp before planting a kiss on her cheek.

"Have a nice day at work, honey." She beamed as I shoved the lunchbox in my briefcase, muttering, "Thanks..."

I then opened the front door and wandered down the garden path, noticing other sons and husbands were also leaving. *This is weird...* I noted, watching everyone do the exact same thing. *Really weird...* Shaking away that contemplation, I turned right once I closed the gate behind me, ignoring mother who still stood by the front door with a radiant smile plastered upon her face.

"Good morning, Nathaniel." Robert greeted with a dazzling smile when I walked past, he was strolling down his garden path with a briefcase in hand.

Forcing a smile, I replied, "Hi, Robert."

"Good morning, Nathaniel!" Thomas hollered with a grin; he then turned back and waved goodbye to his wife and daughter.

"Hi, Thomas." I acknowledged with a dip of my head.

"Good morning, Nathaniel." Donald smiled as he closed the gate behind him, now walking side by side with me.

"Hi, Donald." I greeted with a heavy sigh.

"Rise and shine, it's a beautiful day in Merribridge! The sun is out and there isn't a cloud in the sky!" A plummy male voice rang loud and clear from the speakers along the grass verge.

Suddenly, a young man stepped off his garden path, bumping into my shoulder and dropping his briefcase.

"I'm so sorry!" He apologised with a smile; I couldn't help but huff.

*Every day this happens...* I uttered, unimpressed.

"That's alright..." I grumbled, unable to hide the annoyance lacing my voice, "Just watch out next time, you do this every day..."

The young male gave me an odd look, as if to say '**What are you talking about?**', but his smile never faltered. *Isn't he aware?* I wondered, perplexed. *Does he forget or something?* But I shook off that deliberation, heading on my way again.

"Remember, everyone, keep smiling!" The same plummy voice announced, repeating the broadcast over and over, "Rise and shine, it's a beautiful day in Merribridge! The sun is out and there isn't a cloud in the sky!"

Once I had reached the small town of Merribridge, I had enough of the constant '**Good morning, Nathaniel**', but what puzzled me the most was I didn't even know half of them.

James then clambered out of his car, his eyes landing on me as he greeted, "Good morning, Nathaniel." And I robotically replied, "Hi, James." Before wondering how I knew his name.

*We don't work together... We're not neighbours... Maybe we knew each other when we were kids?*

Stores owners were now opening their shops with a ding, waving at whoever was walking by at the time.

"Good morning, Nathaniel." The butcher smiled, waving his hand that was holding onto a cleaver.

Inhaling a steady breath, I forced a grin and said, "Hi, Jeffrey."

*And I don't know how I know his name either... I've never been in there...* I mulled, shooting his shop a quick glance which was called Six Meat Under.

I then pushed open the door to C.S, releasing a heavy sigh of relief when I came to stand in the reception area. *Thank God I don't have to say hello to anyone else!*

"Good morning, Mr West!" Miss Jones greeted, gaining my attention; she was sat behind her desk glancing down at some paperwork, her startling blonde hair trailed down her petite, porcelain face that reminded me so much of a doll.

*Except for her...*

Taking a step further inside, I replied, "Good morning,

Miss Jones." And she peered up at me before doing a double-take, a horrified gasp escaping her.

"My word!" She declared in coherent shock, slapping a hand over her parted red lips that matched her dress; a badge was fastened just above her left breast, "What happened to your eye?!"

Waving my hand dismissively, I said nonchalantly, "Oh, nothing. I just passed out and smacked my face on the banister." Then I hastily carried on before she could pry anymore, "My father suggested I see the nurse. Can you ask Nurse Lane if she's available to see me?"

Smiling, Miss Jones nodded, "Of course, Mr West! Please, take a seat." And she gestured to a chair in the waiting area, so I immediately headed over while making sure to keep hold of my briefcase.

*I don't want to forget it like I did yesterday.*

"Good morning, Nurse Lane." Miss Jones gleamed down the receiver, twirling the cord with her index finger, "I have a Mr West requesting to see you." There was a slight pause before she nodded, "Yes, Nathaniel." Another pause followed, "Thank you, goodbye." And she hung up.

*I hope she's not going to keep me waiting for long.* I pondered, glancing over at the door that led upstairs. *I really need to get on with my presentat-* Nurse Lane's office door then swung open, and I was instantly blown away by her beauty. *Wow!* I gasped, gazing over her curves that were concealed by her white nurse's uniform. *Is it possible for her to be even more stunning than yesterday?*

Nurse Lane glanced around before her mesmerising green eyes locked onto me, a gasp of shock escaping her, "My gosh!" And she slapped a hand over her gaping mouth, "What on earth happened to you?!"

Just as I was about to reply, the reception door opened and in strolled my colleagues, so I swiftly advanced on her.

"Can we talk about this in your office?" I quietly urged, hoping not to gain any unwanted attention.

Nurse Lane peered over at the door before back up at me, nodding, "Of course!" She then led the way into her office, closing the door behind me.

"Please, take a seat." She insisted, gesturing to the chair in front of her desk, and I obeyed; she then grabbed her own, dragging it round so it was beside me.

"What happened, Nathaniel?" Nurse Lane queried with a worried smile, pulling out a torch from her pocket, "Why is your eye so bloodshot?"

Blinking back the brightness when she shone it in my bad eye, I replied, "Apparently, I passed out when I got home last night."

Now flashing the torch in my eye good, she questioned further, "And what did you hit your face on?"

"The banister." I admitted, a sigh of relief escaping me when she turned the torch off.

Nurse Lane then sat back with a start, pocketing her torch as she explained, "I want to run a few tests." And she pulled out her pen, now holding it in front of my face, "I'd like you to follow the pen with your eyes." And she began moving the pen left and right; I wasn't sure how long for until she instructed, "Now close your right eye."

She repeated the procedure a couple more times before pulling out an alphabet chart from her desk drawer, seeing how far away I could read the letters until they were blurry.

Once Nurse Lane was satisfied with her findings, she discarded the chart on her desk before saying, "Your eyesight is perfect, so it appears only the blood vessels between your sclera and conjunctiva are broken."

*My what and what?* I blinked, baffled.

"Erm..." I murmured, "Is that good or bad?"

"It's relatively good news." She replied, grabbing her chair and dragging it back round behind her desk, "Subconjunctival haemorrhaging, or eye bleeding, is quite common and tends to look worse than it really is."

"So I'm all good?" I asked, sighing a little in relief when she nodded.

"Yes, but it may take a couple of weeks for the blood to clear." She stated matter-of-factly, sitting down and carrying on, "Anyway," And she grabbed the chart, depositing it in her desk drawer, "I need to know why you passed out." But I didn't know. *Everything's a blur...* I uttered, shaking my head.

"Why don't you want to tell me?" Nurse Lane probed, making me realise she thought I had shaken my head as a response.

"It's not that." I explained, waving my hands apologetically, "I just can't remember."

"Could you explain the events leading up to it?" She suggested, smiling softly.

Shaking my head, I apologised, "Sorry, Nurse Lane, but I just can't remember." And she gave me a reassuring smile, "What **do** you remember?"

*Ugh... I'd rather just forget yesterday...* I inwardly cringed, feeling my ears heat up in embarrassment before my face and neck felt impossibly hot.

Grimacing, I gazed down while rubbing a hand round the back of my neck, finally replying, "I remember dressing like an idiot and being late for work..."

"Do you remember leaving work?" She pried, and I diverted my gaze up to meet her mesmerising green ones, nodding, "I do. I remember talking to you."

My comment seemed to make a genuine smile plague her plump, rosy lips but it was gone before I could be certain, replaced with an almost forced grin.

Clearing my throat, I carried on, "I also remember taking two of those tablets like you told me-"

"Hang on!" Nurse Lane intervened, her voice laced with confusion and worry, "What do you mean '**two**'?"

Baffled, I narrowed eyes, stating, "I took two tablets as you said."

"I never told you to take **two**!" She hawked in denial, "Why on earth would I say that when I specifically told you to take **one** twice a day!"

*Ohhhh...* I realised, averting my attention elsewhere. *I think I* know what's happened... And I couldn't help but bite on my bottom lip.

"That explains everything!" Nurse Lane continued in annoyance, her smile never lessening, "You **overdosed**!" Absentmindedly rubbing my eyebrow, I sheepishly admitted, "I must've misread the label..." And I apprehensively circled my gaze back up to her, noticing her eyes soften.

"I guess it could've been worse." She grinned, placing her hands on her desk and entwining her fingers, "So let's move forwards. Have you taken a tablet today?" And I immediately shook my head, lowering my hands to pick my fingers, "I didn't think about it."

A wave of irritation swept across Nurse Lane's features before she asked, "Have you got them on you?"

"I do." I nodded, retrieving the pot in question, "I put them in my pocket this morning."

A smile of relief graced her lips, "Take one now." And she grabbed the pot, shaking out a pink pill, "You may still feel a off today, but you should start to feel... Normal after a couple of days." She then handed me the pill, and I stared at it for a moment.

*I really do hope I start to feel better soon.* I pondered, turning it over. *And I really hope this voice goes as well.* That thought alone gave me the motivation to swallow it.

"Remember," Nurse Lane piped up, gaining my attention as she passed back the pot, "Take **one** tablet twice a day." And I couldn't help but smirk, "I'll try to remember."

Before I could ask any more questions, the telephone started to ring.

"Do you mind if you see yourself out?" She queried, and I shook my head, "Not at all."

I then grabbed my briefcase, quickly adding when she reached for the phone, "Thank you, Nurse Lane."

"My pleasure, Nathaniel." She grinned before answering, "Good morning, Nurse Lane speaking."

I then swiftly let myself out, quietly closing the door before heading upstairs to the offices. As soon as I stepped inside, I saw Mr Sheridan by my desk; he was clad in his iconic sharp grey suit as always. *What does he want?* I mulled, his gunmetal grey eyes landing on me when I was a stone's throw away, his smile shifting into a little '**o**'.

"Goodness gracious me, Mr West!" He blurted, "What on earth has happened to your face?!"

Sighing, I replied matter-of-factly, "I passed out and hit my face on the banister."

Mr Sheridan's lips formed an even bigger '**O**' before he wondered, "Is that why you're late?" And I shook my head, "No, I thought it would be best to see the nurse."

"And you didn't think to inform me of your late arrival?" He countered in a belittling tone, his brow furrowing in annoyance while his smile grew almost otherworldly.

"Honestly, Mr West, I don't pay you to see the nurse, I pay you to process orders!" Mr Sheridan heatedly carried on, irking me, "Do you understand?!" And I had to bite my tongue to stop myself from snapping.

"Yes, Sir." I growled through gritted teeth, "It won't happen again." But my response did very little to pacify him; instead, his cold, grey eyes stared calculatingly at my face.

*What the hell is he looking at?!*

"I'd turn that frown upside down if I were you, Mr West." Mr Sheridan commented in a threatening undertone, "You don't want anyone to think you're like Richard Brown, do you?" And I couldn't help but scoff.

*Why would they think that? I haven't assaulted anyone!*

Folding my arms across my chest, I pointed out matter-of-factly, "Richard Brown attacked people, I haven't."

Slowly, Mr Sheridan took an intimidating step towards me, so I hastily took one back to maintain the same distance between us. *What's he doing?!* I fretted, unable to stop myself from biting the inside of my cheek before suddenly bumping into the desk behind me. With nowhere to go, Mr Sheridan was now practically nose-to-nose with me.

"Richard Brown was a **very** troubled young man." Mr

Sheridan stated in a pitiless undertone, and I couldn't stop my gaze from flitting around the room.
"You're looking awfully nervous, Mr West." He continued, momentarily gaining my attention, "I've never seen a man bite his mouth or fidget as much as Richard Brown. That was until you started doing the same thing." He then abruptly pulled back, giving me some much-needed breathing space.

*What did he mean by that?* I deliberated, mulling over his last comment. *I'm **nothing** like Richard Brown! Richard was possessed by the Devil, and I'm not!* But then the Prime Minister's words came to mind, causing the hairs on the nape of my neck to rise. '**Sometimes, the worst place the Devil can be is inside your head.**'. *No!* I adamantly declared. *I'm **not** like Richard Brown!* But there was no denying the voice inside my head.

"Take a seat, Mr West." Mr Sheridan piped up, dragging me back to the conversation, "I'll arrange for Miss Jones to bring you up a nice cup of tea." And I opened my mouth to object but he had already turned on his heels, disappearing into his office.

Sighing, I stiffly sat down and pulled my paperwork out of my briefcase, all the while hoping the tablet would take effect soon. *Then this voice will go away and I won't be anything like Richard Brown!* But then I started to wonder. *What if this voice never goes away? What if I am just like Richard Brown?* Shaking my head, I realised how stupid that sounded. *No, I'd **never** hurt anyone! Richard Brown killed people while trying to escape!*

I then clipped my briefcase shut before depositing it on the floor beside me, my attention shifting back to my paperwork and presentation draft. *I need to focus on this and forget about the voice for now.* I realised, knowing my promotion could be at stake. *I want this job. I want to make father proud.* I then bundled my papers together, shuffling them into a neat pile just as a green cup was set on my desk, making me jump.

"Here you go, Mr West." Miss Jones beamed, gaining my attention.

"God, you scared me!" I gasped, clearly shocking her.
Wagging her index finger, she scolded with a grin, "Thou shalt

not take the name of the Lord thy God in vain." And I realised she was quoting the bible.

*Oh yeah.* I chided, angry with myself. *How stupid of me. I should know better than to do that.*

Shaking off my annoyance, I grabbed the cup and smiled, "Thank you, Miss Jones." But then the sickly-sweet aroma hit me out of nowhere, making my gag reflexes hypersensitive.

My mouth began to salivate, my stomach churning with every stench that wafted up my nose. *I can't drink this!* I declared, discarding it on the table with a clatter just as a warm ball of vomit suddenly shot up into my throat. *I'm going to be sick!*

Jumping to my feet, I dashed to the nearby window on my left, ripping it open where I vomited down onto the road below. To my relief, no one was wandering the streets, but I wouldn't have been able to stop even if there were. Tears streamed down my cheeks from all the throwing up; my stomach ached and my throat was now raw. *God, I just want today to end...* I uttered, leaning on the windowsill for some much-needed support once the vomiting stopped. *Nurse Lane mentioned I may still feel off, but I never thought she meant* ***this*** *much!*

\*\*\*

*Thank God-* **Goodness** *it's home time!* I sighed in relief while flopping back in my chair, feeling drained from the retching and throwing up all day. *It also probably hasn't helped that I've not eaten...* I mulled, recollecting how I had been unable to stomach my lunch never mind the endless supply of tea Miss Jones had provided. *I just hope this sickness passes soon...* I then shakily packed away my paperwork and presentation draft before wobbly heading to the stairs where everyone was filing out one by one.

"Have a good evening, Mr Smith." Miss Jones bid farewell to everyone in turn, and they too wished her a goodnight.

Her ice blue eyes then landed on me, and she said with a show-stopping smile, "Have a good evening, Mr West."

"You too, Miss Jones." I robotically replied with a forced grin, grabbing the door Mr Smith had held for me.

Just as I was about to hold the door for the person behind me, I remembered. *Oh, the tablet!* And I quickly buried my hand inside my blazer pocket while turning left, plucking out the little pill pot. *I can't believe I almost forgot!* I scolded while making my way passed store owners who were closing their shops.

"Nathaniel?" The butcher called when I walked past, he was locking up his store, "Aren't you going to wish me a good evening, Nathaniel?"
*Urgh...* I inwardly groaned, unscrewing the pot and popping a pill in my mouth. *It starts...* And I shot him a half-arsed smile, hoping that would pacify him, before noticing someone wave at me. *It's James, isn't it?* But I wasn't sure, so I merely gave him an awkward finger wave before heading on my way.

"It's been a busy day in Merribridge! Have a peaceful night's rest ready for a brand-new day tomorrow!" The broadcast rang from speakers fastened to buildings, "Remember, everyone, keep smiling!"

Once I had left the town of Merribridge, I was on the last stretch home. *I'm so hungry!* I groaned and, as if on cue, my stomach started to rumble. *I wonder what mother's made toni-* **BANG!** My briefcase fell to the pavement with a clatter, causing my paperwork to fly out when a young man unexpectedly swung his garden gate into me.

"I'm so sorry!" He apologised with a smile; I merely glowered down at him, pressing my lips together to stop myself from snapping.
*He's **always** doing this!* A tightness started to form in my chest, my pulse quickening the longer I stared at him. *And I'm sick of it!* Oblivious to my anger, the young man bent down to gather my papers, handing them to me; it took every ounce of self-control to stop myself from snatching them. *He's not worth it.* I decided, inhaling a steady breath before carefully taking the papers and shoving them inside my briefcase.

"Thanks…" I uttered before heading on my way.

I hadn't even taken five steps before Donald was suddenly walking beside me, making me jump out of my skin. *Gaaah!*

"You scared me!" I breathed, all the while he just stared at me.

*What's he looking at?* I wondered, taking in his unnerving smile that chilled me to my very core. *Have I got something on my face?* But I didn't get the chance to ask before he queried, "Aren't you going to wish me a good evening, Nathaniel?" And I was so taken aback by his upfront question, I had no idea how to respond.

After an awkward moment of silence where we had come to a halt outside Donald's garden gate, I finally stammered, "Err… Guh-Good evening, Donald."

His smile grew even more as he replied, "Good evening, Nathaniel." Before he disappeared down his garden path, leaving me gawking after him.

*What was all that about?* I deliberated, shaking my head in confusion.

I was then about to continue on my way once more; however, I spotted Thomas at the next house down closing his garden gate painfully slow while blatantly staring at me. *God, that's creepy!* I shuddered, taking in his bright and eerie smile. By now, Thomas had closed his gate but still hadn't swayed from his spot, making me realise he was waiting for me. *But why?* I couldn't help but wonder, furrowing my brow in contemplation before taking a hesitant step towards him.

Once I was within earshot, I asked, "Why are you just staring at me?" Taking Thomas aback.

He was silent for a moment, as if computing what I had said before asking with a one-sided grin, "Aren't you going to wish me a good evening, Nathaniel?" And I couldn't stop a chill from creeping up my spine from those words alone.

*Didn't Donald say the exact same thing?* I debated, my stomach quivering with unease.

Frowning, I cleared my throat before responding with a shaky voice, "Erm… Duh-Does it matter who says it first?"

"Of course it does!" Thomas replied with a dazzling smile, "You've always wished me a good evening first, just like I've always wished you a good morning first. It is what it is, Nathaniel."
*But why?*
When I didn't reply, he carried on in a somewhat pushy tone, "Wish me a good evening, Nathaniel." And I couldn't stop my jaw from dropping.
*He's not serious, is he?* But my shock was swiftly replaced with apprehension; a sense of foreboding. *If I just do what he wants, then he'll go away.* I realised, now grasping my arm that was holding my briefcase by the elbow.
Inhaling a steady breath, I finally said, "Good evening, Thomas."
Smiling from ear to ear, Thomas replied, "Good evening, Nathaniel." He then gave me a wave before wandering towards his front door.
*Good, he's gone.* I sighed in relief, diverting my attention down the road where I saw Robert; he stood in the middle of his garden path staring at me with a show-stopping smile, clearly waiting for me.
*Oh no...* I groaned, hastily avoiding eye contact. *Just walk past and ignore him.* A nauseating feeling rolled in my stomach when I sped past, the feel of his eyes burning a hole through the back of my head swiftly followed. *Just keep walking! Just keep walking!* I chanted. *Just keep walk-* But the squeak of a gate opening made my heart plummet.
"Nathaniel?!" The recognisable voice of Robert hollered, and I apprehensively gazed over my shoulder to see him beaming at me.
Forcing a smile, I innocently asked, "Yes, Robert?"
"Aren't you going to wish me a good evening, Nathaniel?" He queried, his words making my mouth dry and my throat feel constricted.
*Why are they all saying the same thing?* I deliberated, my gaze flitting everywhere but never once landing on Robert.

"Erm..." I uttered, running a jerky hand through my hair before continuing in a slight stammer, "Guh-Good evening, Robert."

Smiling like the cat that got the cream, Robert replied, "Good evening, Nathaniel." Before turning on his heels and disappearing down his garden path.

"It's been a busy day in Merribridge!" The announcement sounded from the grass verge, "Have a peaceful night's rest ready for a brand-new day tomorrow! Remember, everyone, keep smiling!"

**BEEP, BEEP!** Executives and top management started to arrive home, tooting their horns and waving; I gazed ahead and noticed father's car was already on the driveway.

I practically ran the last stretch home, swinging open the garden gate with such force it immediately slammed back into my chest.

"**Ooof!**" I groaned, carefully opening the gate this time.

Dashing for the front door, I pulled out my key, rushing inside when it was barely open a crack where I shut it behind me with an almighty bang.

The stench of meatloaf then suddenly hit me like a slap to the face. *Oh no!* I was unexpectedly overwhelmed by nausea, so much so I began to profusely sweat yet I felt cold and shaky. *Breathe... Breathe...* I murmured, leaning against the front door as I found I no longer had the strength to stand. *I really don't want to be sick!* But then another waft of meatloaf invaded my senses, and I couldn't keep the vomit at bay a moment longer.

I urgently dashed upstairs and ripped open the bathroom door; I couldn't get the toilet seat up quick enough before I collapsed against it, puking. *No more!* I begged but the vomit kept coming; I didn't understand how seeing as I had hardly eaten. *Please stop!* I wept, hating the sting now in the back of my throat from all the heaving, my stomach hollow and achy.

Once I could physically be sick no more, I sat back on my heels only to jump when a hand pressed down onto my shoulder. Peering up, I saw father gazing down at me with a look of concern shimmering in his dark blue eyes.

"Are you alright, son?" He wondered, grinning.

Shaking my head, I didn't dare speak in fear I would projectile vomit all over him. *I just feel so awful...* I groaned, pressing a fist against my lips when my mouth started to salivate. *Please don't be sick! Please don't be sick!*

Sighing, father ran a shaky hand through his coiffed locks before saying, "Go and get some rest." And he gave my shoulder a small squeeze before helping me to my feet.

I merely nodded in response, still not brave enough to say anything. *I just want to lie down...* I uttered, feeling a little lightheaded now I had stood up.

Father guided me into my bedroom where he sat me down on the edge of my bed.

"Are you going to be alright?" He wondered, and I nodded once more.

*I just hope I'm going to feel better tomorrow.*

"Call if you need anything." He said before disappearing onto the landing, closing the door behind him.

When he had gone, I peeled off my shirt and trousers before crawling into bed, feeling both hot and cold all at once. *Please feel better tomorrow.* I chanted, resting my head on the pillow. *Please feel better tomorrow.* And not even a second had passed before I drifted off.

# Chapter Five
## *Father must be so disappointed in me…*

**DING, DING, DING!** *Noooo!...* I griped, tossing and turning in protest. *I just want to go back to sleep!...* But I knew I couldn't risk being late in fear my job application would be withdrawn. *The interview is on Monday, so today is my last opportunity to finish my presentation.* I reminded myself with a sigh.

Throwing back my covers, I wearily swung my legs round to sit on the edge of the bed, switching the alarm off before instinctively turning on my radio.
"Good morning, citizens of Merribridge! It's Friday 10$^{th}$ July in sunny England, and you're listening to 1959's Elation Station!"
**'III've got yooou under my skiiin. III've got yooou deep in the heaaart of meee, so deep in my heart that you're really a paaart of meee. III've got yooou under my skiiin.'.**

Once I made the bed, I hurried over to the wardrobe, accidentally bumping into my nightstand. *Oh no, the radio!* Snatching it in a blind panic to stop it from toppling off, I must have knocked the knobs as the Frank Sinatra song was unexpectedly replaced with the strum of a guitar and bang of a drum. *What's this?* It wasn't calm and relaxing, it was energetic in an almost aggressive way. **'-Would see him sittin' in the shaaade strummin' with the rhythm that the driiivers maaade. The people passing byyy, they would stop and say 'Ooohhh myyy, but that little country boooy could plaay.'.'.** There was something captivating about the music that I couldn't stop my head from bopping even if I tried.

With a newfound surge of energy, I grabbed my navy suit and wingtip shoes, reluctantly turning off the radio before heading into the bathroom.

"Gooooo, Johnny, gooo! Gooo!" I absentmindedly sung while depositing my clothes and shoes, the lyrics forever engraved in my mind.

Turning for the medicine cabinet, I caught my reflection in the mirror. *God, I look awful...* I uttered, peering at my black eye. The bruising had darkened, taking on a more purple colour; the swelling hadn't even gone down. *I really hope it looks better by Monday...* I prayed, noting my eye itself was still bloodshot.

I then brushed my teeth before inspecting the stubble starting to grow through along my jawline, shocking myself that I actually liked the rugged look; I knew I should shave, but I couldn't bring myself to do it. *One day won't hurt.* I decided with a shrug before getting dressed, fastening my tie via the mirror where my green eyes locked onto my dishevelled hair. *Urgh... I really can't be bothered...* I lazily thought; however, the longer I stared at my hair, the more the rakish look grew on me. *It actually doesn't look too bad.* And it didn't take much to convince myself to leave that also.

I swiftly shoved everything back into the cabinet before leaving the bathroom, the sweet aroma of bacon and eggs invading my senses. *God, that smells so good!* I inwardly moaned just as my stomach growled aloud. I then bounded down the stairs, taking them two at a time whilst whistling the tune from the new song I had heard.

I could hear mother and Carmen bustling away in the kitchen as I ambled through the dining room, spotting mother by the hob with her back to me as I came to stand under the archway. *Wow, that's bright!* I gawked, taking in her obnoxiously red dress. *And I have no idea why she does her hair like that, it just makes her head look massive!* I deliberated, now glancing at the bouffant that I hated so much.

The ding of cutlery then echoed in the kitchen; I gazed over at Carmen setting the breakfast table, the ends of her long, blonde hair nearly touching it. Her green eyes then momentarily met mine when I pulled up a chair, a smile growing on her made-up face as she stared expectantly down at me. *Why's she just looking at me?* I mulled, shifting my attention down to her dark yellow dress before back up at her face, now feeling awkward. *What's she doing?*

"Aren't you going to wish me a good morning, Nathaniel?" Carmen finally piped up; I could feel the blood drain from my face, her comment shocking me.

*What did she just say?* A feeling of déjà vu encompassed me.

But I didn't get the chance to respond before mother spoke up, "Aren't you going to wish me a good morning, Nathaniel?" And I peered over to see her facing me, pan in one hand and spatula in the other.

Swallowing a lump that had shot up into my throat, I tremulously replied, "Guh-Good morning, mother. Good muh-morning, Cuh-Carmen."

In unison, they smiled broadly and said, "Good morning, Nathaniel." Before mother turned back to the hob and Carmen began helping her plate up breakfast.

"Where's your father?" Mother queried with a radiant smile gracing her made-up face, hollering, "Jeremiah?!" She then grabbed a plate, setting it down at father's spot.

"Coming, sweetheart!" Father called from the living-room, his shoes suddenly rapping against the dining room floor before he appeared with a newspaper tucked under his arm; he wore the same pale grey suit with a badge fastened to the lapel.

Gleaming, father sat down, "Smells delicious, sweethea-" But he cut himself off when his dark blue eyes landed on me, his smile never faltering but the horror blazing in his blue depths couldn't be ignored.

*Why's he looking at me like that?* I queried, shrinking a little under his scrutinous gaze.

"Nathaniel," Father abruptly spoke after what felt like a lifetime of silence, "Why on earth do you look like **that**?!"

Confused, I wondered. *Like what?* And I peered down, making

sure my suit matched which it did.
Glancing back over at him, I raised a questioning eyebrow and asked, "What are you talking about?"

"Firstly," He heatedly began, "You're not smiling! Secondly, you look like a ruffian with that scruff on your face and the state of your hair!"

*Do I really look that bad?*

"Go and sort yourself out after breakfast!" Father angrily carried on, a smile still plaguing his lips, "Do you understand?!"

Nodding, I stammered, "Yuh-Yes, father…"

"Good." He said before bringing a forkful of food to his lips; his eyes rolled into the back of his head in delight, a pleasing groan escaping him once he took a bite.

"And it tastes just as good as it looks!" He happily proclaimed, dabbing a napkin either side of his thin, beaming lips before tucking it into his light brown shirt.

*I'm so hungry!* I ravenously exclaimed as mother and Carmen dug in; I eagerly snatched up my cutlery, accidentally dropping the fork in my haste where it hit the floor with a clatter. *Damn it!* Leaning down to grab it, my hand brushed against something in my blazer. *What the?* Once I found my fork, I sat up straight and buried my hand inside my pocket, retrieving the pot of Revivamide. *Oh, I forgot about my tablet.*

"What's your plans for the day, sweetheart?" Father asked mother between mouthfuls while I unscrewed the lid.

"Oh…" Mother lazily sighed, smiling, "Well, I plan on-"

"What on earth are you doing, Nathaniel?!" Father interrupted mother just as I tapped a pill out into my palm, his dark eyes then circling down to it, "What is **that**?!"

Furrowing my brow, I replied, "Revivamide, why?"

"Revivamide?" He queried, "Where did you get it from?"

*Hasn't he heard of Revivamide? I mean, I know I've never heard of it, but he's an executive and we produce it at C.S. Don't we?…* I pondered, my mouth turning dry at the prospective that this wasn't a legal drug.

Shaking off the uncertainty that was playing havoc with

my mind, I cleared my throat and said, "Nurse Lane prescribed them to me."

"Nurse Lane?" He repeated, worry now plastered upon his radiant face.
*What... What's going on?* I fretted, my knee now bouncing up and down a mile a minute. *Why does he look so concerned?* I thought I saw the joyous smirk on his lips falter for a split second, but I must have been seeing things as the only tell-tale sign he was on edge were his eyes.

Unexpectedly, father than laid out his hand palm up, gesturing for the pills, "Give them to me, Nathaniel." He insisted, now beckoning with a wave of his fingers, "Before it's too late."
*Too late?* I repeated, confused. *Too late for what?* I didn't like the cryptic undertone to his voice, so much so it filled me with a sense of impending doom. *Are these tablets illegal or something?*

I curiously tilted my head to the side, asking, "What do mean '**Before it's too late**'?" But father ignored my question, gesturing for the pot once more while demanding, "Give me the tablets, Nathaniel!"
Undeterred, I carried on, "But I don't understand. A nurse prescribed these for me, so why are you acting as if she's committed a crim-"

"JUST GIVE ME THE TABLETS!" He exploded with an ever-growing smile, making me flinch back in alarm.
I then sheepishly averted my gaze before slowly sliding the pill and pot over to father, who snatched them out of my hand before they were even halfway across the table.

"Get your briefcase!" Father snapped as he rose to his feet, now towering over everyone, "We're leaving for work now to discuss **this**-" And he glowered incriminatingly down at the pill pot, "With Mr Sheridan!"

*\*\*\**

"Ow! You're hurting me!" I griped as father dragged me by the arm towards C.S once he had parked the car, his iron-like grip making me lose blood circulation.

"Then stop dawdling, Nathaniel!" He bit back with a smile, releasing me when we were outside the entrance.

Giving my arm a brisk shake, I headed inside where I spotted Miss Jones sat behind her desk; she was clad in a dark blue suit dress with a badge pinned above her left breast, her startling blonde hair down in waves.

When the door closed behind us with a gentle bang, Miss Jones gazed over, blatantly blinking at us in confusion before beaming at father, "Good morning, Mr West." Then her ice blue eyes shifted to me, "Good morning, Mr West."

"Good morning, Miss Jones." We said in unison before father carried on, "Has Nurse Lane arrived yet?"

Nodding, Miss Jones confirmed, "She's in her office, Sir."

"Excellent!" Father practically purred in delight, "Tell her to meet me in my office in five minutes." And, without another word, he herded me upstairs.

I didn't get the chance to open the door when we reached the top as father barged past, grabbing me by the arm once more to drag me through into the empty office area.

"Ow!" I growled, trying to shake off his hold to no avail, "**OW!**"

"Stop your complaining, Nathaniel, and smile!" Father barked as he turned on me, his smirk not matching the irate look gracing his face.

*He expects me to smile?!* I gawked, shocked.

Father then released me to scrub a jerky hand through his coiffed, brown locks, wrinkling his brow as he glanced over his shoulder in the direction of Mr Sheridan's room.

"Wait in my office, Nathaniel." He ordered, looking back at me before gesturing with a nod towards his office door along the right-hand wall.

*What's going to happen?* I worried, nodding once before watching father make a beeline for Mr Sheridan's office. *What's going to happen to me and Nurse Lane?*

Clutching the cuff of my blazer with my left hand, I averted my gaze to father's office and reluctantly trudged towards it. Opening the door, I peered inside. The room was identical to Mr Sheridan's; however, there was no window to the left and, instead, there was one along the back wall that had a view of the factory allocated at the rear of C.S.

*Do I sit down?* I mulled, stepping inside, unsure what to do with myself. The trepidation coursing through my veins felt like a parasite, ruthlessly plaguing my mind with worst-case scenarios. *Are they going to fire me?* I panicked, pacing the full-width of the office now I had closed the door. *Or will they think I'm involved in some kind of illegal drug testing with Nurse Lane?* Pinching the skin at my throat, that thought only encouraged me to over-analyse that possibility. *If they do think that, will they get the police involved? And then will they think we're like Richard Brown and get the government involved as well?* But that deliberation was short-lived when the office door swung open and in strolled father.

He wandered round behind his desk, pulling up his plush leather chair while saying, "Take a seat, Nathaniel." And he gestured to the empty chair in front of him.

Hastily plonking myself down, I deposited my briefcase beside me. *What's going to happen?* I fretted yet again, repeatedly smoothing out the creases on my trousers. *And where's Mr Sheridan? I thought father wanted to discuss this with him as well?* And, as if on cue, I heard the recognisable voice of Mr Sheridan behind me.

"Anything else, Sir?" He queried, now coming to stand in my peripheral vision where he placed a hard-looking plastic chair beside me on my left.

Shaking his head, father replied, "That's all, Isaiah. Now we wait for Nurse Lane."

Mr Sheridan didn't reply, he merely closed the door before skulking over to father's desk where he perched himself on the edge, his malevolent, gunmetal grey eyes locked onto me the entire time. Gulping, I had to divert my attention, now taking in his iconic grey suit that made me realise I had never seen him in anything else. *Doesn't he have any other clothes?*

I was then distracted by father when he buried a hand inside his blazer pocket, rummaging around before producing the pot of Revivamide. Mr Sheridan plucked it up just as father deposited it on his desk, turning it over several times before focusing on the label Nurse Lane had written.

"Revivamide?" Mr Sheridan queried with a slight raise of his brow, his grey eyes shifting to me as he probed, "Why do you need these?" And he shook the pot in question, causing the pills inside to rattle.

But, before I had the chance to answer, there was a slight tap at the door.

"Come in!" Father hollered, and I glanced over my shoulder to see Nurse Lane step inside.

Her face was wreathed in smiles but it faltered slightly when her green eyes locked onto Mr Sheridan and then myself; a realisation encompassing her.

"Good, you're here." Father carried on, gesturing to the empty chair beside me with a sweep of his hand, "Please, take a seat." And Nurse Lane closed the door before obeying.

"Whatever is the matter, Sir?" She wondered, curiously gazing at father.

Before he had the chance to speak, Mr Sheridan piped up, "We want to know why you prescribed **these** to Mr West." And he carefully set the pill pot down in front of her.

There was no denying the apprehension swirling in Nurse Lane's green gaze, but that was the only tell-tale sign of her quiet, inner turmoil.

Nurse Lane then slowly sat back, glancing from the pot to Mr Sheridan before calmly responding, "I prescribed these to Nathaniel as he suffers from anxiety, Sir."

"There is no such thing as anxiety, Nurse Lane." Mr Sheridan countered, "It's only in your own mind you've decided what anxiety is, and now you've convinced Mr West that he has it."

"On the contrary, Sir." She radiantly retorted, "I believe his anxiety has been brought on by the pressure of following in his father's footsteps." And her statement caused father's eyes to widen in surprise.

"And as such, you've jeopardised Mr West's opportunity of ever following in his father's footsteps!" Mr Sheridan bit back with a grin; it took a moment for his comment to sink in.

*Hang on, what?!*

Before either of them could retaliate, father piped up with a raise of his hand, "That's enough!" And he glared between Nurse Lane and Mr Sheridan with a toothy grin.

His dark blue eyes then solely focused on Nurse Lane, and he carried on in a menacing undertone, "I don't know where this Revivamide came from and, quite frankly, I do not care. I'm just appalled that you had the audacity to prescribe this placebo to **my** son!" And he slammed a fisted hand onto the desk, practically making me jump out of my skin.

*It's a placebo?...* I mulled, giving Nurse Lane a sideways glance. *Why did she prescribe it to me?* I then slowly circled my attention back over to father, his jaw repeatedly clenching yet the smirk on his face never faltered.

Finally, father concluded to Nurse Lane, "Pack up your desk and bring me the key to the office once you're done."

Furrowing her brow, she countered in a steady voice, "With all due respect, Sir, but you cannot dismiss me. Firstly, you have no other nurse. Secondly, **no one** in Merribridge is nearly half as qualified as I."

"Nurse Hamilton at the rehabilitation centre is more than qualified for your job." Mr Sheridan pointed out with a smug, one-sided grin, crossing his arms over his chest as he done so.

*Hang on, there's a rehabilitation centre? Since when?*

"Nurse Hamilton?" Nurse Lane repeated, her fingers touching her parted, beaming lips, "But her practices are unorthodox, Sir! I've seen first-hand what she does to those poor souls at Merriwell Sanatorium."

Scrunching my brow, I couldn't help but wonder. *What kind of unorthodox practices does Nurse Lane mean?*

Leaning in aggressively as if to challenge her, Mr Sheridan retorted with a sneer, "We're well aware of her practices, Nurse

Lane."

"It doesn't concern you whom we employ, Nurse Lane." Father spoke up, gaining everyone's attention, "Now, I'll ask you one last time, go and pack up your desk." And, without another word, he gestured for her to leave with a sweep of his hand.

Dipping her head in acknowledgement, Nurse Lane rose to her feet and headed for the door; I couldn't stop myself from watching her leave, a sigh escaping me when she closed it behind her. *I wonder if I'll ever get to see her again?* I contemplated, turning back in my seat to face father and Mr Sheridan. *I just want to know why she gave me that drug.*

"You may as well head back to your office, Isaiah." Father said, gazing at Mr Sheridan, "I'll wrap everything up here with Nathaniel."

"Of course, Sir." Mr Sheridan commented, hopping off the desk and heading for the door; he peered over his shoulder when he opened it, wondering, "Is there anything else, Sir?"

"Actually, now that you mention it, there is." Father smiled, adding, "Can you ask Miss Jones to bring a cup of tea up for Nathaniel?"

Mr Sheridan didn't say anything, he merely nodded before closing the door behind him with a gentle bang.

"Nathaniel," Father began with a sigh, gaining my attention.

He was biting the inside of his cheek while, somehow, still smiling. *How does he do that?* I wondered, but then I realised that was the least of my worries judging by the downcast expression plastered upon his beaming face. *What... What's going to happen? Is he going to-* Gulping, I ran a jerky hand through my dishevelled hair. *Fire me?...*

"Nathaniel," Father started up once more, rolling his neck before finally saying almost reluctantly, "I feel after today's events that it may be best to withdraw your application for Quality Assurance Manager." And I couldn't stop my jaw from dropping.

*What?!*

"No!" I blurted, still in shock, "You **can't**!"

I didn't give him the chance to speak before hurriedly continuing, "I've worked hard on my presentation! I **want** the job, father!"

Shaking his head, father curled his hands into slight fists before straightening them, saying, "I'm sorry, Nathaniel, but my decision is final." And he didn't give me the chance to retaliate before gesturing for me to leave with a sweep of his hand, glancing away so to avoid the awkwardness now lingering in the atmosphere; like a massive elephant in the room.

Sighing, I hung my head before grabbing my briefcase and leaving, not even bothering to shoot him one final glance as I shut the door.

*Why is this happening to me?!* I wailed at no one in particular while mindlessly wandering over to my desk, depositing my briefcase before plonking myself down. I then buried my face in my hands, unable to deal with the mountain of paperwork piled up before me. *I worked so hard on that presentation for no reason!* I exclaimed in coherent frustration, unable to stop myself from screaming into my hands just as I heard something put on my desk with a clatter. Gazing up between my fingers, I saw Miss Jones standing there with a radiant smile.

"Your tea, Mr West." She said as I lowered my hands.

Sighing, I replied with a forced smile, "Thank you, Miss Jones."

She then dipped her head in acknowledgement before walking away in the direction of the stairs; I slumped in my chair, my heart thudding dully in my chest. *Father must be so disappointed in me...* I uttered, shaking my head before glancing down at my briefcase; I went to grab it but found my limbs were too heavy to move.

*I just wish today would en-*

"After you, Miss Jones." A silvery voice cut across my thoughts, and I instantly recognised it.

"Why thank you, Nurse Lane." Miss Jones replied as I gazed over my shoulder, the heaviness in my limbs abruptly dissipating.

Miss Jones then disappeared down the stairwell as Nurse Lane made a beeline for father's office; I couldn't tear my gaze away from her no matter how hard I tried.

*Wow! She looks so beautiful!* I gawked, taking in her long, red belted fleece; a brown handbag slung over her shoulder. But then I abruptly scolded. *What's wrong with me?!* And I tore my sights away as she disappeared inside father's office. *She prescribed me a fake drug! I should be mad at her!* But I wasn't; I was more curious why. *But I guess I'll never find out...* I murmured before snatching up my briefcase, opening it with a click. Grabbing my presentation draft and notes, I gave them a quick once over. *I guess I won't be needing these anymore...* I uttered, tossing them into the bin with a heavy heart.

Once I had discarded my briefcase back on the floor, I glimpsed over at my paperwork, making a groan escape me. *I really can't face doing that...* And I swiftly shifted my attention to the steaming cup of tea Miss Jones had left me. *I'll just drink this and get on with some work.* I decided, picking it up and taking a tentative sip just as someone came to stand before me. Peering upwards, I was shocked to see Nurse Lane with a beaming smile plastered upon her beautiful face. *What's she doing here? I thought she was seeing father?*

Lowering the cup, I queried, "Can I help you with anything, Nurse Lane?"

Smiling, she corrected, "**Miss** Lane." And I couldn't stop my jaw from dropping.

*'Miss'?! She's not married?* Gone was my surprise, replaced with delight.

Briskly lowering my cup with a one-sided grin, I carried on in a bubbly tone, "Anything I can help you with, **Miss** Lane?"

"No, I just came to say farewell." She replied with a shake of her head before rummaging in her bag, "And to see if you want this." She then produced something wrapped in tinfoil, confusing me.

"What is it?" I wondered, furrowing my brow, and she replied matter-of-factly, "It's a ham sandwich. I thought you may like it rather than it going to waste."

*What a weird thing to give someone...*

"Oh, erm..." I murmured, "Thanks..." And I apprehensively took the sandwich, placing it down beside the cup of tea.

"Not a problem, Mr West." Nurse Lane beamed, and I was slightly taken aback by her not calling me Nathaniel.
*Well, I guess it makes sense seeing as we'll no longer be seeing each other.*
"Just make sure to eat the sandwich first." She added, "You're looking a little peaky, so get some fuel in your system." And she pushed the sandwich closer while covering the cup of tea with the palm of her hand, sliding it away.

"I'm sure we'll see each other again." Miss Lane concluded before turning on her heels, saying over her shoulder, "Good day, Mr West."

"Good day, Miss Lane." I replied with a heavy heart, watching as she wandered off towards the stairwell before disappearing from view.

I then gazed back down at the tinfoil. *Bit of an odd time to eat a sandwich...* I pondered. *But I am hungry, I didn't eat breakfast today and hardly ate anything yesterday.* And, as if on cue, my stomach started to rumble at the notion of food. *Sod it, I'm eating it now!* And I couldn't have ripped off the foil fast enough.

My mouth salivated as I took in the fresh, vibrant-looking lettuce and thick, juicy ham; however, I wasn't sure if it looked so appealing because I was starving. *I don't care, I'm just so hungry.* And I devoured the sandwich in swift, ravenous bites, even the crumbs littered across my desk weren't safe. *God, that was so nice!* I moaned in delight, scrunching up the tinfoil before tossing it into the bin.

My attention then shifted between the cup of tea and my paperwork. *Right, I'll drink that and then get on with stuff.* I decided while picking up the cup, taking a tentative sip before chugging it back. Begrudgingly, I diverted my focus back upon my paperwork; I knew I couldn't keep procrastinating. *Mr Sheridan won't be impressed if I don't manage to process all these today.* And that thought alone gave me the motivation to crack on.

After I had processed about a dozen orders, I noticed my hands grow cold and clammy yet the heat radiating within me was unbearable. *God, it's getting hot in here...* I whined, loosening my tie with one hand while fanning myself with the other. *I need some air!* I gasped, swiping the back of my hand across my sweaty brow.

I then went to stand but my stomach churned, freezing me where I stood half hunched over my desk. *Oh no, not again!* Inhaling several deep breaths, I slowly tried to sit back down only to stop in fear I was going to throw up when hot sick rushed up my throat. *Don't be sick! Don't be sick!* I begged, swallowing the foul-tasting vomit.

Blood started to pound in my ears, my head now spinning like a vortex. My vision began to blur; I could hardly make out the desk that I was desperately clinging onto. *I need a doctor or something!* I trembled, rapidly blinking in the hopes to see clearly but it didn't work.

Slowly, I glimpsed over in the direction of father's office, knowing he would help me. *I... I just... Just need to get over there...* And I pushed myself up off the desk, but I instantly regretted it as everything around me was now fiercely whirling; I didn't know how I had managed to stay standing. Using the desk as an aid, I staggered round but, as soon as I let go, I felt myself falling backwards before- **BANG!**

# Chapter Six
## We'll reform you before people find out the truth

*Urgh...* I groaned, bringing a hand up to my pounding head. *God, I feel awful...* My body was heavy and achy; my throat so raw it felt as if I'd been screaming at the top of my lungs. *I need a drink or something...* I uttered, blinking open my eyes only to jump with a scream when I saw father perched on the edge of my bed. *Gaaah!* He was peering down at me with an intense, eerie smile gracing his lips. *What the hell is he doing?!*

"Good morning, son." Father beamed, turning to face me, "How are you feeling on this fine Saturday morning?" And he smoothed out the creases on his dark grey slacks, his white and red plaid, short-sleeved shirt tucked into them.

"Uh... Ermmm..." I stammered, now rubbing my forehead in coherent confusion.

*Why is he just sitting on my bed?* I pondered, scrubbing a hand through my bedraggled hair. Then I realised I had no idea how I had managed to get back home never mind into bed. *What happened?*

Ignoring father's question, I queried, "How did I get here?" And I gazed down at myself, noting my pyjamas, "And what happened?" I added, now peering back over at him.

His smile cracked a little when he wetted his lips, and he squeezed his eyebrows together before explaining, "You passed out at work."

I couldn't help but stare incredulously at him. *No!* I declared in denial. *I didn't do that!* But then a wave of doubt crept in. *Did I?*

Before I could interrogate him further, father rose to his feet, saying, "Now I no longer need to keep an eye on you, get dressed and head downstairs."

"But I have so many questions!" I blurted, staring wide-eyed after him as he advanced on the bedroom door, so I hurriedly carried on, "How?! When?! Why?!"
He then faced me when he came to a halt by the door, holding up a hand for me to wait while stating, "All in due course. For now, just get yourself dressed and head downstairs, we'll be in the kitchen." And, without another word, he left, closing the door behind him.
*Why can't he tell me now? I just want to know what happened...*

Shaking my head, I threw back the covers before glancing at the clock, shocked to see it was 10:32AM. *Oh God! I better hurry up!* Panicking, I swiftly got out of bed but instantly regretting it. A dizzy, nauseating spell came over me, so I urgently grabbed the nightstand for some much-needed support, not daring to let go until I felt steady on my own two feet. *Urgg... My head...*

Once everything had stopped spinning, I gingerly staggered towards my wardrobe, snatching out the first things I could get my hands on. *These will do.* I decided, peering down at the white and brown plaid, short-sleeved shirt, cream slacks, and brown and tan saddle shoes. *How can I still be so tired?!* I griped, trying to stifle a yawn. *I've slept for God knows how long!*

I then carefully made my way into the bathroom, depositing the clothes once I had closed the door with my foot. *I need some tablets or something...* I groaned, the back of my head feeling like a massive bruise. Hoping I would find something in the medicine cabinet, I advanced on it only to catch my reflection in the mirror. *God, I look awful!* I gaped. My skin was clammy and pasty, my hair looked as if I had been dragged through a bush backwards. *Why did I pass out?* I wondered, trying to wrack my brains while noting my black eye; it was purple and angry-looking, the white of my eye still bloodshot.

Unable to look at myself a moment longer, I opened the cabinet doors and rummaged around for some tablets but couldn't find any. *Urgh... I just want the headache to go away...* I complained, about to slam the door in a huff but thought better of it. *Maybe there's some downstairs...* I pondered, doubtful. Grabbing my toothbrush, I quickly brushed my teeth, not having the energy to shave or style my hair. *I just want to sit down...* I moaned, pinching the bridge of my nose in the hopes that would lessen the headache.

Once I had put everything back, my green gaze shifted to my clothes; I couldn't be bothered to get changed but knew I had no choice. There was a bit of a kerfuffle pulling on my trousers as I didn't have the balance, and I only realised I hadn't put on my socks **after** my shoes were on. *I just want today to end...* I complained at no one in particular. *I just want to go back to bed...*

I then sluggishly headed downstairs, wandering through the dining room and into the kitchen where I spotted Carmen putting away the dishes; it wasn't hard to miss her as she was clad in a bright pink dress, the ends of her loose, blonde hair almost touching the dirty plates. *They must've finished breakfast...* I deliberated, peering over at mother cleaning the hob; she wore the same obnoxiously red dress from yesterday. *God, that hairstyle...* I murmured, cringing at her bouffant.

I didn't have the energy to speak, so I trudged over to the breakfast table where father was sat reading a newspaper. Pulling up the chair opposite him, I plonked myself down, burying my head in my hands. *Urgh... I just want this headache to go away...*

"You alright, son?" Father queried, and I peered through my fingers to see him glancing over his newspaper at me with a radiant smile.

Lowering my hands, I briefly squeezed my eyes tightly shut before saying, "Just a headache..."

"I'm not surprised." He admitted, folding his newspaper in half before setting it down on the table, carrying on, "From what I heard, you hit your head quite hard yesterday."

*That explains the bruise-like feeling...* I uttered, carefully touching the back of my head with my right hand.

"What happened yesterday?" I queried, bringing my hand round to rub my forehead.

Sighing, father wrapped his left arm around himself, resting his right one on top so he could bring a fisted hand to his lips. I couldn't ignore the apprehension shimmering behind his dark blue eyes, confusing me. *Doesn't he want to tell me?* I mulled, my brow furrowing.

Releasing a heavy breath, father lowered his arm to cross them both over his chest, finally saying, "You passed out at work. You must've hit your head pretty hard because you kept throwing up."

"I hit my head that bad?" I couldn't help but ask, shocked.

Nodding, father carried on in a strained tone, "I was really worried about you. There was nothing I could do; I felt like I failed as a father." And he cleared his throat, emitting a self-deprecating laugh, "But the doctor reassured me you were fine after checking your vitals. He explained it was probably just a bug and to starve you for twenty-four hours to get it out of your system, so I want you to get plenty of rest today."

*He doesn't want my help with the garden?* I deliberated; however, I wasn't going to argue. *Maybe I can just go back to bed for a bit and the headache will go away.*

"But," Father unexpectedly continued in a deep tone, his face reddening with anger but his smile never faltered, "If truth be told, I'm certain it is to do with the Revivamide that miscreant gave you!" And he slammed a fist down onto the table, making me jump and mother and Carmen scream.

"Jeremiah!" Mother hawked, aghast; she turned away from the stove to glower at him, grinning from ear to ear.

Shifting his dark blue gaze to her, father growled, "The hob isn't going to clean itself, Vivian!" And mother swiftly turned back to the stove, wiping it down.

Slowly, father shifted his attention back to me; he opened his mouth to speak but there was an abrupt knock at the front door. *That's strange...* I mulled as he rose to his feet. *No one has **ever** knocked before...*

"I'll get it." Father said before anyone had the chance to speak, adding, "I want you all to wait here." And he disappeared into the dining room; his feet rapped against the floorboards, filling the now eerie silence lingering in the atmosphere.

I heard the front door open with a squeak followed by father saying, "Good morning, Mr Gray. What do I owe the pleasure?"

*Mr Gray?* I repeated, unable to place the name. *Who's he?*

"Good morning, Mr West." Mr Gray replied, his voice like the scraping of a prisons chain chilled me to my very core, "I'm here to talk to you about your son."

*Me?!* I gawked, my heartbeat now racing. *He's here to talk about **me**?! Why me?! What have I done?!*

"Nathaniel?" Father queried in disbelief, "Why?"

"It has been brought to our attention that he is, for lack of a better word, a nonconformist." Mr Gray responded, and I had no idea what he was talking about.

*A nonconformist? What's that?* I deliberated, rubbing my sweaty hands down my trouser legs.

"I beg your pardon!" Father retorted, appalled, "That's **my** son you're calling a nonconformist, and he is nothing of the sort!"

"Then perhaps you'd care to explain why he hasn't been smiling." Mr Gray countered, his voice causing the hairs on the back of my neck to rise, "After all, you know as well as I do that nonconformists don't smile."

"I'll worry about my son, Mr Gray, and you worry about reforming people who actually need it!" Father bit back, his tone laced with animosity.

"Then I needn't remind you that this issue needs to be resolved promptly, Mr West." Mr Gray stated, a bead of sweat now trickled down the side of my face, "Otherwise I shall **personally** deal with him myself."

*'Personally'?!* I panicked. *What does he mean by that?!* And I

couldn't remain seated a moment longer; I hastily rose to my feet, pacing the full-length of the kitchen.

"Don't you dare blackmail me!" Father growled, his voice deepening, "Do I need to remind you who you're talking to?!"
Mr Gray bluntly replied, "I **know** who you are, Mr West. But you're only his left hand and **not** his right."
*Left hand? Left hand to who?* I wondered, hating I didn't know what was going on. *What are they talking about?!* And I came to stand beside the dining room archway, spotting father by the front door but Mr Gray was just out of sight.

"And nor are you!" Father fumed, visibly shaking, "So I advise you respect your superiors!"
"Very well, Mr West." Mr Gray murmured in agreement, "But may I suggest he stick to his routines, unless you wish to arouse suspicion."

"You needn't worry," Father countered in an ominous undertone, "I shall deal with this immediately. Good day, Mr Gray." And he didn't wait for Mr Gray to respond before shutting the door; I couldn't help but emit a heavy breath now he had gone.

I only realised I shouldn't have been eavesdropping when father turned for the dining room, so I hastily headed back over to the breakfast table. As soon as I sat down, he wandered in with a radiant smile gracing his lips.
"Right!" He delightfully exclaimed, clapping his hands together once, "It's a beautiful day, so we better head outside and cut the grass!" And that was when I realised he was talking to me.
*Hang on, but I thought he told me to rest?* I mulled before Mr Gray's advice came to mind. '**May I suggest he stick to his routines, unless you wish to arouse suspicion.**'. Before I had the chance to reply, father turned on his heels and left, leaving me staring after him.
*Well, I guess I don't have much choice...* I uttered, following him.

The front door had been left ajar, so I stepped outside only to be blinded by the sun. *God, my head!* I whined, the brightness stabbing my brain like a thousand shards of glass. Using my hand as a shield, I gazed around before spotting father by the car; he was yanking the pull starter cord on the lawnmower. *It would just be easier if we had our old one...* I muttered, closing the door before noticing other husbands and sons were also tending to their front gardens; most of them had reel mowers, only a few had the lawnmowers with the pull starter cord. *Guess we're lucky we can afford to have it...*

"Nathaniel!" Father hollered once the mower spluttered to life, gaining my attention, "Grab the hedge trimmers!" And he gestured to them laying on the grass beside the car.
I nodded once but instantly regretted it as the shards of glass pierced my brain yet again. *Urgh... I should've asked mother if we have any tablets...* I moaned, pinching the bridge of my nose while advancing on the trimmers.

Once I snatched them up, father began trundling up and down, mowing the lawn; it was only then I realised the grass already looked freshly cut. *Then why's he bothering?* I deliberated, opening my mouth to question him; however, Mr Gray's words came to mind once more. *Routines...* I murmured. *It's like everyone's brainwashed to do and say the same thing every day.*

Sighing, I shook my head and walked past the car, wandering up a little cobbled pathway that ran alongside the house and into the back garden. Hedges were on my right; they were small enough I could see into the neighbour's boundaries.

Once I reached the garden, I noted the light wooden shed in the far, right-hand corner was open. *Guess father forgot to close it.* I mulled, now glancing at the rear hedges that overlooked another neighbour's property. *None of these need cutting.* I noted, shifting my sights to the bushes on my left; they were also small enough to peer over.

Just as I was about to advance on the hedge to my right, I peered around while calling, "Max? Come on, bo-" But then I remembered he was gone, causing a tightness to form in my chest that wouldn't loosen.
*I can't believe he's not here anymore...* Swallowing the lump lodged in my throat, I trudged over to the hedge, my limbs feeling extremely heavy.

As I snipped away the odd twig here and there, I heard footsteps beyond the bush before a shrill voice abruptly sliced through the atmosphere, "Good morning, Nathaniel!"

*Ughhh...* I inwardly moaned while glancing over, spotting the neighbour's twenty-something-year-old son called Charles.

*I'm really not in the mood to talk to him...* I uttered, diverting my attention away from his dark brown eyes, but I could still see from my peripheral vision his chubby, cheery face pulled into an otherworldly smile. His pudgy fingers then brushed back his light brown hair, not that he needed to with the amount of gel slicking it back.

But then I realised I hadn't heard the excited howl from Charles' Golden Retriever this morning, so I shifted my attention back over to him, asking, "Where's Earl?" And a look of confusion now blazed behind Charles' dark gaze.

After a moment of silence, he wondered, "Aren't you going to wish me a good morning, Nathaniel?" Taking me aback.

*Seriously?!* I growled, frustrated.

Shaking my head, I forced a smile, replying in a slightly clipped tone, "Morning, Charles."

"Isn't it a lovely day today?" He queried while snapping away at the hedges with such expertise you would think he were a professional topiary.

"It would be such an ideal day for a barbecue, wouldn't you agree?" He carried on, lowering his own trimmers to rub his stomach; it was barely concealed by his orange and white plaid shirt, which was tucked into his cream shorts.

*It's always about food with him...* I muttered, remembering our never differing conversation every Saturday morning. Ignoring him, I wandered towards the rear of the garden, snipping a couple of twigs that were out of place in the process.

"I'm really looking forward to lunch!" Charles persisted, waddling over like a mother goose.

*Oh just go away!* I inwardly growled.

"Mother is making beef with vegetables!" He continued in apparent delight; I had to bring a hand up to rub my brow, warding off the headache now pounding at full force.

"What's your mother making?" He added, causing the smile on my lips to shift; a twitch now pulsed just underneath my right eye.

*Breathe... Just breathe...*

Once I had somewhat regained myself, I opened my mouth to reply but stopped; a strange look now graced Charles' fat face. *Why's he looking at me like that?* The massive smile on his lips never lessened, but the delight in his brown eyes was replaced with a realisation.

"You're not smiling!" Charles finally announced with a toothy grin, "You're scowling!" And I didn't get the chance to respond before he declared once more in a shrill tone, "He's scowling!"

The rustling of hedges then invaded the atmosphere, causing the hairs on the nape of my neck to lift. Slowly, I glanced over my shoulder to see the other two neighbour's sons peeking over the bushes at me; their hedge trimmers poised mid-cut. *Why... Why are they looking at me like that?!* My stomach turned rock hard the longer I stared at their beaming faces and glinting, malevolent eyes.

"He's scowling!" Charles announced once more, gaining my attention where I saw his father now stood beside him; they looked identical except Charles was slightly shorter and nowhere near as wide, even their clothes were the same.

*Gaaah!* I screamed, jumping backwards and accidentally dropping the hedge trimmers.

"What's the matter, boy?" Charles' father pointedly asked me, his chubby face was wreathed in smiles while his eyes reflected something sinister.

Shaking my head, I hastily stammered, "Nuh-Nothing, Mr Griffin!" And I pressed my elbows to my sides, trying to make myself as small as possible, "I-I've juh-just got to help fuh-father with the errr... The prawn. I mean fawn! **LAWN!**" And I waved a sporadic hand in the direction of the pathway, "The front lawn!"

"But you haven't trimmed **this** hedge." A voice as sharp

as a knifes edge spoke up, and I realised it was the son directly behind me.
Glimpsing over my shoulder, he was grinning radiantly while snapping his hedge trimmers.

"Or **this** side." Another voice creaked like the hinges of a broken door; it was the son from the house to the rear of our garden.
Glancing left, his smile was dazzling but the murderous look gracing his face chilled me to my very core.

*Why are they looking at me like that?!* I fretted before something dawned on me. *Or am I going mad?! Am I just imagining that they want to kill me?!* And that last thought sent shivers down my spine, as if someone had walked over my grave. *I need to go! I can't look at them a moment longer!* And I hastily turned on my heels, running for the pathway where my feet almost slid out from underneath me on the grass. I didn't dare look over my shoulder in fear they were still staring after me.

I came to a staggering halt by the bonnet of the car where I half collapsed on it, desperately catching my breath back.

"Are you alright, son?" Father queried, and I gazed upwards to see him stood on the other side of the car with the lawnmower next to him; he gleamed at me, but there was no denying the look of concern swirling in his dark blue eyes.

Standing up straight, I tried to control my panicked breathing before saying, "Yuh-Yeah, I'm fine."

"Good!" Father grinned, wondering, "Have you finished cutting the hedges?" And I was about to shake my head before realising.
*He'll want me to go back there and finish it, to stick to my routine, but I **can't**! What if the neighbours are still there?!* My hands grew clammy at the notion of facing them once more, so I wiped them down my trouser legs before doing something I've never done before.

"Yup." I lied, "All done." And it felt awful, as if I were going against the very grain of my being.

"Excellent!" Father beamed before glancing over at the

loose blades of grass scattered across the lawn, "Help me clear the garden, it should be time for lunch when we've finished."

I couldn't help but raise a questioning eyebrow. *I thought I was being starved?*

Father must have noticed the confusion upon my face as he swiftly apologised, "Sorry, Nathaniel, I forgot you can't have lunch." He then pressed a reassuring hand on my shoulder, adding, "We'll make sure your mother cooks you a meal fit for a King tonight!"

As soon as we had finished clearing up the lawn, mother was by the front door calling us in for lunch. *I'm starving!* I moaned, my stomach growling in agreement. Brushing the lingering blades of grass off my clothes, I headed inside after father, the tantalising aroma of food making my mouth water. *God, I wish I could have something to eat!* I whined, wandering through into the kitchen where I spotted Carmen dish up lunch; it looked like chicken with vegetables.

I then went to wash my hands but noticed mother peer in the pale blue fridge; it was along the right-hand wall beside the bright yellow counter. *Every week she does this... Goes to the shop because we've run out of milk...*

"Carmen," Mother piped up, closing the fridge with a gentle bang, "Would you be a dear and fetch my purse from upstairs? We've run out of milk, so I need to pop to Merrimart."

Before Carmen could reply, I offered, "I'll go." And they both stared at me in apparent confusion, clearly unsure how to respond.

"I'm not having lunch," I carried on, "So it makes sense for me to go." And a look of unease swept across mother's dazzling features.

After a moment of silence, I urged, "Carmen, go and get mother's purse."

"Of course." She beamed before disappearing through into the dining room.

I couldn't help but notice mother looked a little lost, as if uncertain what to do with herself, so I suggested, "Why don't you finish serving lunch and sit down?"

"Of course, honey." She grinned, but it didn't match the doubt swirling in her dark brown gaze.

While mother finished setting the dining table, I waited by the front door for Carmen just as father emerged from the living-room.

"Nathaniel," He began, gesturing with a nod for me to follow him into the dining room, "Please join us." And I immediately shook my head, explaining, "I can't, I'm going to the shops to get some milk for mother."

My comment may as well have slapped father across the face as he declared in apparent annoyance, "But the women go shopping, not the men!" All the while he had a face like thunder but a smile like a warm summers breeze.

"But it makes sense." I began, trying not to shrink beneath his fierce gaze, "I'm not eating, and it means mother's lunch doesn't go cold." And he opened his mouth to object but clearly thought better of it; he then quickly glanced into the dining room, blatantly staring at mother sat at the table.

After a moment of silence, father peered at me and said in a serious undertone, "Fair enough, but I'm going to explain a couple of ground rules before you leave."

*Why?* I deliberated, narrowing my eyes at him in confusion. *I'm just going to the shop...*

"Firstly, you go there and come straight back. Do you understand?" He began in a sharp tone, rubbing his brows as if to ward off a headache, "Secondly, you **don't** talk to anyone besides Mr Martin or Mr Lester, got it?"

I had no idea who those people were, but I merely nodded in agreement.

"Lastly," Father concluded, running a jerky hand through his coiffed, brown locks, "And I cannot stress this enough. You smile and you **keep** smiling. From now on you smile, I smile, **everyone** smiles. That's how it works." He then stared at me with an almost pained expression; I didn't know what to do or say so I forced a grin, which seemed to pacify him.

Father expelled a huge sigh of relief, his eyes glancing heavenward as he breathed, "Good!" He then pressed a hand to his heart before Carmen descended the stairs, gaining our attention.

"Here you go, Nathaniel." She beamed, handing me some change that I quickly pocketed; she then wandered into the dining room, leaving me alone with father who was peering anxiously at me.

*Why's he so worried about me going to the shop?* I deliberated, involuntarily raising my right eyebrow.

"Right," Father spoke up, now clasping his hands together, "Remember what I said." He then inhaled a steady breath before heading into the dining room, leaving me staring after him.

*What was all that about?* I contemplated, stepping outside and quietly closing the door behind me. *Why can't I talk to anyone else?* Ambling down the garden path, I opened the white gate with a squeak, now noticing mothers and wives leaving their houses. *O... Kay... What are they doing?* Ignoring them, I turned left, my shoes rapping against the pavement while I mulled over father's warnings. *I don't understand what's going on... Why is he so concerned about me smiling? About me going to the shop and not talking to anyone? None of it makes sense!* Then Mr Gray's words echoed in my mind, his voice causing the hairs on the nape of my neck to rise. *'**You know as well as I do that nonconformists don't smile.**'. Who was he and what's a nonconformist?*

I had now reached the quiet T-junction at the end of Paradise Street that joined Faith Road, vaguely aware of the mothers and wives steadily gaining on me. *Are they going to the shop as well?* I pondered, crossing over onto the other side of the road and turning right. *Urgh... This isn't helping my headache...* I griped, bringing a hand up to pinch the bridge of my nose. *I should've asked mother for some money to get some tablets...*

I then saw Merrimart just up ahead on my left when I lowered my hand; it was on the corner of another junction which was called Elysium Mews. The first thing I saw was the name of the shop in thick, black paint along the dark blue wood panelling, framing the door and two windows. One of the windows looked out onto Faith Road, the other Elysium Mews.

As I took several steps closer, I saw posters hung in the glass door, blocking my view of the inside. *Is it even open?* I wondered, unable to see through the windows as dark wooden units were on display; they were cluttered with food and other essential items. Then I saw the open sign hanging in the door, partially hidden by one of the posters.

*Right, get in, get out, and don't talk to anyone.* I reminded myself before pushing open the door, causing the bell to ding. My shoes squeaked against the off-white tiled flooring while I glanced around the small, dark wooden shop, closing the door behind me. Very little light managed to seep through the display units on either side of me, the main light source was from pendants hanging from the ceiling.

My eyes then locked onto the massive shelf on the far back wall; it was filled to the brim with jars of confectionary. *I've not had sweets in years!* I exclaimed in delight, feeling like a little kid again. *I wonder if I'll have enough to get a bag of pic'n'mix?*

Burying my hand inside my trouser pocket, I jumped when two masculine voices spoke in unison, "Good afternoon, Mr West!" And my head snapped over to my right where two men stood behind a glass counter with a till on top, their faces wreathed in smiles.
*How... How do they know my name?...* I mulled, confused. *I've never been here before...*

Turning to better face them, I took in the older of the two who I presumed was the owner; his thin, combed over grey hair barely concealed his balding head. *Why doesn't he just shave it off?* I wondered, taking a step closer when mothers and wives suddenly piled into the shop, now realising he was extremely short. *I doubt he even comes up to my shoulders!* It didn't help he was rather rotund, his protruding stomach emphasised by his red and white plaid shirt that was tucked into his beige slacks. Then I spotted a name badge pinned to his shirt; Mr Martin was written in bold. *Well, at least I know I can talk to him...* I uttered, my mental voice dripping with sarcasm.

"Afternoon." I said with a forced smile, shifting my attention over to the younger of the two.
*Whoa! Check out the guy on those glasses!* I gawked at his massive black, thick-rimmed glasses that looked ridiculous on his gaunt-looking face; his equally dark hair made him look pale. Then I realised I had to tip my head all the way back to look up at him. *How tall is he?!* He easily towered over me and made Mr Martin look like a child. *And I'm just under six foot!* Shaking off my shock, I spotted his name badge pinned to the uniform that matched Mr Martin's. *So he's Mr Lester...*

"What can we do for you today?" Mr Martin queried, gaining my attention.
I noted the shelving unit behind him took up the entire wall, housing tobacco and alcohol. It continued round to the right, attached to the unit in the window that overlooked Faith Road. Shifting my attention back upon Mr Martin, I explained, "I'm just after some milk." And he replied with an otherworldly smile, "Certainly, Mr West!" Before turning to grab a pint of milk out of the glass counter.

"That'll be threepence, please." Mr Lester piped up with a grin, ringing it through the till.
Pulling the money out of my pocket, I handed him the exact change before grabbing the cold pint; the cash register chimed when Mr Lester opened it.

"Thank you." I smiled softly at the pair before swiftly turning to leave; the bell above the shop door dinged, and I accidentally bumped into whoever had entered with an oof.

Once I had regained my balance, I apologised, "I'm so sor-" But I faltered when I realised who it was, now hyperaware of my heart beating just as a warm sensation flooded throughout me.
*I didn't think I'd ever see her again!*
"Nurse Lane!" I exclaimed, a slow smile spreading upon my lips.

"What are you doing here?" I mindlessly carried on, only

realising how stupid I sounded when a genuine smile hooked her succulent red lips.

"**Miss** Lane." She corrected, and my gaze was quick to lock back onto hers where I spotted amusement dancing within them, her black cat flicks making her green eyes pop.
*I never realised how green they were before!*
"And I'm here to purchase some essentials." She added while folding her arms across her chest, drawing my sights down to her-
*Wow! She looks amazing!*

Miss Lane was clad in a blazing red halterneck dress with matching T-bar heels; I noted they were a good few inches high but she still only reached my chin. *They're some heels!* I gawked, my fingers aching with the need to caress her slender legs while she wore nothing but **those** shoes. *What's wrong with me?!* I suddenly snapped, shaking myself out of my daze where I noted a black belt cinched in her already tiny waist, emphasising her hourglass figure.

"What are **you** doing here?" Miss Lane queried, bringing me back to the conversation at hand.
It was only then I realised. *I don't think I've seen her with her hair down.* It was pinned to one side, showing off her beautiful, heart-shaped face.
"Well?..." She probed when I didn't reply, so I quickly held up the milk, "Got milk."
"So I see." She smirked, gazing from the pint back up to my face. *God, she's so beautiful!* I inwardly sighed before taking a step closer to erase the distance between us, my body craving to be touched by hers.

I then opened my mouth to suggest exchanging numbers, but she piped up before I had the chance, "Anyway, I best buy what I need and be on my way. Good day, Mr West." And she dipped her head in farewell before sidestepping past me, advancing on the counter.
*But... But... We've hardly spoken!* I wailed, emitting a heavy breath.

"Good day, Miss Lane..." I muttered before leaving the shop.

*I do hope I see her again.* I sighed, casting one last glance over my shoulder at the shop before making my way back home. *I didn't even get the chance to ask her why she gave me those tablets. What did she hope to gain by giving me some placebo pill?* Now realising I was opposite Paradise Street, I looked both ways before crossing the road. *Maybe it's better I don't know...* I uttered but briskly shook my head of that thought. *I should be mad at her for what she did, but I'm not...*

Opening my garden gate, I wandered up the path towards the front door. *I should just forget about her... I mean, it's not like I'm ever going to see her again.* Burying my hand in my trouser pocket, I rifled around for my key but felt rough paper beneath my fingertips. *What the?* Pulling it out, I was confused to see a folded piece of paper. *What's this?* And I opened it, now realising it was a note. 'Come and see me Monday after work at 10 Amicable Street.'. Remember to wear the badge. *Badge? What badge?*

Fisting the note, I put the pint of milk down by the door before rummaging in my pocket once more, finding the badge in question. Holding it skyward between my thumb and index finger, it was black with gold trim and perfectly circular; roughly the size of a half-crown. The coat of arms emblem was in the middle in gold, then I noticed black writing around the gold edge. *What does it say?* Bringing it closer, I made out the word '**WATCHER**'. *Watcher? What's that?*

I then peered back down at the note, hoping it would shed some light on the situation. 'There are four tablets in your pocket'- *Hang on, what?!* Not even bothering to read any further, I moved the badge into my hand holding the note before searching for these tablets, confused how they had ended up in my pocket in the first place. *I don't understand how this has happened.* I pondered, soon feeling the hard, little capsules beneath my fingertips. *Did Miss Lane do this?* I wondered, pulling a pill out and inspecting it. *How and when?*

Shaking my head in confusion, I then glanced back down

at the note, continuing from where I had left off. -'Make sure to take one tablet <u>TWICE</u> a day! We don't want a repeat of last time!'. *I'm not taking any tablets!* I was about to screw up the note before spotting the next sentence, and I was instantly consumed with curiosity. 'You're probably wondering why you should trust me'- *Too right!* -'But I promise I'll explain everything Monday as long as you take these tablets.'.

Glancing back down at the little pink pill, I couldn't help but wonder. *She'll explain everything?* That was what I had wanted all along, to understand why, so I carried on reading. 'If you don't take them, then you'll probably forget this anyway. I hope to see you. Gloria x'. *Gloria? Is that her name?* But I didn't have time to dwell on that thought as the front door unexpectedly opened, revealing father.

"Nathaniel, why have you been dawdling on the doorstep for the past five minutes?!" He demanded with a radiant smirk, crossing his arms over his chest while his eyes glinted in annoyance, "And what did I tell you about smiling?!"
Immediately forcing a grin, I hastily buried my hands inside my trousers pockets, hiding everything. *What do I even say to him?!* I panicked, now noticing him clench his jaw while impatiently tap his foot.

"Well?" Father urged in a sharp tone, raising his right eyebrow and giving me a glassy stare.

"I-I was just, you know..." I stammered, "I-I just..." And then I did it again, I didn't speak the truth, "I just couldn't find my key." Narrowing his eyes, father countered, "Then why didn't you knock?"
I didn't know what to say, I merely stared at him like a deer caught in the headlights.

After a few moments of silence, father emitted a heavy breath before carrying on, "I was going to drag you back out here, anyway."
Confused, I wondered, "Why?"

"Because you didn't cut the bushes, did you?" He rhetorically asked, taking me aback.

*What?!* I gawked. *How does he know? Unless he-* And a coldness abruptly struck my core. *He must've spoken to Mr Griffin! Oh God, what else was said?!*

"The trimmers are where you left them." Father said, bending down to pick up the milk, "So I suggest you go and cut them before coming inside." He then turned to head indoors, adding over his shoulder, "Make sure you put the trimmers back when you've finished with them, I don't expect to find them laying on the ground again." And he slammed the door shut in my face before I could reply, making me flinch.

Shaking off my unease, I turned away. *Maybe he didn't talk to Mr Griffin?* I mulled while making my way round to the back garden, my shoes echoing along the cobbled path. *If not, then how does he know I didn't cut the bushes? Was mother watching me out the wind- What the?!* I came to a staggering halt when my eyes landed on the hedge to my right; it had twigs poking out left, right and centre. *It was **not** like that earlier!* I adamantly declared, my attention swiftly circling over to the hedges in front of me and then to my left; they too were now unkempt.

*What the hell is going on?! There's no way I would've left them like that!* But then I started doubted myself. *Or did I and I just didn't notice?* Pressing a hand to my head, I suddenly felt sick. *What's wrong with me?!* I wailed, lowering my hand to repeatedly rub my face. *Why is this happening?!* The headache began to increase tenfold, so I pinched the bridge of my nose but it did nothing to alleviate the pain. *I just want things to go back to normal... I just want to be me again...*

***

I had no idea what the time was when I finally finished cutting the hedges; I was so exhausted and feeling faint from not eating all day, the headache now throbbing at my temples. *I can't wait to go to bed...* I groaned, making my way down the little pathway after putting the trimmers in the shed. The front door was unlocked, so I sluggishly made my way inside where I was greeted by the pleasant aroma of meatloaf. *Yes! My favourite!* I exclaimed in delight, closing the door before spotting father in the living-room reading his newspaper.

*Sounds like dinners almost done.* I thought, hearing mother and Carman bustling away in the kitchen, so I decided to head upstairs and get myself cleaned up. Just as I was about to go into the bathroom, I decided. *I need to see if I've got some painkillers in my room.* And I headed straight into my bedroom, yanking open the top drawer on my nightstand; I quickly rummaged around but couldn't find any. *Come on, please!* I beseeched, trying the next drawer down. Nothing. *Urgh... Maybe I just didn't see them in the medicine cabinet earlier...* I murmured, swiftly grabbing the note, badge and tablets out of my pocket, depositing them in the nightstand.

I then trudged into the bathroom while rubbing my temples, hoping the pain would subside. *Please may there be tablets! Please may there be tablets!* I begged, opening the cabinet and searching to no avail. *Damn it!* I growled, slamming it shut with an almighty bang. *I just want this headache to go away!* Holding my head in my hands, I inhaled a deep breath, holding it in for a few seconds before releasing it in one, big huff. *I should've got some from the shop...* I regretted, lowering my hands.

I then minutely shook my head before deciding to wash up, splashing my face with cold water before lathering my hands up with a floral-smelling soap. *Hopefully I'll feel better after having something to ea- Really?!* I fumed when I couldn't find a hand towel. *Didn't anyone think to replace it?* I gazed around in search of something to dry my hands on but couldn't find anything, so I wiped them down my trouser legs only to feel something in one of my pockets. *Huh?* It didn't feel like my front door key, so I buried my hand inside only to pull out one of those pills. *Ha... Guess I didn't get them all out. Better put this away before I forget.*

I was about to turn for the bathroom door; however, that note flashed across my mind. 'I promise I'll explain everything

Monday as long as you take these tablets.'. That was all I wanted, answers. *But do I really want to do this?* I queried, now peering questioningly down at the pink pill pinched between my thumb and index finger. Slowly, my attention then shifted to my reflection in the mirror. *I guess what I need to ask myself is do I want answers or not?* And I would've been lying to myself if I had said no. *I **need** to know why.*

Against my better judgement, I brought the pill to my lips just as I heard footsteps hastily ascend the stairs.
I barely popped it in my mouth when the door swung open and father bellowed, "**NATHANIEL!**" Making me jump and choke on the pill as I swallowed it.
*What the hell is he doing?!* I fumed, seeing him stood in the doorway via the mirror, so I briskly spun round to face him.

"What's going on?!" Father spoke up first with a never dwindling smile; my anger swiftly vanished, replaced with confusion.

"What do you mean '**What's going on?!**'?" I queried in an uncertain tone before he advanced on me; I immediately took a step back to maintain the distance, but the sink was now pressed against me.
Ignoring me, father ordered, "Empty your pockets!" And he gestured down to my trousers with a massive sweep of his hand. I couldn't stop my jaw from dropping, my head jerking back in shock, "What?!" I blurted, staring incredulously at him, "Why?"

Father then took another step towards me, we were now so close we were sharing the same air.
"Just do as I say!" He barked with bared teeth yet, somehow, he still smiled radiantly.
Leaning back slightly, I quickly glimpsed down at my trousers before back up at him, slowly out turning the pockets. My front door key hit the floor with a ding, gaining both our attention. Father then stared hard at my empty pockets for a moment before his dark blue eyes shifted back up to me; I instantly glanced away, staring beyond him at the open bathroom door.

With a frustrated huff, father unexpectedly moved away,

tapping a fisted hand against his lips. *What's he doing?* I mulled as he lowered it, now coming to stand before me yet again.

"You didn't take anything?" He finally asked in an uncertain tone, and I shook my head.

"No tablets? Medicine?" He pried, unconvinced, "Nothing at all?" *What the hell is going on? It's like he knows I've done something!* I fretted while anxiously stuffing my pockets back inside my trousers, shaking my head as I done so.

Narrowing his eyes, father tilted his head to one side before querying, "You wouldn't bear false witness to your own father, would you?" And I was stunned by his question; I couldn't stop my jaw from dropping.

"Of course not!" I blurted, only realising that too was a lie after I had said it.

To my surprise, father emitted a huge breath before bowing his head, as if the weight of the world had been lifted from his shoulders.

"I didn't think so." He beamed, his gaze now returning to mine, "Now hurry up, dinners ready." And, without another word, he turned for the door, closing it behind him.

A few seconds passed before I wondered. *What just happened?* And I narrowed my eyes at the bathroom door. *How did he know about the tablet?* Unable to think of a plausible explanation, I bent down and picked up the key, shoving it in my trouser pocket. Trying not to dwell on my unanswered questions, I headed downstairs into the dining room. Everyone was already sat down waiting for me, so I quickly pulled up a chair opposite Carmen. *Wow! This looks amazing!* I gawked, my mouth salivating at the juicy-looking meatloaf with a side of fresh vegetables.

"Let's say grace." Father said, cupping his hands together and bowing his head, "Bless us, O Lord, and these, Thy gifts, which we are about to receive from Thy bounty. Through Christ, our Lord. Amen."

"Amen." We said in unison followed by the sign of the cross.

I then grabbed my knife and fork, taking a ravenous bite; the flavours overwhelmed my taste buds, making me moan aloud with pure bliss. *God, this tastes **so** good!*

"How was your day tending to the garden, honey?" Mother asked father between mouthfuls, and he dabbed a napkin either side of his beaming lips before answering, "Busy as always, sweetheart. We blah blah blah…" But I swiftly became oblivious to their conversation, too engrossed with dinner.

*This was so worth the wait!* I exclaimed in coherent delight, stuffing more food into my mouth before I even finished the first bite. *I wonder what mother's made for pudd-* **BANG!** I jumped with a scream when father slammed a fisted hand down onto the table, my knife and fork slipping from my grasp and hitting the floor with a clatter.

"Your mother was talking to you." He commented, and I slowly shifted my attention over to her where she was beaming at me. Shaking off my unease, I queried, "Sorry, mother, what were you saying?"

"I asked how your day was tending to the garden, honey." She replied, her unblinking gaze causing an icy chill to creep up my spine, straightening me as if I were a puppet on strings.

"Oh, erm…" I began before clearing my throat, using that as an opportunity to pick up my knife and fork, "It was fine, thanks."

"So you finished cutting the hedges?" Father probed, continuing once I nodded, "And you put the trimmers away?" Casting him a quick glance, I took another bite before replying, "Yes, father, it's all done and everything's put away."

"Good." He smiled, "Hopefully that'll be the last of any aberrations. Tomorrow, everything shall return to normal and you can pray to God for forgiveness."

*Erm… What?* I abruptly stilled, my fork midway to my mouth.

"Forgiveness?" I repeated while lowering my cutlery, looking to father with narrowed eyes, "Why do I need to pray for forgiveness?"

Dabbing a napkin either side of his lips, he explained, "Because you have sinned, Nathaniel." And I couldn't help but jerk my head back in shock.

*But I've done nothing wrong!*

"Do you remember the verse from John 1:9?" Father carried on, oblivious to my controverted feelings, "'**If we confess our sins, He is faithful and righteous to forgive us our sins and to cleanse us from all unrighteousness.**'."

*But I've done **nothing** wrong!* I adamantly declared, discarding my cutlery onto my polished plate with a ding.

"Don't worry, my son." Father said with a sympathetic smile, reaching over to give my shoulder a gentle squeeze, "We'll reform you before people find out the truth."

*Truth? The truth about what?* Then I realised what else he had said. *Hang on, 'reform' me? What does he mean by that?* Before I could ask any questions, father continued to eat his dinner in silence, not even mother or Carmen uttered another word. *Seriously, what the hell is going on? First he interrogates me in the bathroom, and now he wants me to pray to God for forgiveness?* Frowning, I ran a hand through my hair while glancing around as if searching for answers.

Once everyone had finished, father happily proclaimed, "That was delicious, sweetheart!" His dark blue gaze then shifted to me, and he said with a show-stopping smile, "Let's head into the living-room and leave the women to clean up."

Nodding, I got up but stilled when my stomach audibly groaned; violent cramps swiftly followed, then a cold sweat consumed me whole. *Oh no!* I gasped, realising what was happening; I barely managed to slap a hand over my mouth when a sudden rush of vomit erupted up my throat. *Not again!*

Barging past father, I bolted upstairs, shouldering my way into the bathroom where I dropped to my knees in front of the toilet. Burying my head down the bowl, I threw up my guts. *Why?! WHY?!* I bawled, feeling hot tears stream down my cheeks unchecked. *Why is this happening?!* The vomit was never-ending; I couldn't understand why seeing as I had only eaten one meal today.

I then felt a presence beside me long before I finally sat back on my heels; I didn't have to look up to know it was father by the way he pressed a hand down onto my shoulder in comfort.

"I'm sorry…" I uttered, wiping the back of my hand across my moist lips, "I… I don't know why this is happening."
Out of my peripheral vision, I saw him crouch down beside me, his hand no longer on my shoulder.

"I think I might know why…" Father commented, gaining my attention; I couldn't help but gulp when I noted something sinister shining in his dark blue eyes, craftily hidden behind a perfect smile.
"Don't worry, my son." He carried on, giving me a small pat on the back, "Tomorrow's a brand new day."

# Chapter Seven
## Keep! Smiling!

**DING, DING, DING!** *Nooo... I don't want to get up...* I whined before groggily opening my eyes, glancing over at the clock to see it was 8:00AM. *Why does church have to start so early?* Propping myself up onto my elbows, I leant over to turn off my alarm, relieved when the knocking stopped.

I then swung my legs round to sit on the edge of the bed, mustering up the energy to begin the day. *Urgh... Why am I so tired?* I groaned just as my stomach rumbled, and then I realised. *I've hardly eaten these past couple of days, no wonder I feel so exhausted...* I had no idea why until father's voice unexpectedly echoed in my head. **'I'm certain it is to do with the Revivamide that miscreant gave you!'**. And my gaze slowly diverted over to the nightstand where I had discarded the pills last night.

*Maybe father was right.* I pondered, apprehensively opening the top drawer to gaze inside, spotting the three pink pills in question. *Maybe these tablets are making me sick.* But the note then came to mind. 'I promise I'll explain everything Monday as long as you take these tablets.'. *I **want** answers, and I'm not going to get them if I don't take these.* A newfound surge of confidence then enveloped me as I picked up one of the pills, popping it in my mouth and swallowing before I could second guess myself.

*Right, now I better get up.* I decided while shutting the drawer, my eyes quick to lock onto the transistor radio. *And maybe a bit of music will wake me up.* Leaning across, I turned it on and immediately cringed when the never differing Frank Sinatra song played. 'III've got yooou under my skiiin. III've got yooou deep in the heaaart of meee, so deep in my heart that you're really a paaart of meee. III've got yooou under my skiiin.'. *Urgh... Don't they play anything else?* I complained, swift to turn it off.

Once I had made my bed and pulled back the curtains, I turned for the wardrobe, grabbing the navy suit I had worn for the past week. *This'll do.* I decided, snatching up my wingtip shoes before heading to the bathroom, closing the door behind me with my foot.

I then advanced on the medicine cabinet once I set my clothes down, clocking my black eye in the mirror which looked no different from yesterday. *How long did Miss Lane say it would take to heal?* I mulled before inspecting the purple, angry-looking bruise; the white of my eye was still bloodshot. *Hopefully it'll start to look better next week.* I prayed, lightly tapping the bruise with my ring finger but instantly regretted it; it was still tender to the touch, making me hiss in pain. Sighing, I shook my head before grabbing my toiletries, quickly brushing my teeth and styling my hair.

Once I had changed into my suit, I wandered downstairs into the kitchen; the tantalising aroma of bacon and eggs invaded my senses, making my stomach growl aloud. *That smells so good!* I inwardly moaned before my eyes locked onto mother by the hob; she wore a white wool suit dress, making me wonder. *Isn't she hot wearing that?* Then the ding of cutlery distracted me, and I gazed over to see Carmen setting the breakfast table; her long, blonde hair was down in loose curls, almost touching the table top.

Automatically taking a further step inside, I said, "Good morning, mother. Good morning, Carmen."
In unison, they spun round to face me, smiling broadly, "Good morning, Nathaniel." Before turning back and continuing what they were doing.

I then robotically made my way over to the breakfast

table, pulling up a chair just as Carmen finished setting it; the ends of her white dress slightly lifted as she turned to me, a black belt cinching in her small waist. Her green eyes then momentarily met mine, a smile growing on her made-up face before she began helping mother pile the plates up with bacon, eggs, and a side of toast. It was only then I realised. *I can't eat breakfast.* Not because I didn't want to, but because I knew I couldn't miss church.

"Where's your father?" Mother queried with a radiant smile gracing her made-up face, hollering, "Jeremiah?!" She then brushed aside a loose strand of dark brown hair, which had fallen from the pinned up beehive, before advancing on Carmen. Grabbing a plate, she set it down at father's spot opposite me.

"Coming, sweetheart!" Father called from the living-room, his shoes suddenly rapping against the dining room floor before he appeared with a newspaper tucked under his arm; I noted he was clad in a dark grey suit, a black and gold badge pinned to the lapel.

"Smells delicious, sweetheart." He gleamed before sitting down, his dark blue eyes staring eagerly at his food.

Once mother and Carmen had served breakfast and sat down, father brought a forkful of food to his lips; his eyes rolled into the back of his head in delight, a pleasing groan escaping him once he took a bite.

"And it tastes just as good as it looks!" He happily proclaimed, dabbing a napkin either side of his thin, beaming lips.

He then tucked it into his crisp white shirt, hiding his black and gold striped tie from view.

*God, I'm so hungry!* I groaned, watching mother and Carmen dig in. *One bite won't hurt, surely?* But I didn't even get the chance to mull over that thought before spotting father stare at me. *Why's he looking at me like that?* His face was slowly reddening, a bulging vein now pulsing down his forehead; it was right then I knew he was angry. *But why?! What have I done?!*

"Right, young man!" Father began with a raised voice and a beaming smile, his eyes cold and flinty, "What is **that** on your face?!"

*Huh?* Baffled, I brought a hand up to my jaw. *Have I got toothpaste on me?*

"And why aren't you smiling?!" He heatedly carried on, loosening the collar of his shirt as he done so.

Lowering my hand, I brought it round to rub the back of my neck, now acutely aware of my mouth.

"Well…" I began but trailed off, not quite sure which question to answer first, but father growled before I could respond, "Right, that's it!" And he dropped his cutlery with a ding, his smile never faltering, "I've had enough of your antics, young man! I told you how it works; you smile, I smile, just like everyone else!"

Stooping in my chair, my gaze flitted around the room as I apologised, "Suh-Sorry, father…"

"Sorry isn't good enough!" He retorted bitingly, "I explicitly told you yesterday to keep smiling and to shave that scruff off your face!"

Father than inhaled a deep breath, as if to calm himself, before saying, "When we get back from church, you're going to head straight to the bathroom and sort **that**-" He pointed incriminatingly at my face, "-Out before we head to the gentlemen's club! Until then, you will smile and not stop smiling until we get back home! Understood?!" And I promptly nodded.

"Good!" He beamed, picking up his cutlery, "Now eat your breakfast, it's getting cold." And that comment filled me with apprehension.

Running a hand through my hair, I wetted my lips before replying in a slight stammer, "About thuh-that… I… I feel it may be best if I don't."

A look of what could only be described as pure outrage now graced father's radiant face, so I hastily tacked on, "Juh-Just in case I-I'm sick."

He was silent for a moment while tilting his head from side to side, as if weighing up his choices.

Father then slightly shook his head, I presumed that was

his answer until he said, "Hmmm, very well... But this shall be the last time you're exempt from meals. I just hope it's not because you've taken something you shouldn't." And he stared at me hard, as if searching for any tell-tale signs.
Shaking my head, I shot him a forced, dazzling smile, "Of course not, father!" Which seemed to pacify him.

"Good, that's what I wanted to hear." He replied before tucking back into his breakfast, leaving me wondering if he knew about the tablet.

***

*My face is really starting to hurt...* I griped, eager for the church service to end; however, the offering had only just finished and the dark-haired Pastor was about to give a Bible reading. He stood at the front behind a dark wooden podium clad in a black suit with a white collar; a pipe organ was behind him underneath the stained-glass window that took up the entire wall. The choir, who were dressed in white robes, were either side of the organ.

*How am I going to keep this smiling up all the time?* I deliberated while fidgeting on the uncomfortable, dark wooden bench; my family and I were sat at the very back on the left side of the brick-built church that was rammed with everyone from Merribridge. There were another nine rows of benches directly in front of us, so close together my knees were almost touching the back; this was also mirrored on the right-hand side of the church.

"Sit still!" Father scolded in a whisper when I fidgeted again, gaining my attention; he was sat on my right glaring at me through narrowed eyes while the cold, brick wall was on my left.
I couldn't help but run a jerky hand through my hair while flitting my gaze around the room, unable to look at him. *It's really hard to sit still when the bench is like concrete!*
"And keep smiling!" He added with a hard smirk, exhaling

noisily through his nose in apparent irritation when I forced a toothy grin.

*I honestly don't know how I'm going to keep this up, I have no idea when I've stopped smiling!* I fretted, pinching the skin at my throat before spotting Carmen gleaming at me; she was sat in the middle of father and mother. *How can they keep this up all the time?* I wondered while father gestured for Carmen to sit back with a wave of his hand. *My face feels like jelly!*

"Hear the Gospel of our Lord Jesus Christ according to Deuteronomy." The Pastor spoke up, distracting me; sunlight now seeped through the stained-glass window behind him, bathing him and the choir in a kaleidoscope of colours.
"Glory to You, O Lord." He carried on, pushing his black, thick-rimmed glasses up his nose before reading from the Bible, "'**If a man have a stubborn and rebellious son, which will not obey the voice of his father, or the voice of his mother, and that, when they have chastened him, will not hearken unto them: then shall his father and his mother lay hold on him, and bring him out unto the elders of his city, and unto the gate of his place.'.**"

"Keep! Smiling!" Father unexpectedly growled through gritted teeth, distracting me where I saw him frown at me; I quickly forced a grin before circling my eyes back upon the Pastor.

"'**And they shall say unto the elders of his city, 'This our son is stubborn and rebellious, he will not obey our voice; he is a glutton, and a drunkard.'. And all the men of his city shall stone him with stones, that he die: so shalt thou put evil away from among you; and all Israel shall hear, and fear.'.**" The Pastor then closed the Bible with an audible slap, concluding, "This is the Gospel of the Lord, then Praise to You, O Christ."
*That's a really grim passage…*

"Would a member of the council like to come up and explain Deuteronomy?" The Pastor then wondered just as father snapped at me, "Keep smiling! If you don't, so God help me I'll-"

"Ah, Mr West!" The Pastor cut across father with a delighted grin, "Would you care to join me?" I had no idea who he was talking to when he gestured for one of us to come up with a sweep of his hand.

*I'm not going up there!* I adamantly declared while out of the corner of my eye I saw father rub his brow, as if warding off a headache; I was relieved when he eventually rose to his feet, making a huge breath escape me. Father then shuffled out of the pew, his shoes rapping against the red runner that led all the way up to the podium. When he finally came to stand at the front, he and the Pastor spoke in hushed tones for a brief moment; there was no denying the annoyance upon father's gleaming face. *He's not been in a good mood all day…* I mulled before he came to stand behind the podium, gazing out upon the crowd.

"You're all probably wondering why the Pastor chose to preach about such a harsh passage." Father began in a clipped tone while murmurs of agreement echoed throughout the church, "Well, I believe there are some significant considerations that can clarify the text." And the murmurs abruptly stopped; silence now lingered in the atmosphere.

"Firstly," Father carried on, now grasping the edge of the podium with both hands, "Yes, at face value, it does seem a bit of an extreme discipline; however, we need to remind ourselves that the son in question is not a child. In fact, he is a '**young**' man; a delinquent whose decisions can greatly jeopardise not only himself but also his family."

*He got all that from that verse?* I mulled, quietly impressed.

"Secondly," Father continued, "The parents played no role in stoning their son or even the decisions leading up to it; the verdict was made by the elders whom we can presume are similar to our government or even Prime Minister. **They** are the ones who carried out the punishment and warned the citizens of the delinquent son."

*But surely our government wouldn't do something so barbaric?*

"Lastly," Father concluded, "We're all aware some people have recently been amiss. Now, I'm not suggesting they were anything like the delinquent son, but there's definitely a valuable lesson behind Deuteronomy's passage that we can take away today." He then cleared his throat, adding, "My advice would be to make sure your loved ones don't go astray like Richard Brown did; he was the perfect example of a delinquent son." He then pulled away from the podium just as the crowd applauded.

"Thank you, Mr West." The Pastor said from behind the podium while father walked down the aisle.

Once he had sat down, the Pastor carried on, "We are going to conclude today's service by worshipping God through song. In Psalm 98:4, it says to '**Shout to the LORD, all the earth; break out in praise and sing for joy!**', so I would like to invite you all to stand and sing as we worship our God together!"

Everyone then rose to their feet just as the hauntingly beautiful pipe organ came to life.

"Aaaamaaaaaazziiing Graaaace, hoooow sweeeeet the sooound thaaat saaaaved aaa wreeetch liiike meeeeeee!" The choir sang in perfect harmony before everyone joined in, "IIII oooonce waaas loooost, buuut nooooow aaaam fooound. Waaaas bliiiiind buuut nooooow IIII seeeeeee."

It was a little tricky trying to maintain a perfect, unwavering smile while singing; I was so confused how everyone managed it so easily.

*It's impossible!* I adamantly declared, now halfway through singing the second verse before something nudged me in the ribs. Peering down, I saw father's elbow jab me once more; this time a lot harder.

"Ow!" I griped aloud, now noticing him glare at me with protruding eyes.

He then demanded something through gritted teeth; it was difficult to hear him over the singing, but I didn't need to be a lip-reader to know what he had said. *It's because I'm not smiling.*

Ignoring the pulsing vein now zigzagging down father's forehead, I stated, "I **can't** smile!" Which made his face redden in anger before he demanded in a deep baritone, "What do you mean you '**can't**'?!"

*I'm not doing this on purpose!* I growled while minutely shaking my head, which he must have taken as my response.
"Have you not learnt anything today?!" He questioned in a sharp tone, and I couldn't help but force a laugh, "Yeah, that I can't sing **and** smile!" I retorted sarcastically, causing his nostrils to flare.

"I'd watch your tone, young man!" Father snapped, and I didn't like the threatening connotation to his voice, "This isn't the place to act out of sorts!"
"Why?!" I declared, gesturing around at everyone with a sweep of my hand, "Because you're scared people will think I'm like the delinquent son?!" And I instantly regretted saying that as soon as it left my lips.
*What was I thinking?!* I panicked, running a jerky hand through my hair.

Clearing my throat, I hastily apologised, "I'm so sorry, fath-"
"I'll deal with you when we get home!" He cut across while spittle built up in the corners of his mouth; his neck now corded as tendons jumped out.
He then diverted his attention back upon the choir, singing as he done so with a radiant, unwavering smile; it was then I realised everyone was singing the last verse, "Waaaas bliiiiind buuut nooooow IIII seeeeeee." And I couldn't have been more relieved when it was over.

"And now may the Lord bless you and keep you." The Pastor spoke up once the church fell into silence, "May the Lord make His face to shine upon you and be gracious unto you. And may God give you His peace in your going out and in your coming in, in your lying down and in your rising up, in your labour and in your leisure, in your laughter and in your tears..." The Pastor then trailed off, inhaling a steady breath as he done so, "Until you come to stand before Jesus in that day in which there is no sunset and no dawning. Amen." He concluded followed by the sign of the cross.

"Amen." Everyone said in unison while also doing the sign.

Rubbing his hands together in delight, the Pastor then

added, "A few of the ladies have prepared tea and biscuits in the conference room, so please feel free to help yourself before heading home." And he gestured with a sweep of his hand to the grand, double doors behind us that led out into the foyer.

Everyone then rose to their feet, filing out into the aisle one by one; however, father gestured with a raise of his hand for us to wait. Once the majority of people had left, he ushered mother and Carmen to shuffle out; I quietly followed behind him.

The red runner muffled our steps as we left the now vacant church; mottled stone tiles greeted us underfoot when we stepped out into the narrow, brick-built foyer. The lobby was dimly lit; the main light source was from a fancy-looking chandelier that hung in the middle of the vaulted ceiling. *Whoa, that rooms going to be packed!* I exclaimed, eyeing up the throng of people slowly filing into the conference room on my right; the wooden doors pinned back so they wouldn't swing shut.

A heavy sigh then gained my attention, I glanced over to my left to see father eying the crowd in apparent frustration. *I guess he doesn't want to stay...* I pondered. *So we'll have to squeeze through...* And I peered over at the glass, double doors opposite me that led out to the car park, the crowd blocking our escape; even the door on my left that led to the toilets was obstructed.

Shaking his head, father turned to face us, speaking with forced restraint and a show-stopping smile, "Come on, we're leaving." And he spun back around only to accidentally bump into an extremely tall, bald gentleman with a white goatee.

*Whoa!* I gawked, having to tip my head all the way back. *He's massive!*

Father briskly shook off his daze, saying, "My apologies-" But then he abruptly stopped, now seeming to recognise the gentleman who I noted must have been in his late sixties or early seventies.

"Not a problem, Jeremiah." The older-looking man smirked, and I couldn't help but wonder how father knew him; I didn't recognise him as one of father's friends from the gentlemen's club.

*I don't even recognise him from work...* I mulled, taking in his beaming, hatchet-face that was so cold and calculating it felt as if Death was leering over my shoulder; not even his deep, brown eyes melted his icy appearance.

"Are you leaving already?" The older gentleman interrogated while adjusting his navy tie fastened to his crisp white shirt, which was tucked into his light grey trousers.

He then grasped the lapels on his matching grey blazer, a black and gold badge was pinned to the left one; it was only then I saw the burn scars on his hands. *Ouch!* I grimaced. *How'd he do that?*

Before father could reply, the gentleman wondered, "Aren't you at least going to stay for a quick cuppa-" But he abruptly froze when his penetrating gaze landed on me, and not even his smirk was enough to disguise the sinful gleam shimmering in his dark depths.

*Why's he looking at me like that?!* I gulped, running a jerky hand through my hair just as my throat began to feel constricted.

Slowly, the gentleman shifted his attention back to father, querying with a curious tip of his head, "Is this your son?" And father instantly brought a protective arm round, pushing me behind him to block me from view.

*What's going on?* I fretted, my mouth now dry.

When father didn't reply, the gentleman emitted a bark of laughter, "Well, things have just gotten interesting!" And there was no denying the menace lacing his voice.

*What the hell does he mean by that?!* I panicked, now clutching the cuff of my navy jacket.

Father then gazed over his shoulder at mother, Carmen and I, ordering, "Go and wait in the car." Before glancing back up at the older gentleman, requesting, "A word, Doctor Solace?" And he gestured with a nod towards the grand, double doors behind us where we had come from.

*Doctor Solace?* I repeated, peering up at the imposing man. *Father's never mentioned him before, and I'm pretty certain he's never gone to Merriwell Community Clinic, so how do they know each other?*

An ominous smirk then hooked the corner of Doctor Solace's lips before he replied, "By all means." And he immediately advanced on the grand doors just as father turned to us.

"Remember," He quickly said while walking backwards in the direction of the doors, "Go straight to the car." And, without another word, they both disappeared inside.

*What was all that about? Why did that Doctor guy suddenly stop talking when he looked at me?*

"Come on, honey." Mother piped up, gaining my attention; she and Carmen were waiting for me by the exit, the foyer now eerily quiet and empty.

"We better do as your father said." She added, and I merely nodded in agreement.

*I'm already treading on thin ice with him...*

We ventured outside and down the off-white stone steps that led into the car park; it was teemed with a sea of blue Austin Cambridge's. *Which one is ours?* I wondered with a sigh, unable to remember where we had parked; however, mother and Carmen seemed to know. *I don't get how they remember or even recognise which car is ours, they all look the same!*

We walked all the way to the back of the car park before they abruptly stopped by the bonnet of one and, in unison, they turned to face me. *What are they doing?* I mulled, confused. Narrowing my eyes, I questioned mother, "Aren't you going to unlock the car?..."

"I don't have the keys, honey." She replied matter-of-factly, making me inwardly sigh.

*Great... I doubt Carmen has either...* And I looked to her for confirmation; she merely shook her head in response. *Right... I guess I'll be the one who's going back to get them off father...*

Exhaling a noisy breath, I gave them a hard smile before saying, "I'll be back in a minute." And I traipsed across the car park to the church.

*I hope father's not going to be mad at me.* I prayed while trudging up the steps, wandering through the glass doors and into the foyer. My eyes instantly snapped onto the double doors that led into the main area of the church, and I was already dreading the look upon his face when I set foot in there. *Just get it over and done with. Just get it over and done with.* I chanted before bypassing the conference room where there was an abundance of chattering.

I then came to stand in front of the grand doors, sheepishly knocking on it; there was no reply, so I headed inside. "Hello?!" I hollered, but there was no reply again, "Father?!" Nothing, only my voice echoing off the brick walls could be heard. Glancing around, I realised the church was empty. *Where is he?* Even the extremely tall Doctor was nowhere to be seen. *Where did they go?* Not knowing what else to do, I slowly backed out into the foyer, quietly closing the doors as I done so.

*Strange...* I pondered, furrowing my brow before peering over at the conference room. *Maybe they went in there?* And I apprehensively wandered inside where red carpet greeted me underfoot. Sunlight pooled in from the large window along the cream wall directly opposite me, bathing the crowded room in a warm hue. Another smaller window was on the left wall that looked out over the car park, red felted chairs were stacked in front that people were helping themselves to.

*I'm never going to find him in here!* I griped, even scanning for the Doctor to no avail. *Seriously, where did they go?* Taking a further step inside, I sidled past a group of people chatting away while sipping tea and eating biscuits; a table to my right had been set up with refreshments. *God, I'm so hungry!* I inwardly moaned before averting my gaze to avoid temptation. *But I really don't want to risk being sick.* I reminded myself while squeezing through another flock of people to search for father.

Once I had completed a lap of the room, I realised. *He's not here.* And I began to wonder whether he had gone back to the car. *Hopefully he's not going to be mad at me.* I prayed, biting my bottom lip while advancing on the window that overlooked the car park; vaguely aware of a brunette lady clad in a light blue dress trying to pull a chair off the stack.

I barely got the chance to gaze outside before a silvery voice piped up, "Excuse me, would you mind giving me a hand?" And I glanced over at the lady in the blue dress only to do a double-take.

*Miss Lane?!* I gasped, a tentative smile building the longer I peered at her. I noted she wore a halterneck dress with a white belt cinching in her waist, her matching white heels making her almost eye level with me.

When Miss Lane realised who I was, a delighted smile graced her ruby red lips; I was instantly drawn to them like a moth to a flame. *She looks amazing!* I proclaimed just as she swept back her long, brown hair, baring her slender, porcelain neck; I couldn't help but stroke my left arm longingly, as if it were a surrogate for her neck that I longed to caress.

"Nathaniel," Miss Lane abruptly piped up, "What a pleasant surprise!" And just her voice alone made my skin flush. *What's wrong with me?!* I exclaimed, trying to ignore the tingling sensation in my nerve endings.

"Likewise." I instantly responded in a low baritone, all the while my eyes grazed over her bodice, especially her breasts that looked so perky they were practically screaming '**Hello!**' at me. *Snap out of it!* I immediately scolded, shifting my attention back upon her beautiful, made-up face; there was no denying she had caught me staring by the twinkle of amusement dancing in her green gaze.

"Would you mind giving me a hand?" Miss Lane tactfully queried, gesturing with a nod towards the stack of chairs.

I didn't need to be asked twice, I quickly pulled one off while saying, "Of course!" Before setting it down beside her.

Grabbing the chair, Miss Lane turned it to face into the room with the back against the left-hand wall.

"Thank you." She grinned, sitting down and grabbing her brown leather tote bag that was on the floor.

"My pleasure." I grinned, stepping closer to erase the distance between us.

"Are you not having tea and biscuits with your family?"

Miss Lane wondered, blatantly peering around as if in search of them; it was only then I remembered I was looking for father. *Damn it, I shouldn't be here!* And I glanced out the window but couldn't see any sign of him.

"No..." I murmured, trailing off, "I was looking for father after he disappeared with some Doctor guy, but I couldn't find him." And I glanced back down to see a little '**o**' gracing her red lips; cogs evidently turning in her head.

"Oh," Miss Lane said after a moment of silence, her expression downcast before continuing with a show-stopping smile, "Well, I'm sure he'll turn up. In the meantime-" And she patted her tote bag, "-I've got some sandwiches if you fancy sitting and having a chat?"

I couldn't help but furrow my brow as I asked, "Why have you brought sandwiches? There's biscuits over there." And I gestured with a nod towards the table along the right-hand wall.

"Well," She began with a sigh, "I had made them especially for today; however, there wasn't enough room on the table and I really don't want them to go to waste."

Crossing my arms over my chest, I reluctantly explained, "I can't, whatever I seem to eat lately doesn't agree with me."

"I'm sure a sandwich won't hurt." Miss Lane insisted, pulling out a brown paper bag.

"Look, I'm sorry, but I can't." I stated, waving my hands in a no gesture, "I really don't want to be throwing up, especially in the House of God."

"Trust me," She began with a smile, "My sandwiches are the best and won't make you sick." She then plucked one out of the paper bag, passing it to me before I could object.

Gazing at it, I was instantly captivated by the thick slices of ham that were folded amidst just the right amount of cheese. *Oh no!* I gasped, the vibrant-looking lettuce and juicy slivers of tomato that accompanied the main delicacy made my mouth over salivate. *This looks amazing!* And I was torn between doing the right thing or giving into temptation.

"One bite won't hurt." Miss Lane piped up, my attention

unwavering from the sandwich, "**Trust** me." And I couldn't take it anymore, the hunger so unbearable I gave in.

I sunk my teeth into the tasty morsel, but the first ravenous bite wasn't enough; I needed more and tore off another chunk before I had even swallowed the first. *God, this is **so** good!* I moaned aloud, uncaring who heard me.

"Blimey!" Miss Lane exclaimed when I polished off the sandwich, "You really were hungry!" She then rolled down the top of the paper bag, passing it to me while saying, "Here, have the rest."

Shocked, I shook my head, "I can't, they're yours!" Making her scoff, "I'm more than capable of making more sandwiches, so I **insist** you have this." And she stuffed the bag into my jacket pocket, clearly not taking no as an answer.

"Erm, thanks." I replied with a small smile, flattening the top so it was no longer poking out of my pocket.

*I just hope I'm not going to regret eating that.*

"Anyway," I said, changing the subject, "I should probably get going."

"Of course, I understand." Miss Lane commented, "I hope to see you again, Nathaniel."

Hearing those words caused heat to radiate through my chest, a feeling of breathlessness swiftly followed. *She wants to see me again?!* I gasped, overjoyed.

Nodding, I agreed in a bubbly tone, "I hope to see you-" But a strident voice unexpectedly cut across me, "Nathaniel!" And I instantly recognised it as father.

*Uh oh...* I gulped, peering over my shoulder to see him advance on us; his eyes so wide I could see the whites of them.

"What on earth do you think you're doing, young man?!" Father gutturally roared with a radiant smirk, causing a few people nearby to glimpse over at us in apparent shock, "I explicitly told you to wait in the car!"

Pressing my elbows into my sides to make myself as small as possible, I stammered, "Yuh-You didn't give me the kuh-keys, father, so I, erm... I cuh-came looking for you."

"You clearly didn't look hard enough if you're talking to **her**!" He bit back while pointing an incriminating index finger at Miss Lane.

I opened my mouth to reply but she piped up first, "It was my fault, Mr West!" She affirmed with a dazzling grin, now rising to her feet, "**I** was the one who called Nathaniel over to talk to him!"

Turning to better face her, father slowly and deliberately advanced on her, "You stay away from **my** son!" He practically screamed while jabbing his finger in her face, "Do you hear?!" And, without another word, he grabbed me by the forearm and dragged me towards the foyer.

"I don't want you seeing or speaking to that girl ever again!" Father fumed while shunting open the glass, double doors with his free hand, yanking me down the steps into the car park.

"Ow!" I hissed, trying to shake off his hold to no avail.

"She's nothing but bad news!" He continued his tirade once we reached the bottom of the stairs and, when I didn't reply, he pulled me to an abrupt halt and bellowed, "**DO YOU UNDERSTAND?!**" And I immediately nodded.

"Yuh-Yes, father, I-I understand!" I stammered in a shrill tone, relieved when he finally released my arm.

Father then stared at me with eyes so cold and flinty it made me shake uncontrollably, causing my stomach to turn rock-hard.

After a moment, he drew in a quick breath before releasing it, saying, "Come on, let's head to the car." And he turned on his heels, wandering towards the back of the car park; I quietly followed, not daring to say a word in fear he would erupt like a volcano again.

Mother and Carmen were still waiting where I had left them, their faces wreathed in smiles while father unlocked the car.

"Get in." He growled at me, so I swiftly clambered into the back along with Carmen, stiffly sitting on the soft, leather seats that were the same blue as the car.

*I dread to think what's going to happen when we get home...* I gulped, feeling a heated gaze lingering on me. Peering upwards, I saw father staring at me via the rear-view mirror, but he hastily averted his attention when our eyes locked.

We then drove home in silence despite mother attempting to have a conversation with father – *The same one they have every weekend* – but he had been unresponsive. *He really is angry...* I uttered as we pulled up onto the driveway, a sense of impending doom encompassing me. *I dread to think what's going to happen...* I gulped, repeatedly rubbing my face.

Father then switched off the ignition before clambering out the car, slamming the door behind him and making me flinch. *I wish I just listened to him, then none of this would be happening!* I exclaimed in coherent worry while waiting for Carmen to get out before reluctantly following suit, fearful of what awaited me behind closed doors. But then something dawned on me, and a surge of confidence shrouded my apprehension. *I'm a twenty-four-year-old man, not some kid he seems to think I am!*

Closing the car door behind me, I then spotted mother and Carmen advance on the front door where father was waiting; he stared at me like a vulture trying to decide where to peck first. *He'll understand when I talk to him about it.* I positively deliberated, my gaze unwavering from his as I walked towards him. *I hope, at least...* I tacked on while he unlocked the door, taking a step back so mother and Carmen could head inside.

Once they had disappeared, father snapped his attention back to me before barking, "You!" And he pointed at me, "Inside! **NOW!**"

It took every ounce of strength to not run into the house with my tail between my legs; instead, I looked father dead in the eye and said, "Don't talk to me like that." And it clearly took him aback.

Father was stunned into silence for a moment, it felt like a lifetime before he finally hawked, "How dare you have the audacity to talk to me like that!"

The pulsing vein zigzagging down his forehead had returned with a vengeance, his face rapidly reddening by the second.

"I'm at my wits end with you, young man!" He carried on his rant in a deep baritone, "And I've tried my hardest to be understanding and sympathetic, but nothing seems to be getting through to you!"

"Then why don't you try explaining to me what the hell is going on?!" I bit back while crossing my arms over my chest, my words seeming to slap father across the face by the way his jaw dropped and his eyes bulged out of their sockets.

"**GET INSIDE NOW!**" He abruptly snapped, gesturing with a trembling finger towards the hallway; such raw anger consumed him it made my heart race to an extremity I thought it would explode out of my chest.

*I've never seen him this angry before!* I gasped, my hands now so clammy I had to wipe them down my trouser legs.

"I will not tolerate such foul language under my roof!" Father gutturally roared with a dazzling smile, and I couldn't help but blink at him in bafflement.

*Foul language? What foul language?*

Rubbing my forehead in confusion, I queried, "Erm... What foul language?"

"Nathaniel, do as I say and get inside!" He fumed, his muscles and veins now notably straining against his skin.

Gulping, I stammered in a whisper, "Yuh-Yes, father." Before hurrying past him and into the hallway, flinching when he slammed the door shut behind us.

I barely had the chance to turn and face father before he snatched me up by the front of my shirt, making an involuntary gasp escape me. He then dragged me closer, so I hastily gripped onto his wrist with both hands, causing my knuckles to turn white. *What the hell is he doing?!* I panicked, my stomach hardening by the second.

"Now you listen here, young man!" Father started, his flared nostrils not matching the grin pulling at his lips, "Don't you dare utter profanity ever again, do you understand?!"

"Profanity?" I repeated, puzzled, "Since when did I utter profanity?"

Pulling his lips back into a snarl, father raged, "Are you trying to be a smart mouth, Nathaniel?!" And he was now so close his hot breath was beating against my face.

Frantically shaking my head, I urged, "No, no, of course not, father!"

"Then are you just being stupid?!" He retorted, "Or do you honestly have no idea what I'm talking about?!"

"I honestly have no idea what you're talking about, I swear!" I desperately beseeched, and father's grip unexpectedly lessened. He was silent for a while as he just stared at me, his dark blue eyes shifting from anger to dread; a realisation enveloping him.

Finally, father broke the silence lingering in the atmosphere, "I cannot stress this enough, Nathaniel, but no one, and I repeated, **no one** is to hear words such as '**God**', or '**Hell**' come out of that mouth of yours." He then abruptly released me before I could respond, adding, "Now get in the bathroom."

I was slightly confused by his request until I remembered his earlier comment at breakfast. *'**When we get back from church, you're going to head straight to the bathroom and sort that out before we head to the gentlemen's club!**'.*

"Nathaniel!" Father barked, dragging me out of my thoughts, "Do as I say **now!**"

Inhaling a deep breath to calm my inner turmoil, I ran a jerky hand through my hair before saying, "Yes, father." And I didn't shoot him a second glance as I hastily made my way upstairs, shrugging off my jacket as I done so.

*Why can't anyone hear me say '**God**' or '**Hell**'?* I contemplated, mulling over father's comment.

Once I had discarded the blazer in my bedroom, I wandered back out onto the landing only to see father stood outside the bathroom; he was leaning on the doorframe with his arms folded across his chest. *And that's another thing I don't get, why do I have to shave?* I pondered while sidling past him, making a beeline straight for the medicine cabinet where I pulled out my razor and shaving foam

"Stop dawdling, Nathaniel!" Father growled before I even had the chance to close the cabinet; when I did I saw him glaring at me via the mirror, his gleaming face making me shudder.
*God, that's so creepy! How can he be so angry yet look that happy?* I shivered once more before doing as he said; he waited until I had finished before passing me a towel, which I gladly took and wiped my face with.

"Ahhh!" Father purred in delight, turning me around so I was facing him, "You look immaculate, my son!" And he gently placed his hands on my shoulders, giving them a small squeeze.

"Thanks..." I murmured, tossing the towel into the hamper as I done so.

"No!" He scolded in a patronising tone with a shake of his head, "You're supposed to say '**Thank you, father**'. Now, repeat after me, '**Thank you, father**'." And I couldn't help but narrow my eyes at him in disbelief.
*He's joking, right?* I presumed, but then I realised he wasn't when he just stood there staring at me expectantly. *I can't believe my own father is belittling me!* I growled, my gaze flitting upwards in annoyance.

Momentarily clenching my hands, I repeated in a sharp tone, "'**Thank you, father.**'." Which immediately pacified him.

"Excellent!" Father grinned, releasing his hold on me, "Now to put a smile back on your face!" And I couldn't help but furrow my brow at that comment.
*How's he going to do that?*
"Come on," He urged, now standing in the doorway, "Let's head downstairs and get you a nice cup of tea." Before he turned on his heels and left.
*How's a cup of tea going to put a smile on my face?* I mulled, minutely shaking my head before trudging downstairs.

I ambled through into the kitchen only to come to a staggering halt when I saw father lingering by the hob. *What's he doing?* I deliberated, watching as he filled the kettle with water before placing it on the stove. *Why's he making it?* I had never seen him lift a finger in the kitchen, so it had completely caught me off guard when I saw him making a cup of tea.

When father noticed me standing there gawking at him, he suggested, "Why don't you take a seat?" And he gestured to the breakfast table with a sweep of his hand; I wasn't going to argue, I merely nodded before pulling up a chair.

*Strange...* I mulled, even more confused when he only grabbed one cup out of the cupboard. *Isn't he going to make himself one?*

But I didn't get the chance to question him as mother suddenly hollered, "Jeremiah!" Before her shoes rapped through the dining room, "We're just leaving, honey."

She then wandered under the archway into the kitchen just as father gazed over his shoulder, his smile broadening when his eyes landed on her.

Immediately turning from the hob, father advanced on mother while saying, "You have a nice time at the book club, sweetheart." Before pulling her into a tight embrace, planting a gentle kiss on her forehead which took me aback; it was only then I realised I had never seen him kiss her before.

"And you both have a nice time at the gentlemen's club, honey." She replied while briskly stepping out of the embrace, not reciprocating father's affection; I thought I caught a glimmer of sadness flit across his face, but it was gone before I could be certain.

The kettle then whistled and distracted him for a split second, but it was long enough for mother to turn on her heels and leave.

"I'm sure we will." Father commented before gazing back, his face dropping when he realised she had gone.

Rubbing the heel of his palm against his chest, he reached for the kettle; his other now hung limply by his side.

"Do you want me to make it?" I piped up as he poured boiling water into the cup, and he responded in a flat, monotonous voice that didn't match the smile on his lips, "No, no, I'm quite alright."

"Are you sure?" I persisted, watching as he poured the milk.

"Nathaniel!" He abruptly scolded, discarding the teaspoon in the sink with a clatter, "I said I'm quite alright!" And he snatched up the steaming cup before advancing on me.
*He doesn't sound it...* I uttered, choosing not to voice my thoughts out loud.

"Drink this." Father instructed, setting the cup down before pulling up a chair opposite me.
*Why isn't he having a drink?* I couldn't help but wonder once more, now staring sceptically down at the cup of tea; a ludicrous thought then sprung to mind. *He hasn't... Poisoned it, has he?* And my gaze shifted back to father, who just sat there looking at me in anticipation. *No, I'm being stupid.* I reassured myself. *Besides, I didn't see him put anything in it except a teabag and some milk.*

Knowing I was being foolish, I grabbed the cup and raised it towards father, saying, "Thank you." Before taking a tentative sip.
A huge sigh of relief escaped him before he urged, "Drink it as quickly as you can, we don't want to be late to the gentlemen's club."

"I'm drinking it as fast as I can." I stated, "But it's ho-"

"Uh-uh-uh." He interrupted, wagging his index finger as he done so, "All you needed to say was '**Yes, father**'." And I couldn't help but roll my eyes in annoyance.
*I'm getting a bit fed up with him telling me what I should or shouldn't say...* I uttered, bringing the steaming cup to my lips where I blew on it. I then quickly downed it, plonking the cup on the table with an audible thud once I had finished.

"Done?" Father queried and, when I nodded, he clapped his hands together once, "Excellent! I'm proud of you, my son! The first step is always the hardest, but we'll have you reformed by tomorrow." And I was a little taken aback by his comment.
*Reformed?* I repeated, unable to stop myself from shooting him an incredulous gaze. *There's that word again...*

Oblivious to my shock, father then rose to his feet, saying, "Come on now, we better get going." And I couldn't

help but question as I stood up, "What did you mean when you said reform-" But an unexpected gasp escaped me, my hand automatically gripping my stomach.
*No, no, not again!* I fretted as my insides started to roll like choppy waves on a stormy sea, a cold sweat rapidly consuming me. *Please don't be sick! Please don't be sick!* I begged when I felt the tea threatening to resurface.

"What is it? What's wrong?" Father questioned, his dark blue eyes wide in concern as they glanced over me.
I opened my mouth to reply but instantly regretted it, a surge of sick erupted from the pit of my stomach like a geyser; I barely managed to cover my mouth in time.
"Oh no, don't you dare!" Father scolded when he realised what was going on, "You swallow that now!" And I couldn't help but shoot him a disgusted look.
*I'm not swallowing my sick!* I declared while shaking my head.

An audible groan then rumbled from my gut, so I made a dash for the bathroom, having to quickly sidestep past father when he tried to block my escape.
"Nathaniel!" He roared as I took the stairs two at a time, knowing I was a ticking time bomb.
*Please make it! Please make it!* I begged, barely reaching the toilet before another rush of vomit shot into my mouth. Burying my head down the bowl, I heaved my guts up.

*Why?! Why is this happening?!* I wailed before the tablets came to mind, but I hastily pushed that thought to one side. *I just want to stop throwing up!* But the puke kept coming and coming; it felt like a lifetime before it finally stopped. Wiping the back of my hand across my moist lips, I sat back on my heels with a heavy breath. *Thank God it's over.* I then gazed over my shoulder and was somewhat surprised not to see father standing behind me, part of me wondered whether he had decided to go to the gentlemen's club alone. *Surely he would've told me.* I deliberated while gingerly rising to my feet, staggering slightly so I grabbed the sink for some much-needed support. *God, I feel awful...* I groaned, dousing my face in cold water.

Carefully turning around, I decided the best place for me to be was my bed. *I just want to lay down...* Slowly, I wandered out onto the landing but stopped when I heard father's voice coming from his bedroom. *I guess he didn't go to the gentlemen's club.* I pondered, now pinching the bridge of my nose as a headache started to form. *But who's he talking to? Surely mother and Carmen aren't back yet.*

Against my better judgment, I couldn't help but listen in on father's conversation.

"I understand that, but he is my son!" Father proclaimed as I took a curious step closer, "Is there nothing you can do for him, Sylvester?"

*Sylvester?* I repeated, my brow furrowing in confusion. *Who's he?*

"Money is no object, I'm more than willing to pay for the treatment." Father adamantly carried on, "I just want him to be safe, and that's not going to happen unless he's reformed."

*Reformed... He said that earlier, but what does it mean exactly?* I deliberated, taking another step only for the landing to creak underfoot.

"Hang on a minute, Sylvester." Father said, and I could feel my heart plummet into my stomach.

*Uh oh!* Quickly but quietly, I darted back into the bathroom, pushing the door shut with my foot. *What do I do?! What do I do?!* I panicked, blindly turning for the sink where I hastily turned on the cold tap, dousing my face with water yet again.

"Nathaniel?" Father piped up, and I gazed via the mirror to see him open the door with a squeak, visibly relaxing.

"How are you feeling?" He wondered with a smile as I grabbed the hand towel, wiping my face before replying, "Better. Thank you, father."

"Good." He commented, his smile faltering slightly before he added, "Once you're done, go and wait for me downstairs in the living-room. I think we'll give the gentlemen's club a miss today." And, without another word, he left, closing the door behind him; I couldn't help but breathe a sigh of relief.

*Thank God he didn't spot me out on the landing!* But then I recalled his conversation. *Who is this Sylvester guy and why does father want him to treat me? And treat me for what?*

Sighing, I pushed some loose strands of hair out of my face before heading downstairs into the living-room, ignoring the deep, enrooted desire to crawl into my bed and sleep. *I wonder how long he's going to be?* I deliberated while plonking myself down onto the orange Hillcrest chair, waiting for father as he had instructed. *And is he going to talk to me about this treatment he wants me to have?*

The sound of a door closing then echoed above followed by footsteps descending the stairs. Moments later, father appeared and made a beeline straight for his brown club chair; I turned to better face him just as he sat down.

"Nathaniel," He began with a smile, "I understand I've been hard on you, but I want you to know it's because you're my son and I love you."

I couldn't help but jerk my head back in shock. *He's never told me he loves me before.* I pondered, bringing a hand up to touch my throat. *I mean, I know he does, but why's he saying this now?*

"However," Father added, "Your recent behaviour has become a cause for concern, so I have booked you an appointment after work tomorrow to rectify this issue."

*Erm, what?!* My jaw dropped and a sudden coldness struck my core. *An appointment for what?!*

"In the meantime," He carried on, "I need you to try your utmost to keep smiling."

"Hang on," I began with a wave of my hand, my brow becoming knitted as I stared at him with narrowed eyes, "An appointment for what exactly? And with who?"

"Hmmm..." He murmured, as if uncertain whether to tell me or not; he then rubbed a hand across his jaw, continuing with a sigh, "It's with Doctor Solace." And he must have noted the alarm on my face as he swiftly added, "Don't worry, I'll be coming with you. As for why, I think deep down you know the answer."

I couldn't stop myself from sighing heavily, annoyed he couldn't give me a straightforward reply. *Let me guess, it's because*

*I'm not smiling...* I uttered disdainfully, opening my mouth to question him further; however, the front door suddenly opened, distracting both of us.

"Remember, keep smiling." Father briskly instructed in a hushed tone before mother and Carmen strolled into the living-room.

"Welcome home, sweetheart!" He gleamed while rising to his feet, advancing on mother where he pulled her into a one-sided hug; he then released her to plant a kiss on the top of Carmen's head.

"How was the book club this afternoon?" Father queried as they both sat down, and Carmen responded with a smile, "We finished discussing The Fellowship of the Ring."

"How was the gentlemen's club, honey?" Mother questioned with a smile which reminded me to do the same, so I forced a grin.

*I seriously don't understand how they can smile all the time...* I muttered, my cheeks already aching.

"Erm..." Father faltered; I thought I saw his Adam's apple nervously wobble.

*What's wrong with him?* I contemplated; he was silent for a moment, as if mulling over what to say.

"Well..." He trailed off, wandering back over to his chair while scraping a hand through his brown locks, "We... We had some laughs today, sweetheart!"

*Did we?...* I mulled, shooting him an incredulous glance when he sat down and rubbed his hands on his trouser legs.

"Andrew accidentally called his own brother Peter instead of Simon!" Father rapidly spoke with a chuckle, his laughter carrying on longer than normal, "The twins, John and James, were fashionably late as always, and Philip and Thaddeus accused Matthew of being a conniving tax collector!"

*What... What's he doing?* I pondered, slightly puzzled where he was going with this.

"Then James," Father carried on, adjusting his tie again and again, "This is the other James or '**Lesser James**' as we like to call him, told Simon, the other Simon who didn't get called Peter, that Thomas liked Judas' name so much that he preferred it for himself."

*Errrrr... What?* Feeling a little dazed, I began tapping a fist against my lips; I noted even mother and Carmen looked a little baffled. *What the hell is father doing?*

"And lastly," Father concluded, running a hand round the back of his neck, "Bartholomew didn't even show up!"

*But we don't even know anyone called Bartholomew...* I pondered. *Or Thaddeus...* And I rubbed my chin just as father's gaze flitted to me where he did a double-take; his eyes narrowed before he tapped his beaming lips with an index finger, making me realise I was no longer smiling so I quickly forced a grin.

"Oh ermm..." Mother murmured, gaining my attention; her smirk hadn't faltered but there was no denying the concern shimmering behind her dark brown eyes, "That sounds... Lovely, honey..." She then slapped the palms of her hands down onto her thighs before rising to her feet, "Anyway, dinner isn't going to make itself." And she disappeared into the dining room, not even a second passed before Carmen followed.

Once they were out of earshot, father turned to me with a grin, insisting in a threatening undertone, "Don't you **dare** utter a word about this to anyone!"

"Yes, father!" I hastily replied, which seemed to relax him; his head fell backwards as a sigh of relief escaped him, his grin slowly shifting into a smile.

"Good," He breathed, slumping in his chair, "That's what I like to hear." And he pressed the palms of his hands to his eyes.

For a while I just sat there watching him, wondering with a slight shake of my head. *What just happened a minute ago? Why did he act all weird?* But I knew I'd never find out, so I kept my thoughts to myself.

Clearing my throat to gain father's attention, I asked, "Do you mind if I go and lie down for a bit?" And he lowered his hands to peer at me, so I tacked on, "I'm just feeling rundown from earlier."

He was silent for a moment before nodding once, "I'll call you when dinners ready." He then exhaled noisily through his nose, adding, "Not that there'll be much point because you'll probably throw it up." And he forced a laugh, taking me aback.

*Just ignore him.* I told myself while rising to my feet, shooting father a quick smile.

"Thank you, father." I beamed before heading upstairs to my bedroom, quietly closing the door as a headache began to form. *He's been acting weird all day...* I pondered, bringing both hands up to rub my temples. *God, my heads starting to kill...*

Just as I was about to slump down on my bed, I spotted my blazer strewn across it, so I snatched it up only to hear a rustle coming from one of the pockets. *Huh?* I checked one and then the other, finding the bag Miss Lane had given me that I had forgotten about. *Urgh...* I grimaced, the thought of food making my stomach roll. *I've got to throw this away!* Pulling out the brown paper bag, I went to discard it on my nightstand only to get a waft of the ham; all nauseating feelings abruptly vanished, replaced with an insatiable hunger.

My mouth began to salivate, making me realise just how ravenous I was; however, I didn't fancy throwing up again. *But the half I ate earlier didn't make me sick, it was the tea.* And I peeked inside, my stomach grumbling at just the sight of the delectable sandwich. *I shouldn't.* I mulled, now sitting down on the edge of my bed, dropping the jacket onto the floor. *Just in case it was a fluke earlier.* But my hand was already reaching inside, grabbing the other half which looked just as heavenly.

*Maybe one bite won't hurt?* And that thought alone was enough to tip me over the edge where I devoured the sandwich in swift, ravenous bites. *God, that was so good!* I moaned, screwing up the bag and tossing it onto my nightstand. I then kicked off my shoes and laid down on top of the covers, the headache somewhat easing as soon as I closed my eyes. *I dread to think what's going to happen at dinner later...* I pondered, slowly drifting. *I can't keep this up, I feel awful all the time...* Then my thoughts shifted to Miss Lane and the pills she had given me. *If... If I don't get my answers tomorrow, then... Then I'm not... Not taking any more... More of those... Those tab...* But my deliberations trailed off as I finally succumbed to sleep.

# Chapter Eight
## *I knew you weren't like them*

**DING, DING, DING!**
"I'm awake! I'm awake!" I blurted as I sat bolt upright in bed, my tie twisted halfway round my neck, my shirt untucked from my crumpled trousers.
Shaking off my tiredness, I rubbed the sleep out of my eyes before remembering. *That's right, father said he'd wake me up in time for dinner.*
Stifling a yawn, I asked, "What's for dinner?" But there was no reply, "Father?" Lowering my hands, I peered around my bedroom only to realise he was nowhere to be seen.

*Huh? Where is he?* Confused, I now became acutely aware of my alarm clock, the metal hammer ruthlessly knocking between the two bells. *Why's that going off?* I mulled, leaning over to turn it off only to register the time was quarter to seven. *What the? We don't normally have dinner at seven...* But then it dawned on me. *No!...*

Reaching for the window above my wooden headrest, I yanked back the curtains where the morning sun blinded me. ***No!*** I adamantly declared, blinking back the light that now bathed my face. *No, I wasn't asleep for over twelve hours!* And I vigorously shook my head, refusing to believe it was Monday morning. *No, this isn't right! Father was supposed to wake me up for dinner!* But I couldn't ignore the evident truth that was literally blinding me.

Slumping down on the edge of the bed that faced the

wardrobe, I mulled. *Why didn't father wake me?* And I began to think the worst. *Has something happened to him?* Then mother and Carmen came to mind. *To all of them?* My throat started to feel constricted at just the notion my family might be in danger, making my hands so clammy I had to wipe them down my trouser legs. *I've got to make sure they're okay!*

Without hesitating, I jumped to my feet and dashed for the door, ripping it open with such force it hit the bedroom wall with a bang.

"Father?!" I hollered, descending the stairs, "Mother?! Carmen?!" And I came to a grinding halt at the bottom, staring anxiously into the living-room where I saw father sat in his brown club chair reading the newspaper; a sigh of relief immediately escaped me.

*Thank God he's okay!* I breathed just as he peered over his newspaper; his fitted beige suit now on show, a black and gold badge pinned to the lapel.

"Nathaniel?" Father queried, lowering his paper even more, revealing a brown and gold checked tie fastened to his pale blue shirt, "Whatever is the matter, son?"

"You didn't wake me up last night." I pointed out, taking a further step inside, "I was worried something had happened."

"About that," He began with a dazzling smile, folding his newspaper in half and resting it on the arm of his chair, "Something came up at work last night, so I had to go and resolve it." And he crossed one leg over the other, drawing my attention to his brown wingtip shoes.

Curiosity got the better of me, and I opened my mouth to ask but father piped up first, "Anyway, you better get ready for work, you can't go in looking like that." And he gestured with a nod to my dishevelled clothes, adding, "And remember to keep smiling."

*Why?* I couldn't help but wonder, choosing not to voice my thoughts out loud; instead, I forced a grin which seemed to satisfy him.

I then headed back upstairs into my bedroom, dropping

my grin as soon as I closed the door behind me. *What's with all the smiling?* I contemplated while advancing on my wardrobe, grabbing a pale grey suit with black and white checkered braces. *And how is everyone but me managing to keep it up?* I then plucked out a silver tie and light blue shirt before turning to get my black wingtip shoes, which I had kicked off beside my bed last night.

I then snatched up my dirty blazer I had strewn on the floor yesterday, accidentally banging into the nightstand and causing the top drawer to rattle open slightly. Just as I was about to shut it, I remembered. *I better take that tablet...* I didn't want to, but I wanted answers. *Hopefully everything will be explained tonight, I just need to remember to head straight there after work.*

Fully opening the drawer, I rummaged through the assorted pieces of paper until I found one of the little pink pills; a sigh escaped me as I peered down at it. *I really don't want to take this...* My stomach was crying for some much-needed food, but I had to tell myself. *Just got to get through today, then I won't have to take these anymore.* And that thought alone was enough to convince me to pop the pill in my mouth, swallowing it without hesitation.

I then made a beeline for the bathroom, now acutely aware of the tantalising aroma of bacon and eggs lingering on the landing. *Oh God, that smells so good!* The thud of footsteps then echoed up the stairs just as I closed the bathroom door behind me, shocked when I thought I heard my bedroom door open with a squeak. *What the? Why has someone gone in my room?* I deliberated, depositing my clothes before tossing the navy blazer in the laundry basket.

Just as I was about to go and investigate, I heard my bedroom shut followed by footsteps hurriedly descend the stairs. *What was all that about?* I pondered, turning for the medicine cabinet where I clocked my left eye. *God, I still look awful!* I grimaced, taking in the manky yellow-coloured skin around my bloodshot eye; purple bruising was still apparent along my cheekbone. *At least the swellings gone down.* I noted with a genuine smile.

Once I had brushed my teeth and shaved, I swiftly got dressed and styled my hair, putting everything back into the medicine cabinet when I finished. Giving myself one last glance in the mirror, I turned to leave. *Hopefully father will- What's that?* Something above the bathtub was flashing red. Pushing back the lime green shower curtains, I couldn't believe my eyes. *Is that a camera?!* A white, rectangular security camera was fastened to the ceiling; it pointed in the direction of the medicine cabinet.

*No, it **can't** be a camera!* I adamantly declared, my mouth going dry just as a lump formed in my throat. *It wouldn't make sense to have a camera in the bathroom.* But that deliberation was short-lived when it unexpectedly spun round, now pointing down at me. I felt like a deer caught in the headlights, frozen in place as the realisation that someone was watching me sunk in. *Why would someone watch us in the bathro- Oh, God! They've watched us get dressed, have a bath, use the-* And I couldn't help but cringe, instantly feeling sick and violated. *I've got to get out of here!* And I shot out of the bathroom faster than a speeding bullet.

*Does father know about this- There's another one?!* Staggering to a halt, I spotted a camera at the top of the stairs; it pointed down towards the front door. *Why the hell are there cameras in the house?! And how didn't I notice them before?!* Pinching the skin at my throat, I had a horrible, nauseating-feeling grow in the pit of my stomach. *I need to speak to father about this. I need to know if he's aware of these cameras.*

"Father!" I hollered as I descended the stairs, going straight through into the living-room where I saw him sat still reading his newspaper.

"What is it, Nathaniel?" Father spoke through gritted teeth, his dark blue eyes narrowing at me when he lowered the newspaper; annoyance rippled off of him, not matching the smile plaguing his lips.

"Did you know we have cameras in the house?" I implored, my news making his head jerk back in apparent shock.

*So he didn't know about the cameras.* I assumed by the dread plastered upon his beaming face.

Father then ran a shaky hand through his coiffed, brown locks while rising to his feet only to sit back down again, the newspaper now sprawled across the floor.

When he didn't say anything, I spoke up, "Father, what should we do?" And he suddenly seemed to snap back to reality.

Rising to his feet, he advanced on me while saying, "Firstly, you make sure you keep smiling no matter where you are or who you're with, so I suggest you start right now."

*How can he expect me to smile at a time like this?!*

"Secondly," Father carried on when I forced a grin, lowering his voice to a whisper, "Under no circumstances are you to acknowledge the cameras or even look at them. Do you understand?" And I immediately nodded despite the desire to know why.

*So he is aware we have cameras in our house?* I mulled, confused. *But why?*

"Thirdly," He concluded, "This conversation goes no further than the two of us. If I catch wind of you discussing this with **anyone**, so God help me I'll-"

**RING, RING! RING, RING!** The telephone unexpectedly cut across him, causing his face to turn ashen.

Slowly, our attention shifted over to the black rotary dial telephone that was on the table in-between the two chairs, the receiver quivering with every ring. *I don't think I've ever heard the telephone ring before...* I deliberated, circling my gaze back upon father; a bead of sweat trickled down the side of his face.

When I realised he wasn't going to answer it, I asked, "Do you want me to get that, father?" Which instantly snapped him back to reality.

"No, no, I'll get it." He hastily replied, moving towards it while adding over his shoulder, "In the meantime, why don't you go into the kitchen, I'm sure breakfast is almost ready."

I didn't get the chance to respond before he snatched up the receiver, saying, "West residence, Jeremiah speaking."

Shooting father one last glance, I wandered through into

the kitchen where I was hit by the pungent stench of bacon. *God, that smells awful!* I heaved, slapping a hand over my mouth and nose to suppress the odour. *Don't be sick! Don't be sick! I* chanted, resisting the urge to turn tail and leave. *Just breathe! I can get through this!* And I reluctantly made my way over to the breakfast table where Carmen was setting it; her light pink dress complimented her skin tone, a matching bow held her curly ponytail in place.

Carmen's green eyes then momentarily met mine, a smile growing on her made-up face as she stared expectantly down at me.

"Aren't you going to wish me a good morning, Nathaniel?" She queried just before mother piped up, "Aren't you going to wish me a good morning, Nathaniel?" And I peered over to see she had turned away from the hob, the ends of her pale blue dress lifting slightly.

*God, that's so creepy!* I shivered, peering between them.

With a forced smile, I said, "Good morning, mother. Good morning, Carmen." And in unison, they replied, "Good morning, Nathaniel." Before continuing what they were doing; I was left feeling slightly unnerved.

"Where's your father?" Mother queried with a radiant smile gracing her made-up face, hollering, "Jeremiah?!" She then brushed aside a loose strand of dark brown hair, which had fallen from the pinned up beehive, before grabbing a plate and putting it down at father's spot.

"Coming, sweetheart!" Father called from the living-room, his shoes suddenly rapping against the dining room floor before he walked into the kitchen with the newspaper tucked under his arm.

"Smells delicious, sweetheart." He gleamed before sitting down, his dark blue eyes staring eagerly at his food.

Once mother and Carmen had served breakfast and sat down, I couldn't help but retch. *Please don't be sick!* It didn't help when father brought a forkful of food to his lips; I had to look elsewhere in fear I would throw up.

"And it tastes just as good as it looks!" He happily proclaimed, dabbing a napkin either side of his thin, beaming lips before tucking it into his shirt.

Mother and Carmen then dug in; I couldn't even bring myself to look at my food never mind eat it. *Just breathe.* I instructed, pressing a fist to my lips. *In through the nose, and out through the mouth.* But I instantly regretted it as a wave of nausea crashed over me like a tidal wave, so I hastily slapped a hand over my mouth once more. *Don't be sick! Can't be sick!* And it took every ounce of self-control to swallow the lump of vomit that was lodged in my throat.

"Nathaniel," Father then unexpectedly piped up, gaining my attention where I saw him glaring at me with a one-sided smirk, "What do you say?" He carried on in a sharp tone, confusing me.

*Huh?* Raising a questioning eyebrow, I automatically lowered my hand. *What's he on about?*

Father must have grasped my bafflement as he explained, "Say thank you to your mother and sister for preparing your breakfast." And my mouth formed a little '**o**'.
Casting them a sideways glance, I inhaled a deep breath to ward off the sickness before saying, "Thank you, mother. Thank you, Carmen." And in unison, they looked at me and beamed, "I'm glad you're enjoying it." Before continuing to eat.

"What's your plans for the day, sweetheart?" Father asked mother between mouthfuls just as another fetid stench hit me like a wrecking ball, threatening the vomit fermenting in my gut to explode out of my mouth like a geyser.
*No, no! Don't be sick!* I panicked, desperately cupping my mouth and nose to curb the smell.

"Oh…" Mother lazily sighed, her dark brown eyes shifting to father as she smiled, "Well, I plan on making raspberry jam and pottering amid the rosebushes; however, I'm sure Mary will ring and ask me out to play badminton at the club, and then we'll have a spot of shopping with the girls followed by lun-"

"What on earth are you doing, Nathaniel?" Father interrupted with a grin, his dark blue eyes locked onto me in concern, "Why are you covering your mouth?"

I lowered my hand to explain; however, an acidic lump of puke shot up my throat, so I urgently covered my mouth again. *Breathe! Just breathe!* And I closed my eyes while swallowing the sick with a shudder.

"We'll be home late tonight." Father spoke up, and I opened my eyes to see him talking to mother, "I'm not sure what time as Nathaniel has an appointment he cannot miss."

His words from yesterday then came to mind. *'**Your recent behaviour has become a cause for concern, so I have booked you an appointment after work tomorrow to rectify this issue.**'*. And I couldn't help but gulp.

"I'll heat dinner up when you two get home." Mother replied with a smile, but father shook his head, "No need, sweetheart, we'll have something at the appointment." His then attention shifted to me as he said, "I'm driving you to work this morning." And I couldn't stop my hand from dropping as I shot him an incredulous gaze.

*Erm, what?!* I gawked, blinking rapidly at him. *He's **never** driven me to work before!* Then I remembered what he had said the other day, his words echoing in my head. *'**I'm an executive, Nathaniel. You are middle management. During work, we do not socialise.**'. Why is he so willing to take me now?*

***

Once my family had finished breakfast, I quickly headed upstairs to grab my briefcase, relieved to be out of the kitchen and away from the horrid stench of food. *I'm just glad father didn't force me to eat anything.* I pondered, now descending the stairs where I saw him and mother waiting for me by the front door; two metal lunchboxes were in her grasp. *Urgh… I don't know if I'll be able to stomach lunch later…* I uttered, reluctantly taking it before father grabbed his.

After we had put our lunchboxes inside our briefcases, mother spoke up, "Have a nice day at work, honey." And I presumed she was talking to me until father pulled her in for a kiss, so I quickly averted my gaze elsewhere.

"Try not to spend all of the housekeeping money on clothes today." He commented in a serious undertone, and I glanced back to see a smirk on his lips that didn't match the gravity to his voice.

*Pfft! That's not going to happen!*

"Anyway," Father added, taking a step outside, "We best be on our way. Have a nice day, sweetheart." And he turned on his heels, gesturing with a nod for me to follow, but my attention shifted back to mother just as she beamed, "Have a nice day at work, honey."

Forcing a smile, I replied, "Goodbye, mother." Before planting a quick kiss on her cheek.

I then hastily made my way over to father's blue Austin Cambridge just as the engine rumbled to life, discarding my briefcase in the back before hopping in the front.

Shutting the door, I turned to him and said, "Thank you for giving me a ride today, father." And I had expected some kind of response, but he merely reversed off the driveway.

*Is he annoyed or something?* I mulled, my brow furrowing as I took in his iconic vein that pulsed down his forehead. *Have I done something wrong?*

Shifting in my seat, I cleared my throat and asked, "Father, is something the matter?" But he didn't say anything yet again.

He then began rummaging inside his left blazer pocket before switching hands, now searching the right. Narrowing my eyes, I couldn't help but wonder. *What's he doing?*

When he finally retrieved a fisted hand, he held it towards me while querying, "Care to explain why I found this in your bedside table?" And he dropped whatever was in his grasp into my waiting hand; I was stunned into silence when I recognised the little pink pill.

*How did he find this?!* I gaped, my jaw dropping just as my breath hitched in my throat; a heavy feeling grew in the pit of my stomach the longer I stared at it. *He must've been the one who went in my bedroom!* I realised. *He was in and out of there so quickly, he must've known **exactly** where to look! But how?!* Then something dawned on me, causing the hairs on the nape of my neck to rise. *Unless there's a camera in my room...*

"Well?" Father prompted, momentarily distracting me from the tablet; I didn't know what to say, I couldn't even begin to comprehend the possibility there was a camera in my bedroom.

*But where?! And how haven't I noticed it before?!*

"Nathaniel!" He growled, casting me a sideways glance where I noted his eyes were cold and flinty, "Aren't you going to answer me?!"

*What do I even say?!* I gulped, shaking my head in dismay but father must have taken that as my response.

"Right, I've had enough of you, young man!" Father fumed, his face reddening by the second.

"Wuh-What are you doing?!" I stammered when he hastily pulled up alongside the kerb, the wing mirror narrowly missing the throng of pedestrians on their way to work.

Shifting my gaze back to him, I frightfully asked, "Why have we stopped?!"

Ignoring my question, father demanded with a radiant smile, "Who gave you the tablet?!" And I pressed my elbows into my sides, trying to make myself as small as possible.

"I-I don't knuh-know who guh-gave them to me, fuh-father!" I stuttered; it wasn't a complete lie, all the information I had was a letter signed by Gloria.

*Whoever Gloria is...* But I had an idea who it was.

Jerking his head back in apparent shock, father hawked, "'**Them**'?! How many tablets were there?!" And I couldn't help but shrink beneath his hostile gaze, replying in a whisper, "Four..."

"'**Four**'?!" He repeated while spittle built up in the corners of his mouth.

When I reluctantly nodded, he gutturally exploded, "**AND WHAT HAPPENED TO THE OTHER THREE?! DID YOU TAKE THEM?!**"

*What's he going to do when he realises I did?!* I fretted, now clutching my throat with my free hand.

"Well?!" Father urged, and I apprehensively opened my mouth to reply but there was a rapping at his window, distracting us.

I was shocked to see a tall, lean police officer peer inside; the top half of his seemingly gaunt, pale-looking face was hidden by his helmet, but there was no ignoring the unhinged grin plastered upon his thin lips.

*What's going on?* I wondered when the officer gestured for father to roll down the window. With a huff, father pressed his fingers to his eyes while shaking his head, muttering something under his breath. He then lowered his hands, shooting the officer a hard smile before rolling the window down.

As soon as it was open a crack, the officer piped up in a pretentious tone, "Sir, you cannot park alongside the road."

*Why can't we?* I mulled while father clenched his jaw and ground his teeth; it sounded like nails scraping down a blackboard, making me cringe.

"Not only is it a violation of the law," The officer carried on just as father finished rolling down the window, now rummaging inside his blazer pocket, "But you're also showing signs of incrimin-"

"Here." Father interrupted as he pulled out a black, leather-looking wallet, flashing it to the officer.

Peering down at it, the officer tipped his helmet back to get a better look; his sunken, dark brown eyes shimmered with a realisation.

"My apologies, Sir!" The officer beamed before staring past father and over to me; I didn't like the foreboding gleam in his dark, penetrating gaze.

*Why's he looking at me like that?!* I gulped while he adjusted the truncheon hanging from his belt, and I couldn't help but run a jerky hand through my hair.

"And I trust this nonconformist will be reformed?" The officer then queried, shifting his attention back upon father who retorted in a slight growl, "Officer Swanson, I do not tell you how to do your job, and you will certainly not tell me how to do mine!"

*Reformed... That word again...* I murmured, still unsure of the meaning behind it.

"Is that all, officer?" Father questioned in a sharp tone, dragging me back to the matter at hand.

Officer Swanson was silent for a moment before he tipped his hat, saying, "That is all. Good day, Mr West." And he ambled round the front of the car, joining the throng of people strolling towards the town.

"What was all that about?" I wondered, glancing at father just as he pocketed the wallet, peaking my interest, "And what's that?"

"That isn't relevant right now!" He snapped while rolling up the window.

He then minutely shook his head before holding out his hand, urging, "Give me the tablet, Nathaniel." And I gazed down at the pink pill in my sweaty palm.

"**NOW!**" He demanded before I had the chance, causing my heart to beat so fast it felt like it was going to explode.

"O-Okay..." I stammered, dropping it in his waiting hand where he immediately pocketed it.

"Right, you." Father began with a one-sided smirk, glimpsing over his right shoulder before driving off, "You need to keep smiling today. It doesn't matter where you are or who you're with, you **must** smile." And it was right then I realised I wasn't, so I forced a grin which made him tut; his gaze flicked skyward in apparent annoyance.

"Also," Father added once he had inhaled a deep breath, "We're heading straight to your appointment after work, so wait for me in the lobby once you're done." And my smile immediately dropped.

*But I'm meant to be meeting this Gloria person after work to get my answers!* I hawked, forcing a grin when father glared at me. *I can't do that **and** go to the appointment! What am I going to do?!*

"Do you understand?" Father prompted when I didn't respond, so I shot him a dazzling smile and said, "Of course, father."

***

*God, my face hurts!* I griped as we pulled into the executives' car park alongside C.S. *I don't know how I'm going to keep this up.* Giving my jaw a tentative rub, I made sure my smile was still in check before reaching into the back, grabbing my briefcase. I then swung open the door, narrowly missing the brick-built factory wall we had parked parallel to; I couldn't help but inwardly cringe. *Phew! I really don't want to upset father any more than I already have.* And I carefully shut the door before coming to stand behind the car, gazing up and up at the imposing smokestacks that billowed with thick, black fumes.

"Stop dawdling, Nathaniel!" Father abruptly scolded, gaining my attention where he was glaring at me with narrowed eyes and a toothy grin.

He then plucked out his briefcase before shutting the car door, not even bothering to lock it.

"And keep smiling!" He pressed in a sharp tone, gesturing with a nod for me to follow once I forced a dazzling smile.

Passing a service door on my right that led into the factory, we headed around the front to the reception on the high street.

Father went inside first where he was greeted by Miss Jones who was sat behind her desk.

"Good morning, Mr West." She greeted, smoothing out her dark blue dress and adjusting the badge pinned to it just as I came to stand beside him.

She then did a double-take, causing her startling blonde, curling hair to bounce; her bright red, beaming lips formed a little '**o**'.

Once she had dragged herself out of her stupor, Miss Jones swiftly spoke up, "Good morning, Mr West." And father and I responded in unison, "Good morning, Miss Jones."

Father then immediately headed for the door that led upstairs; I quietly followed, our footsteps echoing off the narrow walls like timpani drums.

When we reached the top, father halted me in my tracks with a raise of his hand; he then pointed to his beaming lips, a silent gesture for me to smile. *Am I not smiling?!* I worried, forcing a grin which instantly pacified him. *I **need** to remember to keep smiling!*

Father shot me a warning glance before wandering into the office area; I followed while tentatively rubbing my achy jaw, shocked to see everyone was already sat at their desks. *Damn it, I'm late!* I scolded, my grin faltering slightly but I was quick to rectify it. ***Must** smile!* I urged as father disappeared inside his office, so I advanced on my desk. ***Need** to smile!* And I couldn't help but groan when I saw the imposing pile of paperwork stacked haphazardly.

*Urgh... So many orders to process...* I muttered while pulling up a chair, setting my briefcase down by my feet. *Why didn't anyone think to input them last week-*

"Ah, Mr West!" The recognisable, plummy voice of Mr Sheridan sliced through the atmosphere; I gazed upwards to see him leaning against his office doorframe, his face wreathed in smiles. *Urgh, what does he want?* I murmured, watching him pick invisible crumbs off his iconic grey suit he had paired with the same dark blue tie; a black and gold badge was pinned to the left lapel of his blazer.

I didn't get the chance to respond before Mr Sheridan carried on with an almost maniacal smirk, "I require your assistance this morning. My office needs to be prepared for Tim's presentation." And I instantly didn't like where he was going with this.

*He's not going to ask me to get the chairs ready, is he?* And just that thought alone made my stomach quiver with unease.

Pushing himself off the doorframe, Mr Sheridan advanced on me while saying, "I need you to make sure there are enough chairs and refreshments for the executives."
I wasn't surprised, but there was no denying the annoyance now coursing through my veins. *What do I look like, some kind of P.A?!* I rumbled, briefly clenching my hands into tight fists.

"Oh, and it needs to be ready for 9AM." He tacked on, and my annoyance was swiftly replaced by disbelief.

"**Nine?!**" I hawked, "But that's less than an hour!"

"Is that a problem, Mr West?" He queried, tightly clasping his hands together and causing the knuckles to turn white.
I knew I didn't have much of a choice, so I minutely shook my head while rolling my eyes, "No, Sir." I replied, shifting my attention to the mountain of paperwork, concerned when I was going to find the time to process them.
*Why didn't anyone think to-*

"What was that?" Mr Sheridan cut through my train of thought, distracting me.
*Huh? What's he talking about?*
Peering up at him in confusion, I wondered with a weak smile, "What was what, Sir?"

"That thing you did with your eyes!" He retorted, pointing an incriminating index finger at me and circling it, making me go cross-eyed.
Flinching my head back slightly, I explained, "I... I don't know what you mean, Sir."

Mr Sheridan then opened his mouth but clearly thought better of it; he shook his head once, prompting, "Remember, nine o'clock, Mr West." And he briefly gazed down at his watch, adding, "Chop, chop."
*Did he really just '**chop, chop**' me?!* I fumed, watching him with narrowed eyes as he turned on his heels and disappeared inside his office.

Giving my paperwork one last glance, I inwardly groaned. *I can't believe I'm doing this... Acting as a P.A...* I then rose to my feet, making sure I was smiling from ear to ear before heading downstairs into the reception area, choosing to sort out the refreshments first.

"And he turned up with you know who." Miss Jones giggled, gaining my attention where I noticed she was on the telephone.
*Doesn't sound like a business call...* I commented as she twirled the cord with her index finger. Shaking my head, I then advanced on the door in the left-hand corner that led to the kitchen.

The door opened with a groan as I stepped into the dimly lit kitchen that had burnt orange walls; it was barely big enough to swing a cat. *God, how does everyone manage to fit in here during lunch?* I pondered before taking a further step inside, causing my shoes to squeak against the red and white lino flooring. *Right, better get the refreshments ready for Tim's stupid interview...* I bitterly uttered, closing the door behind me a little too hard.

Bypassing the fridge on my left, I immediately grabbed the kettle that was on the hob beside it. Two square-shaped windows with blue and white mottled curtains were directly above the cooker, they looked out to a dark, dank alleyway that led to the factory. Turning for the sink that was built into a white counter along the back wall, I passed a black table on my right that had hard-looking, plastic chairs tucked underneath it. An idea then came to mind, and I couldn't help but grin. *I can use these awful chairs for Tim's interview.*

Plonking the kettle in the sink with a ding, I turned on the tap before grabbing mugs out of the white cupboard fastened to the wall in front of me. *Mr Sheridan... Mr Carter... Mr Campbell...* I muttered, lining the cups up. *Mr Patterson... Father... Is that everyone?* Then I abruptly remembered. *Oh, I forgot about Tim...* And I hastily grabbed another before turning off the tap, taking the kettle back over to the cooker where I set it down and lit the hob.

While the kettle was boiling, I snatched the milk out of the fridge before wandering back over to the mugs. *Now for the pièce de résistance, the teabags.* Opening the cupboard,

I rummaged around but couldn't find them. *Where would Miss Jones put them?* I hummed and hawed, now pulling cups to the front to see if the teabags were behind them.

"Where are they?" I muttered under my breath, grabbing an unopened jar of coffee from the top shelf before spotting the pot of teabags hidden at the very back, "Ah-ha! Found you!"

Grasping the pot, I set it down before grabbing a spoon out of the drawer; the kettle then whistled, distracting me. *Better get that before it boils over.* And I hurriedly discarded the spoon on the side, accidentally knocking the pot off the counter in my haste. It hit the floor with a smash; glass and teabags scattered everywhere like shrapnel.

"Damn it!" I growled, emitting a heavy sigh, "Just what I need..."

Just as I was about to search for a dustpan and brush, a feminine voice unexpectedly piped up, "Are you alright, Mr West?" And I glanced over my shoulder to see Miss Jones stood in the doorway; she had a glass plate in one hand with a chocolate cake on top.

Turning to better face her, I scrubbed a hand through my hair, hurriedly replying, "Yeah, just fine..." But she didn't seem convinced; it was the eerie, almost otherworldly gleam in her ice blue eyes and the radiant smile plaguing her lips that chilled me to my very core.

With a curious tip of her head, Miss Jones queried once more, "Are you sure, Mr West? I'm just a tad concerned as you're not smiling." And her comment was like a blow to the gut.

*I'm not?!* I gawked, now hyperaware of the frown on my face. *Father's going to be mad if he finds out I'm not smiling! I need to focus! I need to concentrate!*

Forcing a show-stopping smile, I countered, "Of course I'm fine, Miss Jones. I was just in a hurry to make the refreshments for Tim's presentation that I accidentally knocked the jar on the floor." And I gestured to the mess with a sweep of my hand.

"You're doing the refreshments for the interview?" Miss Jones wondered, the inhuman look in her eyes long gone.

Nodding, I replied, "Indeed, I am." And, without explanation, she handed me the chocolate cake.

*Why's she giving this to me?* I mulled in confusion, eying the delicious-looking dessert.

"This is for Tim." She stated, gaining my attention, "After all, he's bound to get the promotion seeing as he is the only one who applied." And I couldn't stop my jaw from dropping.

*Erm, what?!* But my shock was hastily replaced with anger; I had to refrain myself from baring my teeth and exploding like a bomb. *I also applied for the role, not just Tim!*

"Can you cut it up for me, please?" Miss Jones carried on, my hold on the glass plate increasing tenfold, "I want to make sure everyone gets a slice."

*Is she seriously asking me to cut up her Goddamn cake?!* A red mist began to cloud my sights just as I heard something crack like ice, distracting me. Gazing down, I realised it was the plate, making me inwardly gasp. *I need to calm down!* And I inhaled a few steady breaths before carefully depositing the plate on the table, fearful I would break it.

I then diverted my attention back upon Miss Jones, smiling through gritted teeth, "Of course I can."

*But Tim can have the smallest slice.* I wickedly decided.

"Thank you, Mr West!" She gleamed before turning on her heels, leaving without another word where an agitated huff escaped me.

*What's the point in Tim doing this stupid presentation if he's* ***'bound'*** *to get it?!* I griped, kneeling to gather up the teabags still scattered on the floor. I then hastily tossed them in the bin by the table before searching for a dustpan and brush, which I found in the cupboard underneath the sink.

*Right... Better clean this mess up before someone comes in...* I sighed, briskly sweeping up the glass. Once I had put the dustpan and brush away, I removed the kettle from the hob and began searching for more teabags in the top cupboard, relieved when I found an unopened box tucked away. *How much time do I have left before the interview?* I mulled, glancing over at the clock above the table while mindlessly ripping off the packaging. *Got just under forty-five minutes...*

    I then plucked out a teabag, about to drop it in one of the cups but noticed it felt lumpy. *What the?* And I gave it a couple of squeezes but had no idea what it was; it felt like a small stone or even a pebble, something that was roughly the size of a shirt button. *What the hell is it?* Without thinking twice, I ripped it open, shocked to see a half-crushed tablet amid the tealeaves. *How did it get in there?* I deliberated with a tilt of my head, narrowing my eyes at the box. *I wonder if there's any more like it?*

    Setting the suspicious teabag aside, I grabbed another only to realise that too had a lump; I immediately pulled it apart to find yet another mangled tablet. *Why are there pills inside?* I queried with a slight shake of my head, shifting my attention back upon the box. *They can't all be like this, can they?*

    Apprehensively, I grabbed another and another and another, tearing them open only to find they all contained broken tablets. *I... I don't understand... Is someone trying to poison us?* I contemplated, staring at the mess littered across the countertop before thinking better of it. *Don't be so stupid, Nathaniel. It's probably just a faulty batch-*

"What on earth are you doing, Mr West?!" Hollered a plummy male voice, making me jump out of my skin.

Spinning around, I came face to face with Mr Sheridan; he was smiling from ear to ear but there was no denying the shock blazing behind his gunmetal grey eyes.

    Pinching the skin at my throat, I glanced over at the mess dashed across the countertop before peering back at Mr Sheridan, panicking, "Errr... I was just, errr..."

*What the hell do I say?!* I knew I couldn't keep him waiting judging by the slight tap of his foot and the unimpressed look growing on his beaming face.

    Then, without thinking, I said the first thing that came to mind, "Brewing!" And Mr Sheridan's face shifted to confusion.

"'**Brewing**'?" He repeated, furrowing his brow.

Nodding, I hastily replied, "I much prefer brewing the leaves than boiling them in those bags, Sir." And I quickly forced a toothy grin just as his head flinched back in apparent shock; a look of '**What the hell are you talking about?!**' grew on his radiant face.

Mr Sheridan then snapped himself out of his stupor, commenting, "Just use the teabags like a normal person, Mr West." And he turned to leave but halted when he spotted the cake.

Rubbing his hands together in delight, he smirked, "And do remember to bring up some of that delicious-looking cake."

I couldn't help but glare at the chocolatey goodness with animosity.

Gritting my teeth, I diverted my attention back upon Mr Sheridan, uttering, "Yes, Sir…"

"Excellent!" He purred before advancing on the door once more, adding over his shoulder, "And make sure to bring a slice for Tim seeing as it is his celebration cake."

Just those words alone filled me with an indescribable bitterness; my hands curled into tight fists, causing my nails to bite into my palms.

*He may as well tell Tim not to bother with the interview then seeing as he's handing him the job on a plate!* I seethed, glowering at the cake just as Mr Sheridan stopped in his tracks once more.

Slowly, he turned to me, asking in a cutthroat undertone that didn't match the grin on his lips, "What did you just say, Mr West?"

Blinking at him in confusion, I wondered. *What's he on about?*

"I didn't say anything, Sir." I replied before Mr Sheridan advanced on me; I hastily took a step back to maintain the distance between us, feeling the counter now pressed against me.

"I'd watch your tongue if I were you, Mr West!" He threatened with a growl, "If I decide to hand Tim the job on a plate, that is of no concern to you!" And it was right then I realised I had spoken aloud.

*Have I accidentally said anything else?!* I panicked, my stomach turning rock-hard.

"I suggest you keep your opinions to yourself in the future!" Mr Sheridan carried on before turning to the door, saying over his shoulder, "Chop, chop, Mr West, I have more tasks that need your attention today!"
*What?!* I gawked, blinking at him in bewilderment. *More?!*
"But, Sir, what about my orders?!" I hollered, "Who's going to process them?!"
"Ask William or Jerry to do it." He replied matter-of-factly, not even bothering to look at me as he opened the door.
Taking an urgent step forward, I croaked, "But what about my clients?! They don't know William or Jerr-"
"Mr West," Mr Sheridan interrupted with an audible huff, now standing in the doorway with a radiant smile on his furious face, "I don't have the time to worry about **your** clients, just see to it that they're processed before the end of the day!" He then briefly clenched his hands, adding, "And remember to come and see me once you're done here."
"But-" I didn't get the chance to finish as he abruptly left, leaving me staring after him in disbelief.
Scraping a hand through my hair in irritation, I turned for the counter, clocking the mess. *Urgh...* I groaned. *I completely forgot about this...* Inhaling a huge breath through my nose, I quickly tidied up before making the drinks and cutting the cake. *I better hurry, it's almost nine.* Once I had taken them upstairs to Mr Sheridan's office, I returned for the horrible plastic chairs, placing them in a semi-circle in front of his desk. *Done!* I breathed, staring around at my handiwork in admiration.
"Excellent work, Mr West!" I heard Mr Sheridan, and I gazed over my shoulder to see him in the doorway.
Smiling, I said, "Thank you, Sir." And then I remembered, "You mentioned other tasks that needed my attention?"
"Ah, yes!" He exclaimed, clapping his hands together once, "Please, sit down." And he gestured to one of the plastic chairs; I perched on the edge as he wandered round behind his desk
"I need you to organise a celebration party for Mr Miller." Mr Sheridan stated as soon as he sat down; it took a moment for

his words to sink in but, when they did, I blurted, "What?"
*He's joking, right?!* I gawked, shocked and utterly confused. *So not only is he giving Tim the job, but he's also throwing him a celebration party?!*

Taken aback, Mr Sheridan hawked, "What do you mean '**what**'?!"

"He's not even had the interview yet!" I countered, "And you're already talking about a celebration party!"

"Mr West, it is of no concern to you whom I decide to throw a celebration party for!" He retorted, his eyes narrowing but his smiling never lessening; I opened my mouth to bite back but there was a sudden knock at the door.

"I suggest you start smiling, Mr West…" He uttered before diverting his gaze, and I instantly brought a hand up to my lips, feeling the scowl.

*How long haven't I been smiling?!* I fretted, lowering my trembling hand.

As soon as I forced a grin, Mr Sheridan beckoned, "Come in!" And the door opened with a squeak.

He then hastily rose to his feet with his arms outstretched, happily proclaiming, "Ahhhh, Mr West, Mr Campbell, Mr Carter, Mr Patterson, do come in!" And I looked over my shoulder to see the beaming executives pile into the room one by one, immediately diverting my gaze when I saw father.

*Need to keep smiling! Need to keep smiling!* I chanted, fearful I would let him down.

Mr Sheridan then gestured with a sweep of his hand towards the empty chairs beside me, "Please, gentlemen, take a seat." And they all sat down without so much as giving me a sideways glance, except for father whose dark blue eyes swirled with confusion.

*Maybe I should leave?* I deliberated, tugging the cuff of my jacket.

I then went to stand but didn't get the chance as Mr Sheridan carried on, "Mr West," And I wasn't sure whether he was talking to myself or father until his gunmetal grey eyes landed on me,

"Can you tell Tim we're ready for his interview."
*Why me?* I mulled, but I wasn't going to argue; I was silently relieved to be dismissed.

Nodding once, I said, "Of course, Sir." Before leaving the office where I came to stand in the main room.
My eyes instantly circled over to Tim sat behind his desk on my left; his interlocked hands resting on top as he clearly waited for something. *Or someone...* Shaking off my unease, I advanced on him just as his head snapped over in my direction, his stone-cold eyes clocking me. *God, that smile is so creepy!* I shivered, taking in his long, chiselled face that was graced with a merry grin, chilling me to my very core.

When I came to stand in front of him, I cleared my throat and said, "They're ready for you." And I gestured to Mr Sheridan's office with a nod of my head.

"Excellent!" Tim exclaimed in delight, slapping his hands down onto his desk as he stood up; it was then I noted his dark brown suit and pale brown shirt, which had a black tie fastened to it.

Tim then nimbly plucked up his briefcase, adding with a smirk, "I do have an **awfully** good feeling about this!" And I couldn't help but glower at him as he advanced on Mr Sheridan's office, scraping a hand over his dark brown hair that was swept to one side.
Turning for my desk, I inwardly growled. *That should be me! I should be having an intervie-*

"Mr West!" The plummy voice of Mr Sheridan struck me like a bolt of lightning; I apprehensively peered over to see him stood in the doorway to his office.
Sighing, I couldn't help but wonder. *What now?...*

"What are you doing?" Mr Sheridan queried in an uncertain tone as I faced him, his grey eyes narrowing in confusion.

"Erm..." I murmured, slipping my hands into my trouser pockets, "I, erm... I'm going back to my desk to process my orders, Sir."

"Did I tell you to return to your desk and process orders?" He curtly asked, but he didn't give me the chance to respond before snapping, "No, I didn't! So get in my room this instant!"

Mr Sheridan then sharply gestured to his office with an index finger; I knew better than to argue, so I swiftly followed him inside where he slammed the door behind us, making me jump.

When the executives and Tim glanced over, Mr Sheridan bluntly explained, "Mr West shall be joining us for Tim's interview." And I was completely taken aback; I couldn't stop my jaw from dropping.

*But why? Why does he want me here during Tim's interview?*

Running my fingers through my hair, I implored, "But it's not my place to be here-"

"Are you questioning my orders, Mr West?" Mr Sheridan intervened as he sat down behind his desk, interlocking his hands before leaning forward.

I didn't get the chance to reply as one of the executives murmured, "Why isn't he smiling?" It sounded like Mr Patterson but I wasn't sure, then it dawned on me what he had said.

*I'm not smiling?!* And I immediately forced a grin, hoping it would be enough to convince them. *I **need** to focus!*

Ignoring Mr Patterson's comment, Mr Sheridan prompted, "Mr West, sit down, you're making the room look untidy."

I couldn't help but shoot him a bewildered glance, making sure my smile didn't falter as I challenged, "**Where?!**" And I gestured at the occupied chairs with a sweep of my hand; I knew it didn't go down well by the slight raise of his eyebrow.

"On the floor by my desk!" Mr Sheridan retorted in a sharp tone before father unexpectedly piped up, gaining everyone's attention, "Mr Sheridan, I feel it may be best Nathaniel processed his ord-"

"Jeremiah," Mr Sheridan abruptly cut across, causing my head to jerk back in coherent shock.

*Did he really just interrupt an executive?!*

"He may be your son," He carried on, his cold, grey eyes boring into father's dark blue ones, "But during the hours of eight and five he is **my** employee."

Mr Sheridan didn't give father the chance to reply before shifting his glassy gaze upon me, exhorting, "So, Mr West, take a seat." And he gestured to the floor beside his desk; I couldn't help but shoot him an incredulous glance.

*He can't be serious, can he?*

But I knew he was by the twisted grin plaguing his lips; however, I didn't get the chance to move before he banged his fists down onto his desk, yelling, "Don't just stand there like a chucklehead! Do as you're told!"

There was no denying the initial shock that consumed every fibre of my being, but it was swiftly replaced with annoyance. *Did he really just insult me?!* I growled, my hands briefly clenching into fists.

"Isaiah!" Father heatedly intervened in a deep baritone, "He may be your employee between the hours of eight and five, but he will **always** be my son and I will not tolerate anyone being disrespectful to him!"

Slowly, Mr Sheridan diverted his penetrating gaze upon father, his eyes so wide I could see the whites of them.

"Very well…" He uttered, his neck becoming corded while his beaming lips pulled back, baring his teeth, "I'm sure this will be a discussion for another time…"

Mr Sheridan then shifted his attention back to me; I couldn't help but avert my gaze elsewhere.

"Mr West," He began in a bitter tone, not continuing until I looked at him, "Go and process your orders. I'll call for you once the interview has ended."

*\*\*\**

'**Congratulations, Mr Miller!**' was all I could hear echoing around the office once Mr Sheridan had announced Tim was the new Quality Assurance Manager. I wasn't surprised he had been promoted, but it didn't make the truth any easier to swallow. *That could've been me!* I bitterly exclaimed, glaring at Tim from the corner of my eye where I sat at my desk; he was merrily talking to the crowd gathered around him by Mr Sheridan's office.

But then I minutely shook my head, correcting myself. *No, **should've** been me!* And I fisted the wad of papers in my grasp, trying my hardest not to pound the desk. *I should've been the new Quality Assurance Manager! I'm more experienced, I've been with the company longer, and I know all the products we sell!* But I knew there was nothing I could do, so I pinched the bridge of my nose and squeezed my eyes tightly shut. *I'm just going to have to accept the fact that he's my new manager...* I uttered, opening my eyes and smoothing out the papers I had scrunched up just as Mr Sheridan's door opened, gaining my attention.

I watched as father strolled out grinning from ear to ear, but there was no denying the frustration blazing behind his dark blue eyes. *Why does he look so annoyed?* I mulled as he went to close the door; however, he stopped mid-swing and immediately turned for his office. Narrowing my eyes, I couldn't help but wonder. *What was all that about?* And my unspoken question was swiftly answered when Mr Sheridan appeared in the doorway, his gunmetal grey eyes circling away from father and over to me.

A sly, one-sided smirk then hooked the corner of Mr Sheridan's cruel, thin lips as he said, "Mr West, a word in my office." And he gestured inside with a sweep of his hand.
*Why? What now?* My stomach instantly rolled with dread, I couldn't help but wish time would just speed up so I could get whatever this was over and done with.

"Yuh-Yes, Sir." I stammered with a weak smile, an ache forming in the back of my throat as I followed Mr Sheridan inside his office, closing the door behind me.
"Take a seat." He urged while advancing behind his desk; I felt as if I had no choice but to obey, so I sat down on the horrid, plastic chair that was directly in line with his plush, leather one.

*Why has he called me in here?* I fretted while biting the inside of my cheek, crossing my arms in front of my stomach in a protective huddle.

"So, Mr West." Mr Sheridan began once he plonked himself down, sliding over a pen and paper, "Write down what I'm about to tell you for Tim's celebration party." And I instantly remembered Tim's stupid party.

*Why do I have to sort it out?!* I grumbled, abruptly realising I was chewing the inside of my cheek when the taste of copper lingered on my tongue. *Hasn't Mr Sheridan rubbed enough salt in the wound?!* I fumed, pressing a fist to my lips while trying to ignore the headache steadily forming in my temples.

Once I had lowered my hand and picked up the pen, Mr Sheridan carried on, "You need to choose a venue where the party will be held, and then a date and time."

*Blah, blah, blah…* I uttered, mindlessly writing down whatever he said.

"You need to decide what theme this party will be, and then make a guest list." *Tim is **soooo** special…* "Decide on a budget and then discuss the budget with me before you purchase anything." *I love Tim… Tim, Tim, Tim…* I griped, mimicking Mr Sheridan's plummy voice.

"Once you've done that, send out the invitations." Mr Sheridan resumed, oblivious to my inner resentment, "On the day of the party, you need to prepare and set out the food and arrange the decorations. Understood?" He queried, not giving me the chance to respond before concluding, "Good."

Lowering the pen, I couldn't help but wonder. *Why am I doing this? I'm not a P.A…* But I chose to keep my opinion to myself; instead, I forced a radiant smile and tried my hardest not to frown.

"I won't let you down, Sir." I spoke in a sharp tone, rising to my feet so I could head back to my desk.

*I just want to get this over and done with…* I murmured, snatching up the paper that I immediately fisted.

"Er, I beg your pardon!" Mr Sheridan hawked, stopping me in

my tracks, "Where do you think you're going?!"

"What do you mean?" I questioned, baffled, "I'm going back to my desk to start organising the party, Sir." And my response may as well have been a slap to the face, Mr Sheridan was aghast.

"I don't think so!" He countered, his beaming lips pulled back, baring his teeth, "You will be sitting in here and organising it!" Jerking my head back in coherent shock, I couldn't help but gawk. *Erm... What?*

"But..." I began, shooting Mr Sheridan an incredulous glance, "But this is your office, Sir."

"I'm well aware this is my office, Mr West!" He bit back, exhaling a noisy breath in apparent irritation.

I didn't get the chance to retort before he slammed a fist down onto his desk, exploding, "**JUST DO AS YOU'RE TOLD AND SIT DOWN!**" And I couldn't have sat quick enough.

Once he had calmed down, Mr Sheridan spoke with a delighted grin, "It is better this way."

*Better for who?...* I couldn't help but wonder, but I didn't dare ask.

"And I'll be right here if you need anything." He concluded, staring at me unblinking.

*O... Kay...* I gulped, smiling weakly at him. *That's just creepy...* And I averted my gaze down to the list in my tight grasp, which I swiftly smoothed out on the desk.

*Why am I doing this? Or, more importantly, why is he doing this to me?* I deliberated, glancing back up to see Mr Sheridan still smiling radiantly at me, so I peered back down at the list. *God... Why is this happening to me?...*

***

*Thank God it's home time!* I breathed a sigh of relief when five o'clock rolled round; the sound of footsteps in the main office swiftly followed. I couldn't help but gaze longingly at Mr Sheridan sat before me, hoping he would give me the go-ahead to leave; however, he was too fixated on a letter he was writing. *Urgh... I just want to go...* I griped, glancing down at the list, silently impressed with how much I had managed to organise in such a short space of time.

I had persuaded Mr Sheridan to host the party at the office, seeing as it had plenty of space in the reception as well as a kitchen for all the food and drinks. *Which means I don't have to hire a venue.* I inwardly grinned, unable to stop it from spreading from ear to ear. *And I can't believe I convinced him to throw the party Friday afternoon, meaning we don't have to work!* I had then suggested the party should be a surprise, which Mr Sheridan happily agreed to. *Thank God I don't need to worry about a theme! The most decorating I'll have to do is a few balloons!* Lastly, I had also organised the guest list. *Which is everyone from work, so I don't understand why he told me to make one...* When I had shown Mr Sheridan the budget, he was delighted the only expenses would be the food and drinks.

I then diverted my gaze back upon Mr Sheridan who was still busy scribbling away; I couldn't help but minutely shake my head in annoyance. *I'm not waiting any longer, I'm leaving.* I decided, snatching up the list and rising to my feet just as his gunmetal grey eyes snapped up to meet mine.

"Where do you think you're going, Mr West?" Mr Sheridan queried, lowering his pen as he done so.

"It's five o'clock, Sir." I pointed out while he interlocked his fingers, his gaze unblinking and filling me with a sense of impending doom; I couldn't help but avert my eyes elsewhere.

"Did I give you permission to leave?" He asked, not giving me the chance to reply before growling, "Sit down!" And I begrudgingly obeyed.

*I should've asked his permission!* I gulped, my foot anxiously bouncing up and down while Mr Sheridan continued to write his letter. *How long is he going to keep me here?* I contemplated. *I've got to go; I'm meant to be meeting this Gloria person to get my answers.* Whoever Gloria was, even though I had my suspicions, was the light at the end of my tunnel. *I just want to know what's going on!*

Once Mr Sheridan had finished, he looked at me and said

with an otherworldly grin, "You may leave, Mr West." And it took every ounce of self-control to stop my jaw from dropping.
*What?!* I gawked, shocked. *Did he really just make me sit here until he finished writing his stupid letter?!*
But I refused to show him how much he had bothered me; instead, I shot him a dazzling smile and said, "Thank you, Sir. Have a good evening." Before rising to my feet.

"Leave that here, Mr West." Mr Sheridan commented, and I had no idea what he was referring to until he gestured with a nod towards the list still in my grasp, "You'll be back in my office tomorrow morning."
*Great… Another day with him just staring at me…* I griped before discarding the list on his desk, making sure my smile didn't falter as I done so.
With a nod, I said, "Good evening, Mr Sheridan."

"Good evening, Mr West." He replied before shifting his attention back down to the letter, neatly folding it in half.

Without shooting him a second glance, I eagerly left. *What's the time?!* I worried, glancing over my shoulder at the clock hanging above his office door, shocked to see it was nearly quarter past five. *I can't believe he kept me behind for so long!* I grumbled while ripping open the door to the stairwell, taking the steps two at a time in my haste to leave.

A sigh escaped me when I realised everyone had left, even Miss Jones wasn't lingering in the reception area. *Good!* I purred in delight.
Grabbing the door, I yanked it open and was greeted by the speakers echoing off the buildings, "It's been a busy day in Merribridge! Have a peaceful night's rest ready for a brand-new day tomorrow! Remember, everyone, keep smiling!"

*Must keep smiling! Must keep smiling!* I chanted, making sure I was grinning from ear to ear while heading in the direction of Amicable Street. *It was Amicable Street, wasn't it? Number ten?* I mulled but didn't have the letter to check; I knew I had no other choice but to go with my gut instinct. I continued onwards as if I were heading home, Amicable Street was just a road or two over from where I lived.

*I can't believe I'm finally going to get my answers.* I pondered just as an unexpected wave of tension was released from my body, making me feel a little giddy. *Then all of this, whatever **this** is, will be over and done with.* I couldn't help but emit a moan as my eyes turned heavenward, the realisation sinking in.

Once I was at the top of Amicable Street, I glanced to my right and saw number two; number ten was just a stone's throw away. Hurriedly weaving past all the people making their way home, I advanced on the white gate and tugged it open, making a beeline for the front door where I knocked twice. Not even a second passed before it opened with a squeak, revealing- *Wow!* I gawked at Miss Lane who was smiling from ear to ear. *She looks amazing!* And I couldn't stop myself from staring her up and down.

Miss Lane's long, brown hair was swept to one side, tumbling over her bare, slender shoulders in curls. *I wonder how soft it is.* And my fingers tingled with the need to comb through her luscious locks. A warm sensation then flooded my body when my eyes shifted to her soft, mesmerising green ones, noting the black flicks that made the green pop. *God, I just want to kiss her!* I inwardly moaned, my attention momentarily flicking down to her vibrant red lips before I realised what she was wearing, instilling me with a carnal urge I had never felt before.

Miss Lane was clad in a lacy black, off-the-shoulder dress paired with patent red, peep-toe heels. *God, I want her so bad!* And I had to fight the desire to just grab her and kiss her, hold her and never let her go. *Stop it!* I abruptly scolded, feeling my cheeks heat up.

"Mr West!" Miss Lane abruptly gasped, her radiant smile never lessening, "What a pleasant surprise!" And I couldn't help but furrow my brow.
*What?* My mouth suddenly turned dry, my throat feeling constricted, as it dawned on me that she wasn't Gloria. *Then who*

*the hell is?!*

Stepping aside, Miss Lane then gestured for me to enter while saying, "Please come in." And I couldn't bring myself to say no, so I quietly obeyed and stepped inside; I instantly realised the house was identical to mine from the layout to the colour scheme and furniture.

Once she closed the door, Miss Lane then offered with an outstretched hand, "Your jacket, Mr West."
*No, I can't stay.* I decided, regretfully shaking my head while making sure my smile didn't falter. I wanted nothing more than to stay, just the sight of Miss Lane made all my nerve endings stir and tingle, but the need for answers greatly outweighed the longing in my heart that grew with every beat.

Inhaling a deep breath, I reluctantly responded, "I can't sta-" But Miss Lane wasn't taking no for an answer, she gestured for my blazer once more with a firm wave of her hand while reiterating, "Your jacket, Mr West." And I felt I had no choice but to comply.
Inwardly sighing, I shrugged it off and handed it to her, explaining, "I can't stay for long."

"That's a shame." She said, turning to hang up my jacket, "I guess I'll have to make it quick." And she turned back to face me; I couldn't stop my jaw from dropping when I realised she wasn't smiling.
*She's not smiling!* I gawked, taking several steps back where I staggered into the door with a bang. *How the hell isn't she smiling?!*

Pointing a trembling finger, I blurted, "Wha- How- Whe- You're not smiling! Why aren't you smiling?!"

"I must keep up appearances." Miss Lane explained with a one-sided grin, adding, "I knew you weren't like them." Which confused me.

"Like who?" I wondered, "What do you mean?"

"Like everyone else. You're not smiling." She stated, making my heart plummet.
*I'm not?!* And I forced a weak grin, feeling the corners of my

mouth tremble.

"You don't need to worry about smiling while you're here." She carried on, "But I'm glad you've learnt to do that."

*How the hell isn't she smiling?! What's going on?!* My chest tightened as my mind raced, searching for answers.

I eventually shook my head and ran my fingers through my hair, murmuring, "I… I don't understand…"

"It's okay." Miss Lane smiled, it was so genuine it reached her eyes, "I'll explain everything. After all, I did say I would in that note I gave you." And I sighed in relief, glad she was Gloria.

She then took me by the hand, leading me into the living-room where she gestured for me to sit down on the pink tufted sofa; I couldn't get over how weird it felt to be in a house identical to mine.

"Tea?" Gloria offered while I plonked myself down, depositing my briefcase on the floor.

Shaking my head, I said while gazing around, "No, thank-" But I froze when I saw a camera directly above the brown club chair; it pointed in the direction of the hallway.

*She's got cameras too?!* I declared in coherent fright. *What the hell do I do?!* And I did the first thing that came to mind, I smiled from ear to ear.

"What are you doing?" Gloria wondered before following my line of sight, her attention snapping back to me where she insisted, "I told you, you don't need to smile here."

Furrowing my brow in disbelief, I couldn't help but ask, "Why should I believe you?"

"Because I'm the only hope you've got if you want to stay alive." She replied matter-of-factly, and I was stunned into silence.

When it eventually sunk in, I couldn't help but think. *What? What does she mean?*

Bringing a hand up to rub my forehead, I queried in an uncertain tone, "What's going on?" And Gloria automatically sighed, as if she had been dreading this question.

"Well," She apprehensively began, now sitting down next to me on my right, "I'm going to be matter of fact with you as there's no easy way to say this, but the government are drugging everyone in Merribridge."

*Erm... What?... She's joking, right?* But I realised she wasn't by the worry blazing behind her green eyes.

"Hang on," I began, my voice laced with uncertainty, "The government are drugging Merribridge? How? Why?"

"Well, it all started with C.S." Gloria started, wetting her lips, "The government tasked them with the production of a drug, which is now used as a '**supplement**' in all of our food." And she quoted using her middle and index fingers.

*C.S?* I repeated, unable to ignore the fluttery feeling in the pit of my stomach. *As in the same C.S I work for?*

"Why, we're not sure." Gloria carried on, and I couldn't help but wonder who '**we**' were, "We presume for control. There's no theft or murder in Merribridge, everyone's always punctual, and work is always running smoothly. It's as if everyone's a robot."

Unconvinced, I pressed, "And what is this drug exactly?"

"We're not sure." Gloria replied, and I was left wondering who '**we**' were again, "We don't know how C.S made the drug or even what it's called, all we know is it literally drugs people. They can no longer think for themselves, they just live the same routine day in and day out like they've been programmed."

*How do I know if what she's saying is true?* I mulled, furrowing my brow in contemplation. *I've never heard of this drug, and I can't recall processing any orders for something out of the ordinary...*

Narrowing my eyes, I probed, "How do you know all this?"

"I used to work for Merriwell Sanatorium..." Gloria regretfully began, "I've seen first-hand what they do to people who are no longer under the influence of the drug, no longer under their control..."

*Hang on, if she worked there, then how doesn't she know what this drug is or what it's called?*

Shaking my head, I commented, "How don't you know anything

about this drug if you worked there?"

"There's only three people who know." She swiftly responded, listing them off on her fingers, "The Prime Minister. His right hand. And his left hand."

*Riiight...*

Raising my right eyebrow, I said, "This all sounds too-"

"Convenient?" Gloria finished, and I merely nodded before she continued, "I would've thought the same if I were in your shoes, everything suddenly changing and a voice now in my head-" *Wait, she has a voice inside her head too?* "-But they slowly weaned me off of the drug when I was chosen to be a nurse nearly fourteen years ago. Any profession, doctors and nurses, police, they're weaned off of the drug just like the government and Watchers." And I couldn't help but blink at her in bafflement.

*Watchers?... What the hell are those?*

"And what's a Watcher?" I queried in uncertainty, and Gloria explained, "They do as their title suggests, they **watch** for people not smiling." And I could vividly remember the black and gold badge with '**WATCHER**' around the gold edge.

"Their job is to report nonconformists', people like us-"

"Hang on a minute!" I interrupted with a raise of my hand, "What **exactly** is a nonconformist?"

"Someone who is no longer under the influence of the drug without due reason."

"Then how are **you** a nonconformist?" I pried with a furrowed brow, making Gloria sigh, "Because I'm an inside eye for the People's Guild."

*The People's what?* I deliberated; it was now sounding ridiculous. Gloria must have sensed my doubt as she carried on, "It's a safe haven for all those who are no longer under the influence." And I suddenly found myself with more questions than I had to begin with.

She then opened her mouth, but I swiftly held up my hand and firmly said, "Don't!"

*This is too much...* I murmured, pressing my index fingers to my temples while closing my eyes. *So there's Watchers* who watch for people who aren't smiling, and the people who aren't smiling are nonconformists? Then there's a guild to help nonconformists, and a sanatorium to cure nonconformists? Have I got that right?

Slowly, I opened my eyes and finally asked, "Why did you give me those tablets?" And Gloria shifted uncomfortably in her seat; she was strangely quiet for a moment before replying, "I... I can't say. Not because I don't want to, but because I can't."

*She **can't** or **won't**?!* I fumed, shaking my head in annoyance. *This is ridiculous! She said she was going to explain everything! Not that I think I'd believe her anyway! She's got some elaborate imagination with Watcher's and a guild and this mind manipulating drug! How stupid does she think I am?!*

Expelling a frustrated huff, I abruptly stood up with a growl, "Right, this has been a waste of time!" And I snatched my briefcase before marching towards the front door.

"Nate, wait!" Gloria begged; I was immediately taken aback.

"'**Nate**'?!" I repeated in disbelief, now peering over my shoulder at her, "Who's Nate?!" But then I realised that was the least of my worries, "You know what, I really don't care, I've just got to go."

*I can't believe I was so stupid to think I'd get answers!* I fumed, my heart now pounding as anger consumed me.

"Where are you going?!" Gloria desperately asked, nimbly slipping past me and blocking the front door, "You can't leave!"

Shrugging on my blazer, I said through gritted teeth, "Watch me!"

"No, just wait!" She beseeched, slapping the palms of her hands against my chest when I was mere inches away.

*What the hell does she think she's doing?! She can't keep me here!*

Gloria must have sensed my animosity as she hurriedly exclaimed, "I know I can't stop you, but **please** put that badge on before you walk out the door!"

"You mean the one you subtly slipped into my pocket?..." I uttered, searching my blazer but couldn't find it, "I don't think I brought it with me-"

"You fucking idiot!" She unexpectedly exploded, the rage lacing her voice completely blowing me away, "Do you realise how much you're putting your life at risk by not having it with you?!" *What... What did she just say?...* I deliberated, my brow knitting in consternation. *Is '**fucking**' even a word?*

"I **specifically** gave you that badge so the government wouldn't notice you on their cameras!" Gloria angrily carried on, her neck corded and her nostrils flared; I couldn't help but scoff.

"And how's a badge going to stop them from noticing me?!" I retorted, and Gloria swiftly countered, "It acts as a form of pass when detected on the cameras, exempting them from suspicious activities such as curfew!" And I couldn't help but laugh.

*Pfft! Like a badge is going to do all that! And curfew? What the hell's she on about? There is no curfew!*

"You need to leave!" Gloria suddenly declared, "You need to leave now before it's too late!" And she ripped open the front door, shunting me outside before I had the chance to process what was going on.

Spinning back round to face her, I fumed, "What are you doi-**AH!**" I gasped when I noticed the unnatural, eerie smile gracing her red lips, making me shudder.

"Watchers patrol the streets at night." Gloria stated matter-of-factly; I couldn't help but note how her tone of voice and demeanour had drastically changed.

"If you hear someone following you, don't look back." She ominously carried on, "If a car pulls up beside you, keep walking."

*She can't be serious, can she?!*

"I'd head straight home if I were you, Mr West." Gloria implored, "You know where to find me if you decide you want my help." And, without another word, she slammed the door in my face.

*She's... She's joking... She **must** be joking!* I tried to convince myself, but the niggling feeling in the back of my mind refused to budge. *She's just trying to scare me, that's all.* I decided with a shake of my head. Turning on my heels, I advanced down the garden path where I was blinded by the summers sun that was still riding high in the sapphire sky.

*I can't believe I thought she could help me!* I fumed, ripping open the gate; however, the anger coursing through my veins swiftly vanished as soon as I heard it swing shut behind me, the notion someone may be watching caused an indescribable fear to consume every fibre of my being. *I've got to get home! I've got to get out of here!* And I immediately turned left, heading straight towards the end of the road where I had come from earlier.

*Do Watchers really patrol the streets?!* I fretted, glancing all around only to realise there was not a single soul in sight and the speakers were silent; the chilling sound of my shoes rapping against the ground now acutely echoed all around me. *Hang on, what the hell am I thinking?! There's no such thing as Watchers!* And I hastily crossed the road to my right, heading towards the next intersection. *I can't believe she managed to get in my head with all her lies!* I seethed, my house now a stone's throw away.

When I was within reach of the garden gate, I realised father's car was nowhere to be seen. *Isn't he home yet?* I deliberated, my fear now replaced with concern. *Has something happened to him?* Tugging my jacket more firmly into place, I tried to ignore the quiver in my stomach as I made my way up the garden path. *Maybe he's just working late...* I pondered, my hands fumbling for the key in my blazer pocket. *I'm probably just overreacting...*

Once I had unlocked the door, I inhaled a deep breath before stepping inside, making sure my smile was still in check.

"I'm home!" I absentmindedly hollered, closing the door behind me.

"Welcome home, Nathaniel!" The distinct voices of mother and Carmen replied before the unease started to creep in once more.

*What if something has happened to father?* I worried, biting my bottom lip while mindlessly heading upstairs into my bedroom. Discarding my briefcase by the door, I shrugged off my jacket and tossed it on the bed. ***No**, I can't think like that!* I scolded, ignoring the apprehension building within. *He's fine! He'll be home soon!* And I vigorously shook my head before wandering into the bathroom, deciding to splash my face with some much-needed cold water; the coolness instantly calmed me.

Reaching for the hand towel to dry my face, I breathed. *That's bette-*

"Nathaniel?" The recognisable voice of father cut across my thoughts, and I instantly dropped the towel with a gasp.

"Father?!" I gawked at him via the mirror before spinning round to face him, "You're home?!"

*Thank God he's okay!*

"And where have you been?!" He demanded with a radiant smile, his face reddening by the second, "I've been searching high and low for you!"

*What... What does he mean? Why's he been looking for me?*

"Why weren't you waiting for me in the lobby?!" Father carried on while loosening his tie, his dark blue eyes now cold and flinty as he glared at me; it was only then I realised why he was so angry.

*Uh oh... I completely forgot about the appointment with Doctor Solace...*

"Well?!" He urged when I didn't reply, impatiently tapping his foot as he done so.

Rubbing a hand round the back of my neck, I tried to calm my rapid breathing, "I-I-I... I-I-"

"Come on, spit it out!" Father impatiently growled, so I inhaled a slow, steady breath before replying, "I... I completely forgot, father." And it wasn't a lie, I had been preoccupied with the desire to find out answers.

*Which was a waste of time...* I uttered in annoyance.

"You forgot?" Father abruptly queried, his eyes wide in shock.

*What do I even tell him?! I can't tell him it was because I needed to find out what was going on, that I needed answ-*

"What were you doing that was so important you forgot your appointment?" He interrupted, and I couldn't help but inwardly moan as dread consumed me.

*Oh God, what do I say?*

"Wuh-Well," I began with a weak smile, running my now clammy hands down my trouser legs.
*Think, Nathaniel, think!* I couldn't lie to him, mother and Carmen knew I had returned home late.
"The thing is... I-" But then Gloria's words came to mind, causing an unexpected release of tension.
**'They can no longer think for themselves, they just live the same routine day in and day out like they've been programmed.'.** *That's it! I just need father to think I'm acting normal!* And then his own words came to mind. **'Remember, routine is key.'.**

A slow smile graced my lips as I calmly said, "I just went about my routine, father. I left work and took a stroll home like normal."
*It's not like he's going to find out I went to Gloria's...*

"Hmm..." He murmured, rubbing his jaw in uncertainty as he done so, "Very well... I shall try to rearrange your appointment for a day I won't be finishing late." He then lowered his hand while saying, "We may as well join your mother and sister for dinner seeing as we're home in time."
*Is that it?* I wondered, silently surprised he had accepted my explanation so readily.

"Come on," Father urged with a nod of his head, "Let's head downstairs." And he left without another word, the rap of his shoes echoing across the landing.
Once I had picked up the towel, I wandered downstairs and into the dining room, hearing father's irate voice resonate from the kitchen, "What do you mean you've eaten all ready?!" And I realised he was talking to mother when I came to stand in the archway.

Mother was trying to wash up while father stood directly beside her, practically invading her personal space; Carmen was on her other side drying up the dishes.

"I'm sorry, honey." Mother apologetically began, removing her marigolds as she turned to face him, "I thought you told me not to cook for you tonight." And there was no denying the sincerity to her voice which didn't match the radiant smile gracing her lips.

Father then opened his mouth to object but clearly thought better of it; instead, he inhaled a steady breath before calmly saying, "You're right, I did say we would be eating at Nathaniel's appointment. However," And his dark blue eyes shifted to me, narrowing slightly as he uttered, "Something came up…" He then circled his attention back to mother, adding in an almost upbeat tone, "We'll just have to make do with a cup of tea tonight."

*Why can't we just cook something?* I wondered, intently eying the cupboards just as my stomach grumbled.

"Of course, honey!" Mother beamed, already pulling mugs out, "Go and make yourself comfy in the living-room and I'll bring them in in a jiffy!"

"That sounds perfect, sweetheart!" Father happily proclaimed, turning to me as he said, "Come on, let's retire to the living-room and leave the women to finish cleaning." And he gestured for me to lead the way with a nod of his head.

"So," Father began as soon as we sat down, "I shall organise another appointment with Doctor Solace once I've checked my work schedule tomorrow. This time you **will** wait for me in the lobby, understood?" And I nodded before he carried on with a grin, "Good!" He then reached for the newspaper on the wooden side table in-between us, leaving me to quietly mull over my thoughts.

*I can't believe I was so stupid to think she could give me answers!* I fumed, my toes curling in on themselves as shame consumed me. *I should've listened to father, then none of **this** would've happened!* And I couldn't ignore the tension building between father and I just as mother and Carmen wandered in; they each held a cup with steam rising from the top.

"Here you go, honey." Mother smiled, passing the mug to father when he set his newspaper down while Carmen handed me mine, the cup instantly warming my hands.

Without another word, they then disappeared in the direction of the kitchen and I was left gazing apprehensively down at the cup of tea.

"Aren't you going to drink your tea, Nathaniel?" Father queried, gaining my attention where he gazed quizzically between myself and the cup in question.

"Of... Of course I am, father." I hesitantly responded with a radiant smile.

*Will things go back to normal if I drink this?* I mulled, slowly bringing the cup to my lips while father watched me like a hawk. Then Gloria's words came to mind. '***The government tasked them with the production of a drug, which is now used as a 'supplement' in all of our food.***'. *Will I get my old life back?* And just that thought alone was enough for me to take a tentative sip.

***

"Would you like me to turn the television on, father?" Carmen queried, making a beeline for the television.

"Oh, yes, of course!" Father exclaimed, as if suddenly remembering, "We don't want to miss the broadcast!"
Carmen hurriedly twisted the knobs until she tuned into the live broadcast; she then dashed over to the sofa, slumping down beside mother.

"Citizens of Merribridge!" The Prime Minister began, grinning from ear to ear, "Last night, Kathleen Sarah Long was apprehended where she was condemned to die by fusillading, a sentence imposed by myself under Deprived of Existence Act." He then fell silent for a moment, as if allowing his words to sink in, "I pray to the Lord every night that the Devil doesn't corrupt another unfortunate soul." Another moment of silence filled the atmosphere before he finally concluded, "I'd like to wish you a goodnight. Remember, keep smiling!" And as soon as he had finished, Carmen got up and turned off the television.

"Right!" Father proclaimed, slapping his hands down onto his thighs, "It's time to turn in for the night." He then stood up and switched off the lamp, all the while we each said goodnight to one another.

I then followed Carmen upstairs, watching as she disappeared into her room; I quickly went into the bathroom to get ready for bed.

Once I had finished, I headed to my room, switching on the bedside lamp and drawing the curtains. Grabbing my suit jacket, I hung it up so not to crease it. Finally, I clambered into bed, fluffed up my pillows, and switched off the lamp.

# Chapter Nine
## He's a Watcher?!

**DING, DING, DING!** *Urgh... It can't be quarter to seven already, can it?* Groggily opening my eyes, I stared over at my alarm clock, groaning in dismay when I saw 6:45AM. *Feels like I've hardly slept...* I uttered before something suddenly dawned on me. *The voice! It's back!* And I was instantly wide awake. *Why's it back?! I drank the tea last night, so why haven't things gone back to normal?!* Running my fingers through my hair, I could feel my throat closing up at the notion of having to spend the whole day pretending again.

*How has this happened?!* I fretted, turning off my alarm with a shaky hand. *Why didn't it work?!* I continued to worry while getting out of bed, pulling back the curtains where sunlight smacked me in the face. *Now I need to remember to keep smiling...* I murmured, grabbing my pale grey suit from yesterday as well as my wingtip shoes. *Just keep smiling. Just keep smiling.* I chanted with a wavering grin.

I then made my way into the bathroom, closing the door behind me and depositing the clothes. Grabbing everything out of the medicine cabinet, I went about my usual morning routine. *Just keep smiling! Just keep smiling!* I carried on, struggling to maintain a full-blown grin while brushing my teeth. *I **can** do this!* Even when I noted the yellow bruising around my bloodshot eye I wasn't swayed from my determination.

Once I had returned everything to the cabinet, I pulled off my pyjama top only to abruptly remember. *I forgot I'm being watched!* Slowly, I circled my gaze up to the camera above the bathtub, my smile cracking; I instantly felt sick and violated. *What do I do?* But then I realised there was nothing I could do, so I reluctantly changed into my grey suit. *This is wrong! So wrong!*

With a shiver, I couldn't leave the bathroom fast enough where the tantalising aroma of bacon invaded my senses. *Oh God, that smells amazing!* I moaned in ecstasy just as my mouth began to salivate. Eagerly taking the stairs two at a time, I wandered through the dining room and into the kitchen where I spotted mother by the hob. *Oh, I've never seen her put her hair up like that before.* I deliberated, noting her dark brown hair was in a bun; then I realised her floral dress matched the flowery apron tied around her tiny waist.

Automatically taking a further step inside, I said, "Good morning, mother. Good morning, Carmen."
In unison, they spun round to face me, smiling broadly, "Good morning, Nathaniel." Before turning back and continuing what they were doing.

I then robotically made my way over to the breakfast table, pulling up a chair just as Carmen finished setting it; she wore the same light pink dress as yesterday, but her hair was down in waves today. Her green eyes then momentarily met mine, a smile growing on her face that had very little make-up before she began helping mother pile the plates up with bacon, eggs, and a side of toast. *God, I'm so hungry! I can't wait to eat something!*

"Where's your father?" Mother queried with a radiant smile gracing her made-up face, hollering, "Jeremiah?!" She then grabbed a plate and set it down at father's spot.

"Coming, sweetheart!" Father called from the living-room, his shoes suddenly rapping against the dining room floor before he appeared with a newspaper tucked under his arm; he wore the same beige suit as yesterday.
"Smells delicious, sweetheart." He gleamed before sitting down, his dark blue eyes staring eagerly at his food.

Once mother and Carmen sat down, father brought a

forkful of food to his lips; his eyes rolled into the back of his head in delight, a pleasing groan escaping him once he took a bite.

"And it tastes just as good as it looks!" He happily proclaimed, dabbing a napkin either side of his thin, beaming lips before tucking it into his pale blue shirt.

Mother and Carmen then dug in; however, I was a little sceptical. *If what Gloria said was true about the drug being in our food, then there's no going back if I do this...*
But I was so desperate to have my old life once again, so I snatched up my cutlery while saying, "Thank you, mother. Thank you, Carmen." And in unison, they looked at me and beamed, "I'm glad you're enjoying it." Before continuing to eat.

"What's your plans for the day, sweetheart?" Father asked mother between mouthfuls.

"Oh..." Mother lazily sighed, her dark brown eyes shifting to him as she smiled, "Well, I plan on making a chocolate cake and doing a spot of sewing; however, I'm sure Betty will ring and ask me out to play tennis at the club, and then we'll have a spot of shopping with the girls followed by lunch." And the usual conversation swiftly followed.

*Well, here goes nothing...* I mulled, apprehensively taking my first bite; the flavours tantalised my taste buds, making me moan aloud. *God, I've missed this so much-*
"Now look what you've made me do, Vivian!" Father unexpectedly growled in annoyance; egg yolk had dripped down the lapel of his blazer, so he snatched the napkin free from his shirt to wipe it away.

But I had to do a double take when I noted a badge; it was black and gold with writing around the edge. *What does it say?* Squinting to get a better look, the toast in my hold dropped with a splat when I realised what it said. *No!* I hawked, my jaw dropping as a cold sweat consumed me. ***NO!*** The word '**WATCHER**' was as clear as day staring back at me.

*Oh my God! What Gloria said was true!* And just that notion made me snatch up my napkin, spitting out the food still lingering in my mouth. *He's a Watcher?!* I declared in coherent fright, my heart now racing, threatening to explode out of my chest. *My own father's a Watcher!*

Suddenly, father tucked the napkin back into his shirt, hiding the badge from view once again.

"Nathaniel," He began, gaining my attention, "Why aren't you smil-" But then a shimmer of realisation flashed across his dark blue eyes when he grasped what I had been staring at; it was in that split second he figured out I knew and understood what he was.

*What am I going to do?!* Gulping, I diverted my gaze, unable to look at him a moment longer. *My father's a Watcher!*

"Nathaniel..." Father finally spoke up, gaining my attention once more, "You better leave for work if you hope to finish organising the party for Mr Miller..." And I thought I saw a glimmer of fear sparkle in his blue eyes.

Nodding, I immediately darted upstairs to grab my briefcase. *I need to see Gloria! I need to tell her my father's a Watcher!* And I grabbed the badge from my bedside table before leaving for work.

*\*\*\**

*Just keep smiling. Just keep smiling.* I chanted, trying to ignore my aching jaw which felt like jelly. I hadn't met anyone else on my journey to work, but the speakers abruptly came to life as soon as I was a stone's throw from C.S.

"Rise and shine, it's a beautiful day in Merribridge! The sun is out and there isn't a cloud in the sky!"

Ignoring the obnoxiously loud announcement, I opened the door to the reception, spotting Miss Jones slip off her long, black belted fleece; underneath was a bright red dress that matched the lipstick on her made-up face.

"Good morning, Miss Jones." I beamed, startling her where she dropped her coat with a small scream.

Clasping the front of her dress with a fisted hand, Miss Jones gawked with a dazzling smile, "Goodness gracious me, Mr West!

You scared the life out of me!"

"My apologies." I said, watching as she picked up her coat; she then folded it in half, tucking it under her desk once she pulled off a badge pinned to it.

"You're early." Miss Jones changed the subject while fastening the badge to the front of her dress, and I replied with a hint of sarcasm, "Can't let Tim down for his surprise party!"

"Very well, Mr West." She grinned, clearly oblivious to my bitterness, "I'm very much looking forward to Mr Miller's surprise party." And she brushed a loose strand of startling blonde hair behind her ear, which had fallen from her pinned up beehive.

*Of course you are...* I grumbled.

"Good day, Miss Jones." I bid farewell before wandering upstairs, making a beeline for Mr Sheridan's office where I knocked twice.

*Guess he's not in yet...* I deliberated when there was no reply. *Do I wait out here? Go inside?* Casting a quick glance around the empty office, I gingerly opened the door and stepped inside, shivering against the chill lingering in the dark room; a sinister vibe surrounded me, making my skin prickle with goose bumps. *God, his room is so creepy!* Flipping on the light switch, I sighed in relief as all my nerves seemed to dissipate along with the darkness.

Shifting my attention to Mr Sheridan's desk, I pulled up a chair and discarded my briefcase by my feet. *I can't believe I'm expected to organise this stupid party!* I groaned, snatching up my notes with an audible huff. *At least all that's left to do is the guest list-*

"Mr West?" The recognisable, plummy voice of Mr Sheridan interrupted my train of thought, stilling me.

Snapping my head over my shoulder, I saw him stood in the doorway, his gunmetal grey eyes were wide in surprise while a massive grin plagued his thin lips.

"You're early!" Mr Sheridan carried on, taking a further step inside where I realised he was clad in his never differing attire; a sharp grey suit and dark blue tie.

Hurriedly standing to better face him, I began with a slight stutter, "Wuh-Well, Suh-Sir, I just wanted to make sure everything was in order fuh-for Tim's party, Suh-Sir!" And I anxiously sat back down once he plonked himself in his plush, leather chair behind his desk.

Shocked, Mr Sheridan's lips formed a little '**o**' while he, somehow, still managed to smile. *That's so creepy!* I shivered, diverting my gaze back down to the list.

"What have you got left to do?" He queried after a moment of silence, gesturing to my notes with a nod of his head.

"Just the invitations, Sir." I replied, my attention momentarily flicking back down to the list.

"Good!" He beamed, leaning back in his chair, "Chop, chop then, Mr West. The sooner we get them out, the better." And I couldn't help but grit my teeth when he told me to '**chop, chop**'.
*I hate it when he says that!*

Ignoring Mr Sheridan's comment, I merely nodded. *The sooner I get this done, the sooner I can get back to my orders.* I mulled while he adjusted his tie, distracting me where I saw a black and gold badge pinned to the lapel of his jacket. It took a while for it to sink in, but when it did- ***No!*** An involuntary gasp escaped me; I could feel the blood drain from my face. *He's a Watcher too!* Terrified, I hastily circled my sights back down to the list, hoping Mr Sheridan hadn't noticed my prying eyes. *I can't believe he's a Watcher!* I panicked once more. *Actually, I can believe it!*

"Is something the matter, Mr West?" Mr Sheridan suddenly piped up.
Gulping, I slowly lifted my gaze, meeting his gunmetal grey ones.
Shaking my head, I replied tremulously, "Wuh-Wuh-Why would something be the muh-matter, Sir?" And I ran my clammy hands down my trouser legs.

"You look awfully pale." He commented, a genuine look of concern gracing his face.
*I do?!* I fretted, swiping the back of my hand across my sweaty

brow. *I can't let him know somethings wrong!*

"I'm fine, thank you, Sir." I replied in barely a whisper, but he didn't seem convinced.

"Are you sure?" He pressed once more, leaning forward to better look at me, "Because you're not smiling." And a sinister grin hooked the corner of his thin lips.

*I'm not?!* I exclaimed, forcing myself to smile from ear to ear. *I need to concentrate! I **can** do this!*

Grinning like a madman, I firmly stated, "Positive, Sir!" And I circled my sights back down to the list.

*Just keep smiling! Just keep smiling!*

\*\*\*

"All the invitations have been handed out, Sir." I commented, closing Mr Sheridan's office door; he was sat behind his desk with a beaming smile.

"Excellent!" He purred, peering down at his watch, "And just in time for lunch!" And just the thought of food made my stomach rumble.

*God, I'm so hungry!* But then I remembered I had nothing to eat; I had left home in a hurry and forgot my lunchbox. *Great...* I groaned before everything that had happened this morning came rushing back. *Everything's just so complicated...* I uttered, catching a glint of Mr Sheridan's pin badge; it was another reminder of how difficult my reality had now become. *I need to speak to Gloria. I need to figure out what I'm going to do.*

"You may carry on with processing your orders after lunch, Mr West." Mr Sheridan spoke up, dragging me back to the conversation.

"Thank you, Sir." I replied with a nod, turning to leave.

"Oh, and one more thing, Mr West." He added just as I opened the door; I gazed quizzically over my shoulder to see him rummaging around in his desk drawer.

"I need you to sign this." He explained, pulling out a handmade card which he set on his desk, pushing it towards me with his index fingers; I instantly knew it was a congratulations card for Tim.

"Sign it, Mr West." Mr Sheridan urged, passing me a pen which I reluctantly took.

*First a cake, then a card... What next?* I bitterly thought, glancing back down at the card and scanning the other comments; I immediately spotted father's handwriting. *What did he put?* 'Congratulations, Tim! Best wishes, Jeremiah.'. *Simple and straight to the point.* Then I glimpsed at another; it was so hard to read I had to squint. 'Congratulations, Tim! Best wishes, Isaiah.'. *God, whose awful handwriting is this?!* I gawked before moving onto an easier one. 'Congratulations, Tim! Best wishes, Marjorie.'. *Miss Jones has always had such neat writing.*

"Today, Mr West..." Mr Sheridan piped up, bouncing a fisted hand against the desk in apparent frustration.

*I better do this before he loses his patience.* I decided, gazing back down only to realise everyone had written the exact same thing. *But why?* Then it hit me. *Because of the drug... Everyone does the same thing...* I inwardly sighed while searching for an empty space, quickly signing the card only for Mr Sheridan to snatch it back before the pen had barely left the paper.

"Thank you, Mr West." Mr Sheridan hurriedly said, shoving the card in a brown envelope, "Now can you put it on Mr Miller's nice, **new** desk in his nice, **new** office." And I didn't like how he was purposely trying to aggravate me.

Clenching my jaw, I inhaled a deep breath. *Just ignore him. He's doing it to get a reaction.* And I slowly exhaled before discarding the pen on the desk.

"Of course, Sir." I finally replied in an upbeat tone, taking the card from Mr Sheridan's grasp; I then turned on my heels, leaving.

*He's doing this on purpose!* I growled, my free hand briefly clenching into a fist. *Rubbing salt in the wound just to try and get a reaction!* My eyes then narrowed on Tim's office in the corner by Mr Sheridan's, and I instantly spotted the shiny new golden plaque on the door. Timothy A. Miller was engraved into it with

Quality Assurance Manager underneath.

*This could've been my office...* I murmured as soon as I stepped into the dimly lit, square-shaped room. The blinds along the far back wall shuttered the window from view, so I flipped on the light switch. I could feel a pulse in my throat as I stared around in defeat, taking in the dark green walls decorated with black and white photos; the colour made the office feel much smaller than it was.

*Would I have been offered the promotion if I hadn't been taking those tablets?* I couldn't help but wonder while advancing on the mahogany desk in the middle of the room. *Or had Mr Sheridan always planned for Tim to be the Quality Assurance Manager?* I mulled further, tracing an index finger along the dark red, leather chair that was tucked in front of the desk, a matching one was on the other side.

I then placed the card on the desk when I came to stand behind it, straightening the envelope so it was sitting perfectly centre. *I guess it doesn't really matter now...* I continued to ponder, burying my hands inside my blazer pockets. *What's done is done...*

With a sigh, I peered around the room once more before wandering towards the door, pulling my hands out of my pockets where I felt something accidentally slip out, hitting the floor with a clack. *Huh?* Glancing down, I spotted something small and pink just to the right of the desk. *What is that?* Bending down to get a better look, I recoiled when I realised what it was. *A tablet?!* I gawked. *But how did it end up in my pocket? I gave the last one to fathe-*

"Mr West?" The plummy voice of Mr Sheridan abruptly sliced through my thoughts, and my head snapped up to see him standing in the doorway.
*What's he doing here?!* I panicked, standing up straight.

"Yuh-Yes, Sir?" I queried, a bead of sweat now trickling down my brow.

"Would you care to join me for lunch?" He asked just as I took a step forward, hiding the tablet from view.

"Luh-Lunch?!" I stammered, shocked.
*He wants to have lunch with me?!*

Mr Sheridan shot me an incredulous glance, clearly taken aback by my question. Knowing I couldn't turn down his offer, I enthusiastically nodded, "I'd love to have lunch with you, Sir!"
*I'll just have to remember to grab the tablet afterwards!*

"Excellent!" He purred, gesturing with a nod for me to follow; I tried my hardest not to shoot the pill one last glance as I closed the door behind me.

During the entire lunchbreak, I couldn't help but think. *Why does he want to have lunch with me?* It had felt almost pointless. We had ended up retreating into Mr Sheridan's office due to the kitchen being crowded, and I got the impression he only wanted to have lunch with me to push a few buttons. He was constantly talking about Tim. *Tim's new office. Tim's new role.* Everything was about Tim. *And don't get me started on the excuses I had to make about why I wasn't eating!* I was more than relieved when he told me to return to my desk and process orders.

*Now to get that tablet!* I instructed, closing Mr Sheridan's office door behind me. My attention then shifted over to Tim's office, and I could feel the blood drain from my face when I realised the door was open. *Oh no! No, no, no!* I panicked, taking a step closer where I saw him milling about inside.

Suddenly, I was overwhelmed with worry. *What the hell am I going to do?! How am I going to get it out without him noticing?!* Running a jerky hand through my hair, I struggled to maintain my composure as well as not let my smile falter. *Oh God, what do I do?!*

The squeak of a door then gained my attention, Mr Sheridan strolled out of his office with a black folder in his grasp. *I better head to my desk.* And I hastily advanced on it before Mr Sheridan could question what I was doing. *I'll just wait until he's gone- Wait, where's he going?!* I declared when he made a beeline for Tim's office, causing my stomach to turn rock hard. *No, no!* I cried in fear, my knees so shaky I collapsed onto my chair.

I couldn't help but watch with wide eyes as Mr Sheridan knocked twice on Tim's door, asking, "Are you ready for our meeting, Mr Miller?"

*Please be in Mr Sheridan's office! Please be in Mr Sheridan's office!* I prayed, jamming my hands into my armpits.

I couldn't see Tim, but I heard him respond in an upbeat tone, "Of course, Sir."

***Please** be in Mr Sheridan's office!* I begged, swiping a hand across my sweaty brow.

"Excellent!" Mr Sheridan purred, and my heart plummeted when he took a step inside.

*No, no, no!* I wailed, feeling the hair lift on the back of my neck. *What am I going to do if he sees the tablet before I get the chance to grab it?!* He then took a further step inside, closing the door behind him; it was in that instance I couldn't handle the fear building within a moment longer. *It'll only be a matter of time until he sees that tablet!*

***

The afternoon dragged before five o'clock finally arrived. I had been worried Mr Sheridan was going to storm out of Tim's office and drag me away, but he didn't; in fact, he and father had been in there all afternoon. *And they're still in there now...* I mulled, recollecting the apprehension etched on father's gleaming face when he disappeared inside. *What's going on?* Running a jerky hand through my hair, I shot Tim's office one last glance before grabbing my briefcase and heading downstairs.

"Have a good evening, Mr Smith." Miss Jones bid farewell to everyone in turn, and they too wished her a goodnight.

Her ice blue eyes then landed on me, and she said with a show-stopping smile, "Have a good evening, Mr West."

"You too, Miss Jones." I grinned, grabbing the door and holding it for whoever was behind me.

Once they had grabbed it, I turned left and made my way

passed store owners who were closing their shops; their voices but a distant echo as troubled thoughts plagued my mind. *I need to speak to Gloria now I know she wasn't lying and figure out what I'm going to do.* I just prayed she was going to be home.

Once I reached the top of Amicable Street, I anxiously buried a hand inside my blazer pocket where I felt the cold, metal badge against my fingertips. **'It acts as a form of pass when detected on the cameras.'.** Gloria's voice came to mind. **'Exempting them from suspicious activities such as curfew.'.** *I guess there's only one way to find out if that's true...* And I fastened the badge to my lapel before weaving past all the people making their way home.

My shoes rapped against the pebbled path once I opened the white gate, making my way towards Gloria's front door where I knocked twice. *Please be in!* I wasn't sure how much time had passed, but I began to lose hope; my stomach clenched as I ran a hand round the back of my neck in disappointment. *Well I guess that's that then...* Just as I turned to leave, the door opened; a slow smile graced my lips as I faced Gloria. *Thank God she's in!* I breathed, an unexpected release of tension dispersing from my body.

"Can I come in?!" I blurted before Gloria had the chance to speak, the confusion plastered on her made-up face didn't match the smile gracing her ruby red lips; shock blazed behind her mesmerising green eyes.
After a moment, she nodded and I immediately took a step inside where I carried on, "I need to talk to you." But it was only then I realised how stunning she looked.
*Whoa!* I gasped as she closed the door. *She looks- Wow!*

Gloria was dressed to the nines with her bright red, off the shoulder wiggle dress that hugged her every curve; she had paired it with black, open toe heels. *How the hell didn't I notice what she was wearing?!* I gawked, trailing my eyes up where I noted her brown hair was up in a beehive, a few loose tendrils graced her slender neck. *She's just so beau-*

"What did you want to talk about?" Gloria queried, cutting across my yearning thoughts.

Shaking off my heated desires, I explained, "I need your help."
A small, triumphant smirk graced Gloria's lips while I deposited my briefcase by my feet.

"What changed your mind?" She probed, and I went on to reveal how I had found out my father and Mr Sheridan were Watchers.

"Now I don't know what to do!" I concluded before Gloria herded me into the living-room where I slumped down onto the sofa; she was silent for a moment before asking, "Do you happen to know whether either of them have reported you?"

"I don't think so." I replied with a shake of my head, making Gloria sigh in relief.

"Good!" She breathed, "The last thing we want is for Doctor Solace to be involved." And just the mention of that name had my flesh tingle with goose bumps.

Gulping, I brought a hand up to pinch the skin at my throat, tremulously wondering, "Wuh-Why? What wuh-would happen if he were to be involved?"

"He is the head doctor at Merriwell Sanatorium." Gloria ominously began, "He oversees all the ruthless treatments inpatients undergo. His personal favourite is electroconvulsive therapy."

*Electroconvulsive?!* I gaped, unable to stop a shudder. *Does father know what this doctor does?!* I fretted. *'**I have booked you an appointment.**'.* His words echoed in my head. *'**It's with Doctor Solace.**'.*

"It'll only be a matter of time until either one of them reports you." Gloria carried on, dragging me out of my deliberations, "So I need to speak to the guild about our plan of action before that happens."

"Can't things just go back to the way they were?" I queried, and Gloria shook her head, "No, you know too much now."

"Then what I am supposed to do?!"

"Just continue with your routines until I tell you otherwise." She firmly stated, "But under no circumstances are you to eat or drink anything that is offered to you. Tap water is fine, they've not managed to get the drug into the water system yet."

I couldn't help but stare at Gloria in disbelief. *How the hell does she expect me to stick to my routines if I can't eat anything?! What am I going to do during breakfast and dinner, pretend?!*

Gloria must have noted the doubt on my face as she quickly inputted, "I can make you some food for tonight and lunch for tomorrow." She then rose to her feet before I could object, adding, "I'll be back in two shakes of a cat's whisker." And she disappeared in the direction of the kitchen.

*Can I actually trust her?* I couldn't help but wonder. *What if there is no guild? And how are they even going to help me?* Anxiously running my fingers through my hair, I then peered down at the badge pinned to my lapel. *I still can't believe father's a Watcher...*

"Eat this." Gloria piped up as she wandered into the living-room; a plate in one hand and a brown paper bag in the other.

Passing me the plate, I was delighted to see it was one of her delicious ham sandwiches. *God, this looks amazing!* I exclaimed, my mouth instantly salivating.

"This-" She carried on, distracting me where she held up the paper bag, "-Is for lunch tomorrow. I'll put it in your briefcase so you don't forget it." And she disappeared into the hallway.

"Thank you!" I called after her, now diverting my attention back down to the sandwich.

Grasping it with both hands, I took a huge bite. *God, it tastes so good!* I inwardly moaned, my eyes rolling into the back of my head.

"Pfft! It's not that good!" Gloria scoffed in amusement when she sat back down, making me jump, "It's probably because you've hardly eaten."

Swallowing my mouthful, I nodded in agreement, "Probably, but it's still so good!" And I took another ravenous bite, making her giggle.

"Once you're done, I suggest you head home." Gloria instructed, a soft smile gracing her red lips, "Seeing as your father's a Watcher, we can't compromise your routines; it's too risky!" Her mesmerising green eyes then grazed over me, locking onto my chest.

"I'm glad to see you remembered it." She commented; I followed her gaze to the badge as she continued, "Just don't forget to take it off before you go indoors." And I couldn't help but raise a curious eyebrow as I shifted my attention back to her.

"Why?" I questioned through a mouthful, and Gloria explained, "While the general public won't bat an eyelid, Watchers' know their associates." And she swiftly took the plate once I polished off the sandwich, carrying on, "So never, **ever** wear the badge or suit in the presence of another Watcher."

"Suit?" I repeated, confused, "What suit?"

"Haven't I told you?" She queried, "They have special suits they wear to their monthly meetings; they're black with gold ties." And she waved her hand dismissively, "Not that you'll probably ever see one."

"Anyway, you ought to go." Gloria finished, rising to her feet, "But do come back tomorrow, hopefully I'd have spoken with the guild by then."

"Hopefully." I reiterated, following her into the hallway where she passed me my briefcase.

She then opened the door, an unnatural smile gracing her lips that sent a shiver up my spine. *God, that's creepy!*

Forcing a grin, I stepped outside where the warm summers breeze tickled my skin.

I then faced her, saying, "Goodnight, Gloria." And she hesitantly closed the door while replying, "Goodnight, Mr West."

*Just one more night.* I deliberated, advancing on the garden gate; I wasn't surprised the streets were dead and the announcement had stopped, the silence chilling me to my very core. *Just one more night and then everything will no longer be up in the air.* Closing it behind me with a squeak, I immediately turned left, picking up the pace. *I better hurry before father gets suspicious.*

A sigh of relief escaped me when I set foot on Paradise

Street; my house was a stone's throw away when I noticed father's car wasn't on the driveway. *Where is he?* I couldn't help but bite my bottom lip when worry started to set in. *Has something happened to him?* It was out of character for him to be late. *Except for yesterday...* Reluctantly tearing my gaze away, I opened the white gate. *I hope he's okay.* I prayed, clutching at my blazer and realising I was still wearing the badge. *God, I can't believe I almost forgot to take it off!* Stuffing it inside my jacket pocket, I retrieved my keys at the same time.

Unlocking the front door, I stepped inside and saw mother and Carmen clearing up the dinner table. *Huh? What are they doing?* I pondered, rubbing my chin before closing the door behind me, gaining their attention; they stared at me for what felt like a lifetime. *Why are they just looking at me?*
Then I remembered my routine, so I blurted, "I'm home!" And they replied in unison, "Welcome home, Nathaniel!" Before continuing to clear the table.

I then came to stand in the dining room once I discarded my briefcase by the bottom of the stairs, watching mother and Carmen with great intent. *Have they eaten?* I mulled, noting only two spaces had empty plates.

"Where's father?" I instantly asked, looking to mother for confirmation as she stacked her plate on top of Carmen's.

"He's working late, honey, and told us to eat without him." She explained, heading into the kitchen and leaving Carmen to wipe down the table; I hastily followed like a bloodhound that had caught the scent of its prey.

"If I had known you weren't with him," Mother added while washing the dishes, "I would've made dinner for you."

"It's fine," I replied with a beaming smile, secretly glad I didn't need an excuse not to eat, "I can wait until tomorrow."
*I just need a plan for the morning...*

"Anyway," I resumed, turning for the hallway, "I'm going to get washed up." And I didn't wait for her to reply before heading upstairs with my briefcase in hand, unable to ignore the worry slowly eating away at me.

*Why hasn't father come home?*

# Chapter Ten
## Where's Tim?

**DING, DING, DING!** The dreaded sound of the alarm woke me with a start. *Oh God...* I groaned, rubbing the sleep out of my eyes. *It feels like I've hardly slept...* I had been tossing and turning all night, worried about father's whereabouts. *Did he even come home?* I contemplated, reaching over to turn the alarm off. *Or has something happened to him?* Shaking off my unease, I couldn't sit in bed a moment longer; I immediately got up and opened the curtains, blinking back the suns blinding rays. *God, it's so bright!* Turning for the wardrobe, I grabbed my pale grey suit and wingtip shoes before heading to the bathroom.

*Just keep smiling. Just keep smiling.* I chanted once I closed the door behind me and deposited my clothes, glimpsing at the camera above the bathtub as I went to the medicine cabinet. *How many cameras are in the house?* I couldn't help but wonder as the one on the landing came to mind. *I've just got to keep smiling and act normal.* I reminded myself, grabbing the toiletries and putting them on the little shelf underneath. Closing the mirrored door, I grimaced at the state of my black eye; the white of my eye was red and looked painful, the skin around it now a faded yellow. *Maybe I should ask Gloria if there's anything I can do to reduce the redness.*

Once I had finished my morning routine and got dressed, I headed downstairs where the sweet fragrance of bacon lingered up my nose. Passing the living-room, I couldn't help but peek inside, a sigh of relief escaping me when I saw father sat reading his newspaper. *Thank God!* I breathed, letting my head fall back for a brief moment before making my way into the kitchen.

Mother was stood by the hob wearing the same floral dress from yesterday; her dark brown hair down in a hideous bouffant. *How am I going to get away with not eating?* I deliberated while taking a further step inside, feeling my skin crawl when mother suddenly faced me; an expectant look on her face. *What's she-* Carmen then swiftly turned away from the breakfast table, her white and yellow plaid dress fanning around her; she too stared at me in anticipation.

Then I realised what they wanted, so I swallowed the lump in the back of my throat and said with a weak grin, "Good morning, mother. Good morning, Carmen." And in unison, they smiled broadly, "Good morning, Nathaniel." Before turning back and continuing what they were doing.

*God, that was creepy!*

With a shiver, I slowly ambled over to the breakfast table, pulling up a chair just as Carmen finished setting it; her curly ponytail swayed from side to side whenever she moved, a matching white and yellow plaid bow held it in place. *I've just got to act as normal as possible.* I mulled while Carmen's green eyes momentarily met mine, a smile growing on her face that had very little make-up before she began helping mother plate up. *God, that smells so good!*

"Where's your father?" Mother queried with a radiant smile gracing her made-up face, hollering, "Jeremiah?!" She then grabbed a plate and set it down at father's spot.

"Coming, sweetheart!" Father called from the living-room, his shoes suddenly rapping against the dining room floor before he appeared with a newspaper tucked under his arm; he wore the same beige suit.

"Smells delicious, sweetheart." He gleamed before sitting down, his dark blue eyes staring eagerly at his food.

Once mother and Carmen sat down, father brought a forkful of food to his lips; his eyes rolled into the back of his head

in delight, a pleasing groan escaping him once he took a bite.
"And it tastes just as good as it looks!" He happily proclaimed, dabbing a napkin either side of his thin, beaming lips before tucking it into his pale blue shirt.

My breath hitched in my throat when mother and Carmen dug in; I knew it would be a matter of time until father asked why I wasn't eating. *What excuse will he believe today?* A bleeping noise then unexpectedly sliced through the atmosphere; my attention shifted to father as he buried a hand inside his blazer pocket. *Since when did he have a pager?* I queried when he pulled it out.

"Sorry." Father apologised, rising to his feet, "I've got to take this." And he swiftly left the kitchen.
*I don't think I've ever seen him use it...* I murmured, my gaze lingering on the dining room archway. *Does he have it because he's a Watcher?* Then I wondered. *Does Mr Sheridan have one?* Before I suddenly realised. *Hang on, why am I just sitting here when now's my chance to leave!*

"I've got to go!" I blurted at mother with a radiant smile, pushing back my chair and causing the feet to squeal, "I can't be late for work! I have countless orders to process!" And I didn't wait for her to object before swiftly heading upstairs, grabbing my briefcase.
*I can't forget the badge.* I reminded myself, making sure it was in my blazer pocket.

Just as I was about to thunder downstairs, I heard father's voice coming from his bedroom, stopping me in my tracks.

"I assure you, if there are no further improvements by the end of the week, I **will** dispose of him myself."
*Who's he talking about?* I wondered. *It's not me, is it?* And that thought alone instilled me with an indescribable feeling of fear.

*I-I-I better go before he comes out!* And I quickly but quietly rushed downstairs, ripping open the front door. Once I had made it out the garden gate, my worries carried me away. *Would he really dispose of me?!* I panicked, feeling beads of sweat now line my brow; oblivious to the empty street and silent speakers. *Don't be so stupid!* I scolded. *Father wouldn't kill me!* I was so lost amidst my thoughts, I almost walked past C.S.

*I need to focus!* I growled, yanking open the door and stepping inside. I had expected to see Miss Jones sat behind her desk, greeting me with her unwavering, dazzling smile; however, the reception was empty. *I guess she's in the kitchen.* I pondered with a shrug, so I headed upstairs. Just as I opened the door at the top of the stairwell, I jumped back in fright when I came face to face with Mr Sheridan. *God, he scared me!* I gasped, clutching at my chest with my free hand; I noted he wore his iconic sharp grey suit. *What's he doing here so early, anyway?* I mulled, now aware he looked just as shocked as I was.

"Mr West?" Mr Sheridan finally queried with a Cheshire-like grin, "You're here early?"
Nodding, I explained, "I was hoping to catch up with my orders, Sir."
*Seeing as you've been stopping me from processing them...* I quietly added.

"Very well." He beamed, "Then I expect them **all** to be processed by lunchtime." And I couldn't stop my jaw from dropping.
*He can't be serious, can he?!* But there was no denying the gravity blazing behind his gunmetal grey eyes.

"But-" I began just as Mr Sheridan abruptly cut across me, "Anyway, Mr West, I've got a meeting to attend to." And, without another word, he barged past and disappeared down the stairs, leaving me gawking after him.
*A meeting at this hour?* I deliberated; aware it wasn't even eight o'clock yet. *Who has a meeting at this time?* But then the little pink pill came to mind, filling me with dread. *What if he's having a meeting to discuss what to do with me?*

*\*\*\**

*Where's Tim?* I wondered for what must have been the hundredth time; it was nearly lunchtime, and I still hadn't seen him. *Maybe he's been in meetings all morning?* But I doubted that as the plaque on his office door had been removed an hour ago.

I had tried to distract myself with processing; however, something deep down was niggling me. *What if something has happened to him?* But then I realised how stupid that sounded; Tim was a perfect role model employee. *I need to focus and get these orders processed!* I scolded, putting my worries about Tim to the back of my mind.

*Mr Sheridan wanted them completed by lunchtime, and I'm running out of tim-* The bang of the stairwell door interrupted my train of thought followed by the rap of shoes; I had to stop myself from gazing over my shoulder so not to arouse suspicion.

"I do **not** agree, Jeremiah!" The recognisable voice of Mr Sheridan growled, and father curtly responded, "But I **am** the executive, a job entrusted to me, so get him in your office!" There was a moment of silence before Mr Sheridan gravely replied, "Very well... But I'd watch that tone if I were you..."

*What's going on?* I wondered as father stormed past, disappearing inside Mr Sheridan's office; my heart plummeted when Mr Sheridan came to stand by my desk. *Oh God, it must be about that tablet! They know it's mine!*

"My office, Mr West." Mr Sheridan ordered, and I peered up to see him beaming down at me.

"What about my orde-" But he ignored me before I could even finish; I merely watched as he wandered into his office without so much as shooting me another glance.

Shaking my head, I put the order I had been processing to one side before following him, closing the door behind me.

"Sit down." Mr Sheridan implored; he was perched on the edge of his desk while father sat on the plush leather chair.

"So," He carried on once I sat down, as if whatever he was about to say was a massive inconvenience, "I'd like to be the first to congratulate you on your new position as Quality Assurance Manager."

It took a moment for the news to sink in but, when it did, I couldn't help but shoot him an incredulous glance. *Err... What?*

"This is a joke, right?" I blurted, unable to stop myself.

"This isn't a joke, Nathaniel." Father stated matter-of-factly, gaining my attention where he entwined his fingers on the desk, "We've called you in here to explain what we expect from you as Quality Assurance Manager."

Every fibre of my being wanted to jump for joy; it was my dream job, yet I couldn't help but wonder. *What about Tim?*

"As a manager of quality assurance, you are to make sure all external and internal requirements are met before our products reach our clients." Mr Sheridan started, my eyes locking onto his gunmetal grey ones, "And some of your responsibilities will include planning procedures to inspect and report quality assurance issues, supervising all procedures that affect quality, and monitoring and guiding inspectors, technicians and other staff involved in the procedures."

I merely nodded, but whatever he had said went through one ear and out the other. *I don't understand what's going on... Why have they given me Tim's job?*

"You will also need to guarantee the reliability and consistency of production by checking the processes and final output." Father added, my attention shifting to him just as Mr Sheridan swiftly carried on, "You will need to make sure all our clients are satisfied, and report all malfunctions to make sure immediate action is taken."

"We expect you to collect and analyse quality data and review current standards and policies." Father resumed, followed by Mr Sheridan, "You must keep records of quality reports, statistical reviews and necessary documentation."

"Make sure all legal standards are met."

"And communicate with Quality Assurance Officers during inspections."

*Is that it? Are they done?* I wondered when neither spoke for a while; they merely stared at me, clearly waiting for a response.

"What about Tim?" I queried and silence filled the room, instilling me with uncertainty.

*I... I don't like this...* I uttered, having to stop myself from biting the inside of my cheek so my smile didn't falter.

Father and Mr Sheridan then exchanged brief glances, and there was no denying the concern shimmering in father's dark blue eyes. *What's going on? What's happened to Tim?*
Before I could question them, father spoke up, "Okay, lets head down to the factory and discuss the procedures."

After they had showed me around, explaining how the procedures worked and what they wanted me to implement, we headed back upstairs where father eagerly herded me towards Tim's office. *Correction, **my** office.* But it didn't feel right, not even when I saw Nathaniel J. West engraved on the golden plaque. A pain formed in the back of my throat; I had to advert my gaze when guilt overwhelmed me. *What happened to Tim?*

"Nathaniel," Father beamed, dragging me out of my thoughts, "Take a look at your new office." And he opened the door, gesturing for me to go in.
Inhaling a deep breath, I closed my eyes and stepped inside.
"Well, what do you think?" He eagerly asked, and I opened my eyes to see the window directly in front of me was no longer shuttered; it overlooked the factory workers.
*I still have no idea why I've got this promotion...* I murmured, trailing a finger along the mahogany desk until I came to stand behind the leather chair.

"Well?..." Mr Sheridan urged when I didn't say anything, and I peered over at them with a show-stopping smile.
"I-It's perfect!" I stammered, struggling to hide the guilt lacing my voice, "Thuh-Thank you, father!"
"Excellent!" Father purred, momentarily glancing down at his watch only to do a double-take, "Oh crumbs! I've got a meeting with clients." He then hastily turned to leave, quickly adding over his shoulder to Mr Sheridan, "Make sure Nathaniel has everything he needs." And, without another word, he left.

"You may as well have your lunch, Mr West." Mr Sheridan commented, distracting me where I saw he had a face like a beaming slapped arse.

*How he manages to look so angry and happy at the same time, I have no idea...* I deliberated, watching as he leant on the doorframe with his arms folded across his chest.

"And make sure you take all personal possessions out of your old desk." He carried on, "It'll be cleared out this evening."

"Which reminds me," Mr Sheridan brusquely added, "I expect your orders to be processed by the end of the day. Understood?"

*There's not enough hours left in the day to finish processing them!* Gritting my teeth, I nodded, "Yes, Sir."

"Good." He beamed, pushing himself off the doorway, "You know where to find me if you need anything." And I was silently grateful when he left.

*Anyway...* I uttered, emitting a heavy sigh. *I best empty my desk before I forget.*

It felt surreal coming to stand in the main office. *This... This doesn't feel right.* I mulled before glancing over at Tim's empty desk. *What happened to you, Tim?* I pondered, guilt consuming me once again. With a grimace, I averted my gaze while making my way to my desk, spotting father usher a group of men towards his office; I presumed they were clients. *They don't look like they're from around here...* I deliberated, but then I realised how stupid that sounded. *They must be from around here.* No one from another country had ever visited Merribridge. *Just like no one has ever left.*

I was about to sift through my orders but froze, unable to stop staring. *Hang on, is that a black man?!* I gawked, my jaw dropping. *I've never seen one before!* His pale grey suit and matching waistcoat complimented his dark skin. *I can't believe he's dressed smarter than that guy!* I declared in coherent shock, now gaping at a man with curly, dirty blonde hair who was vigorously shaking father's hand.

"It's nice ter finally meet yah, Mr West!" The man with the dirty blonde hair gleefully exclaimed in a strange drawl, causing his tweed jacket to slip from his shoulder and reveal a black turtleneck with matching slacks.

*What accent is that?* It was as if he hadn't opened his mouth, the words just blended together, and the end of his sentences had a rising inflection.

"Yes, yes..." Father growled with a smile, unimpressed, "It's a pleasure to meet you too, Mr Knight." He then yanked his hand free before holding the door open, gesturing for everyone to go inside.

Once they had all disappeared, I decided to leave the orders. *I'll need to process them here, anyway.* I then gathered my belongings and returned to my office, sitting down on the plush leather chair while depositing my briefcase by my feet. *I just need to find a home for these.* I mulled, glancing at the stationery I had discarded on my desk, surprised to see built-in drawers. *Why couldn't my old desk have had drawers?*

Opening the top one, it was inundated with notepads and pens. *Well, I guess I don't need these then...* And I glimpsed at the stationary on my desk with a shake of my head. *I may as well just keep them...* I then opened the middle drawer, which contained a pile of documents for discontinued products. *Urgh... Why hasn't this been emptied?* Flicking my eyes skyward in annoyance, I slammed the drawer before moving onto the bottom one. It was a little stiff to open, but after several firm yanks it eventually did where a large black folder slid to the front.

*What's this?* I wondered, picking up the folder only to note it was untitled, so I opened it to see an index page. C.S (Controlling Substances) Clientele was predominantly titled; it was only then I grasped what C.S stood for. I then glanced down at the first few names on the list underneath. *Is this a folder on all our clients?*
Australia – Knight, Ian
Belgium – Bélanger, Alexandre
Canada – Hayward, Zachary
China – Wong, Yazhu

*I never knew we dealt with other countries...* But then the guy with the dirty blonde hair came to mind. *Didn't father call him Mr Knight?* I mulled, peering back at the list. *Does that mean he's from Australia?* So many questions bombarded my brain; I had to pinch the bridge of my nose just as something flashing red caught my eye. Gazing up in the direction of the door, the hairs on the nape of my neck rose when I saw a camera pointing into the room.

*NO!* I fretted, my stomach turning rock hard. *How didn't I notice that before?!* Then I realised I was no longer smiling. *Need to smile! Can't forget to smile!* Forcing a toothy grin, I wiped my clammy hands down my trouser legs. *I just need to remember not to do anything stupid-* But then I remembered the little pink pill, causing my chest to painfully tighten. *Oh no! What am I going to do?! Someone would've seen me drop it!* I panicked, swiping the back of my hand across my sweaty brow. *It'll only be a matter of time until father and Mr Sheridan find out!*

***

*How many more orders are left?* I wondered, thumbing through the remainders. *Two, six, nine, fourteen, eighteen. Urgh... I'm not going to finish them in-* And I glanced over at the clock hanging above Mr Sheridan's office, shocked to see it was nearly five o'clock. *Should I just come in early tomorrow?*

As soon as it struck five, everyone immediately filed out and I was left staring at my pile of paperwork. *What do I do?* Mr Sheridan's office door then opened as I pressed a fist against my mouth, his gunmetal grey eyes locking onto me.
"Finished?" He questioned with a twisted, one-sided smirk, as if he already knew the answer.
Making sure my smile didn't falter, I replied with a shake of my head, "No, Sir. I've got eighteen more to process."
He clearly wasn't surprised, which only irritated me. *What else did he expect? I've not been given the time to do them!*
"Then you should be grateful I'm staying late." Mr Sheridan commented, irking me even more.
*Grateful?!*

"I'll be leaving at six." He carried on, "I expect them to be finished by then."
*But that's still not enough time!* I grumbled, my gaze flicking upwards in annoyance.
"Bring them to me once you're done." He concluded, disappearing back inside his office.

*This is stupid!* I growled, my fingers restlessly tapping the desk. *If he had given me enough time, then I wouldn't need to stay late-*

"Nathaniel?" A masculine voice sliced through my train of thought, making me jump with a gasp; it was only then I spotted father stood beside me.

"You scared me!" I breathed, running a shaky hand through my hair.

"I didn't mean to." He apologised with a toothy grin, "But I wanted to catch you before you left."

*Why?* I wondered, raising a questioning eyebrow just before a sense of impending doom ignited in my gut. *He looked at the camera!* I panicked, my heart threatening to explode. *He knows the tablet is mine!*

"I'm leaving now." Father started, "So I'll drive you home." And I couldn't help but jerk my head back in shock.
*He's... He's not here to talk about the tablet?* I gaped, staring incredulously up at him, unable to speak. *He doesn't know it was mine?*

When I didn't reply, father prompted, "Well, aren't you going to say anything?" And I instantly shook off my daze.

"Sorry, father, and thank you, father, but no, father." I blabbered, which I immediately regretted by the confusion plastered upon his beaming face.

Father then opened his mouth, but I quickly intervened, "I've got to finish processing these." And I gestured to the orders with a sweep of my hand.

"Are you staying late?" He probed in disbelief; I had never worked late before, which I knew would ring alarm bells.

"I am." I replied matter-of-factly, shooting him a dazzling smile in the hopes that would ease him.

"But how are you going to lock up?" Father countered, "You don't have a key."

"Mr Sheridan's staying until six." I explained, and his scepticism was swiftly replaced with exasperation.

"Very well…" He uttered, "But you are to be home no later than half six, understood?" And I nodded again, "Yes, father."

"Good." He bluntly replied, "I'll see you soon." And he dipped his head in farewell before advancing in the direction of the stairwell.

*Right…* I sighed, pinching the bridge of my nose. *I better get back on with these…* And I glanced down at the orders in question. I processed them as quickly as I could, not checking for any mistakes as I knew the clock was ticking. Once I had finished, I couldn't help but sigh in relief. *Thank God they're done!* And I slumped back in my chair, peering over at the clock. *Ten minutes to spare.* I thought with a smirk.

Shuffling the orders together, I headed to Mr Sheridan's office where I knocked on the door.

"Come in!" He hollered, and I opened it with a squeak.

"I've finished, Sir." I commented, glancing over at him sat behind his desk; there was no denying the shock plastered upon his radiant face.

"You've **finished**?" He queried doubtingly, sitting upright in his leather chair to better look at me.

Nodding, I carefully placed the orders on his desk, "Yes, Sir. They're all processed." And I took a step back, as if to admire my work.

Mr Sheridan was silent for a moment as he peered over the orders, but his attention finally settled on me as he said, "Very well, then you may leave." And he carried on with whatever he was doing.

Dipping my head, I replied while walking backwards out the office, "Thank you, Sir."

*That showed him!* I grinned while closing the door, now wandering into my office and grabbing my briefcase. *And I should still have enough time to see Gloria.* Giving the clock one last glance, I rushed towards the stairwell, taking the stairs two at a time.

As soon as I stepped out onto the eerily quiet and empty high street, I buried my hand in my blazer pocket, rummaging for the badge. *Where is it?* Panic started to set in before the cool metal graced my fingertips. *Thank God! I thought I lost it!* Quickly pinning it to the lapel of my jacket, I made my way to Amicable Street.

When I finally turned onto Gloria's road, I pondered. *Hopefully she's got an answer from the guild.* I then opened the gate with a squeak, my shoes rapping against the cobbled path until I came to stand outside her front door, knocking twice. A few moments passed before it opened, my head jerking back in shock when I saw Gloria. *Whoa! I mean- Whoa!* There were no words to describe how completely blown away I was.

Gloria's brown hair was down in curls with the sides pinned back, her succulent red lips moving but I couldn't hear a word she was saying; I was lost amidst her beauty. *How does she look so good all the ti-* **SLAP!** Gloria's hand struck me across the face, snapping me back to reality where my eyes locked onto hers, noticing the black cat flicks. *Did... Did she just hit me?* And I pressed a hand to my throbbing cheek.

"Are you just going to stand there like a lemon?" Gloria heatedly asked, "Or are you going to come in?"
Enthusiastically nodding, I blurted, "Yes, yes! Of course!" And I stepped inside, all the while my eyes refused to budge from her.
It was her breasts I now couldn't stop staring at, they looked like they were going to burst free from her dark green rockabilly dress; her cleavage ensnaring me like a Venus flytrap goading its next victim. *Why am I just staring?!* I had **never** looked at a woman which such yearning.

"You're a tad late." Gloria commented, shutting the door and gaining my attention once more, "I didn't think you were coming."
"Wuh-Well..." I began, glimpsing at her breasts.

*What's wrong with me?!* I growled, averting my gaze to the black silk ribbon cinching in her waist.

"I just had to..." I carried on but needed to erase the distance between us, so I edged closer.

"Had to what?" Gloria impatiently asked, tapping her foot where I saw her black and white patent heels; my breath quickened as I stared at those shoes, a heat creeping across my cheeks.

*If she wore just them and nothing else-* I couldn't help but inwardly moan at that thought.

"You just had to what?!" Gloria snapped, distracting me yet again; her hands now firmly planted on her hips.

*I need to focus!* I scolded, shaking off my heated desires.

"I had to work late." I stated, discarding my briefcase underneath the coat hooks just as she repeated, "Late?" And I got the sense that she didn't believe me.

"Yes. Late." I confirmed, "Mr Sheridan needed me to finish processing orders."

*Which I could've done tomorrow if I hadn't been promoted...*

"Well... It is awfully late, Nate." Gloria explained, "But I have spoken to-"

"It wouldn't have been an issue if I wasn't promoted to Quality Assurance Manager!" I interrupted, defending myself.

*I didn't **want** to work late! I had no choice!*

Then I noted the shock blazing behind her mesmerising green eyes, so I hastily apologised, "Sorry, I didn't mean to cut across you. You were saying something about talking to someone?"

"You... You were promoted?" She queried, biting her bottom lip when I nodded.

Pushing the matter, I prompted, "You said you spoke to? ..." And Gloria exclaimed with a dismissive wave of her hand, "Oh! No one, I spoke to no one." And she immediately turned for the kitchen, "I cooked you dinner." Before disappearing.

*O... Kay... What just happened?* I deliberated, venturing into the living-room where I sat down on the sofa. *Why is she acting strange?*

When Gloria reappeared with a tray in her grasp, she commented, "It may be a tad cold."
Taking the tray, I asked, "Have you spoken to the guild?" But then I was distracted by the food.
*This is a bit... Different...* It was red peppers stuffed with rice, cheese, and olives.

"Erm..." She murmured, dragging me back to the conversation, "Nuh-Not yet, no." And she apprehensively sat down, shuffling her feet.

"You do remember my father's a Watcher, right?" I countered, speaking through a mouthful of delicious food, "And that he knows I know? It's only a matter of time until I'll slip up!"

"I know..." Gloria sighed, crestfallen, "But it's just not that simple..."
*What's not that simple?* I mulled, taking another ravenous bite. *What isn't she telling me?*

"Just stick to your routines as much as possible." Gloria resumed; I couldn't help but scoff.
*That's easier said than done!* I fumed with a shake of my head.
"Look," She swiftly added, clearly sensing my annoyance, "You may not believe it, but I **am** really trying for you. It would be much easier if you weren't..."

"Weren't?..." I urged when she trailed off, but she merely snatched up the tray as soon as I finished the last bite.
Rising to her feet, she said, "I'll be back in two shakes of a cat's whisker." And she disappeared in the direction of the kitchen.
*Weren't what?* I contemplated, confused by her comment. *What the hell is going on?*

Not even a minute passed before Gloria returned with a brown paper bag in hand, passing it to me as she said, "This is your lunch for tomorrow."
Taking it, I murmured, "Thanks..."

"My pleasure." She beamed yet the sincerity didn't quite reach her eyes.
*What game is she playing? She said she'd explain everything, but I've just got more questions that I've had answers!*

"It's getting late." Gloria hinted, hovering by the hallway, "But come back tomor-"

"You're joking, right?" I intervened, emitting a huff in disbelief, "I can't keep coming here when I'm meant to be sticking to my routines! And you said you'd explain everything, that you'd speak to the guild, but you've done none of that!"

Shaking my head in irritation, I questioned further, "What's going on?"

Gloria notably clenched her jaw before she morosely explained, "I-I'm sorry, Nate. I don't mean to be act aloof, but things have taken an unexpected turn."

Again, I was left with more questions. *An unexpected turn for what?*

"But I **promise** I'll speak to the guild before I see you tomorrow." And a stupid part of me believed her.

*Just one more night.* I mulled, emitting a heavy breath. *Then I'll know what's going on.*

"Okay, fine." I replied while slapping my hands down onto my thighs, pushing myself up, "But if you haven't, then you won't see me again." And it pained me to say that, but I couldn't take any more risks.

"You've got my word!" Gloria insisted as I packed away the brown paper bag into my briefcase, "You can also tell me all about your new job." She added, "Like all the interesting things you're doing, and if there's anything new you've learnt about the company."

Just the mention of '**interesting**' and '**new**' reminded me of the foreign clients, so I immediately replied, "Actually, I did learn something today. I learnt C.S deal with clients from other countries. There's a whole folder with loads of names in it and where they come from." And I gestured with my hands the size of the folder.

"No!" Gloria gaped, frightened, "They're selling to people overseas?!" And I slowly nodded.

"Can... Can you bring the folder tomorrow?" Gloria questioned after a moment of silence; I couldn't help but jerk my head back in shock, blurting, "What?" And I shot her an incredulous gaze as I asked, "Why do you want to see the folder?"

"Well," She began, carefully selecting her words, "As a nurse, if C.S are shipping medicinal supplies overseas, then I'd like to make sure it isn't illegally." And I was a little stumped by her response.

*I guess that makes sense...*

"Erm..." I murmured, running a hand round the back of my neck, "I'll see what I can do..."

"Anyway," Gloria carried on, ushering me towards the door, "You should leave."

"Hang on-" But she swiftly opened it before I could react, stepping aside with an unnerving smile now gracing her ruby red lips.

"Goodnight, Mr West." She said when I spun back to face her; I didn't even get the chance to reply before she slammed the door in my face.

*I'm starting to think this was just a waste of time...* I uttered, storming down the garden path where I closed the gate behind me with an audible bang. *Perhaps I should just forget her and start eating again.* But then Gloria's words came to mind. *'**You know too much now.**'. Damn it! Why can't things just be simpler?!*

Once I turned onto Paradise Street, I immediately removed the badge from my blazer now I was a stone's throw from my house.

"I'm home!" I hollered as soon as I unlocked the front door, and everyone replied in unison, "Welcome home, Nathaniel!"

Just as I was about to wander upstairs, I spotted my family sat at the dining table, their half-eaten plates making a sigh of relief escape me. *Thank God I don't need to make up an excuse for tonight!*

"Nathaniel, join us!" Father beckoned when he gazed over his shoulder, adding with a radiant smile, "We only need to heat yours up."

"It's okay," I insisted with a shake of my head and a show-stopping smile, "I'm not hungry." But father wasn't having any of it, "Nonsense! Don't be so ridiculous! All it needs is a little time in the oven." His attention then shifted to mother as he commanded, "Vivian, go and heat it up!"

*No, no, no!* I panicked as mother stood up, her face wreathed in smiles.

"No, it's okay, father!" I blurted, waving my hands in a no gesture, stopping mother in her tracks, "I-I didn't eat all of my lunch, so, erm... I ate the rest while I was processing."

"Oh." Father spoke, clearly taken aback, so I hastily tacked on before he could say anything, "I'll wait for you all in the living-room once I've washed up." And I briskly darted upstairs before he could object.

Once I had deposited my briefcase and slipped off my blazer, I quickly splashed my face with cold water before heading back downstairs; shocked to see father already sat in his club chair. *I wasn't upstairs for that long, was I?...* I murmured, my ears pricking at the sound of cutlery clattering against plates coming from the kitchen.

"Did you get all of your orders processed?" Father enquired with a radiant smile, leaning on the armrest of his chair just as I sat down.

"Yes, I did." I replied before mother and Carmen wandered in; mother drew the curtains while Carmen made a beeline for the television.

"Would you like me to turn the television on, father?" She queried.

"Oh, yes, of course!" He exclaimed, as if suddenly remembering, "We don't want to miss the broadcast!"

Carmen hurriedly twisted the knobs until she tuned into the live broadcast; she then dashed over to the sofa, slumping down beside mother.

"Citizens of Merribridge!" The Prime Minister began, grinning from ear to ear, "It is with a heavy heart another has fallen victim to the Devil." He then fell silent for a moment, as if allowing his words to sink in.

Biting my bottom lip, I couldn't help but worry. *If they're managing to find all these nonconformists, it's only a matter of time until they find me...*

Clearing his throat, the Prime Minister then carried on, "I have a few words I would like to say. Not only was he a colleague, a neighbour, and a friend, but he was also a brother, a husband, and a father..." Another moment of silence filled the atmosphere before he resumed, "Timothy Albert Miller was apprehended last night where he was condemned to die by fusillading, a sentence imposed by myself under the Deprived of Existence Act."

**WHAT?!** I gaped, an involuntary gasp escaping me. *Tim's dead?!* And I peered at father who was cupping his mouth, remorse glistening in his dark blue gaze.

"Hopefully tomorrow will bring brighter news." The Prime Minister concluded, gaining my attention, "I'd like to wish you a goodnight. Remember, keep smiling!" And as soon as he had finished, Carmen got up and turned off the television.

"Right!" Father proclaimed, slapping his hands down onto his thighs, "It's time to turn in for the night." But there was no way I could sleep.

*Tim's dead?!* I still couldn't believe it. *How?! Why?!* It didn't make sense. *He was* - For lack of a better word - *Perfect! It just doesn't make any sens-*

"Nathaniel?" Father's voice sliced through my thoughts, bringing me back to reality, "Aren't you going to say goodnight to your sister?" He queried, making me realise Carmen was standing right in front of me.

*I need to snap out of it!* I scolded, shaking off my daze. Standing up with a radiant smile, I robotically said, "Goodnight, Carmen." Before kissing her on the forehead.

I then said goodnight to mother and father before retreating upstairs with Carmen hot on my heels, all the while I couldn't help but wonder. *What did Tim do to deserve to die?*

# Chapter Eleven
## *Delirium?*

**DING, DING, DING!**
"I didn't mean it! I swear, I didn't mean it!" I gasped awake, sitting bolt upright before realising I was in bed.
*Oh God...* I breathed, bringing a hand up to rub my face. *It was just a dream...* But there was no shaking the guilt that consumed me, especially when all I could hear as the metal knocked against the two bells on my alarm clock was '**TIM! TIM! TIM!**'. Hastily turning it off, I pulled at the collar of my pyjama top. *I... I can't believe he's dead...* I tried to ignore the shame by reminding myself it wasn't my fault; however, there was a little voice in the back of my mind that made me doubt myself. *What if it was?*

Shaking my head, I inhaled a deep breath before getting out of bed, making sure I was smiling from ear to ear. Once I had pulled back the curtains, I turned for my wardrobe. *Just keep smiling. Just keep smiling.* I chanted, grabbing my pale grey suit, crisp white shirt, and wingtips shoes I had been wearing the past week. *Just keep smiling.*

I then made a beeline for the bathroom where I closed the door behind me, depositing my clothes. *Right...* I muttered, feeling the camera burn a hole in the back of my head. *Just get it over and done with...* Once I had reluctantly gotten dressed; I then shifted my attention to the medicine cabinet, spotting my reflection. *God, my eye still looks awful!* I grimaced at the whites of my eye that was still bloodshot, the skin around it was no longer yellow. *Hopefully it'll look better by next week.* I positively thought while carrying on with my morning routine, putting everything back in the cabinet when I had finished.

I then opened the bathroom door to the sweet, mouth-watering scent of bacon. *That smells **so** good!* I moaned, descending the stairs while my stomach growled. I tried to ignore the hunger consuming me, trying to think of an excuse to skip breakfast but nothing came to mind. *God, what am I going to do?* I fretted, pinching the skin at my throat while casting a sideways glance into the living-room, spotting father sat reading the newspaper. *What can I say that'll convince him?* I mulled before wandering through into the kitchen.

Mother was stood by the hob. *What is it with her and that awful bouffant?* I cringed with a shake of my head, the ding of cutlery momentarily distracting me where I saw Carmen setting the breakfast table.

Taking a further step inside, I forced a radiant grin, "Good morning, mother. Good morning, Carmen."

In unison, they spun round to face me, smiling broadly, "Good morning, Nathaniel." Before turning back and continuing what they were doing.

Shaking off my unease, I walked over to the breakfast table, pulling up a chair just as Carmen finished setting it; her hair was up in a curly ponytail, the pink bow that held it in place matched her dress. Her green eyes then momentarily met mine, a smile growing on her face that had very little make-up before she began helping mother plate up.

"Where's your father?" Mother queried with a radiant smile gracing her made-up face, hollering, "Jeremiah?!" She then grabbed a plate and set it down at father's spot, her dark blue and white polka dot dress fanned whenever she moved.

"Coming, sweetheart!" Father called from the living-room, his shoes suddenly rapping against the dining room floor before he appeared with a newspaper tucked under his arm; he wore the same beige suit.

"Smells delicious, sweetheart." He gleamed before sitting down, his dark blue eyes staring eagerly at his food; I couldn't help but inwardly cringe when he notably – *And audibly* - inhaled the meaty aroma lingering in the kitchen.

Once mother and Carmen sat down, father brought a forkful of food to his lips; his eyes rolled into the back of his head in delight, a pleasing groan escaping him once he took a bite. *Does he put this on every day?* I couldn't help but wonder. *And how can he eat without being affected?* It just didn't make sense.

"And it tastes just as good as it looks!" He happily proclaimed, dabbing a napkin either side of his thin, beaming lips before tucking it into his pale blue shirt.

Mother and Carmen then tucked in, but I was a little hesitant. *What do I do? Pretend?*

Picking up my cutlery, I peered between them, forcing a grin while saying, "Thank you, mother. Thank you, Carmen." And in unison, they looked at me and beamed, "I'm glad you're enjoying it." Before continuing to eat.

"What's your plans for the day, sweetheart?" Father asked mother between mouthfuls.

"Oh…" Mother lazily sighed, her dark brown eyes shifting to him as she smiled, "Well, I plan on making strawberry jam and pottering amid the rosebushes; however, I'm sure Doris will ring and ask me out to play badminton at the club, and then we'll have a spot of shopping with the girls followed by lunch."

"The jam isn't going to make itself." Father grinned, and mother briskly added, "But the shopping tempts, so I acquiesce. Lordy, last time I recklessly spent two thirds of the housekeeping money on a black handbag, a red ribbon hat and a pair of long gloves."

*Must've been expensive if only three things cost that much!* I exclaimed, cutting my food into tiny pieces while they carried on as usual.

Father then glanced over at me, commenting, "We'll be leaving earlier today." And I was a little confused when he said '**we**', but he must have sensed my confusion as he explained, "Now you're no longer middle-management, you may carpool with me."

"Oh!" I gasped, shocked, "Thank you, father."

"Now hurry up." He added, pointing to my breakfast with his knife, "We'll be leaving shortly."

I had managed to hide the majority of my breakfast underneath the slices of toast, silently relieved father hadn't noticed. Once we had said goodbye to mother and were given our lunchboxes, father quickly ushered me towards his blue Austin Cambridge.

"Come on! Come on!" He urged, "We can't be late for your appointment with Doctor Solace." And my heart plummeted as soon as he said that name.

*What!* I gawked, shocked. *No! This can't be happening!*

"He has agreed to meet us at work." Father carried on once we were in the car; he was just about to reverse off the driveway but paused to better look at me, earnestly adding, "I love you, Nathaniel, and I don't want anything happen to you. But don't put me in a position where I have to choose between your life and my life." And there was something to his voice that instantly filled me with fear.

*What... What does he mean?...*

Neither of us spoke another word by time we arrived at work; frantic thoughts plagued my mind, fearful of what awaited me.

"Come on, Nathaniel!" Father urged, shunting me through into the lit, empty reception, "We don't want to be late for your appointment with Doctor Solace!" Again, just that name alone made my heart plummet.

*What's going to happen?!*

"Come on!" Father fumed when I didn't move, grabbing my arm and dragging me towards the nurse's office; his fingers dug into my skin, making me wince.

"Ow!" I growled, trying to tug my arm free but he was fairly strong, "**OW!**"

"Quit your whining!" He scolded, reaching for the handle but a plummy male voice stilled him, "Good! You're early!" And we glanced over our shoulders, spotting Mr Sheridan storm towards us with a wad of papers in his grasp; he was clad in his iconic sharp grey suit.

"Did you finish processing these yesterday?!" Mr Sheridan demanded with a dazzling smile; I didn't know who he was talking to until he thrust the papers into my chest, an oof escaping me.

"Now isn't the time, Isaiah." Father spoke while I hastily gathered the papers, and Mr Sheridan's cold, grey eyes snapped to him as he spat, "And why's that, Jeremiah?!"

"Nathaniel has an appointment with Doctor Solace." Father explained matter-of-factly, making Mr Sheridan gasp in in disgust, "On company time?! I don't think so! You can rearrange the appointment in your own time, not mine!" And I couldn't stop my jaw from dropping.

*He **didn't** just talk to an executive like that!*

"But I'm trying to fix **this**!" Father angrily retorted, gesturing at me with a sharp wave of his hand; he then pointed an index finger at his beaming lips, making me realise I wasn't smiling.

*Damn it!* I vented, forcing a grin. *I need to focus!*

"That's not my problem." Mr Sheridan countered, his gunmetal grey eyes shifting to me as he ordered, "In your office, **now**!" And I shot father a sheepish glance before following Mr Sheridan upstairs.

As soon as we set foot inside my office, Mr Sheridan demanded, "Why are they incorrect?!" And he pointed an incriminating finger at the papers in my sweaty grasp.

*Incorrect?!* I gaped. *No, they can't be! I've never made a mistake before!*

"Are you sure they're incorrect?" I responded, making him growl, "Don't patronise me, Mr West! Just take a look for yourself!"

Nodding, I glimpsed at the first order in the pile, skimming over it only to realise he was right. *I... I can't believe I inputted the wrong item!* I then glanced at the rest. *They can't all be wrong, can they?*

Peering at Mr Sheridan, I hesitantly wondered, "Are... Are they all wrong?" Which clearly irritated him.

"I've just told you to look for yourself!" He retorted bitingly, his tone dripping with sarcasm when he added, "Or shall I just amend them for you?!"

"No, no, no, Sir!" I hastily blabbered, shaking my hands negatively and causing the orders to flutter, "I-I-I just thought I'd ask!"

"**All** of them need to be amended and processed by twelve o'clock!" He furiously declared, now coming to stand so close we were sharing the same air, "You have just over three hours. I'd get started if I were you."

*\*\*\**

*Thank God I finished them in time!* I breathed, glancing at the clock hanging above Mr Sheridan's office as I advanced towards it, noting it was 11:36AM. Firmly grasping the wad of orders with both hands, I confirmed. *I've checked and double checked and triple checked, these are all faultless-* **BANG!** Mr Sheridan's office door swung open into me when Miss Jones walked out, causing the orders to burst out of my hands like a flock of doves. Then I clocked a cup slip from her grasp, hitting the floor with a smash; tea flowed everywhere. *No, no, no!* I panicked when the orders fluttered down. I tried to snatch them out of thin air but wasn't quick enough; they landed in the puddle of tea, soaking it up. *They're ruined! All ruined!* I exclaimed in dismay, scooping them up where tea dripped with an audible pitter-patter.

"You should really watch where you're going, Mr West!" Miss Jones abruptly scolded with a dazzling smile, taking me aback where I just stared at her in disbelief.
"And look what you've done!" She heatedly carried on, gesturing to her red and white polka dot dress that was stained with specks of tea, "You've ruined my nice, new dress!"
Shaking my head in annoyance, I snapped, "I don't have time for this!" And I turned for my office.

*I've got to try and fix these orders before twelve!*

"Where do you think you're going?!" Miss Jones barked, pulling me to a halt when she clasped a firm hand on my left shoulder, "How are you going to resolve this?!" She spoke to me as if I were a child, gesturing to her attire with a sharp wave of her hand, "You've ruined my dress!" And I couldn't take it anymore, something deep within just switched and I exploded, "AND YOU RUINED MY GODDAMN ORDERS!"

Gasps of shock erupted throughout the room followed by whispers of '**What did he just say?**'. Glancing around, I noticed everyone was staring at me; even the executives had opened their doors with a squeak, poking their heads out to see what the commotion was about. *Why... Why are they all looking at me?* ... Then I heard the rap of shoes before Mr Sheridan came to stand in his office doorway; a triumphant look blazed behind his gunmetal grey eyes.

"Inside, now." He instructed, and I quietly followed, closing the door behind me.

"Well, well, well!" Mr Sheridan purred in delight as he sat down behind his desk, a Cheshire-like grin growing on his face, "I've been waiting, and waiting, and waiting for you to eventually slip up."

*Slip up?* I repeated, confused. *What the hell's he on about?*

"Erm..." I murmured, bringing a hand up to touch my brow, "Wuh-What... What do you mean, Sir?"

"'**What do you mean**'?!" He hawked, clearly shocked, "You spoke profanely, Mr West!" Then his eyes unnervingly lingered on my mouth, "Not only that, but you're also not smiling!"

*I'm not?!* I gaped as a malicious smirk spread across his face; I instinctively lowered my hand, feeling my lips tremble in fear.

"I suggest you sit down, Mr West." Mr Sheridan urged, entwining his fingers, "You're going to be here awhile." And I couldn't help but gulp.

*What's going to happen to me?!* I nervously exclaimed, trying to still my shaky legs once I sat down, placing the sodden orders on the floor.

"Now," Mr Sheridan carried on, resting his hands on his desk where he slightly inclined forward, "Where are they?"
Shooting him an incredulous glance, I asked, "Where are who, Sir?" And he banged a fist down onto the desk; I couldn't help but recoil as he snapped, "Do **not** take me for a fool, Mr West, I know you're working for the guild! Now, I'll ask one last time, where are they?"

**THUD!** The office door unexpectedly swung open; I gazed over my shoulder and was relieved to see father stood in the doorway, as if he were my knight in shining armour.
His dark blue eyes landed on me before circling over to Mr Sheridan, demanding, "What's going on?!" And he placed a consoling hand on my shoulder when he took a further step inside.
Mr Sheridan's cold, grey eyes lingered on father's hand for a heartbeat before he urged with a twisted grin, "Why don't you ask your son? Or better yet, why don't you ask **everyone else**?"

Slowly, father's hand dropped from my shoulder like deadweight as he probed, "What did he do?" And Mr Sheridan stated matter-of-factly, "Your son spoke profanely, Jeremiah. You know what that means." There was no denying the delight lacing his voice.

"It doesn't matter whether he spoke profanely or not, Isaiah." Father retorted with a slight growl, his smile never lessening, "There will still need to be an investigation!"
*Investigation?* I repeated, clasping my shaky hands, trying to still them. *An investigation into what?*

"That shan't take long." Mr Sheridan commented with a bloodcurdling smirk, "A day at the most. It's just a shame he's been found guilty of such a diminutive crime, unlike that pill we found in Mr Miller's office." His gunmetal grey eyes then shifted to me while he said to father, "I swear it was similar to the one your son was given by that nurse." And when he shot me with a wicked grin, I knew he knew it was mine.

"Until then he will be detained where I see fit!" Father demanded before his dark blue eyes shifted to me, "Go home,

Nathaniel. Go home and stay home."
I didn't need to be told twice and nor was I going to argue with him, I merely nodded before rising to my feet.
"Remember!" He added, pointing to his beaming lips, "Keep smiling!" And I shot him a dazzling grin before leaving.

As soon as the door closed behind me, it felt as if the weight of the world was on my shoulders. *I can't believe this is happening!* I fretted, aware of the sweat now lining my brow. Jamming my clammy hands into my armpits, I made a tremulous dash for my office. *What's going to happen when it's confirmed I spoke profanely?!* Pulling back the plush leather chair, I went to grab my briefcase but stopped mid-reach, my eyes clocking the large black folder. *No, I should just go home!* I insisted but knew this was my last chance to get answers.

Without thinking twice, I swiftly shoved the folder inside my briefcase.

***

*I hope Gloria's in!* I prayed when I reached the top of Amicable Street, swiftly fastening the badge to my blazer before making a beeline for her house. *Come on!* I desperately banged on the door. **Come on-** *What was that?!* I nervously glanced over my shoulder when I thought I heard the clip clop of shoes, but there was no one around. *Stop it!* I scolded, snapping my eyes back on the door. *No one's watching me and no one's following me!*

Just as I was about to bang on the door again, I heard the distinct sound of heels on the other side. *Thank God she's in!* I breathed, letting out a huge breath as Gloria opened the door, shock gracing her beaming, made-up face.
"Nate?!" She queried in disbelief, jerking her head back, "What are you doing here? Shouldn't you be at work?"
"Can... Can I come in?" I asked, itching to get out of the open.
"Erm..." She murmured, twisting a strand of dark brown hair that was down in waves, "Suh... Sure..." She hesitated, her smile threatening to crack as she stepped aside, allowing me access.

"Can I get you a drink?" Gloria wondered, closing the door as I turned to face her; I barely registered the lowcut front on her dark green dress that had three-quarter length sleeves. Shaking my head, I replied, "I'm alright, but thank you."

"Are you sure? Because I was about to get myself a glass of water." She persisted, carrying on when I shook my head once more, "Suit yourself." And she wandered off in the direction of the kitchen; I followed like a lost puppy when I deposited my briefcase by the front door.

"Why are you here?" Gloria questioned, getting straight to business while grabbing a glass out of the cupboard, "I thought you were promoted? So why aren't you learning the ropes?" And she briskly added before I could reply, "Speaking of your new role, do you have access to all the products?"

I couldn't help but furrow my brow. *What a random thing to ask...* I found it strange; of everything she could ask, she wanted to know that.

"Ermm..." I uttered, running a hand round the back of my neck, "Yeah, but-"

"So you'd be able to take any product?" Gloria interrupted, turning for the sink.

*What's she after?...* I suspiciously pondered.

"Yeah, I guess." I responded dryly, watching as she filled the glass with water, "**Why?**"

Setting the glass down, Gloria was silent for a moment before retrieving a piece of paper from inside her bra, shocking me. *What the-*

"The guild will require you to obtain these as hard evidence you're not working against us." She explained, handing me the paper where I peered down at it.

Fertquiliser
Reme-Tea
Dental Dose
Delirium

*Delirium? What the hell is Delirium?* But then I realised what she had said.

"Hang on!" I blurted, fisting the note, "Why do I need to provide hard evidence?! I wouldn't even be in this predicament if it weren't for you-"

"It's because of who you are!" Gloria swiftly interrupted, and I hawked in annoyance, "Because of who I am?! What does that even me-"

*Ohhh...* But then it dawned on me. *It's because father's a Watcher...* And I glimpsed down at the note. *They want to make sure I'm loyal to them and not reporting back to him...*

Shifting my attention to Gloria, I stated, "Look, I can't get these for you."

"Why not?" She pried, picking up the glass and bringing it to her lips.

I knew there was no easy way to explain this, so I ripped off the Band-Aid and bluntly replied, "Because I spoke profanely at work."

**SMASH!** The glass slipped from her hand, scattering across the floor like shrapnel.

"**YOU DID WHAT?!**" Gloria hawked when she rounded on me, her face reddening by the second, "What the hell is wrong with you?! Do you know how much shit you're in?! **URGH!**" And she stormed past before I had the chance to respond.

"Gloria, wait!" I insisted, hurriedly following her into the living-room where she picked up the telephone.

*Wait, what is she doing?!* I panicked; my mouth now so dry I yearned for that glass of water.

"What are you doing?!" I anxiously demanded, "Who are you calling?!" And I tried to snatch the phone out of her grasp, but she was surprisingly strong and shunted me back.

"Don't!" Gloria exclaimed, but I wasn't backing down.

Lunging for the phone once more, there was a bit of tug-o-war before she snapped, "I'm trying to help you!" And I couldn't help but stare at her with wide, disbelieving eyes for a heartbeat. *She... She is?...*

Slowly, I released the phone where Gloria pressed it to her ear, dialling. *Can I really trust her?* I couldn't help but wonder, clutching at the cuff of my blazer.

"It's me." She spoke to whoever was on the other end, "I need you to do me a massive favour." There was a moment of silence before she growled in frustration, "Now isn't the time for jokes! I need you to hack into C.S's mainframe and gain access to their cameras."

*Hang on, what?!* I gawked, shocked. *Who's she talking to?!*

"I need you to access all of the cameras between 8AM and now-ish. Replace them with old footage or make it look like a connection was lost."

Then it dawned on me what she was doing. *She's trying to hide the incident! Make it seem like it never happened! But how? Who does she know that can do that?*

"Perfect!" Gloria exclaimed in delight, shooting me a reassuring glance, "You're the best, Wes!" And I couldn't help but wonder who Wes was.

*She's never mentioned them before... Are they part of the guild?*

"I'll speak to you later." She gleamed, now grasping the phone with both hands, "I owe you big time!" And then she hung up, leaving me staring at her in both amazement and uncertainty.

*Did she really get it resolved just like that?*

When Gloria faced me, I automatically blurted, "Who was that?" And she waved a dismissive hand, replying, "Oh, just an old friend."

*An old friend?* I pondered, narrowing my eyes.

"And is this '**old friend**' part of the guild?" I pried, and Gloria nodded, "Yes, they're one of the council members."

*Council?!* I gasped, shooting her an incredulous glance. *How big is this guild?!* I had only envisioned a handful of people.

"Without being rude, you should probably leave." Gloria reluctantly piped up, her green eyes momentarily turning downcast, "There's nothing more I can do for you now. If anyone followed you here after what happened, I'm running the risk of exposing the guild."

"Wait, so all of this has been for nothing?" I queried, desperately carrying on when Gloria nodded, "Even if I can provide evidence, you can't help me?"

"You said it yourself, Nate." Gloria dejectedly said, "You can't get the products for us."

"But what if I could give you that folder?" I countered, her eyes widening in curiosity.

When Gloria opened her mouth, I held up my index finger for her to wait before dashing into the hallway, snatching up my briefcase.

"I hope this is enough hard evidence for your guild." I commented as I sat down on the sofa, pulling the briefcase up onto my lap where it opened with a click; a gasp escaped her when I retrieved the large clientele folder.

"You... You brought it?!" Gloria gaped, sitting down beside me where I handed it to her, "I didn't think you'd actually bring it!"

"Well, I did." I replied, watching as she urgently flicked through, reading over a contract for someone called Mahesh Joshi from India.

"So is this proof enough that I'm not working against you?"

Reluctantly tearing her gaze away, Gloria murmured, "I... I hope so, I really do hope so, but I don't know if it's too late now because of what's happened." And just that comment alone reminded me of the investigation.

*What's going to happen to me?*

"I should probably go." I said, rising to my feet with my briefcase in hand, "I'm already in enough trouble as it is; I can't risk father finding out I haven't gone home."

Setting the folder aside, Gloria followed me into the hallway where she stared anxiously up at me, "I hope this isn't the last time I see you." And my heart lurched when her comment sunk in.

*What if this is the last time?* I deliberated, my eyes shifting from hers down to her ruby red lips. *I never got the chance to know her...*

Shaking off my melancholy, I forced a smile and replied upbeat, "Don't worry, this won't be the last time." But even I could hear the uncertainty lacing my voice.

Opening the door, Gloria grasped it with one hand, smiling weakly, "Goodbye, Nate." It sounded so mournful, as if she were bidding farewell to a dying relative.

Swallowing a lump lodged in my throat, I croaked, "Guh-Goodbye, Gloria." And she slowly closed the door before I reluctantly turned on my heels, heading home.

*What's going to happen to me after the investigation?* I fretted. So many questions plagued my mind, I almost forgot to take the badge off when I was outside my front door; my body must have gone into autopilot.

Once I removed it, I unlocked the door and stepped inside, hollering, "I'm home!" But there was no reply, confusing me.

*Where's mother and Carmen?* I then searched the house but they weren't home. *I guess they've gone out to do some shopping.*

I kept myself busy the rest of the afternoon by sorting through my wardrobe, discarding any clothes that no longer fitted on the bed. *Now what?* I mulled once I had finished, turning to neatly fold the clothes only to jump back in fright when I saw father stood in the doorway. *What's he doing home so early?* I mulled, glimpsing at the clock on my nightstand that read 15:47PM.

"Nathaniel." Father spoke as he took a step inside, closing the door behind him, "We need to talk." And I instantly felt my entire body freeze, dread consuming me; I clutched at my tie that hung loosely around my neck.

"As you're aware," He began, now coming to stand at the end of my bed, "There was an investigation as soon as you left, which was meant to be concluded today."

*'Meant to be'?...* I repeated, narrowing my eyes questioningly. *Does that mean the investigation is still ongoing?*

"But why?" I spoke up, tilting my head to one side.

"All the footage on the CCTV cameras came up negative." Father explained before inhaling a deep breath, as if to calm himself.

*But surely that's a good thing?* I deliberated, trying to stop a triumphant smirk from gracing my lips. *Thank you, Gloria!*

Choosing to act dumb, I probed, "What do you mean '**negative**'?"

And father stated, "There was no footage, no evidence to prove you committed a very serious offence." His brow then wrinkled with worry.

"But surely that's a good thing?" I voiced my thoughts out loud, and father instantly shook his head, "Not when there's plenty of witness statements against you, Nathaniel."

He then ran a jerky hand through his coiffed, brown locks before continuing, "For now, the investigation has purely been extended."

*Extended?* I mulled, now anxiously wringing my hands. *For how long?*

"Then now what?" I queried as father emitted a heavy breath, replying downbeat, "Nothing." Taking me aback.

"Nothing?!" I gawked, insisting, "Surely there's something we can do?" And there was no denying the look of irritation that crept upon his gleaming face.

"What do you think I've been trying to do?!" He barked, his smile faltering, "I've tried steering you back onto the safest path **countless** times!" He then regained himself before adding, "I've got one last trick up my sleeve, as long as everything goes according to plan when we arrive at work tomorrow."

*Hang on, 'we'?!* I gaped with a questioning raise of my right eyebrow. *I thought I was being detained here until after the investigation?!*

"Wait!" I intervened when father opened his mouth to speak, which clearly irked him judging by the pinched expression upon his face, "What did you mean when you said, **'When we arrive at work tomorrow.'**?"

"I need to keep a close eye on you until a decision has been made." He responded in a sorrowful tone while folding his arms across his chest.

*I... I guess that makes sense...*

"Anyway," Father sighed, turning for the door, "I've got to get my affairs in order. Do as you wish for the rest of the day, but you are **not** to leave the house."

*Do as I wish?* I echoed, baffled. *Is he serious?*

"What do you mean?!" I called after him when he stepped out onto the landing; he then turned to better face me, scrubbing a hand across his jaw.

"How else am I supposed to word it?" He rhetorically asked, "Do whatever you want. Stay up here until tomorrow morning for all I care." And I couldn't help but shoot him an incredulous glance.

"But what about dinner?" I countered, and father retorted, "What's the point if you're not going to eat it? I don't have the energy to argue with you when this will be our last night as a family."

*Wait, what?!* I opened my mouth to question him but didn't get the chance as he swiftly left, leaving me gaping after him. *What did he mean when he said '**This will be our last night as a family.**'?*

# Chapter Twelve
## A Watcher were murdered

**DING, DING, DING!** The metal hammer on my alarm clock ruthlessly knocked between the two bells; I was already wide awake, dreading today. *What's going to happen after the investigation?* I fretted, feeling my stomach roll. *And what's going to happen to me?...* I quietly added, now reaching over to turn the alarm off with a trembling hand. Inhaling a deep breath, I reluctantly got up and pulled back the curtains, squinting against the morning sun.

Once I had grabbed my grey suit and wingtip shoes, I made my way into the bathroom, closing the door behind me before depositing my clothes. *Do I still need to keep smiling?* I mulled, peering over at the camera above the bathtub with a forced grin. *I probably should, just in case...* I then swiftly got dressed before diverting my attention upon the medicine cabinet, clocking my reflection. *Well... That still looks awful...* I uttered, taking a step closer to inspect my eye; it was still bloodshot but the bruising had gone.

When I had finished my morning routine, I gave myself one last despairing glance before stepping out onto the landing; the sweet smell of bacon smacked me in the face. *God, that smells so good!* I moaned, heading downstairs where I spotted a black suit with a gold tie hanging up by the front door. Ignoring it, I wandered through into the kitchen.

Mother was stood by the hob, her cream, lacy dress complimenting her dark brown hair that was up in a beehive.

The ding of cutlery then distracted me; I glanced over to see Carmen setting the breakfast table.
Taking a further step inside, I forcefully smirked, "Good morning, mother. Good morning, Carmen."
In unison, they spun round to face me, smiling broadly, "Good morning, Nathaniel." Before turning back and continuing what they were doing.

*Will father expect me to eat this morning?* I deliberated while advancing on the breakfast table, pulling up a chair just as Carmen finished setting it. Her green eyes then momentarily met mine, a smile growing on her face that had very little make-up before she turned to help mother, causing her pink skirt to fan; a white bow that matched her blouse held her curly ponytail in place.

"Where's your father?" Mother queried with a radiant smile gracing her made-up face, hollering, "Jeremiah?!" She then grabbed a plate and set it down at father's spot.

"Coming, sweetheart!" Father called from the living-room, his shoes suddenly rapping against the dining room floor before he appeared with a newspaper tucked under his arm; he wore the same beige suit.
"Smells delicious, sweetheart." He gleamed before sitting down, his dark blue eyes staring eagerly at his food.

Once mother and Carmen sat down, father brought a forkful of food to his lips. *I still don't understand how he can eat and not be affected.* His eyes then rolled into the back of his head in delight. *Does he take something to stop it affecting him?* A pleasing groan escaped him once he took a bite. *And how does he manage to keep smiling all the time?*
"And it tastes just as good as it looks!" He happily proclaimed, dabbing a napkin either side of his thin, beaming lips before tucking it into his pale blue shirt.

Mother and Carmen then tucked in; I looked to father for guidance but he merely flicked his eyes skyward in apparent annoyance. *I guess he's given up...* I uttered, dejected, as they carried on with their usual routine.

\*\*\*

"Remember," Father began with a radiant smile as soon as we pulled into the car park, "Just stay in your office. I don't want you talking to anyone." He then reached into the back to grab his briefcase, accidentally knocking the black suit hanging up.
*Do I get on with work or just sit there?* I deliberated as we ambled round to the reception.

Just before father opened the door, he turned to me and said in a morose undertone, "Nathaniel, I promise to try my utmost to protect you but, **please**, don't make me regret this decision." And I couldn't ignore the sadness shimmering behind his dark blue eyes, not matching his beaming lips.
*Decision? What decision?* I wondered as he gave my shoulder a gentle squeeze.

We then headed inside where I saw Miss Jones sat behind her desk, she was smoothing out the creases on her pale blue dress.
Her ice blue eyes then locked onto father when the door closed with a gentle bang, her smile growing as she greeted, "Good morning, Mr West!" She then tucked a strand of startling blonde hair behind her ear, which had fallen from the sleek bun.

"Good morning, Mr West!" Miss Jones gleamed when her eyes shifted to me, but there was no denying the loathing that simmered in her icy cold depths.
*I guess she's still upset about her dress...* I pondered.

"Good morning, Miss Jones!" Father and I replied in unison before venturing upstairs.

Once we reached the top, father grasped my shoulders, halting me in my tracks. *What's he doing?!* I panicked, suddenly aware of my feet precariously tittering on the edge of the step.

"Now I need you to listen carefully." He began, "There will be a meeting this morning, which you are **not** to attend." He then gestured with a nod towards the main office area before resuming, "Everyone will be gathered up here, so you'll need to wait downstairs in the kitchen until I come for you."

*A meeting?* I inquisitively deliberated. *A meeting for what?*

Father must have sensed my curiosity as he commented with narrowed eyes, "You're probably wondering why, aren't you?" And he didn't give me the chance to respond before carrying on, "As you're aware, the investigation is ongoing, so the government are coming in to interview everyone."

Just the mention of the government had me stiffen, my stomach turning rock hard. *Oh God, what's going to happen to me?!*

Father then released my shoulders, "I'll come and escort you downstairs in two hours." He then opened the door as I asked, "What am I-" But he disappeared inside, leaving me staring after him until the door slammed shut in my face.

*But what am I going to do in the meantime? Do I just sit there or get on with stuff?*

My eyes momentarily turned downcast before I apprehensively headed inside. A few people were already busy working, so I lowered my head and hurriedly advanced on my office, not wanting to make eye contact after what had happened yesterday. *What do they think of me now? That I'm some kind of criminal?* I couldn't open my door quick enough, relieved to be away from prying- *What the hell's he doing in here?!* I hawked, spotting Mr Sheridan rummage through my desk drawers; he was clad in his iconic sharp grey suit.

As soon as I closed the door, I blurted, "What are you doing?!" And Mr Sheridan's head shot up, his gunmetal grey eyes wide like a deer caught in the headlights.

A realisation then graced his face before he retorted with a smug smirk, "I could ask you the same question."

Mr Sheridan then straightened to his full height before explaining, "I was looking for a specific folder."

Tipping my head, I queried, "Folder? What folder?" And he responded a little snappily, "A very important folder, Mr West, you wouldn't understand!" But then he watched with great interest when I rested my briefcase on the desk.

"Do you mind?" He questioned, gesturing to my bag with a wave

of his hand; it then dawned on me what folder he was after.
*The clientele folder!* I was just relieved he couldn't pin the blame on me as I had given it to Gloria.

Shooting Mr Sheridan a triumphant grin, I replied, "Of course not, Sir." And I eagerly opened the bag, turning it to better face him.

He hastily rummaged inside, not caring about the scrunched-up paperwork he left in his awake; my metal lunchbox tossed aside on the desk with a ding. Once he had emptied it, he grunted in disapproval, shoving the briefcase towards me once he was done.

"Well," Mr Sheridan began in detest, "If you happen upon any folders, be sure to let me know." And, without another word, he left, slamming the door behind him and causing the photo frames to rattle.

*Thank God he's gone!* I breathed, slumping against the desk in relief. But then the quietness dawned on me, and I knew the next couple of hours would drag.

***

*Any minute now...* I worried, biting my lip as I glanced at the clock hanging above my office door which read 10:04AM. *Why isn't he here yet?* I fretted further, standing up only to abruptly sit back down again on the plush leather chair, knowing it was out of character for father to be late. *What's going to happen to me once the government have come to a decision?!* I panicked, pinching the skin at my throat before standing up once more, pacing the full length of the room. *Will I be shipped off to the sanatorium? Or-* And I gulped. *Or will they kill me?*

**BANG, BANG, BANG!** Knocking at the door made me jump; I tumbled backwards into the window that overlooked the factory, causing the blinds to rattle against the glass.

"Nathaniel?" The recognisable voice of father called, instilling me with fear, "Are you in there?"

Unable to speak, I just stared at the door.

"Nathaniel?" Father spoke up once more, so I hastily cleared my throat and croaked, "Yuh-Yes, come in!" And the door opened with a groan.

Slowly, father poked his head inside, a smile on his lips that didn't match the anguish glistening behind his dark blue eyes.

"It's time." He said morosely, his words chilling me to my very core.

*Oh God, it's actually happening!* My heart thudded violently against my chest while I struggled to maintain my smile. Father then gestured with a nod for me to follow, and I reluctantly obeyed. As soon as I took a shaky step into the main office, I felt everyone's eyes snap to me; their accusing gazes contradicting their radiant faces. *I dread to think what they're going to say about me!* I worried while descending the stairs, the echo of mine and father's footsteps imitating my racing heart.

Once we reached the bottom, father opened the door and I wasn't surprised to see the reception dead, so quiet I could hear a pin drop. *Where's Miss Jones?* I wondered, spotting a closed sign had been put in the entrance door, making me realise how real this situation had become. *All because I spoke profanely...*

"Come on." Father spoke as he advanced towards the kitchen, distracting me; I quietly followed where he closed the door behind me.

"Take a seat." He urged with a sweep of his hand, waiting for me to sit before continuing, "I'll be back once the government have gone."

Clutching at the cuff of my blazer, I stammered, "O-Okay..."

Father then gave my shoulder a gentle squeeze before leaving, the bang of the kitchen door making me flinch.

After what felt like a lifetime of silence, I eventually uttered, "This is it... It's happening..." And I buried my head in my hands.

*Now it's just a waiting game...* I tried to pull myself together by scrubbing a hand through my hair. *God, what am I going to do with myself?!* I dreaded, now glancing around the kitchen only to notice- *What the?* C.S factory workers were filing past the window that was stationed above the kitchen sink, heading towards the high street. *What are they doing? Why are they leaving?* Then I heard voices in the reception, it sounded like Mr Sheridan greeting people.

Then it hit me. *Hang on, why does the government want to speak to the factory workers when they weren't there?!* A growl escaped my lips, my nails biting into my palms when I clenched them into fists. But I soon realised there was no point getting angry. *There's nothing I can do about any of this...* And I slumped in my chair, burying my head in my hands, feeling my hair slither in-between my fingers.

*I wonder if I'll get a chance to say goodbye to anyone.* I mulled, unable to imagine never speaking to mother or Carmen again. *What if this morning was the last time?* And I couldn't help but wince, now staring down at my empty hands as the severity of the situation came crashing over me like a tsunami. *Surely father would let me say goodbye to them.* I thought, hopeful, before doubt crept in. *Wouldn't he?* But I was quick to shake off my sorrow, remembering they weren't the only people I longed to say goodbye to. *I'd regret not seeing Gloria one last time.* And a heaviness formed in my chest at that notion.

*Maybe I will get the chance.* I mentally crossed my fingers before realising. *No one should have to go through all this. I don't even know if I'll get to see my family again, all because I'm no longer under the governments control.* Then an idea came to mind. *What if I could stop this from happening to someone else?* Pulling the note out of my pocket, I swiftly glanced down the list.
Fertquiliser
Reme-Tea
Dental Dose
Delirium

*No one's in the factory...* I mulled, slipping the note back into my pocket. *And I know all the orders are stored on the walkway, so it should be easy to grab what I need and leave.* A triumphant smirk now plagued my lips. *If this will help the guild stop the government, then it'll be worth it!* Without thinking twice, I abruptly advanced on the kitchen door, unable to hear anyone on the other side so I opened it a crack. To my relief, the reception was empty. *Thank God!* I breathed, quietly closing the door behind me before skulking towards the exit.

The high street was dead and the speakers were silent, filling me with an unease I just couldn't shake. *I better hurry up.* I instructed, turning right out the door and then right again down the alley alongside the building, my shoes rapping against the ground. Further down on my right was the factory's thickset, metal door; it opened with a groan, the metal shrieking against the concrete ground and making me tense. *I hope no one heard that!* I prayed, peering inside the brick-built building that was twice the height of the office block only to sigh in relief. *Thank God no one's here!* And I took a step inside.

Once I carefully closed the door, I headed right towards the stairs that led up to the metal, wireframed walkway, bypassing about a dozen wooden work benches on my left as well as two large generators; another two were mirrored on the other side. My shoes dinged against the steps when I took them two at a time, my hand grazing along the ice-cold rail.

Once I reached the top, I froze when I saw the executives' office windows. *I forgot they can see in here!* I panicked, staring at the window directly in front of me that wasn't shuttered, now recognising it was my office. Peering further down at the others, I sighed when I realised all the blinds had been pulled. *Thank God!* It was then I spotted all the client orders neatly packaged up against the far wall to my left.

*Just grab what I need and go.* I instructed, now coming to stand on the walkway with the windows to my right, the orders directly ahead like a light at the end of the tunnel. Gripping the handrail on my left, I tried to ignore the imposing drop while quickly but carefully advancing on the packages. *Don't look down. Don't look down.* I chanted but couldn't help it, I briefly glanced over only to see the hatch that belonged to a large, bright blue impact crusher; a small, wooden platform with control panels was attached to it. *Don't look down!* I commanded, circling my attention back upon the orders drawing ever closer.

As soon as I came to a halt in front of the packages, I pulled out the list, refreshing my memory. Pocketing the note, I gazed back down at the orders. *Where to start...* I mulled, grabbing a small box that was on top, carefully opening it and pulling out the invoice. *Cigarettes, no. Coffee, no. Selection of tinned foods, no. Ugh...* And I shoved the invoice back inside before grabbing box after box, scanning the invoices for the products.

By the time I had filtered through the smaller boxes, I had only managed to find the teabags and toothpaste, which I had stuffed inside my blazer. *Urgh! This was meant to be easy!* Frustrated, I snatched the largest box and ripped it open. Scanning the invoice, I was shocked to see it contained Delirium. *Finally!* Then I saw underneath in red writing was '**WARNING! DELIRIUM IS A HAZARDOUS POWDER! USE ONLY AS A SUPPLEMENT!**'. *Hazardous? Why is it hazardous?*

Setting the invoice down, I began sifting through the products. *I have no idea what I'm looking for...* I murmured, pulling out products I didn't recognise until I found a little white pot with Delirium written on the lid. *This is it!* I gasped, stuffing it inside my blazer before hurriedly repackaging the box. *I can't believe I found it!* And a delighted smile graced my lips just before I heard the ding of footsteps ascend the metal stairs.

"Nathaniel?" The voice of father made me freeze, a cold dread now consuming me.

*What's he doing here?!* I panicked, now peering over the handrail where I noticed he was nearly at the top. *How long has he been looking for me?!*

Once father reached the walkway, he glanced at the open packages; a look of disbelief graced his radiant face as he asked with a wavering smile, "Why aren't you waiting in the kitchen?" And his attention circled over to me.

*Oh God, what do I do?!* I fretted, repeatedly rubbing my face. *What do I even say?!*

Before I had the chance to respond, father spoke through gritted teeth, "Don't make me have to ask again." And I wracked my brains for what felt like a lifetime, trying to figure out the best excuse; however, I soon realised I didn't want to keep lying to him.

Wringing my hands, I dropped my smile and anxiously stated, "Because it's wrong what the government are doing. **No one** should have to live in a society that is controlling people." When father didn't reply, I inhaled a steady breath and carried on, "If the People's Guild can stop the government from controlling everyone, then I'm going to help them."

Father still didn't say anything, he merely brought one hand up to cup his mouth, leaving only his horrified eyes on show. *Isn't he going to say something? Anything?*
"Father?" I urged when he lowered his hand only to fist it, now resting it against his mouth.
His dark blue eyes then stared off, looking anywhere but at me. *What's he thinking?* I then opened my mouth just as his hand dropped like a deadweight; his smile was gone, replaced with a frown. *Gaaah!* I gasped, taking a step back only to stagger into the boxes. *He's not smiling!*

"Isaiah was right..." Father uttered, snapping me back to the conversation, "It's too late for you..." And I couldn't help but blink at him in confusion.
*What's too late for me?* I deliberated, feeling a tightening in my chest.
"What... What do you mean?" I questioned in uncertainty, "What's too late for me?"
Father's glazed eyes then locked onto mine, making me wonder. *Is he going to cry?*

"I tried **so** hard to steer you back onto the safest path." Father ruthfully began, "But Nurse Lane made matters worse when she prescribed you **that** drug." Something unexpectedly switched within his dark blue eyes, and he carried on with animosity lacing his voice, "And then everyone started to notice you, so I had to step in before you made matters worse!" He then angrily advanced on me, his shoes clipping against the metal walkway; I immediately shuffled back only to feel boxes against my legs.

"Not only did you disobey me at church!" Father bellowed, making me shrink beneath his protruding glare, "But you had the audacity to strut around with scruff on your face like a ruffian!"

My whole body quaked uncontrollably, my knuckles turning white as I gripped them into fists, stammering, "I-I-I'm suh-sorry!"

"And don't get me started on Mr Miller's interview!" Father furiously snapped, "I had to put my neck on the line because you couldn't- No, **wouldn't** sit down!"

"But I didn't get the chance!" I desperately pointed out, "You jumped to my defence before I could do anything!" And I jammed my hands into my armpits when father shot me a scornful look.

"You backchatted a manager in front of the executives!" Father heatedly retorted, his face reddening by the second, "And then you just stood there with a stupid look on your face! I had to draw the attention away from you before they noticed something was wrong!" He then came to a halt before me; I could feel the hatred he emanated.

Averting my gaze downcast, I stuttered, "I'm suh-sorry, father." And he must have believed me as his rage dissipated, replaced with remorse.

"And then..." Father croaked, "And then you realised I'm a Watcher..."

I immediately peered at him, noting his eyes shimmered with anguish; his neck corded as he clenched his jaw.

"I... I should've disposed of you." He continued, the word '**dispose**' instilling me with an indescribable fear, "But I couldn't because you're my son, so I decided to get you help instead."

*But I didn't think Watchers' killed people?!* I proclaimed just before Gloria's words came to mind. *'**Their job is to report nonconformists**'.'*

But it soon dawned on me what father had said, and I couldn't help but shoot him an incredulous look as I blurted, "Help? You mean with Doctor Solace?"

Again, Gloria's words infiltrated my mind. *'He oversees all the ruthless treats inpatients undergo.'.*

"You think sending me to someone who uses electroconvulsive therapy is '**help**'?!"

A scowl now graced father's face as he snapped, "Who told you that?!" And I replied without hesitation, "Nurse Lane. She told me all about Doctor Solace and his ruthless treatments on inpatients."

"Oh for crying out loud!" Father seethed while scrubbing a hand over his face, "She's telling you that because she's using you, Nathaniel!"

"Why would she use me?!" I countered, clenching my jaw in annoyance, and he bitingly retorted, "Because she knows you're **my** son, which makes you a valuable asset to nonconformists!"

I didn't get the chance to retaliate before father angrily continued his tirade, "I **explicitly** told you not to see or speak to that girl again, but you blatantly ignored me! And, in doing so, made a mockery out of me!"

"A mockery?!" I repeated in disbelief, "How did **I** make a mockery out of you?!" And my retort seemed to tip father over the edge; spittle built up in the corners of his mouth as he exploded, "BY PROVING TO THE GOVERNMENT THAT I, JEREMIAH WEST, CANNOT REFORM HIS OWN **FUCKING** SON!"

*I've never seen him this angry before!* I panicked, staggering backwards out of pure shock and fear, almost tumbling into the parcels.

Unexpectedly, father then rummaged inside his jacket pocket, his neck corded and his nostrils flared. When he pulled something out that looked like a black cigar case, I couldn't help but wonder. *What's that?* Then he slowly opened it, producing a- *Is that a needle?!* The hairs on the nape of my neck rose when he held the needle skyward, showcasing a pink liquid inside the syringe.

"Wuh-What's that?" I stuttered, swiping a hand across my now sweaty brow.

Father then hastily shoved the black case back inside his blazer, momentarily glaring at me before shifting his attention back upon the syringe.

"Wuh-What are yuh-you doing?!" I panicked when he gently squeezed it, causing some of the liquid to spurt out the tip.

"It's better I do this than them…" He quietly uttered, his rage long gone and replaced with an undeniable look of dread.

*Them?! Who's them?!* I fretted, pressing my back against the wall when he took a decisive step forward.

"I'm sorry, Nathaniel." Father apologised, his chin quivering while a deep, enrooted sorrow blazed behind his eyes, "But I have no choice. It's either this," And he gestured to the needle, "Or you'll be sentenced to die by fusillade."

Then the realisation of what was happening finally dawned on me. *He's… He's going to kill me! My own father's going to kill me!*

"Please!" I sobbed, struggling to stop my legs from quaking, "Don't do this!"

"I-I'm sorry, Nathaniel." Father stammered, unable to look at me, "Just remember I'll **always** love you." And, without warning, he lunged towards me, clutching me by the front of my shirt and choking me.

"Stuh-Stop!" I wheezed while he raised the needle with his free hand, a gasp escaping me when he drove it towards my neck. I hastily snatched his arm out of thin air, our bodies shaking from tension while I croaked, "Pluh-Please!"

Copious amounts of sweat now seeped through my suit.

"I-I'm suh-suh-sorry!" I desperately pleaded, but father ignored me and shunted me against the cold, brick wall.

The needle steadily drew closer; I was no match for him while he leered over me with all his body weight.

"Stuh-Stop!" I begged, but he continued to ignore me so I shoved the heel of my palm into his throat, making him stagger backwards while spluttering and wheezing.

Gasping in lungful's of air, I realised now was my

opportunity to escape while father was hunched over rubbing his throat. Darting past, I charged towards the stairwell, my shoes dinging against the metal walkway that matched my racing heart. *I can't believe he's trying to kill me!* I panicked, hearing the thud of footsteps gain on me. Glancing over my shoulder, I saw father rapidly approaching. *How fast is he?!* I gawked just before he snatched my elbow, dragging me to a staggering halt.

"Get off!" I cried, ramming father in the chest where he stumbled backwards, hitting the railing with an oof.
Everything then happened in slow motion; he lost his balance and tumbled backwards over the rail headfirst. I tried to grab his outstretched hand, but his fingers slipped through mine at the last second.

"**NOOOO!**" I cried, clutching onto the handrail as I peered over the edge, "**FATHER!**" But I recoiled when his legs hit the impact crusher with a bone crunching crack.
Another evident snapping noise shattered the atmosphere when he fell legs first into the hatch, all I could see now was his upper body slumped over the gaping entrance. *Oh no! No, no, no!*
"FATHER!" I wailed again, watching – waiting – for him to do something - say something - but he was motionless like a ragdoll.

"No, no, no!" I panicked, charging down the stairs, "Please be okay! Please be okay!" I prayed, now clambering up onto the wooden platform that was attached to the impact crusher.
"Father?!" I called, looking up at him and noticing he was as white as a ghost.
Then it dawned on me. *I... I've killed him!* A pain now lingered in the back of my throat, guilt consuming me as I tugged at the collar of my shirt.

*I never wanted to hurt him-* Movement suddenly caught my eye, I glanced at father again to see him stir.
"Father?!" I gasped, emitting a huge sigh of relief, "You're alive! Thank God you're alive!"

"Nah-Nathaniel?" He croaked, his dark blue eyes peering down at me in confusion.

"I'll get you out of there!" I vowed, leaning over the control panel that was in my way to grab his clammy hand. "Take my hand!" I urged, giving it a brisk shake, but father was clearly disorientated; it took him a moment to register what was going on before reaching down, a torturous cry erupting from him.

"What is it?! What's wrong?!" I panicked, aware father was paling by the second.

"Muh-My-My leg!" He groaned, struggling to string a sentence together, "I-I thuh-think it… It's bruh-broken!"
*Broken?!* I gaped, running a jerky hand through my hair at father's confession. *How am I going to get him out without causing him more pain?!* Another agonising scream dragged me out of my deliberations.

"I'll get you out, I promise." I affirmed, shunting my trepidation to the back of my mind, "You've just got to trust me, okay?" And father merely grunted in response, clearly trying to control his tremulous body.
Leaning over the control panel once more, I implored, "Take my hand!" And I gave it another firm shake, "You can do it!" I encouraged when he reached down, my fingertips narrowly missing his, "Almost there! Just a little more!" But his deafening scream had me tense; it echoed around the factory like a banshee beckoning Death.

"I-I-I cuh-can't!" Father panted, sweat now lining his pasty brow, so I insisted, "Yes, you can!" And I inclined forward even more, "Take my hand!"
He then inhaled a shaky breath before stretching down with a harrowing cry, finally managing to get a firm hold.
"Yes! That's it!" I beamed, "Now I'm just going to pull you out, okay?"
When father nodded, I summoned all of my energy, feeling him slowly slip free from the confines of the hatch.

"We're nearly there!" I exclaimed, ignoring his

insufferable cries, "Just hold on a bit longer!"

"NATHANIEL, STOP! JUST STOP!" Father howled, trying to release my hand but I wouldn't let him.

"We're nearly there!" I reiterated, "Just a little-" But my hand slipped free from his clammy one, and I accidentally fell onto the control panel with a thud; the impact crusher roared to life and father's heart-wrenching screams could be heard over the machine.

"**MAKE IT STOP! MAKE IT STOP!**" He shrieked, fighting against the crusher to no avail; he was slowly being dragged down the hatch, his nails audibly scraping against metal.

*I need to turn it off!* I panicked, staring down at the buttons but had no idea which one to press.

"WHICH ONE DO I PRESS?!" I frightfully demanded, looking to father for confirmation as he screaked, "**NATHANIEL! TURN IT OFF!**" Blood spurted from his lips, hitting my face.

"I'M TRYING! I'M TRYING!" I cried, scanning the buttons yet again before spotting a turnkey, but father's torturous cries abruptly stopped; I didn't get the chance to turn the machine off before blood erupted out of the hatch like a bomb detonating.

I watched in horror as gore hit the floor with a pitter-patter, staring between the bloodstained hatch and my grisly suit once it had stopped. *I... I killed him!* I gasped, my breaths bursting in and out. *I killed father!* **SPLAT!** The sound of father's minced remains slopping into the metal trough attached to the crusher caused vomit to shoot up into my throat. I tried to avert my gaze but the noise was too much; I couldn't stop the puke from gushing out of my mouth, hitting the wooden platform with a squelch.

Tears now streamed unchecked down my cheeks as I stared around at the carnage once more. *What have I done?!* I then peered down at my tremulous, blood specked hands and equally peppered suit; it was right then the stench of gore hit me like a wrecking ball, causing another rush of puke to burst out of my mouth and over the control panel.

*I've got to get out of here!* I panicked, staggering off the platform. I zigzagged over to the service door in the far, right-hand corner that led to the car park, now acutely aware of the blood on my hands, my suit feeling contaminated. *I need to get out of these!* I retched, itching to tear off my clothes. Shunting open the heavy metal door, I stumbled outside and breathed in some much-needed fresh air to no avail; the smell still lingered up my nose. *Don't be sick! Don't be sick!* I chanted when another wave of nausea crashed over me.

*I've got to go!* I sobbed when I had somewhat regained myself. *I've got to get as far away from here as possible!* Then my eyes landed on father's car and I charged towards it, stones skidding across the ground underfoot. I couldn't yank open the door quick enough only to realise when I sat down. *The keys! I haven't got the keys!* A despairing groan escaped me while I searched the glove box, the sun visor, even under the seats. *He must've had them on him!* And I sunk deeper into the seat as the weight of the world came bearing down on me.

*What am I going to do?!* Tears gushed down my face like a waterfall. *I can't stay here! And I certainty can't go home!* The only person I could turn to was- *Gloria! She'll know what to do!* Sniffing back my tears, I sat up straight only to spot father's black suit hanging in the rear-view mirror. *I... I could wear that.* I didn't want to but had no other choice; I changed inside the small car, discarding my bloody suit underneath the driver's seat once I had emptied the pockets.

I then quickly inspected my face in the mirror, wiping off the few specks of blood I could see before adjusting the gold tie. As I stared at my reflection, I couldn't help but think. *I... I look just like him...* I didn't know if it was the suit that made me think that or the guilt that consumed me, but I couldn't stop seeing similarities. *Snap out of it!* I scolded, quickly glancing out the window to make sure the coast was clear. *I can't think like that when I need to focus on getting out of here!*

To my relief the car park was empty, so I hastily got out only to notice how small the suit was; the sleeves came up past my wrists and the trouser legs showed off my white socks. *I look ridiculous!* I griped just as a blue Austin Cambridge pulled into the car park, making my heart lurch when I realised it was Mr Sheridan. *Oh no!* I panicked, spotting three other people in the car. *What do I do?! Do I look okay?!* And I glanced in the wingmirror, giving myself another once over as car doors slammed, making me flinch.

"Mr West?" The plummy voice of Mr Sheridan rattled my eardrums, and I turned around to see him gleaming at me in confusion.

Making sure I was smiling from ear to ear, I enthusiastically greeted, "Mr Sheridan! What a pleasant surprise!" And even I could hear the sarcasm lacing my voice.

*Please just go away!* I begged while his gunmetal grey eyes blatantly took me in. *What's he staring at?* I wondered, now acutely aware of the other people hovering behind him; I was shocked to see one of them was Miss Jones. *What's Miss Jones doing with Mr Sheridan and two executives?*

"Have you changed your suit, Mr West?" Mr Sheridan queried, distracting me.

"Huh?" I blurted, and then it sunk in what he had asked.

*Oh God, what do I say?!* I fretted, clutching at the cuff of my blazer. *I can't tell him I have; he'll want to know why!*

Clearing my throat, I repeated, "Have I changed my suit?" And I shook my head, pinching the skin at my throat, "Wuh-Why would I change suits, Sir?"

"I thought you were wearing a grey one earlier." He commented with a shrug, turning to leave.

*Thank God!*

"Anyway," Mr Sheridan annoyingly carried on, facing me once again, "I trust your father has discussed the outcome with you while everyone was on lunch?" And I impulsively blurted, "What?"

*Father was going to discuss the outcome with me?* I pondered, biting my bottom lip. *What was the outcome?*

"What do you mean '**What**'?!" Mr Sheridan snapped, his smile cracking slightly, "Did he talk to you or not?!"

*I can't tell him no! He'll get suspicious!*

"Yes, of course he did, Sir!" I lied, and he curiously wondered, "And what are your thoughts?"

*My thoughts?!* I repeated, rubbing an eyebrow. *What the hell do I say now?!*

I could see Mr Sheridan was slowly getting impatient, so I hastily replied, "Erm, I'm delighted, Sir!" And my response surprised him.

*Oh God, did I say the wrong thing?! Should I have been disappointed?!*

"Delighted?" He repeated in disbelief, his eyebrows shooting halfway up his forehead, "You're delighted?"

*I definitely said the wrong thing!*

I opened my mouth to correct myself, but Mr Sheridan shook his head, uttering, "Very well... Where is your father, anyway? I need to discuss his resignation with him."

*Wait, what?!* I gawked, blinking in confusion. *His resignation?! Why has he resigned?!*

Then I realised Mr Sheridan was waiting for a reply, so I said the first thing that came to mind, "Erm... I believe he left for lunch, Sir."

"Well, when you see him, tell him we need to talk." He commented, "In the meantime, clear out your desk."

He then turned to leave only to do a double-take, his brow furrowing as he stared at my face. *What's he looking at now?* I fretted, biting my bottom lip.

"You've got something on you." Mr Sheridan stated before, unexpectedly, reaching for my face, wiping something off with the pad of his thumb.

*What the hell is he doing?!* I gawked, pulling away from his lingering hand.

He inspected his thumb for a second before giving it a quick sniff, asking, "Is that blood?"

*Wait, what, blood?! I thought I got it all off!* And I brought the cuff of my sleeve up to my face, rubbing the spot Mr Sheridan had touched.

"Well?" He urged after a moment of silence, and I hastily shook my head, replying, "It's probably red ink, Sir."
He clearly wasn't convinced but merely said, "Very well."
He then turned to leave yet again, heading in the direction of the main entrance.
"Mr Campbell, Mr Patterson." I heard him pipe up, gesturing for them to follow with a nod of his head, "Get the workers back in the factory, we cannot waste any more time."
"Yes, Sir." They replied in unison, shocking me.
*Wait, why is Mr Sheridan telling the executives what to do?* And then it dawned on me what Mr Sheridan had said. *I better go! It'll only be a matter of time before they find father!*

Once they had disappeared, I darted towards the high street, hoping no one inside C.S spotted me speedily walk past. *I don't know what I'm going to do!* I panicked, fearful to glance over my shoulder in case someone was following me. *Mr Sheridan's going to know I killed father!* I fretted further, remembering how he had wiped the blood off my face. *And then he'll piece it all together! It'll only be a matter of time until the government come for me!*

***

**BANG, BANG, BANG!** I desperately knocked on Gloria's front door. **BANG, BANG, BANG!** Repeatedly glanced over my shoulder, fearful someone had followed me. *It's only a matter of time!* **BANG, BANG, BANG!** *Come on! Open up!* **BANG, BANG, BA-**
"I'm coming! I'm coming!" Gloria exclaimed as she ripped open the door, her beaming red lips cracking when she saw me.
"Nate?!" She gaped, a few strands of her loose, long brown hair falling, framing her face, "What are you doing here?!" And worry swiftly engulfed me, constricting my throat.
*What the hell do I say?!*

Running a jerky hand through my hair, I forced a laugh, "I told you you'd see me again!" But I presumed my comment didn't go down well when Gloria folded her arms across her chest with a huff.

I then noticed her lowcut black blouse, which was tucked into a pink rockabilly skirt, before glancing over my shoulder when I thought I heard footsteps; relieved nobody was there.

"Can... Can I come in?" I asked, peering back to Gloria; her smile was long gone, replaced with dread.

*Why's she looking at me like that?* I fretted before she snatched my arm, dragging me inside.

"Whoa! What are you doing?!" I gasped, spinning round to face her when she released me in the hallway.

*What was all that about?!*

As soon as she slammed the front door, Gloria rounded on me, snapping, "What the hell are you wearing?!" And I followed her gaze down to my suit, wondering while glancing back up, "What do you mean?"

Gesturing to my clothes with a wave of her hand, Gloria declared, "**That's** a Watcher's suit!" And I peered back down at the suit in question.

*It is? How does she know?* I opened my mouth to ask, but I suddenly remembered her comment from the other day. **'They have special suits they wear to their monthly meetings; they're black with gold ties.'**.

"If another Watcher were to see you wearing it," Gloria carried on, dragging me back to the conversation, "They'll know you're a nonconformist and report you to the government!" And I instantly jammed my hands into my armpits, my heart threatening to explode out of my chest.

*'Have you changed your suit, Mr West?'.* Mr Sheridan's words ploughed through my mind like a freight train.

"I need to know why you're here!" Gloria piped up, snapping me back to reality once more, "And why you're wearing that suit!"

*What do I tell her?!* I panicked, repeatedly rubbing my face while gazing anywhere but at her.

"I... I need your help." I anxiously began, constantly clearing my throat as my mouth felt dry.

"Help?" She repeated, "Why, what's happened?"

Lowering my gaze, I pulled at the collar of my shirt, croaking, "I-I... I duh-did something buh-bad..." And Gloria wondered, "Bad? What do you mean '**bad**'?" But my voice cracked whenever I tried to tell her; I found it hard to admit the truth that my father was dead.

Shifting from foot to foot, I said, "I-"

**RING, RING! RING, RING!** But the telephone unexpectedly rang, gaining both our attention.

"I better get that." Gloria commented with a sigh, disappearing into the living-room where her black T-bar's clipped against the floorboards, "Hello?"

I apprehensively followed, noting a frown on Gloria's face before she glanced over at me in confusion.

"Erm... He's here with me..." She trailed off, rubbing her chin in uncertainty, "Why?"

*Wait, who's she talking to?* I deliberated, incredulously staring at her. *Why are they talking about me?*

"Who are you talking to?" I couldn't help but ask just as Gloria gasped, "What do you mean there's an emergency at C.S?!" And the hairs on the nape of my neck instantly lifted and a cold sweat consumed me; I knew exactly what the emergency was.

*What's going to happen to me?!* I fretted, a thickness forming in my throat. *I didn't mean to kill him!* A vivid stench of blood then suddenly wafted up my nose, it took everything I had not to retch.

"What do you mean you can't tell me?!" Gloria heatedly snapped, gaining my attention, "And why do we have to leave?!" She added, baffling me.

*Leave?* I queried, narrowing my eyes. *And did she say '**we**'?*

"Wes, wai-" But she cut herself off with a growl before slamming the receiver down, uttering under her breath, "Damn it!" I presumed whoever she was talking to had hung up.

Once she had inhaled a deep breath, Gloria rounded on me, "What's happened at C.S?" And that question made my stomach turn rock hard.

"I-I duh-didn't mean it!" I blurted in a shrill tone, swiping the back of my hand across my now sweaty brow, "I didn't muh-mean for any of it tuh-to happen!"

"You didn't mean for what to happen?" She pried with a raise of her brow.

*How do I tell her what I did?! That I killed someone!* But I knew I needed to tell her the truth, she was my only hope.

Clearing my throat, I stammered, "I... I-I kuh-kuh-"
**BEEP, BEEP!** But a car horn tooting cut across me; there was no denying the relief that enveloped me, but it was swiftly replaced with curiosity when Gloria peeked through the curtain.

Turning back to face me, she stated, "We've got to go." And she disappeared into the hallway.

"Go where?" I questioned, following Gloria where her hand lingered on the doorknob.

"I promise I'll explain everything." She began, "But you've got to trust me."

*What other choice do I have?*

Nodding, I replied, "Okay, I trust you." And my response made her smile.

Gloria then opened the front door where I spotted a blue Austin Cambridge waiting outside her garden gate. Grabbing my arm, Gloria tugged me towards it, opening the door and ushering me inside with a sporadic wave of her hand.

"Get in!" She urged, and I quickly clambered inside, bouncing down on the backseat; I was a little surprised she had chosen to sit in the front.

As soon as she shut the passenger door, Gloria gazed at the male driver who was dressed head to toe in black, "Take us to the guild." She ordered, and I blurted, "The guild?!" A sudden coldness struck my core.

*Did she say the guild?!*

Glancing over her shoulder, Gloria nodded, "Yes, I've got no other choice but to take you."

*No other choice?* I repeated. *Doesn't she want me to go?* And I opened my mouth to ask but she had fixed her sights upon the road when the driver pulled away.

With a sigh, I peered out the window, watching as the town of Merribridge was soon left in our wake. *What's going to happen now?* I worried, clutching at the cuff of my blazer. *Will I ever get to go home again? Or is this it? Have I literally just left everything behind?* Then a realisation dawned on me, making a painful lump form in the back of my throat. *What's mother and Carmen going to think when they find out I killed father?!* I inwardly sobbed, vaguely aware of the luscious green countryside now stretching as far as the eye could see. *If I could go back in time, I'd find help instead of trying to get him out myself!*

Suddenly, my mind was plagued with harrowing screams, making me recoil. **'MAKE IT STOP! MAKE IT STOP!'**. Father's cries echoed inside my head. *I tried, father, I tried!* I declared, trying to swallow the lump in my throat to no avail. **'NATHANIEL! TURN IT OFF!'**. Then the stench of blood invaded my senses, making me retch.

"Nate, are you okay?" The concerned voice of Gloria dragged me back to reality; she was staring over her shoulder with worry shimmering in her green gaze.
*I... I can't tell her!* I gulped, tugging at the collar of my shirt.
Nodding, my voice cracked, "Yuh-Yes, I'm fuh-fine. I just get a luh-little car sick."

"Well, we're almost there." She smiled softly, gesturing with a nod towards the alpine trees now looming in the distance, taking my breath away.
*Whoa!* I gasped, noting they expanded across the horizon line.

Reluctantly tearing my gaze away, I asked, "Is that where we're going?" And Gloria nodded, "Yes, the guild is in the heart of the forest."
*I'm guessing that's why they haven't been caught, the government can't find them.*

As soon as we entered the dark forest, a thin layer of fog pranced around the alpine trunks, parting for us like the Red Sea. The road swiftly became a bumpy dirt track; I couldn't help but yelp as I violently bounced up and down, grasping each side of

Gloria's seat for some much-needed support.

"We're. Almost. There." She said between each bump; I noticed she too was gripping onto her seat for dear life.

Fragments of light soon appeared up ahead, breaking through the dense foliage and creating shards of divine light. I inwardly gasped when the forest unexpectedly opened into a gigantic glade, a cobbled path circled the clearing along with timber framed houses.

"Are we here?" I couldn't help but ask as the driver took the right-hand path.

Nodding, Gloria replied, "Nearly."

Once we reached the other side, the driver then turned right down another cobbled road hidden between two houses. *Wait, where are we going now?*

"What are we-" But I was stunned into silence when we pulled up outside a large, half-timbered farmhouse on our left.

*That's a big house!* I gaped, shifting my attention to the adjacent barn.

Gazing over her shoulder, Gloria smiled, "Now we're here." And I had expected to feel some kind of relief, but all I felt was apprehension.

*Was this the right thing to do?* I contemplated, clutching at the lapel of my jacket before feeling something in one of the pockets. Peering inside, I noted it was the products I had managed to grab. *What am I going to do with thes-*

"Ready?" Gloria wondered, distracting me.

*I don't really have much choice...* I pondered, smiling weakly.

"Ready." I replied, clambering out after her.

Once Gloria had waved goodbye to the driver, who turned around and disappeared in the direction of the glade, we then advanced on the farmhouse veranda. *Does she still want these?* I mulled, fiddling with my jacket pocket.

"I've... I've got something for you." I commented, now walking so close our arms were brushing.

"Oh?" Gloria queried in surprise, knocking on the dark wood front door that had a frosted glass panel down the middle, "Do you?" And she gazed up at me inquisitively.

Reaching inside my pocket, I said, "I managed-" But the door suddenly opened, revealing a petite woman with long, wavy red hair.

"Give it to me later." Gloria hurriedly commented just as the redhead gasped, "Glory?!" And whatever she was holding hit the dark, hardwood floor with a smash, causing glass to scatter like marbles.

"What... What are you doing here?" The redhead sceptically queried, ignoring the glass, "And who's he?" She tacked on, her light brown eyes narrowing up at me.

*I could ask the same question...* I murmured, watching as she crossed her arms over her chest, crumpling her white blouse that was tucked into a black rockabilly skirt.

Sighing, Gloria stepped over the glass and came to stand just inside the farmhouse, uttering, "I presume Wes hasn't told you what's going on..." And the redhead wondered with a tip of her head, "Told me what?" It was only then I noticed the abundance of freckles peppering her nose and cheeks.

"Told you why I'm here." Gloria replied, gesturing with a nod for me to follow, and the redhead murmured while closing the door behind me, "Nuh-No... I haven't spoken to him since Sunday..."

Once I came to stand in the red walled lobby, I noted dark wooden stairs were in the far, left-hand corner that circled up to the right; a red leather, wingback chair was tucked underneath facing into the room. *Wow!* I gawked, gazing up at the open-planned landing with a fancy-looking banister.

"I'm just a little concerned you've brought a Watcher here." The redhead carried on, brushing aside the glass with her black and white patent heels; her eyes never lingered from me as she spoke to Gloria, "Or is he working on the inside as well?"

*Inside?* I repeated, confused.

"He's **not** a Watcher." Gloria swiftly replied, "And nor is he working on the inside."

"Then **who** is he?!" The redhead demanded, raising her voice and taking me aback; it was so loud for someone so small.

Before Gloria had the chance to respond, a sophisticated male voice hollered, "Ruby?!" It was coming from behind the door on my left, which was at the bottom of the stairs, "What's with all the racket?!"

The door then opened, revealing an elderly gentleman; his steely grey eyes instantly locked onto me, and it was right then I knew he was a force to be reckoned with.

When the gentleman came to stand before me, he questioned, "Who are you?" And I had to tip my head back as he was a good few inches taller than me.

*Is he in charge around here?* I deliberated, taking in his weather-beaten face and halo of white hair that encompassed his bald head; it was such a startling white, it matched his crisp shirt.

I then opened my mouth to reply, but Gloria piped up, "Ralph, this is Nate." She now stood beside me, also staring up and up at the elderly gentleman.

"Nate?" Ralph repeated in distaste, as if he had eaten something bitter, "What kind of name is '**Nate**'?"

*Why does she keep calling me Nate?!* I growled, watching as he clutched the checkered braces attached to his black slacks.

"My name's Nathaniel. Nathaniel West." I stated matter-of-factly, shooting Gloria a warning glance when I added, "**Not Nate.**"

A gasp sounded from the redhead just as Ralph took a sudden step back; his black shoes squeaked against the floorboards. *Did I say something wrong?* I worried, bringing a hand up to the base of my neck.

"As in **the** Nathaniel West?!" The redhead gawked just as Ralph shifted his attention to her, "Ruby, call the council for an urgent meeting!"

"Wait!" I blurted, jerking my head back, "What's going on?!"

But my question must have fallen on deaf ears as Ruby hurried through a door on my right, which was opposite the one at the bottom of the stairs, while Ralph diverted his attention to Gloria.

"Gloria," He began, "Take Mr West to the guestroom, lock

him in."

"**Lock** me in?!" I hawked, my jaw dropping, "You can't be serious!" But he ignored me and carried on, "The meeting will commence shortly."

"Wait!" I urgently exclaimed as Ralph advanced on the door Ruby had disappeared through, "You can't-" But he slammed the door shut in my face, leaving me standing there with my mouth agape.

*Who the hell does he think he is?!* I fumed, now glaring at Gloria who looked a little apprehensive.
Pointing an incriminating finger towards the door, I growled, "What the hell was all that about?!"

\*\*\*

*I can't believe she locked me in here!* I fumed for what must have been the hundredth time, glaring over at the mahogany door in the bottom, right-hand corner. I was pacing the red walled guestroom, my wingtip shoes rapping against the dark, hardwood floor. *It's not like I can even climb out the windows!* I complained, turning my back on the door to stare at the locked, square-shaped window. It was in the middle of the back wall with brown curtains tied either side; a double bed was underneath with crisp white sheets. *Not that I'd be able to climb out in* **these***!* I bitterly added, glowering down at the tight blue jeans I had been forced to wear; my father's suit folded neatly in the middle of the bed.

Unable to rein in my anger a moment longer, I mentally declared. *I JUST WANT TO KNOW WHAT'S GOING ON!* And I slumped down onto the bed facing the rectangular window on the left-hand wall; brown curtains were tied either side with a dark wood vanity table underneath. *Why am I being treated like a Goddamn prisoner?!* Pounding a fist against my thigh, I swiftly realised. *I should* **never** *have come here!* And that thought alone made a dejected sigh escape me.

I then rose to my feet, advancing on the rectangular

window to gaze out at the dark, imposing forest. *I wonder what happened at C.S after I left...* I murmured, recollecting Gloria's shocked telephone conversation. '**What do you mean there's an emergency at C.S?!**'. *Have they told mother and Carmen yet?* And my stomach rolled with dread at that notion, the distinct sound of the impact crusher suddenly roaring to life inside my head.

'*MAKE IT STOP! MAKE IT STOP!*'. Father's torturous cries echoed all around me, as if I were reliving it. *I tried!* I sobbed before the feel of his hot blood peppering my flesh swiftly followed, making me choke in revulsion. *I tried to stop it but couldn't!* Another gag broke my hold; I couldn't bear the thought of anything touching my skin a moment longer. *I need this off!* Ripping off the heavy leather jacket, I tossed it onto the bed as if it were doused in gore, but I soon realised that wasn't enough. The white t-shirt felt foreign against my skin, making my toes curl in disgust. *I just need it off!* My hands went for the ends, pulling it up over my head just as I heard the bedroom door open followed by a gasp.

With the t-shirt now in hand, I found myself staring at Gloria whose eyes were fervently locked onto me. *What's she looking at?* I deliberated, momentarily gazing down at my toned torso before back at her.

"What are you looking at?" I queried, feeling a little uncomfortable with her eyes roaming over me.

When she didn't reply, I growled, "Gloria, what are you doing?!" Which seemed to snap her back to reality.

A flush crept across her cheeks as she briskly retorted, "I... I-I could ask you the same thing!" And she gestured at me with a sharp wave of her hand, "Why are you getting undressed?!"

"I wasn't!" I lied, hastily pulling the t-shirt back on.

Gloria then opened her mouth to speak, but I swiftly changed the subject, "So what's going on? What happened in the meeting?"

"I can't discuss it, Nate." She stated matter-of-factly, my head jerking back in shock when I pried, "What? Why?" And I shot her an incredulous glance.

"Because it was about you, about who you are." She explained, and I was stunned into silence.
*About me?* I repeated, but I soon grasped what she meant.

"Because my father's a Watcher?" I presumed.
**Was...** A little voice piped up. *Was a Watcher...* And my chest tightened as guilt consumed me.
Nodding, Gloria explained, "Which means the government will be on the lookout for you. What we discussed could be used against you if they apprehend you, so I'd rather not tell you."
*But that doesn't explain why she locked me in here.*

"Can you at least tell me what's going on here?" I urged, gesturing around at the guestroom, "I feel like a prisoner."

"You're **not** a prisoner." Gloria corrected, "You're our guest."
*But that still doesn't explain anything!* I fumed.
"Which reminds me," She carried on before I could inquire further, "Dinners ready." But the thought of food make my stomach churn.

"I'm fine but thank you." I replied with a shake of my head, but Gloria grinned defiantly, "Well tough! You've got to eat something!" And she gestured with a nod for me to follow her, "Come on."

"But-" I began; however, she had already disappeared onto the landing.
Shaking my head in annoyance, I reluctantly followed. A lush, cream carpet was now underfoot; the red walls continued from the bedroom with timber struts holding up the vaulted ceiling. Ignoring the dark wood door directly on my right, I followed Gloria left.

"Can you at least tell me what's going to happen after dinner?" I pressed, tension notable in my voice as I continued, "Am I going to be locked up again?"

"I wouldn't have thought so." Gloria answered as we passed more doors on our right, "Unless Ralph says otherwise."
The fancy-looking banister was soon on our left, overlooking the lobby below.

"I'm guessing this Ralph is in charge of the guild?" I presumed as we descended the stairs.

"Yes," She nodded, "He's the founder of the People's Guild."

Once we reached the lobby, Gloria headed through the door on our left. The smell of beef and chicken invaded my senses as soon as I set foot in the open-planned living/dining room, the hardwood floor carrying on from the lobby. *God, that smells good!* I inwardly moaned, noticing the light brown walls made the living-room feel much smaller than it was.

Then I spotted two people sat on a musky orange sofa directly across from me; it was underneath a square-shaped window with dark red curtains tied either side. An identical window was to my right overlooking the veranda, matching orange chairs were either side with a mahogany coffee table in-between. *Who are they?* I couldn't help but wonder, staring intently at the woman who took up over half the sofa; her potbelly emphasised by her red, high-waisted pencil skirt.

"Kent, Darlene," Gloria piped up, gaining the two people's attention, "This is Nate." And she gestured to me with a sweep of her hand.

"Is this him?!" The rotund woman, Darlene, eagerly queried, gawking at me as if I were the Messiah, "Is this **the** Nathaniel West?!"

*'The' Nathaniel West?* I repeated. *Why am I being called 'the' Nathaniel West?*

Nodding, Gloria replied, "Indeed, it is." And Darlene instantly fanned her silky, pale blue blouse that was tucked into her skirt.

"Well, you better make a move before Mama Darlene does." The rotund woman advised, her green eyes furtively glancing at me as she spoke to Gloria, "Because he's yummier than my homemade banana cream pie!" And she unexpectedly made nom nom noises, her tongue darting out to lick her red lips.

*God no!* I cringed, watching as she brushed her wavy, dark brown hair off her shoulder, exposing her flush neck. *She's old enough to be my mother!*

"I'm right in thinking his dad is the Head Watcher,

right?" The man, Kent, piped up for the first time, gaining everyone's attention.

*'Head' Watcher? I echoed, puzzled. What does he mean by- How old is he?!* I couldn't stop my jaw from dropping as I took Kent in for the first time; he had such a young-looking face it would put a baby's to shame. *He looks twelve!* I gawked, covering my slack mouth with my hand.

*He's definitely no older than eighteen-* But I was soon distracted when he brushed a hand through his shiny, luxuriant brown hair that was coiffed to perfection. *What's that on his arm?* I wondered, squinting to get a better look. The sleeves of his white shirt, which was tucked into his black slacks and partially hidden underneath a dark blue, button up vest, were rolled up to his elbows. *Are those bruises?* I deliberated, staring at the purplish splotches that marred his left arm. *Or is it a birthmark?*

"Wait, he doesn't know?!" Kent gaped in disbelief, snapping me back to the conversation.

Shaking her head, Gloria replied, "No, but that's a matter for another time." And I knew they were talking about me by the way Kent openly stared at me.

"Hang on!" I piped up before anyone could change the subject, "What don't I know?"

"Dinners ready!" A woman unexpectedly hollered, and I glanced over at the dining room to my left.

Ruby was stood beside a long, dark wood table with plates in her grasp; eight chairs were tucked underneath, three on each side and one at either end.

"Ooooooh!" Darlene chanted breathily, "Dinner, dinner, dinner!" And she rubbed her hands together in delight as Ruby set the plates down; I couldn't help but shoot the rotund woman a questioning glance.

Once Ruby had disappeared through a door on her right, Darlene made a dash for the dining table. *I've never seen someone move so fast!* I gawked, my eyebrows rising in amazement.

"Nate?" Gloria queried, gaining my focus where I noticed she and Kent were advancing on the table, "Come on." And she beckoned me over with a nod of her head.

Drawing closer, I exclaimed. *Oh wow, the food looks good!* The two plates Ruby had put down either end were piled with vegetables, roast chicken, and sliced beef. *But I still don't think I can stomach anything...*

*Diverting my attention away from the food, I realised Gloria had sat in the middle with her back facing the door Ruby had disappeared through; Darlene was opposite while Kent seemed to linger. Does it matter where I sit?* I pondered, pulling up the chair on Gloria's left before Kent decidedly sat across from me. *Why was he waiting for me-* **BANG!** The door behind me burst open, making me jump.

"Almost ready!" Ruby affirmed as she barrelled through with two plates in her hands, depositing them in front of Gloria and I before returning to the, I presumed, kitchen.

"Sooooo," Kent fervidly piped up, bouncing his fork with his index finger; I instantly didn't like the way he looked at me with his big, brown doe eyes.

"Tell me about yourself, Nate." He carried on, "Or do you prefer Nathaniel?"

"I prefer Nathaniel." I bluntly replied, ignoring his other question.

*What's with this guy?* I mulled, aware his gaze was exploring every inch of my face almost suggestively. *And why does he keep staring at me like-* **BANG!** The kitchen door swung open again, startling me. *God, why does she keep doing that?!* I growled as Ruby hurried through balancing three plates, giving one to Kent and the other to Darlene. She then set the last plate down to Darlene's left, pulling up the chair as she done so. *Hang on...* I noted, counting seven plates. *If one is for Ralph, then who's the other for?*

"So, what are we talking about?" Ruby queried, looking between each of us before Kent replied, "I was just asking Nathan-" But he immediately fell silent when the door to the lobby opened with a squeak.

*Why's he stopped talking?* I mulled before Ralph stepped inside, closing the door behind him. *Isn't he allowed to talk or something?* I pondered further, watching as Ralph visibly breathed in the meaty aroma that lingered in the atmosphere.

"Ahhh! Suppers ready!" Ralph purred in delight, a grin manifesting on his weather-beat face as he ambled over.

He then pulled up the chair that had its back to the living-room, his steely grey eyes landing on the unoccupied one across from him.

"I see we're waiting for Wesley yet again..." He tutted, expelling an exaggerated sigh, "It's becoming a bit of a habit, us waiting for him..."

"He did have that emergency, remember." Gloria swiftly pointed out, and Ralph murmured, "Everything's an **'emergency'** with him..." He then minutely shook his head in annoyance before picking up his cutlery, "Let's just start without him."

"Can't we wait five more minutes?" Ruby queried, making Ralph jerk his head back as he rhetorically asked, "And allow dinner to go cold?! I don't think so!" He then immediately tucked into his roast just as I heard a rumble come from Ruby.

*Did she just growl?!*

"So, Nathaniel," Ralph spoke between mouthfuls once everyone, excluding Ruby, had grabbed their cutlery, "What's the emergency at C.S?" And I involuntarily sat up straight, as if I were a puppet and my strings had been pulled.

*What do I tell him?!* I fretted, a sudden and overwhelming sense of dread encompassing me; I couldn't stand the thought of being here a moment longer. *I've got to go! I need to get out of here!*

Dropping the cutlery with a ding, I rose to my feet just as the lobby door opened, stilling me.

"'ope I didn't keep yer lot waitin'." The newcomer spoke in a thick accent, taking me aback.

*Why's he talking like that?* I deliberated as he strolled over clad head to toe in black; it emphasised his muscle-bound body that would put a superhero's to shame. *Who is he?* I pondered further, watching as he pulled up the chair opposite Ralph.

"You always keep us waiting, Wesley…" Ralph uttered, his fingers impatiently tapping the table top, "It's becoming a regular occurrence."
*This* is *Wes?!* I gawked, shocked; I hadn't known what to expect. *But not **this**!*

"Me apologies, Ralph." Wes commented with a smirk, accentuating his sculpted face and sun-kissed skin that was like a Grecian God's, "Next time, right, I'll tell Mr Gray I've got reservations and can't be late." He then brushed back a slither of his dark, thick, glossy hair that had fallen from its slicked back style, making Ruby swoon.

"So what was the emergency at C.S?" Ralph pried, his nose wrinkling in disgust when Wes used his fingers to eat the chicken that was slathered in gravy.

"Oh, right!" Wes recollected, licking his thumb and index finger before picking up the cutlery, "A Watcher were murdered."
Gasps filled the room as all eyes turned to him.

"Murdered?!" Darlene hawked in disbelief, gaining Wes' attention; I noted his striking, devilish eyes were such a vivid dark brown.

"Yeah," He replied with a nod, "Turns out it were the 'ead Watcher Jeremiah West."
*I've got to go!* I trembled, aware all eyes were now on me. *I can't stay here a moment longer!*

"I've got to go!" I blurted, not giving anyone the chance to object before I darted towards the lobby, bumping into furniture as I made my escape.

*What am I going to do?!* I fearfully exclaimed, the bang of the front door a distant echo as I stepped out into the chill night air. Jamming my hands into my armpits, I shakily made my way towards the glade. *Where am I even going to go?! I **can't** go home!* And then it dawned on me I had nowhere, no one, to turn to.

*\*\*\**

I had no idea how long I had been sat on the edge of the glade, watching the mist prance around the alpine trunks and the dimly lit wooden houses. I had no mode of transport and no idea how to leave the forest; I felt trapped, unable to escape the horrors of my reality.

*I should never have come here...* I uttered, holding my head in my hands. *What am I going to do-*

"Nate?" A silvery voice called, stilling my thoughts.

Lowering my hands, I glanced over my shoulder to see Gloria approach from the direction of the farmhouse. *What's she doing?* I wondered, my eyebrows rising in surprise.

"Have you been out here this entire time?" She pried, awakening the memories of why I had left.

*Oh God...* I worried, my gaze flitting around the glade, unable to settle on her even when she sat down beside me. *Does she know?*
...

I could feel Gloria's eyes roam over me before she said, "Wes told us what happened." And that ignited the panic within. *Oh God, no!* I frightfully exclaimed, bringing my hands up to hide my face.

"You know it's not your fault, right?" She reassured, grabbing my hands and lowering them; I was completely taken aback by her comment.

*What does she mean?* Then I saw an almost understanding look in her eyes, detonating a deep, enrooted anger I didn't know was waiting to surface. *How the hell would she know?! I don't need her Goddamn pity!*

"And how the hell would you know?!" I snapped, yanking my hands free from hers.

Shocked, Gloria explained, "It was just an accident, Nate. You shouldn't blame yours-"

"Stop trying to justify **my** actions!" I sharply cut across, glaring at her with cold, flinty eyes, "You're not the one who killed a person never mind someone you actually care about!"

"You know fuck all about me!" Gloria retorted with animosity lacing her voice, an unspoken remorse shimmering in her green gaze.

*Wait, has she killed someone?!* Pressing a fist to my mouth, I couldn't help but stare at her with wide eyes. *No, of course she wouldn't!* I insisted, but a doubtful voice swiftly inputted. *Would she?...*

"Anyway," Gloria tactfully changed the subject, rising to her feet, "Let's head back inside, it's nearly bedtime."

"Whoa, hang on a minute!" I exclaimed, swiftly following after her where I grabbed her by the wrist, pulling to her a halt. "What were you trying to say?!" I pried, searching her eyes for any tell-tale signs but she had abruptly closed herself off, her face now blank of all emotions.

After a moment of silence, Gloria commented, "That's a story for another time." Before tugging her hand free and wandering back in the direction of the farmhouse.

*Who?* I pondered, staring after her. *Who did she kill and why?* Part of me refused to believe it, yet another part knew by the remorse in her eyes that she was hiding something.

Shaking off my unease, I swiftly caught up with Gloria just as we were a stone's throw from the farmhouse; the lobby dimly lit and eerily quiet when we stepped inside. *Has everyone gone to bed?* I mulled, straining my ears but couldn't hear anything. *What time is it?*

Glancing over my shoulder at Gloria as she closed the front door, I queried, "Where is everyone?" And she replied with a shrug, "They've probably gone to bed."

"Besides," She added, advancing on the stairs, "It's been a long day, so we should probably do the same."

*She's right.* I breathed, following after her. *It has been a long day...* But I soon became acutely aware of how it had felt like days, even weeks since I was in the factory. *'MAKE IT STOP! MAKE IT STOP!'*. Father's echoes of pain haunted me with a vengeance; I had to grasp onto the banister for some much-needed support as I almost toppled backwards. *I tried!* I assured, but even I wasn't convinced by the shrill voice echoing in my ears. *I really tried!*

"Tried what?" The curious voice of Gloria sliced through my mental suffering; I blinked up to see her stood at the top of the stairs.

Confused, I asked, "What did you just say?"

"You said you tried." Gloria explained, tilting her head to one side, "Tried what?" And then it dawned on me I had spoken my thoughts out loud.

*Oh God, what else have I said?!* I fretted, repeatedly rubbing my face before ascending the last few steps.

"Nothing." I lied, bypassing her and advancing on my bedroom door before she could pry any further.

*She may know what happened, but I'm not ready to talk about it just yet.* I then opened the door and instantly spotted father's suit laying in the middle of the bed; I was overwhelmed with such sorrow that I had to steady myself on the doorframe. *It's all my fault!* I berated, feeling a lump form in the back of my throat. *He'd still be alive if it weren't for me!* And I didn't try to hide the few stray tears that rolled down my cheeks.

"You really need to stop beating yourself up." Gloria commented, gaining my attention where I noticed she stood beside me, "You were just another nonconformist to him." She added, and I couldn't stop my head from jerking back in shock. *She seriously can't think that, can she?!* Animosity began to bubble in my veins, making my muscles quiver and my heart pound. *I wasn't just a nonconformist to him; I was his son!*

Unable to stop myself, I snapped, "I'm not a murderer like **you**! I never wanted to kill my father!" And I didn't give Gloria the chance to respond before thundering into my room, flipping on the light switch; I about to slam the door but she was standing in the way.

"Look!" She heatedly began, but I retorted with a deep growl, "Just leave!" And I turned on my heels, storming over to the bed where I slumped down, burying my head in my hands.

"Fine, whatever..." She uttered, "I'll see you in the morning then..." And she closed the door with a squeak; the evident sound of a key swiftly followed.

*Has she just locked me in?!* I fumed, glaring at the door in question.

A heavy sigh was expelled from my lips as I stomped over, giving the knob several sharp turns but the door didn't budge. *Great, just great!* I seethed, briefly clenching my fists. *I should **never** have come here!* I declared, turning back to the bed where my gaze instantly locked onto father's suit. My heart suddenly grew heavy as the anger vanished, thudding sporadically against my chest. *None of this would've happened if it weren't for me!* I sobbed, collapsing down onto the edge of the bed. *It's all my fault!*

A whimper left my lips as I dragged the jacket closer, bringing it into a tight embrace where I was brought up short when I felt something bulky inside. *What the?* Then I remembered as soon as I pulled out the white pot of Delirium. *Oh, I forgot about these...* I sniffed, wiping away a few lingering tears.

*What do I do with them now? Give them to Gloria?* I mulled while retrieving the Reme-Tea, now searching for the Dental Dose but felt something else tucked away with it. *Huh? What's this?* And I pulled out an envelope with my name on it; it was written in father's scrawl. Confused, I gingerly turned over the envelope, opening it to find a letter. *Why's father written me a letter?*

'Nathaniel,
I am writing this letter after today's meeting with the government where I renounced my position as executive for C.S as well as my duties as a Watcher.'.
*So what Mr Sheridan said was true, he really did resign.* I noted, shaking my head in disbelief. *But why would he quit his job? What happened?* So many questions infiltrated my head; I carried on reading to quench my curiosities.

'This evening I shall be sentenced to death by fusillade, my life in exchange for your life.'.
An uncontrollable shudder swept throughout my body, my eyes just staring at the letter but unable to take any more in. *He... But... Why?...* Then father's words from the other day came to mind. **'But don't put me in a position where I have to choose**

***between your life and my life.'.*** I didn't understand what he meant at the time, but now I do. *He... He was going to sacrifice his life for me?* And I brought a hand up to grip my throat, not wanting to read any more but unable to stop myself.
      'After careful negotiation, it has been agreed that you'll be sent to Merriwell Sanatorium for rehabilitation. This is my last chance to protect you after countlessly trying to steer you back onto the safest path. '.
'***I tried so hard to steer you back onto the safest path.'.*** Father's voice echoed in my mind, making my eyes water with remorse.
'Don't worry about your mother or sister, they will be looked after during your absence.'.
*It's because of me he isn't here to look after them!* I cried, momentarily covering my face with my hand before reading the last passage.
      'I am aware we don't live in an ideal world where we can choose our own way of living, and I highly doubt anything will change during your lifetime.
Always remember that I love you no matter what.
Father'.

## Chapter Thirteen
### *There's no escape now!*

**BANG, BANG, BANG!** Knocking startled me awake; I stared bleary eyed around the room, trying to get my bearings. *God...* I groaned, shifting on top of the bed. *Did I fall asleep?* And I gazed down at my dishevelled clothes, my father's letter resting on my chest. *What time is it?* I wondered, rubbing the sleep out of my eyes.

"Nate?" The silvery voice of Gloria called, my attention snapping to the bedroom door when I heard a key rattle, "Can I come in?"

"Erm..." I stalled, snatching up my father's letter and hiding it under the pillow, "Yuh-Yeah, sure, that's fine." And I swung my legs round to sit on the edge just as the door opened with a squeak; Gloria stepped inside, her red T-bar heels clipping against the floorboards.

"I've brought you a clean change of clothes." She beamed, but I was too distracted by what she was wearing.
*Wow!* I gaped, my eyes suggestively exploring her breasts that were emphasised by a lowcut, red and white polka dot blouse. *They look mass-*
"What are you looking at?" She interrupted my perverted thoughts, giving herself a once over.

"Nothing!" I blurted, hastily averting my gaze as a heat emanated from my cheeks.

*I hope she didn't catch me staring!* I anxiously prayed, noting her dark grey, cropped trousers when she set the clothes down next to me on the bed. I then slowly shifted my attention back upon her face, our eyes locking for what felt like an eternity. *Does she feel the same way about me?* I wondered, hopeful.

"So how did you sleep last night?" Gloria queried, brushing her long, wavy brown hair from her shoulder; it only just hit me how tired I was.

"Erm, not brilliant." I admitted, rubbing a hand across my stubbled jaw.

I then spotted a questioning gleam in her green eyes, which were accentuated by black cat flicks, so I swiftly added, "I've just got a lot on my mind." And I automatically glanced at the pillow that concealed father's letter.

*I still can't believe he was going to sacrifice his life to save me...*

"I'm sorry to hear that." Gloria commented, gaining my attention, "Hopefully you'll feel better after some break- What are those?" And I followed her gaze to the three products discarded at the foot of the bed.

"I managed to get hold of some of the things you asked for." I replied, making Gloria gasp in delight, "You got them?!" She giddily exclaimed, snatching up the Dental Dose and Reme-Tea to inspect the ingredients.

"**Some** of them." I reiterated just as she picked up the white pot, turning it over where she spotted the name Delirium written on it.

"You... You got it?!" Gloria gasped in disbelief, her eyes widening, "You got the drug?!"

*The what?* I pondered before she suddenly turned for the door, disappearing onto the landing with the products still in hand. *Wait, where's she going?* The urgent rap of heels then descended the stairs, making me shake my head in annoyance. *Fine... She's clearly got what she wanted...* I uttered, shifting my attention to the clean clothes beside me. *I better get changed and find out what's going on.* I decided, taking off my dirty clothes and discarding them on the floor beside the bed.

Just as I pulled on the dark wash jeans, a strange voice

piped up from the doorway, "'ave yer seen Glory?" And I peered over to see Wes.

Grabbing the white t-shirt, I bluntly replied, "Downstairs." And I became acutely aware of him just staring me up and down, his hands buried in his dark denim jeans.

*What the hell's he looking at?!* I bristled, tugging on the t-shirt as I done so.

Glaring at him, I fumed, "What?!" Which I instantly regretted when he took a further step inside, his brown boots thudding intimidatingly against the floorboards as he advanced on me.

*I shouldn't have snapped!* I gulped, pinching the skin at my throat.

When Wes came to a halt before me, he crossed his arms over his tight, white t-shirt - which emphasised his defined abs – and sternly asked, "Are yer wearin' me t-shirt and jeans?"

It took a moment for it to sink in but, when it did, I couldn't help but gape. *Wait, what?!*

"**Your** t-shirt and jeans?" I repeated as I sat on the edge of the bed, pulling on the scuffed, dark brown boots Gloria had also provided, "I don't think so-"

"Wait a minute!" Wes interrupted, now inspecting the boots with his dark, penetrating gaze, "They're me shoes!" And I was instantly chilled to the very core when his attention snapped up to glower at me.

*He's... He's joking, right?!* But I could tell by his reddening face and cold, flinty stare that this wasn't some kind of shaggy-dog story.

"Who the fuck 'as given yer me kit?!" Wes demanded, now stepping into my personal space where I had to tip my head all the way back to look at him, "I'm bloody well not a fuckin' charity!"

"I-I didn't knuh-know they were yours!" I desperately beseeched, waving my hands apologetically.

"We look like Tweedle fuckin' Dee and Tweedle fuckin' Dum!" He irately carried on, gesturing between us with a sharp wave of his hand.

"I-I'm sorry!" I urgently apologised, but he merely shook his head before asking, "Glory gave 'em ter yer, didn't she?" And I didn't know what else to do besides vigorously nod my head.

Unexpectedly, Wes' anger seemed to subside; he inhaled a deep breath and closed his eyes.

"I-I can give them back if you luh-like." I hastily stammered, frantically grasping the ends of the t-shirt.

A twisted look of irritation grew on Wes' face as his eyes flew open, "Nah, keep 'em." He growled down at me, "Don't fancy another dude's junk in me jeans."

*Junk?* I repeated, confused. *Does he mean-*

"Anyway, I ought ter go." Wes interrupted my ponderings, turning for the door as he done so, "I need ter speak ter Glory before breakfast." And, without another word, he left.

*Thank God he's gone!* I breathed a sigh of relief, an unexpected release of tension escaping me when I heard him descend the stairs. *But why did Gloria give me his clothes?* I deliberated, peering down at the clothes in question before wondering. *Where did she go, anyway?*

Rising to my feet, I headed onto the landing and gazed over the banister, spotting the living-room door was ajar. It was only then another thought occurred to me. *Am I even allowed out of my room?* But I soon remembered what Gloria had said last night. **'You're not a prisoner. You're our guest.'**. *Not that I've been treated like a guest...* Shaking off that contemplation, I decidedly made my way downstairs where I heard voices coming from the living-room, a man and a woman. *Wes did say he wanted to talk to Gloria.* But it soon became apparent that the man wasn't Wes by their strident, articulate tone.

"I don't care, he can't stay here!" Ralph declared, my feet now rooted at the bottom of the stairs, "They will scour every inch of Merribridge for him!" And I instantly knew he was talking about me, "If he stays here, I'll be putting the guild at risk!" He heatedly added.

*Oh God, he wants me gone!* I panicked, my hands clenching by my sides as an overwhelming sense of dread consumed me. *What am I going to do?!*

"Then what do you suggest?!" The intense voice of Gloria retorted, "That we just hand him over to the government?!" And it felt like a cold bucket of ice had been thrown over me.
*She's not serious, is she?!* I fretted, bringing a hand up to bite my thumb before realising. *Don't be so stupid! She wouldn't turn me in!*
"That's not a half bad idea." Ralph thoughtfully commented, causing my chest to tingle as fear crept in.
*Wait, what?!*
"Wesley can take him," He decisively added, "It'll stand him in good stead."
*Stand him in good stead?!* I gawked. *In good stead with who?!*
But I soon realised that was the least of my worries when Ralph resumed, "Go and fetch the boy now. Whatever you do, don't tell him."
*I need to go! I need to get out of here!* And I made a dash for the front door, ripping it open so fast I swore I heard the hinges creak in protest.

The morning sun shimmered through the branches overhead, blinding me momentarily as I urgently stepped off the veranda. *What the hell do I do?!* I anxiously thought, staring around for some kind of sign. *Where do I go?!* But I froze when I spotted a black car outside the adjacent barn; I instantly recognised it as a Bentley S1, a car only the government were permitted to drive. *Oh no! Oh God no! The government are here to take me away!* My throat started to tighten, feeling as if someone were choking the life out of me.

*Oh God, oh God, oh God! What do I do?!* It felt like a lifetime I was stood there like a deer caught in the headlights, waiting for men in black to rush out and drag me away. *What are they waiting for?!* I cried when no one got out, so I took a shaky step closer only to realise the vehicle was empty. *Wait, where are they if they're not in there?!* Anxiously peering around, I knew I was living on borrowed time.

*Maybe I can use that to get out of here?* I pondered, glancing back at the Bentley. But a numbness abruptly consumed me, my entire body feeling heavy as the reality – my reality – dawned on me. *If... If this is it, then I need to say goodbye...* Burying my head in my hands, a dejected sigh leaked from my lips. *I need to say goodbye to mother and Carmen while I've still got the chance.* And I lowered my hands, my eyes locking onto the car once more. *I just hope the keys are inside.*

***

Darkness loomed on the horizon line; I watched the storm threaten to roll in as soon as I pulled up outside my house. *You wouldn't think it was the middle of July...* I muttered, shivering against the chill lingering in the air. *I think it might rain...* I pondered further, but I knew it was just a distraction from the inevitable; a sad goodbye. Momentarily covering my face with my hands, I gazed sullenly at the front door; it was just a stone's throw away but knew it would feel like miles as soon as I stepped out of the car.

But then what? I deliberated, shifting my attention down to my hands. *I can't keep running.* I had no food, no money, and the car would eventually run out of fuel. *And there's no way they'd rehabilitate me now after what happened to... To father...* There were only two outcomes I could see. *I either keep running until they find me, or I turn myself in and accept my fate...* Shaking my head at that thought, I decidedly pushed it to the very back of my mind. *Right now I just want to say goodbye to my family...* And with a dejected sigh, I finally got out the car.

I noted the speakers were dead as I apprehensively wandered up the garden path, the gate swinging shut behind me in the wind that was slowly picking up. The thud of my boots on the cobbled stone echoed along the eerily silent street. Reaching with a heavy hand for the front door, I knocked twice, knowing mother and Carmen would be home. *Unless they've been taken by the government for questioning.*

Just as I was about to try the knob, the door opened with a squeak, revealing mother who had a massive, almost otherworldly grin gracing her ruby red lips.

"Nathaniel!" She gleamed, brushing aside a loose strand of hair that had fallen from her beehive, "You're just in time for lunch!" And I was immediately taken aback.

*Wait, isn't she going to ask where I've been?* Then another thought came to mind. *Do they even know what happened to father?* But I soon realised none of that mattered. *I'm here to say goodbye.*

"Whatever is the matter, honey?" Mother queried, drying her hands on her floral apron that concealed her light blue dress; I presumed she could see the sadness of my unspoken farewell brimming behind my eyes.

*What do I even tell her?* **How** *do I tell her this is it, that I'm leaving and she'll never see me again?*

"You're not smiling." Mother carried on when I didn't respond, making me realise my presumption was wrong.

*I'm not?!* Panic erupted within; it felt as if something were smothering me as I could no longer breathe. I then immediately smiled from ear to ear, hoping it would be enough to pacify her. It took every ounce of self-control to prevent my hands from clenching into fists, to stop the quick, shallow breaths that wanted to escape me; instead, I stared into mother's inquisitive green eyes that didn't match the joyous grin gracing her red lips. *I need to say something before she gets suspicious.*

"I-I-I need to talk to you!" I hastily blurted, gesturing inside with a nod.

"Of course, honey!" Mother beamed, stepping aside and granting me access without question; I instinctively closed the door behind me while she wandered off in the direction of the kitchen.

Following her, I came to stand under the archway, wondering, "Where's Carmen?" Then the sweet scent of chicken smacked me in the face, making my mouth water.

*God, that smells so good!* I inwardly moaned, watching with hungry eyes as she plated up the chicken with a side of vegetables.

"She's upstairs, honey." Mother replied without glancing

at me; I noticed she had grabbed a third plate, but I didn't have the heart to tell her I wasn't staying.

*I just need to say goodbye and go.* I reminded myself with a sigh, reluctantly tearing my gaze away.

Inhaling a steady breath, I piped up, "I'll go and get her as I need to speak to both of you."

I then turned for the dining room, making my way heavy-footed to the stairs, my hand barely gracing the banister before the moaning of an air raid siren whirred to life outside. *What the?* Squishing my eyebrows together in confusion, I glanced over my shoulder at the front door. *What the hell's going-*

**BANG!** I practically jumped out of my skin when I heard a thump from upstairs, as if someone had fallen over. *Carmen!*

Frantically ascending the stairs, I hollered, "Carmen?!" But the clang of metal from the kitchen distracted me, as if pans had scattered everywhere; I couldn't help but envision mother dropping a pot of boiling hot water.

"Mother?!" I bawled, rushing back down in a blind panic, "Are you okay?!" But I didn't get the chance to set foot in the dining room before a voice sounded in the living-room, making me jump in alarm.

A sense of protectiveness enveloped me as I investigated, gazing quizzically around before noticing the TV was on and the Prime Minister was giving a speech.

"This is an emergency broadcast asking for you all to step forward and help bring justice to the town of Merribridge!" He began, his face wreathed in an otherworldly smile.

*An emergency?* I pondered, now coming to stand directly in front of the TV. *What's happened?*

"Deprive of Existence Act has been sanctioned by the government until Nathaniel Jeremiah West has been executed for the death of his father – Jeremiah Arthur West!"

*Executed?!* There was no denying the shock and horror coursing through my veins despite the fact I had planned to turn myself in, but now it was beginning to feel all the more real.

"He is no longer a colleague, a neighbour, a son,

or a brother; the Devil has tarnished his soul that must be cleansed by the hands of God's disciples!" The Prime Minister enthusiastically carried on, dragging me out of my presentiment, "So for justice and for principles, he must atone for his sins!"

*I can't listen to this anymore!* I panicked, everything was moving too quickly for me to process.

"And without further ado, I'd like to wish you all a good hunt." The Prime Minister concluded, "Remember, keep smil-" And I turned off the TV with clammy hands, jamming them into my armpits once the living-room fell into silence; all I could hear now was the air raid siren echo outside.

It felt like a lifetime before I deliberated. *I need to say goodbye now before the government turn up!* And I turned for the hallway only to jump back with a gasp when I saw mother standing beside the sofa. *God, she scared me!* I breathed, bringing a hand up to clutch my chest before something dawned on me. *How long has she been standing there?* And panic swiftly set in.

Gesturing to the TV with a shaky hand, I anxiously asked, "How much of that did you hear?" But she didn't reply; instead, all I could hear was her heavy, rasping breaths linger like phlegm in the back of her throat.

*Is... Is she okay?...* I contemplated, taking unsteady steps towards her before realising. *Oh God, she's disappointed of me because of what I did!*

Just as I came to stand before her, I desperately began, "It's not what it see-" But she unexpectedly struck my left shoulder; the impact had me stagger backwards where I fell down onto father's chair with an oof.

*What... What just happened?...* Dazed, I peered over at mother, noting her harrowing smile. *Did she just punch me?* But something deep down didn't feel right, as if my soul had been speared.

Slowly, I gazed down at my shoulder; it felt warm - really warm - like water trickling down it. It wasn't until I saw the blade, which was a good nine or ten inches long, that a throbbing pain consumed me.

"Wuh-What the hell?!" I choked just before feeling unbearably hot, and I couldn't stop myself from throwing up all over the floor.

*She... She stabbed me!* I frightfully exclaimed as blood oozed through my white t-shirt like ink seeping into a piece of parchment.

"He is no longer a son." Mother's cryptic voice distracted me; I glanced upwards to see her beaming, delusional face just staring at me while she slowly but surely advanced on me.

*What the hell is wrong with her?!*

"Or a brother." Another equally eerie voice piped up, and I stared beyond mother to see Carmen; she was clad in a white floral dress, her long, blonde hair down in loose curls.

*Why... Why's she looking at me like that?* I couldn't help but gulp as I rose to my feet, staring into my sister's animalistic green gaze that was paired with a chilling smile.

"What's going-" I began but they unexpectedly cut across me, declaring in unison, "He must atone for his sins!"

*What the hell are they doing?!* I screeched when they sprung at me. I then spotted a flash of metal in Carmen's grasp; I couldn't stop my jaw from dropping when I realised it was a pair of scissors poised ready to stab me. *What the?!*

"STOP!" I fearfully cried when Carmen went to stab my neck; I barely managed to catch her wrist where our bodies shook with tension.

"**Pluh-Please!**" I sobbed, "Let me explain!" But I was offered no mercy as mother ripped the knife from my left shoulder, making an involuntary gasp escape me.

My entire arm felt ablaze with agony; I barely had the strength to push Carmen back before my legs buckled underneath me, collapsing on father's chair once more.

"WHY ARE YOU DOING THIS?!" I blurted out in one breath, unable to stop the shrill tone from lacing my voice.

Mother then raised the knife high above her head when she came to tower over me, and I held up my right hand in a stop gesture.

"Let me explain!" I beseeched, but she ignored me and swung the knife down where I regretfully caught it by the blade, its sharpened edge slicing mercilessly into my palm.

"MOTHER!" I screamed, prying her fingers off the handle with my left hand, "**PLEASE!**" But nothing was getting through to her, so I shoved her backwards once the knife was free from her grasp.

*I've got to get out of here!* I declared, rising to my feet while shifting the knife into my left hand; I couldn't help but groan as the blade glided free from the oozing wound left in its wake. Then I heard the clip clop of heels hurry towards me; I barely had the chance to gaze upwards before Carmen collided into me with such force I almost fell backwards into father's chair yet again. Something warm and wet then dripped down my fingers that were holding the knife just as Carmen's entire body tensed, her scissors hitting the floor with a clatter. Peering down between us, I saw the blade was buried to the hilt in her stomach. *What have I done?!*

An uncontrollable shudder swept throughout my body; I immediately released the knife and clamped a hand over my mouth to stop myself from being physically sick, watching with wide eyes as Carmen's face swiftly became blank of all emotion except for that unnerving smile plaguing her lips. Her knees then buckled; I couldn't help but grimace when she hit the floor with a bang, wanting to look away but unable to. *I... I killed her!* Just mentally admitting that made a scream erupt out of me.

"The Devil has tarnished his soul!" Mother's ghoulish voice announced, distracting me, "That must be cleansed by the hands of God's disciples!" She then bent down, scooping up the scissors in one swift motion.

*No, no, no!* I worriedly sobbed, bringing a hand up to pinch the skin at my throat as mother raised the scissors. *No more!*

"Just stop!" I fearfully implored, but my words may as well have fallen on deaf ears as mother thrusted the scissors at me; I barely dodged the attack by ducking out of the way.

*I've got to get out of here!* I then made a dash for

the front door, my fingertips barely brushing the knob when an impenetrable force bulldozed me from behind, sending me flailing into the dining room where I hit the table with a bang. *God...* A groan was the only thing I permitted to leave my lips. *My ribs...* Then the rush of footsteps behind me gained my attention. Peering over my shoulder, I saw mother lunge at me with the scissors outstretched. *Not again!*

Pushing myself off the table, I swiftly made a beeline for the patio doors in the kitchen, seizing the handle when mother propelled herself into me once more. **SMASH!** We both flew through the glass doors that shattered on impact, littering the paving slabs and grass like shrapnel. I gasped in pain when I hit the ground with a thud, my entire body singing with unbridled suffering.

Another groan escaped my hold as I pushed myself up onto my knees, the glass scratching into my palms before a harrowing cry of agony burst from my lips. *Why does my stomach hurt so much?!* Staring down, the first thing I saw was red; it steadily trickled down the right side of my white t-shirt. *Is that blood?!* But that thought was short-lived when I saw a protruding shard of glass, instilling me with fear and I could no longer think straight. *I've got to get out!* Grasping the shard with a shaky hand, I was just about to pull it out when I heard the sound of glass scraping underfoot.

Slowly, I gazed upwards to see mother wobble to her feet, my jaw dropping in shock. *Is she okay?!* Her once perfect beehive was now a bedraggled mess, splinters of glass plentifully bestrewn it like confetti, and her once flawless blue dress was torn and frayed, the loose garments flapping against the wind.

"Are you okay?!" I blurted before noticing mother's bleeding hands, the blood hitting the paving slabs like soft rain. *Oh God, she's bleeding! I need to get the first aid kit!* I didn't think twice as I shakily rose to my feet, grasping my bleeding stomach with a hiss when the glass snagged at my flesh.

"I'm going to get the first aid kit!" I announced as she scooped something up off the ground, but that was the least of my worries.

I then hobbled towards the kitchen, doubled over in agony. *I need to get this out!* I winced, glimpsing down at the shard in question. As soon as I stepped inside I heard the crunch of glass. Peering over my shoulder, I saw mother shuffle towards me with- *Is that glass?!* She was firmly clutching a lengthy piece that must have been from the smashed patio door. *What the hell is she going to do with that?!* But I already knew the answer, making me gulp.

Turning to face her, I took slow and steady steps back while trying to reason with her, "Mother, I know you're angry because of what I did!" And I stiffly held up my left hand, gesturing for her to stop, "But, **please**, just put the glass do-"

"**HE MUST ATONE FOR HIS SINS!**" She cut me off with a primal scream, lunging for me with the shard hacking thin air.

"JUST STOP!" I hawked, staggering backwards where I collided into the kitchen wall with a grunt; a terrified gasp escaped me when she aimed for my face, but I managed to side-step where the glass stabbed into the wall.

*What's wrong with her?!* I questioned, watching as she tried to pry the shard out to no avail. Shaking my head in uncertainty, I knew if I didn't escape now she would kill me, so I made an arduous dash for the dining room. Unexpectedly, cold, dead-like hands snatched me backwards by my bicep; the abrupt movement jerked the glass still in my side, making me yelp.

*Why won't she listen to me?!* I cried when mother spun me round to face her; I couldn't ignore the bloodlust in her terrifying gaze, as if she were possessed by the Devil himself.
"PLEASE! JUST STOP!" I begged before she snapped her hands around my neck, cryptically declaring, "The Devil has tarnished his soul that must be cleansed by the hands of God's disciples!"

*I can't breathe!* Wheezing against her surprisingly strong hold, I grabbed her hands. *I CAN'T BREATHE!* I continued to panic while dots fizzled in my sights; I could hear my heartbeat pound in my head. ***I CAN'T BREATHE!*** And I urgently pried her fingers off one by one, gasping in lungful's of air once I was finally free.

*I need to get out of here while I still can!* I promptly thought; however, mother lurched for me once more.
"What are you doing?!" I hawked, snatching her by the wrists when she went for my throat again, "**JUST STOP!**" And I abruptly shoved her away, instantly regretting it when her feet skidded out from underneath; her arms helplessly flailed as she fell backwards, smacking her head on the corner of the kitchen counter with a blood chilling crack.

"OH GOD!" I screamed, slapping a hand over my mouth when she hit the floor with a thud; the reality of my actions dawned on me when she didn't stir.

*No, no, no, this isn't happening!* I repeated over and over while grasping the sides of my head, trying to regain control. *This isn't happening!* My chest became unbearable tight the longer I stared down at her, so much so I could hardly breathe. *What have I done?!* Her neck was unmistakably broken, twisted at such an awkward angle it made my stomach roll.

An overall feeling of numbness churned within; I couldn't stop the tears from cascading down my cheeks as grief consumed me. *First father... Then Carmen... Now mother...* Rubbing at my wrists with shaky hands, a shudder swept throughout my body. *I... I killed my family!* And that realisation made me choke, feeling the burn of bile in the back of my throat. *I'm a murderer!*

I desperately tried to figure out when I could have prevented any of this from happening, but it soon dawned on me I should have listened to father all along. '**She's using you, Nathaniel!**'. His voice echoed in my mind and, if I had believed him, then it just might have saved his life. *It's **my** fault he's dead!* I broke down, unable to stop my chin from quivering. *I wish I had listened! I wish I had believed him before it was too late!* Instead, I had chosen to side with a woman I hardly knew.

Anger crashed over me like a tsunami when I thought of Gloria. *Why me?!* I couldn't help but furiously wonder, recollecting how I had asked her the same question. '**Why did** *you give me those tablets?'.* And that's when I realised where it had all begun; I could have prevented the death of my family if my curiosities hadn't got the better of me. *'I... I can't say. Not because I don't want to, but because I can't.'.* Her response swiftly followed, and it only became apparent now why she couldn't.

*'Because she knows you're my son,'.* Father's bona fide words answered my unspoken recognition. *'Which makes you a valuable asset to nonconformists!'.* And I instantly remembered when I had first met Gloria in the nurse's office, how she had changed her tune as soon as I told her who I was. *Father was right, she was using me!*

**BANG! BANG!** *What the?* A heavy knocking was coming from the front door, I barely heard it over the air raid siren still whirring outside. *It sounds like someone's trying to break it down...* I mulled, brushing away my tears while gingerly venturing into the dining room. **BANG! BANG!** More thumping followed, so I peeked out the window only to see a horde of people gathered outside. *What the hell?!* Their radiant, malevolent faces were staring expectantly at the door where two people were trying to break it down with a mallet and axe. Then, as if they had heard my thoughts, the entire crowd slowly shifted their attention to me. *Gaah!* I felt like a deer caught in the headlights, so I hurriedly pulled the curtains as if that would make them forget I was inside.

*God, what am I going to do?!* I worried, pinching the skin at my throat just as the door creaked in protest; I knew it wouldn't be long until they managed to break it down. *I've got to get out of here!* Turning tail, I rushed back into the kitchen, not even daring to glance down at mother one final time. **THUD!** It sounded like the front door had finally been knocked down followed by the pitter-patter of footsteps.

"He is no longer a neighbour!" A choir of voices resonated in the dining room, chilling me to my very core.

Hurrying outside, glass skidded across the paving underfoot, the obnoxiously loud air raid siren drowning out the voices gaining on me. *What the hell do I do?!* I mentally shouted while peering around the eerily dark garden, trying to hear myself think to no avail. *Where do I go-* **BOOM!** A clap of thunder roared in the lightning spangled black clouds overhead, making me jump in alarm and almost slip on the glass.

"The Devil has tarnished his soul!" I faintly heard the voices chant, "That must be cleansed by the hands of God's disciples!" And I gazed over my shoulder to see a mass of shadows seep into the kitchen, making the hairs on the nape of my neck rise.

*I've got to go!* I fearfully declared, glancing at the hedge to the rear of the garden just as the heavens above opened; the unexpected downpour drenched me in seconds. *I've got to go* ***now!***

I then ran headlong towards the hedge, carelessly flinging myself over where an agonising cry burst from my lips when I landed in the neighbours garden with a thud, the burning-like pain from the glass still embedded in my right side crippling me. *Oh God, it hur-*

"So for justice!" Cryptic voices infiltrated my thoughts; I glanced upwards to see faces peering over the hedge in apparent delight, "And for principles!"

*Oh no!* I frightfully exclaimed, forgetting the glass and struggling to my hands and knees.

"He must atone for his sins!" They carried on as I tremulously scurried away, wincing when I applied too much weight onto my throbbing right hand.

*Please don't climb over!* I hopelessly begged, making a beeline for the path alongside the house only to freeze when I spotted four silhouettes gathered on the garden patio. Staring through my sodden hair that clung to my face, I instantly recognised them as the neighbours – the Williamson's; they each held something but I couldn't quite tell what in the dark azure. *And I'm not going to stay to find out!*

Before I had the chance to rise to my feet, Mr Williamson shifted the garden rake in his grasp before forebodingly proclaiming, "He is no longer a neighbour!" And then his wife swiftly added while thrusting her butchers knife skyward, "The

Devil has tarnished his soul that must be cleansed by the hands of God's disciples!" The metal glinted whenever there was a flash of lightning.

"So for justice!" Their son abruptly declared, gaining my attention where he slowly advanced on me while snapping a pair of hedge trimmers.

"And for principles!" The daughter carried on, slapping a rolling pin in the palm of her hand as she followed her brother's lead.

"He must atone for his sins!" The family announced in unison before charging towards me with their weapons raised.

"**PLEASE!**" I desperately beseeched over the siren, staggering to my feet and waving my shaky hands in a no gesture, "JUST STOP!" But I wasn't getting through to them; it were as if they were stampeding bulls and I was the antagonising red flag.

*They're going to kill me if I don't get out of here!* I panicked, feeling a spike of adrenaline course throughout my body.

Turning to flee the way I came, a gasp of fright escaped me when I saw ruthless, gleaming faces still peering at me from over the hedge. *Gaaah!* Skidding to a halt, I stared over my shoulder at the Williamson's who now had me surrounded. *What am I going to do?!*

Facing them, I cupped my hands together as if in prayer, begging, "Pleas-"

**THWACK!** Black dots clouded my vision when the rolling pin was smacked across my face. Wind rushed past me as I fell backwards, hitting the ground with an audible thud; a tortuous cry leaked from my lips when the glass in my stomach sliced deeper. Groaning, the dots began to fade just as something abruptly hurtled towards my face. *What the?* Then I gasped. *Oh God!*

"STOP!" I shrilled at the daughter, catching the rolling pin with my dominant right hand which I instantly regretted; I couldn't stop a hiss, my palm painfully stinging with an ever-growing fieriness.

But the suffering in my hand was soon forgotten when her

brother and parents came to tower over us; I couldn't help but sob. *This is it! I'm going to die!* All the while I still fought against her, my entire body shaking with tension.

"PLUH-PLEASE!" I fearfully pleaded, unable to stop my chin from trembling, "JUST STOP!" Then I saw the glint of a blade moments before it struck the rolling pin, cleanly slicing through the middle of my fingers like butter.
A harrowing scream erupted from me; it felt as if I couldn't breathe while watching my dismembered limbs hit the ground with a pitter-patter.

"**MY FUH-FINGERS!**" I hysterically sobbed, staring wide-eyed at Mrs Williamson who was struggling to pull the knife out of her daughter's rolling pin, "**YOU CUT OFF MUH-MY FINGERS!**" And I brought my impaired, bleeding hand to my chest, muttering to myself over and over, "I've got no fingers! She cut off my fingers! I've got no-"

"He is no longer a neighbour!" The voice of Mr Williamson interrupted my hysteria; I squinted against the rain pummelling my face, watching as he hoisted the rake skyward with the wooden handle pointing downwards.

"The Devil has tarnished his soul," His son inputted, gaining my attention where he ferociously snapped the hedge trimmers, "That must be cleansed by the hands of God's disciples!"

Gone was my hysteria when Mr Williamson brought the rake down towards my chest, replaced with unquestionable fright.

"DON'T!" I shrieked, swiftly rolling out of the way, the pain in my hands and stomach long forgotten.
I then staggered to my feet, gasping when I came face to face with the son who snapped the hedge trimmers; I could have sworn I felt the tip of the blades graze my nose when I jumped out of harm's way.

"So for justice!" Mr Williamson boorishly declared, gaining my attention where he rushed at me with the broken handle of the rake aimed for my chest.

"And for principles!" The son promptly added, my eyes circling

to him as he ran at me thrusting the blades.
*They're going to kill me!* I gulped, my gaze darting between them. When they were mere inches away, they proclaimed in unison, "He must atone for his sins!" But I quickly leapt aside, causing them to collide into one another with an almighty thud; it was in that moment I knew now was my chance to escape.

I made a dash for the pathway alongside the house, my boots pounding against the cobbled path before I came to an abrupt halt by the blue Austin Cambridge on the driveway. *What the hell do I do?!* I panicked, my body trembling as the lingering pains steadily ignited once more. *I can't go back for my car, those people will still be in my house!* Then my eyes landed on the Austin Cambridge beside me. Without thinking twice, I stumbled round to the driver's door, ripping it open and gracelessly clambering inside. I cackhandedly dabbed the ignition with my left hand, a sigh of relief escaping me when I felt the key. *Thank God!*

"He is no longer a neighbour!" I faintly heard the Williamson's over the rain thrashing against the windscreen; worry enveloped me when I saw them trudge down the pathway towards the car.
I hurriedly turned the key while biting my bottom lip. *Come on! Come on!* But the car choked, fear now consuming every fibre of my being. *Oh no! No, no, no!* I turned it once more. Nothing. *Why won't you start?!*

"The Devil has tarnished his soul that must be cleansed by the hands of God's disciples!" The Williamson's continued to chant, their voices eerily close.

"COME ON!" I frightfully cried, their shadows slithering across the bonnet as I turned the key again, "JUST START!" All the while they recited, "So for justice and for principles!"

"FOR CRYING OUT LOUD, **JUST START**!" And I forcefully twisted the key, this time the car spluttered to life.
*Yes!* I gasped in relief, a slow smile creeping along my lips. *Thank God, yes!*

I then shunted the gearstick into reverse and slammed

my foot down on the accelerator, causing the car to rocket backwards across the street; I almost didn't brake in time, narrowly missing the neighbour's fence. *Phew! That was close!* And I let out a huge breath before shifting the gearstick into first, peering out the window where I saw the Williamson's advance on me. *What the?!* But I had to do a doubletake when I spotted families from neighbouring houses now converging towards me as well.

"He must atone for his sins!" The Williamson's finished their chant before every single person along the street recited together, "He is no longer a neighbour!" Their creepy tone chilled me to my very core, my heart now beating so fast it gave me chest pains.

"The Devil has tarnished his soul," They all carried on, "That must be cleansed by the hands of God's disciples!"

*I've got to go! I need to get out of here now!* And I sped off as fast as I could; the car tyres screeched in protest, leaving the stench of burning rubber in my wake. *Where do I go now?* I pondered, flipping on the wipers as the rain still ruthlessly pummelled the windscreen. *I can't go back to the guild, and I've got no one to turn to.* I added, switching on the headlights, now recognising Merribridge town centre.

*Thank God I got out of ther-* **BANG!** The whole car shook when something collided into the passenger side as I was driving over a crossroads. Panic engulfed me when I lost control, struggling to stop the car from frantically spinning when I saw-*Uh oh!* **CRASH!** The bonnet smashed into a brick building and I was flung forwards, my nose crunched mercilessly against the steering wheel. Warm fluid poured down my mouth; I didn't realise it was blood until the copper tang made me gag.

A groan seeped from my lips as I slumped back into the seat. *What... What happened?* I wondered, noting the distinct smell of smoke lingering in the atmosphere mingled with blood. *Is something burning?* Then I saw smoke billow from the bonnet. *Oh God, the cars on fire!* I fretfully presumed, reaching for the door but it was ripped open before I got the chance. *What the?!*

Unexpectedly, a hand lurched inside and ferociously dragged me out by the front of my t-shirt.

"LET GO OF ME!" I shrilled before coming face to face with a man, his hold on me impenetrable.

He then rammed me up against the car, a cry breaking my hold when the glass tugged at my stomach. *Who is he?!* I exclaimed in coherent fright, blinking at him through my sodden hair that clung to my face. The first thing I noticed were his stone-cold, murderous blue eyes; they struck such fear in me I thought I was going to die. *What does he want with me?!* I continued to panic, now acutely aware he wasn't smiling; his thin, unkind lips were pulled in a frown, giving his sculpted, sun-kissed face a dark, threatening glow.

Suddenly, he brought his hand up, making me squirm in fear he was going to hit me.

"PLEASE DON'T HIT ME!" I shrieked, squeezing my eyes tightly shut, but nothing happened.

Blinking them open one at a time, I watched as he swept aside his wet, dirty blonde hair that was stuck to his brow.

"So," He began in a brusque tone, which sounded like the scraping of a prisons chain, "**You're** Jeremiah's son..." And he disdainfully stared me up and down, as if I were lower than the dirt on the bottom of his shoe.

Quickly drawing my head back, I gaped. *I... I know that voice!*

"This would've been resolved by now if you weren't..." He carried on while burying a hand inside his fitted, black blazer pocket, the white shirt underneath stretching across his musclebound body.

*Oh my God!* I frightfully screamed when he pulled out a gun; I would have crumpled to the ground if he still didn't have me pinned against the car. *He's going to kill me!*

"Pluh-Please!" I whimpered, flinching when he sneered at me.

"You're pathetic!" He growled, adding contemptuously, "Just like your father was!" And he raised the gun; I couldn't stop the full body tremors from consuming me.

Pulling back the hammer, he reflected, "I should've personally dealt with **you**." He then pressed the barrel of the gun to my forehead just as the screeching of car tyres invaded the atmosphere; I didn't dare peer over my shoulder in fear the gun would go off.

The slam of a door pierced through the drumming rain and whirring siren before an eloquent male voice piped up in delight, "Anthony!"

*Anthony? I repeated, staring at the man with the cold, murderous eyes before me. Is that his name?*

Lowering the gun, Anthony – I presumed – uttered in distaste, "**Mr Simmons**, what a pleasant surprise..." And his blood chilling voice gave me goose-bumps.

"Sorry to interrupt," The man with the eloquent voice began, and I followed Anthony's gaze to the rear of my car where I saw-

*What's **he** doing here?!* I gawked, shocked to see Wes who was clad in a fitted black suit, white shirt and matching black tie.

"But the Prime Minister has requested that Mr West is to remain unharmed and **I'm** to bring him in for questioning." Wes carried on in that same articulate tone, confusing me further.

*What the hell has happened to his voice?!* Gone was his accent, now he sounded just like everyone else. *Why's he talking like that?!* Then it dawned on me what he had said. *Wait, questioning?!*

"Uh-huh..." Anthony murmured, clearly unconvinced, "Considering I've only just been given **my** orders, I'm going to have to clarify that. You won't mind, would you?"

Shaking his head, Wes replied with a roguish smirk, "Of course not." And Anthony shot him an incredulous glance before abruptly releasing me, wandering towards the back of my car where Wes still stood.

*Are they going to question me about father?!* I worried, bringing a hand up to bite my thumbnail while Anthony advanced on the car that crashed into mine; it looked like a Bentley S1.

Just as he opened the driver's door, Wes piped up, "Oh,

Anthony?" And Anthony spun round to face him, growling through gritted teeth, "What?!"

"Say 'ello ter Eddie for me." He replied in his thick accent, grinning guilefully as he ripped out a gun from inside his blazer, shooting Anthony in-between the eyes; I couldn't help but scream when he collapsed against the car with a thud, sliding down where he crumpled to the ground.

*Oh God!* I bawled, slowly backing away. *He killed him!* My heartbeat thrashed in my ears, a pain now lingering in my chest the longer I stared unblinking at the blood streaming down Anthony's face. *I can't believe he killed him!* And I pressed a fist to my mouth, uncertain if I could keep the vomit at bay.

"Nate," Wes spoke, distracting me just as he pocketed the gun, "We need ter leave." And he gestured to a car – an Austin Cambridge - with a nod, pulling out a packet of cigarettes and a lighter as he done so.

Taking another step back, I blurted with a shaky voice, "You... You killed him!" And just announcing it aloud made me feel suddenly cold.

"It were either us or 'im." He responded through his cigarette, lighting it, "And I much prefer the latter."

Wes then pocketed the lighter and took a big pull of his cigarette, exhaling a cloud of noxious smoke and adding, "So come on, we've got ter go."

"Go?" I repeated, confused, "Go where?"

"I'm takin' yer back ter the guild." He explained matter-of-factly, and I immediately exclaimed, "No!"

*There's no way I'm going back!* I adamantly declared, remembering how Gloria had suggested they hand me over to the government.

"Nah?!" Wes spouted, clearly taken aback; he then lowered his cigarette, asking, "Wotcher mean '**nah**'?"

"I overheard the conversation this morning!" I heatedly began, ignoring the bafflement growing on his face as I continued, "I heard Ralph say you're to hand me over to the government, so why would I want to go anywhere with **you**?!"

Jerking his head back, Wes stated in a high-pitched tone, "But I ain't 'andin' yer over ter the government!" And he took another pull on his cigarette, "Glory sorted that-"

"And why should I believe you?!" I sharply intervened, clearly offending him as he snapped, "Yer fink if I 'ad every intention of 'andin' yer over, I'd 'ave shot one of them in plain view of the bloody cameras?!" And he gestured around at the cameras fastened to nearby buildings, "I've just blown me fuckin' cover for yer!"

"**BUT I DIDN'T ASK YOU TO!**" I exploded with frustration, shocking Wes; his mouth formed a little '**o**', the cigarette falling to the ground where the embers dwindled.

*None of this should've happened!* I vented, flexing my trembling hands and instantly regretting it; the pain ignited once more, making me inwardly hiss. *Breathe! Just breathe through it!* I instructed, inhaling several deep breaths which also calmed the rage bubbling within.

Once I had somewhat regained myself, I carried on, "I didn't ask for any of **this**." And I gestured around with my left hand at nothing in particular.

Sighing deeply, Wes nodded in understanding, "I know yer didn't... None of us did..." And that's when I realised I wasn't the only one whose life had been turned upside down.

*Was he not given a choice as well?*

I then opened my mouth to question Wes; however, lights loomed towards us, distracting me. *What the?* Squinting to try and make it out, my jaw dropped when I realised it was three, maybe four vehicles honing in on us.

"We 'ave ter leave!" Wes urgently declared over the downpour, retrieving his gun and instantly putting me on edge. *Who the hell are they?!* I panicked, staring back at the impending vehicles with a gulp.

"Nate!" He desperately cried, his voice almost lost amidst the ongoing siren, "We 'ave ter leave **now**!" And he pulled back the hammer of his gun when the vehicles screeched to a halt just beyond the wreckage that was once my getaway; a mass of men in black then swarmed out of the cars.

"Nate!" Wes bellowed while I backed away with quick, jerky steps, terrified when the men in black pulled out their guns in unison.

*I'm going to die if I don't get out of here!* I fearfully exclaimed, my breaths now rasping in my throat.

"**NATE!**" Wes screamed once more; I immediately flinched when he rushed towards me, grabbing me by the forearm and yanking me towards the Austin Cambridge.

"Get in the car!" Wes demanded, gesturing with the barrel of his gun towards the driver's side, "Or they'll kill us-"

**BANG! BANG, BANG! BANG!** Gunfire abruptly exploded; I couldn't have bolted to the car fast enough, clambering in when Wes ripped open the door for me. *Arrghh!* I cried in pain when the glass dug deeper into my side.

"Oi!" Wes seethed when he hopped into the passenger's side, stilling me from pulling it out, "What the fuck are yer doin'?!" And he gestured at the men in black looming towards us, slamming the door while hollering, "Fuckin' drive!"

Forgetting the shard, I hastily shunted the car into reverse; bullets peppered the windscreen with an almighty smash as we flew backwards down the road. *Oh God, we're going to die!* I thought, terrified. I couldn't see behind us, having to duck my head to avoid gunfire; all I had to rely on were the ridiculously tiny wingmirrors. I didn't dare move until the whistle of bullets were drowned out by the air raid siren, even then I was scared I would get shot.

Rain battered my face when I sat up straight, shunting the gearstick into first when we came to a crossroads.

"Where am I going?" I asked, automatically turning left which led out of town.

When Wes didn't reply, I urged once more, "Where am I going?!" Nothing, "Wes?" And I peered over to see his motionless body slumped against the passenger door, my eyes widening in shock when I saw blood seep through his crisp white shirt.

*No! He... He **can't** be!*

"Wuh-Wes!" I tremulously hawked, shaking my head in denial, "Wake up!" Nothing.
*No, no, no! He can't be dead! He just can't-* Headlights blinded me via the rear-view mirror; I instantly knew it was the men in black fast approaching. *Oh God, what do I do, where do I go?!* I frantically panicked, clenching my hands around the steering so tight my knuckles turned white.

My eyes darted everywhere as I sped out of Merribridge, ignoring the wind and rain that whipped at my face. The town was soon long behind me, the air raid siren fading in the distance. *Everything will be okay! Everything will be okay!* I repeated, gasping to try and control my hectic breathing.

Buildings were long gone, replaced by a black abyss as far as the eye could see. *Where am I going?* I deliberated just before a dark mass loomed on the horizon line, filling me with trepidation. *What is that?* But that thought was swiftly forgotten when the headlights rapidly gained on me; it took every ounce of self-control to stop my limbs from shaking. *Oh God, what do I do- Hang on, is that the forest where the guild is?* I pondered, realising the dark mass were alpine trees. *But how?* I wondered further. *We didn't go this way yesterday.* Then I noted the trees expanded across the entire horizon line. *Must be a pretty big forest...* Which gave me an idea. *I can lose them in there!*

Pressing my foot down hard on the accelerator, I hurtled towards the forest where a thick, impenetrable haze enveloped the Austin Cambridge as soon as I entered; not even my headlights could penetrate through it. *God, I can't see!* I griped before the car violently hopped along the uneven track, causing Wes' body to bounce around like a ragdoll; his gun toppled off his lap, disappearing in the footwell with a clatter.

The impending headlights began to fade, making a sigh of relief escape me. *Thank God!* And a slow smile grew on my lips just before the car unexpectedly choked, causing the headlights to flicker. *What?!* Panic set in. *What's going on?!* Then I spotted the fuel gauge, the white arrow was on the E, and my heart plummeted. *No, no, no! This can't be happening!* The headlights wavered a couple more times before the car died, rolling to a stop and leaving me stranded in darkness.

"**NOOO!**" I cried aloud in frustration, running my hands through my sodden hair.

*What do I do now?!* I wailed just before lights glinted in the rear-view mirror; I knew the men in black would be here in a matter of seconds. *I've got to get out of here!* Shunting open the door, I staggered out, momentarily blinded by the headlights rapidly approaching. *Oh God, they're here!* Diving into the undergrowth, I sprinted as fast as my legs would carry me; a distinct crisp, earthy fragrance wafted up my nose.

**THUD! THUD, THUD!** The slam of car doors echoed behind me followed by the crunch of footsteps charging through the leaf littered shrubbery.

"He went this way!" Someone hollered, but it was swiftly drowned out by the blood pounding in my ears.

*I just need to lose them, then everything will be okay!* I chanted over and over while blindly running, desperately trying to make my way through bushes that snagged at my skin.

"I see him!" Another announced when the warm glow of torches hit me like a bullseye.

*Oh God, they're gaining on me!* I panicked, hissing against the sharp stab of thorns before breaking free from the thicket where an unexpected slope was on the other side. A scream escaped me when stumbled all the way down, crying aloud when I felt the glass in my stomach embed deep.

"Where did he go?!" I faintly heard someone holler, but I ignored them as I staggered to my feet with a groan, wincing against the pain coursing through my body.

"He must've gone down here!" A voice from the top of the slope declared.

*I've got to go!* I hurriedly exclaimed, now glancing around where I realised I was standing in a clearing with a- *What the hell is **that**?!* A concrete wall, at least sixty feet high, was just on the other side of the expanse, easily hidden amongst the alpine trees.

*There must be a gate or something to get to the other side!* I assured, feeling a spike of adrenaline surge within as I charged towards the wall. As I came to stand before it, there was no end in sight either way I glanced. *There **must** be a gate somewher-*

"THERE HE IS!" A voice abruptly declared before the click of hammers being pulled back on over a dozen guns stilled me.

"PUT YOUR HANDS UP WHERE WE CAN SEE THEM!" The same voice commanded, and I slowly raised my tremulous hands before turning to face the men in black who were now gathered in the clearing.

"PUT YOUR HANDS BEHIND YOUR HEAD!" They added, and I immediately complied.

*This... **This** is it!* I fearfully thought, struggling to keep a whimper at bay. *This is where I die!*

"Nathaniel Jeremiah West!" A plummy male voice spoke up before they stepped away from the assembly, their gun readily poised at me; I couldn't help but raise my eyebrows in shock when I recognised him.

*What the hell is he doing here?!*

A triumphant smile grew on Mr Sheridan's cruel, thin lips as he carried on in delight, "You have been condemned to die by fusillading, a sentence imposed by the Prime Minister under Deprive of Existence Act! Is there a statement you'd like to say before the sentence is carried out?"

I didn't have anything to say, I was too terrified. *There's no escape now!*

"No?" He prompted after a moment of silence, clicking back the hammer of his gun before saying, "Then it was a pleasure knowing you, Mr West."

Printed in Great Britain
by Amazon